V.M. MOUCHAS

MEMORIES OF A MAD MAN VOL. 2

Published in 2020

Special thanks to the following

Jessica Green
Izaiah Ferguson
Emma Newton
Angel Brittony Adams
Shiloh Roper
Covid-19 For giving me so much time to work on this.

CHAPTER ONE: PORCELAIN MADE PERFECTION

???? ATC

It was dark when The Cartographer awoke. A sweeping, cold, endless darkness that he didn't recognize.

Where was he?

Where was the rest of his party? The Archaeologist's Guild?

The man tried to sit up, only to find his head brushing immediately against the ceiling. Was this some kind of container he was in?

"Anybody?!" He called out.

He waited.

Nothing.

He frowned and pressed his hands against the material in front of him. It was some kind of smooth stone and cold. Solidly constructed and smelled strongly of dusty clay. Struggling, The Cartographer tried to rock himself back and forth in the confines, but found the box was sturdy, as if it were being held in place by some means.

The Cartographer tapped the dark hard clay with a hand and listened quietly. There was no response, and he tried his best not to panic at the situation and tried to figure a way out of this. Perhaps this was a prank by some of the mercenaries that had accompanied him and his guild members to the largely unmapped Great Eastern Forest of Posiil.

"ANYBODYYYYYY?! HEY! HELP!"

His throat was sore from yelling. From screaming for help. From cursing and snarling and kicking at the hard porcelain. The nameless man gave a shout and feebly struck the door in front of him. It didn't budge.

He lost track of time as he kept pounding away at the confined space with nothing but his bare bleeding knuckle. The box was a decent sized cube, almost similar to a small cell, he could get some decent weight behind a hit, all he had to do was lean back against the wall and he could get a good kick in.

Was this a punishment of some kind? Some terrible punishment for all the things he'd screwed along the journey? Perhaps it was getting them lost just a few days earlier.

Why had no one come to his help?

"ARGHHH! ARGHHH...!"

The Cartographer pressed his hands into the hard clay and pushed. Hard.

He pushed with all his might, giving it everything he had.

"ARGHHHH...!"

Angry sobs followed by a flurry of punches in the darkness.

It seemed like forever, punching at one particular spot until it cracked, dust seeping from it and coating his fist.

BOOFMCRACK.

White dust coated the floor window, and, and he was surrounded by shapes of white and black.

The Cartographer found himself naked, stripped of all of his gear, his skin deathly pale, and standing in a length of a corridor, many boxes much like his own lining the walls.

How long had it been since he had seen the sun?

Wait.

Noise.

Run. Now.

This place beat like a heart, cyclical, always punctual. A strange metallic rhythm, grinding, the distant sounds of hot liquid metal being poured, a throbbing telling the nameless man something was working in the deepest reaches of this place. He looked at the porcelain cubes he was trapped in, and the geometry of this place, and concluded he had to be trapped in a much bigger porcelain cube than the one he was confined in. Further proved as he wandered, slowly and cautiously.

The Cube was completely decentralized and everything looked almost the same.

His breath, heartbeat, heaving offered the only echoes of life here, sans the distant noises of work, reverberated against the bony walls of the halls he passed through.

He passed through strange structures made of bone, metal, hard porcelain and what appeared to be a spiderweb-like membrane that covered almost everything.

The Cube's noises grew stronger, louder, and closer. At first a low, monotonous beat, it now thumped like a giant drum against the alien architecture caging him. Low, high, long, short, it never stopped.

This was a nightmare. He had to run. Run. As fast as he could anywhere.

Run.

Escape.

He ran until he reached the center, and saw it.

A massive, far-spreading chamber of porcelain, all kinds of liquid metal being poured into various mixing pots, flesh like cables that pumped a bright blue liquid throughout the massive cube and then his captors...

Along the walls surrounding the massive chamber were slots, and in them porcelain, doll like humanoid creatures with features of various races from the planet Laguna combined into almost all of them. Some had the draconian tails of Pryldahnians, combined with the large elvish ears of the Alphonse Island elves, paws from the reclusive Parudese panther people tribes, and tusks and large bodies of Greentusks, and the features of various humans, flesh still showing and slowly being reworked into pseudo-living statues. The armor that was grafted onto them was pure white metal that looked like it was halfway between bone and porcelain, and every one of them was in varying condition. Some had bits of paint and other decorations on them.

The strange cables of bright blue wonder fluid pulsed and wobble, alive and well. Bravely, he peered over the edge to see what was below.

Mountains of bones being crushed down into dust, and turned into the clay. Varying races pumped full of the wonder fluid and brain washed, their natural bodies had been seemingly torn apart and reconstructed, with entire limbs and large sections of their skin replaced with the same porcelain-like metal, leaving gaps of their muscle and sinew exposed as they were being worked on by the porcelain monsters.

And all he could do was stare in horror and short breath.

Go.

Run.

He turned his back to the scene before him and ran, all before one of them jumped from a level above and right in front of the nameless man.

Only this one was much more unique than the others.

This one was a seven foot tall porcelain humanoid, with refined cat like ears atop it's head and a long cat like tail that resembled more of a spine now, it's body set against a white veneer with gold inlay with proportionate flower like adornment running up it's side, symmetrical and perfect in every way. It's grey face was featureless aside from lilac markings that depicted a flaming lotus, associated with the long disappeared Kundalandian race.

"Wha- Wha- Wha-" The Cartographer could barely gasp as the unique porcelain creature approached him.

"PRISONER ESCAPE!"

About a dozen Luektorem all began to stir from their stasis along the walls, starting to march towards the nearest set of stairs towards their leader who cornered the lone man, blocking any escape.

"What are you?" The Cartographer finally choked out, falling back and frozen in fear, now noticing the leader was simply wearing a mask, as he could see where the white porcelain armor ended and the grey stone of the featureless mask began.

"We are The Luektorem... We will return you to clay. Remake you, remold you, make you perfect." The leader spoke with a deep, smooth hypotonic voice.

The leader pointed to himself, porcelain fingers clacking against porcelain armor.

"As for myself... I am THE Luek."

The Luek seized the man by one of his arms and hauled him to his feet, and all he could do was scream and flail to avail.

"There is something we are searching for, something hidden within the minds of a select few... We will see if you hold this secret. If you not know this secret, then you will become part of us..."

"Perfection made porcelain."

CHAPTER TWO: SHADOW OF A GODDESS

???? ATC

A soft, steady rain that slowly seeped into the land and wet the spring grass in a sea of dewy green. The wet air was cold and smelled strongly of loam. Birds and animals were hidden away from the miserable weather. And fled from the sounds of battle that rang through the trees.

The old warrior ignored the pain, his adrenaline fueling him. He pulled the blade toward him with enough force to break bone. The greentusk stumbled to the ground, its muscular legs splayed in front if it once the deformed orc hit the wet forest floor with a splat, it's crude spear falling along with it.

"Arrghhh...!"

The Slave Paladin rushed to the side to dodge the crude club of a second towering orc, long silver beard swaying in the wind, and then chopped at it's hand before pushing forward to duel it.

The Slave Paladin wielded a unique longsword with a stone blade, with a collection of flesh growing at the hilt, swung through the air and plunged into its target, causing the lumbering brute to scream and shout, using one arm to grip the man's sword arm whilst he had his sword plunged through his chest.

The Slave Paladin struggled as the orc raised his club above his head. In response he raised his free hand as well, a magical golden spear up at it's pudgy face, maiming him and stunning him for a few long precious moments.

"Come now, my patience is longer than your lifespan, beast..."

It shrieked and stumbled back, the Slave Paladin's soul fueled sword sliding out of it's chest with ease. He ran forward again, charging the blade with the same wispy magical lilac aura and slicing through it's legs with ease.

Once it fell to the ground, crippled and screaming he chopped at it's hand to disarm it, before holding out his left hand, which was one enveloped in a bright green aura.

The Slave Knight plunged his sword into the orc's heart and the light left it's eyes. But, before it died the armored man held out both hands and slowly brought them towards his chest, making a crushing motion. Black flames with white outlines burned in his palm, trapping it's soul into physical form. It appeared as a wispy green ball, his hungry blade absorbing some of it's wispy life force.

The old man stepped off the corpse and reclaimed his blade and sheathed it onto his side, letting the soul float there for now.

Feeling the immense power flow through him. His sword, old and worn was starting to supernaturally deform and bloat with the blood and souls of those he had slain.

As the adrenaline left his body, the knight in ancient, well maintained shining armor found himself huffing and puffing for air and a burning sensation in his chest. He noticed there was a great gash in the side of his armor and blood was flowing from his torso.

"There it is... The blood..."

The cold rain showered down upon him as he sat with his back against a tree in the overgrown ruins of the fort that resided within the Great Eastern Forest.

His tattered lilac cloak flapped against the wind along with his silver beard, but he ignored it and continued to sit quietly after the battle, staying as stoic as ever in his brass armor, which was cared for and shined religiously, a flaming lotus symbol was prominently displayed in the middle of the chest, and he wore a set of chains around his chest piece that formed an X over the symbol. His armor, his cloak and his hungry blade were the only relics of his past, and all that he had.

Moss and vines covered nearly every inch of the ancient fort nearby, and the stone beneath him had sprouted a thick coat of dirt and grass. It was beautiful, in its own way.

The sound of metal clinking and clanking pierced the tranquil air as he silently watched each blade of grass move with the wind, the cold droplets from above washing the blood off his armor. Blood mixing with rain and mud beneath the Slave Paladin as he sat with his back against the ancient tree.

Suddenly, the sound stopped just in front of him. A shadow of a girl fell over him while a figure knelt in front of him.

"You poor thing..." Said a sweet voice.

His eyes slowly opened beneath his lilac hood. His body was sore, very sore, he felt stiff as if she was an unoiled machine that had rusted over the years. And yet, he kept going, always.

That's when a small jolt of pain went through his body.

The Slave Knight felt as his ankle throbbed, as did his head.

"Here, this thing should help with the pain for now." The voice spoke still muffled yet familiar.

He felt the cool electric tingles of the soul flow across his body as it soothed his old nerves. The Slave Knight sighed as the pain dissipated into a memory within a few short moments.

Slowly he opened his eyes again, it's color and features hidden in shadow beneath his pointed hood.

In front of the old knight knelt St. Holly, the human Goddess of Forgiveness. Behind her sat the waning moon its fading smile lighting the sky in a quiet glow making the woman all the more beautiful.

The old man slowly sat up, struggling as he stared into those beautiful opal pools. It was so hard to even move as he was lost in them.

Tentatively St. Holly lifted a hand to The Slave Paladin's cheek. The old man leaned into the goddess's warm touch reaching up a gloved hand of her own to place upon hers.

Clear as day in his tired old eyes was love but something darker sat behind the loving glow that came from his lidded eyes.

Devotion.

"Hey..."

And the goddess was gone just like that. A vision, an illusion? A ghost?

The rain was falling faster now, cascading over his worn body in cold, wet, droplets. His cape and hood became heavy, as he let out a sigh, his head falling back to the dark sky.

"What are you doing?" A ghost of his younger self asked, his armor looking new as the day it was forged and his cloak and hood bright all in one piece, his face hidden in shadow beneath the hood.

"What are you doing? Repeating the same mindless tasks, day after day? Wandering? Is that even living?"

The Slave Paladin had to admit he had forgotten his purpose, it all was a fog now. Days had turned to weeks, weeks into months, months into years, and years into decades. Maybe even centuries, or millennia. He wasn't sure. He wasn't even sure of his name anymore, only that he was timeless.

Timeless...

And that the Goddess of Forgiveness had a mission for him. A mission he had long forgotten. The only idea he had was his rare, ancient ability to trap souls. A forbidden spell. He was always hungry for the energy that lay within all living creatures... But why?

It was an endless hunger for the Timeless Slave Paladin, it was his mission.

"Aren't you tired? Don't you wish it could end?"

She began to walk away, and the old paladin rose to his feet.

"Wait, where a you going?"

Where was he going?

His life before was nothing more than a distant dream. The memories of his golden age had grown hazier and hazier, and he became old, scatter brained and decrepit, and yet, he retained his strength and lived longer than he should have.

Age had no effect on him.

"Promise me, when you see a lilac lotus, you'll think of me. Notice, this ghost of the lotus..."

The old man ran after the shadow of the girl, through the trees until he found himself by the river, staring down into the steady stream, leaves of amber gently falling around him, the setting sun reflecting.

Here he was. A slave to his past, a devoted servant for longer than anyone could remember. Longer than himself, perhaps. At times his thoughts weren't even coherent, and time no longer had any meaning for him.

A slave to his goddess.

The Slave Paladin had started to forget his purpose. Even his name. No one had used his name in such a long time...

What was it?

The Old Paladin had no quality of life. He was completely reduced to only the most primitive functions. He existed in this land only to wander and kill, to consume soul after soul of almost every living thing he encountered...

His memory began to fade. The souls of those he had consumed always shouted in his ear and flooded his mind with strange visions... He could remember a few key things, but he was always uncertain if they were true or not.

How long was it before he just turned into a rabid monster? Much like the greentusks he had put down?

The humans of this world had their St. Holly. But he was convinced she was something else, someone else. A false goddess... The gods of Laguna chose never to intervene and only empower their followers rarely, the people will choose to follow anyone who answers their pleas.

The goddess of forgiveness and compassion, patron of humanity St. Holly was nothing more than a false memory of a powerful, long forgotten woman from an ancient civilization. One simply had to dig beneath the surface...

He was part of it, but that was so long ago that most of his memory had deteriorated.

Beneath the mud.

Raising his sword he slowly stuck the blade into the water until it reached the bottom, sliding the blade across and tearing the mud, and the molten mass of souls within the blade spoke to him and showed him the veiled curtains to the other side.

And Slave Paladin knew what to do next.

CHAPTER THREE: STARFLIES

The Dragon's Head Tavern and Inn, Vorland, 1437 ATC

Kari Fullbuster-Karkaldwin soaked in her tub the same way her thoughts soaked in her mind; completely.

She was a cryomancer, a protector by trade. And she was a young woman in her twenties, with a candid complexion, icy blue eyes, and hair so blonde it looked white. Almost like a porcelain doll in appearance

From the way her hair floated on the surface, her entire body submerged below, it might've seemed that the young mother had drowned in her bath... But as she broke the surface and sucked in a breath, it seemed she lived to see another day. Her water had grown lukewarm, though it had been near-scalding when she'd climbed in an hour ago. It was time to get out, she knew, but she didn't want to. It was perhaps the last thing she wanted to do, besides the conversation she would soon be having. With a sigh she lifted herself from the tub, water streaming down over her skin while her long, snow colored hair clung to her damp skin. Reaching out, she grabbed her green silk robe and wrapped it around herself, wringing out her hair onto the washroom floor. She lingered as she padded across the wet floor, barefoot and dripping. Exiting the bathroom and down the hall, slipping back into her room. The door was slightly open as she laid out her clothes. She sighed. "It's just a bit longer than usual."

"Mommy!" The twins exclaimed as they ran into her room, dressed in their footy pajamas followed by their father, who wore pink bunny pajamas with feet and a hood. He had a party horn in his mouth and he blew it hard. "We're having a super slumber party! Wanna join us?" He asked scooping the twins up in his arms, nuzzling them. The twins squealed happily and smiled warmly to their mother.

She hadn't been expecting the twins to burst in, she shrieked again at Venser's party horn being suddenly blown. "Oh ah! Knocking would be good sweetie before you scare me like that!" Time to turn it into a lesson. Clearing her throat, she smoothed out her robe as Venser cuddled her, as well as their kids.

"I would love to." The cryomancer answered. "As long as you all learn to knock before entering a lady's room, kids. Ven." She pointed that particular word at the bunny-esque Venser, taking note of his strange pajamas. "Nice ears," She commented. "You need to buy me a pair too!" Kari couldn't help but giggle.

Traveling was one of the worst ways a girl could spend her days. Being on the road for four days now, the patron Elly was just about fed up with sleeping on the cold and hard ground, so it was with great relief that she entered the Dragon's Head Tavern and Inn. With a little pouch tied around her waist, filled to bursting with coin, the young girl made her way further inside, her small boots clicking with purpose. She stopped after she had made her way into the middle of a large room, and she glanced around to see who might be able to assist her.

Venser blew the party horn again then spat it out of his mouth. "Goodie!" He set the twins down and they ran over to Kari, hugging her legs. "Just let yourself go floppy, for now this is your chance, pretend you have no bones and do the rubber chicken dance!" Venser said picking up Lucinda and waving her about before setting her down. He pulled out a rubber chicken wearing a bowler hat and tossed it on Kari's bed beside her.

"Dance Lord Bowler!" The rubber chicken levitated up into the air and began to flop around with no rhyme or reason. Venser wasn't controlling it. Venser the head bartender was absent from the bar, and so the shadow tendrils manifested themselves in an old silhouette replica of the serpent eyed bartender. Complete with his battle skirt, messy hair, right shoulder cape, gauntlets, and shoulder pad. The shadow replica stared at the patrons at the bar, expecting them to order.

"Hello. My name is Elly, and I am seeking lodgings and a small meal." The young girl hadn't been away for long, and so she had barely any experience with strangers. She hadn't even had enough common sense to hide any of her belongings underneath her green dress as she was among a few other patrons, who looked like they were from the local towns much like her.

Kari reached down to ruffle the twins' hair as they hugged onto her legs. She smiled down at them before Venser's song drew her eyes upward, as did the ridiculous rubber chicken. "What in Laguna is that chicken?" She couldn't help but laugh at the dancing rubber chicken, grabbing Soarin's tiny hands to dance around the

"I don't know! I was, something from back home." Venser said watching the rubber chicken with the bowler hat dance about on the bed. "Dance wif me mommy Dance wif me!" Lucind begged hopping up and down while Soarin giggled dancing with the white haired girl. "I'm needed at the bar, hold on love." Venser said before disappearing in a puff of thick red smoke. He reappeared behind the bar and shooed the shadow replica away. "Someone say they needed a room and a stable?"

Kari obliged, taking Lucinda's little hand and making a ring with the two of them. She spun them around, singing some little nonsense song to fuel their dancing.

"What do we do with a drunken Venser? What do we do with a drunken Venser? What do we do with a drunken Venser early in the mor-nin'?" She spun with them as Lord Bowler danced, eventually scooping up both twins and blowing raspberries on their chubby little cheeks.

A strange furry creature popped out from a tiny chaos portal underneath a set of barstools, waddling out into view and trying to make a beeline towards Venser and clinging to his leg, looking up at him with two big yellow cat eyes. Much to everyone's shared confusion, looking around the semi-crowded bar area and listening to everyone.

The bearded man sorted through the room cards and set a key down in front of the girl, scooping up the payment. "Right hall, second door on the right." He said looking to the rest of the bar. "Anyone need anything else?" Venser paused and looked down, prying the furry shapeshifter, Silca off his leg. "Hmmm... I think you'd make a great gift for my kids."

The twins giggled and squirmed in Kari's grasp. "Can we go outside?" Soarin asked in his tiny voice.

The strange small furry creature flailed her tiny arms while being picked up, the tiny shapeshifter fluffing up now.

"So late? Well, yeah. Just like the party last night." Not minding that she was still in little more than a green silken robe, Kari nudged open the door with her foot and carried both twins out into the hallway. Knowing Soarin liked to run everywhere, she lowered him to the floor and let him blaze the trail to the front door while she carried Lucinda on her hip. She still hummed her little tune as she escorted the children out into the cool night. The stars were shining, and a few lone fireflies drifted here and there. One settled on Lucinda's nose while a few others twirled around Soarin, as if challenging him to a race.

"Yes, yes. We have some stables beside the tavern." Venser said setting Silca down and looking through the room cards again. "Occupied... Occupied... Roselie's room... Occupied... Ah." He passed a woman a key. "Right hall, fifth door on the right." He then turned around and grabbed a metal tankard, filling it with ale. "Three silver." He said setting it down in front of her.

Silca hid behind his legs while holding onto a coin that had been forgotten beside the bar counter wall. Holding the small piece of shiny silver close.

"Moe... What are dey called again?" Lucinda asked, crossing her eyes, smiling in awe at the hovering, glowing bugs. Soarin laughed and was chasing one around, trying to catch it as he ran around out front.

"They're star flies! Sometimes called fireflies." Kari answered, touching her nose to Lucinda's cheek for a moment with a grin. "They glow, like stars. Except these you can touch, sweetie." Reaching out, she snatched the one from Lucinda's face and held it out so she could see, the tiny bug lighting up between her fingers in a soft pulse. Barefooted, the white haired girl followed along behind Soarin with Lucinda still on her hip, not letting her boy get too far ahead.

Silca started to waddle off in search of more coins or even some food crumbs. Waddling passed an oddly dressed stranger with a large hat and even making her way passed a witch with closed eyes, not even paying attention to what was going on save for the fact she was hungry.

"Where dey come from?" Lucinda asked, poking the glowing bug, it flew away from her and past Soarin. Who jumped up and caught it in between his hands.

"Yes!" He uncovered his hands and he had crushed it on accident "... Oh..."

"Silca?" Ven asked, raising a brow pointing to the little cat creature munching away at the coin on one of the tables.

Little Silca would fluff up her thick red and black fur upon the mentioning of her name, slowly turning her silver gaze on Venser and the woman in question, giving a very eeric stare as she did so her teeth would take a clean bite through the coin now.

The bearded bartender looked away from Silca, then to one of the patrons, a woman from the town nearby, before picking up the glass and refilling it with wine. "There ya go."

"Well... Like, some people think they're tiny little pieces of stars themselves that float down and grow wings." She watched it fly away before it met its early end by Soarin's hand. Moving over, she gently peeled off the bug carcass from his palm and dropped it into the grass. "Careful now, sweetie," she murmured. "You have to be careful..." Another starfly drifted over their heads and she guided Soarin's hand upwards, gently closing his fingers around the bug. "Like so..."

The static and chaos energy would gather in her thick fur just enough that the tiny furry shapeshifter would begin to float off of the table and away, bouncing up and down as she did

"What happen to it?" Soarin asked in his tiny voice looking down to the crushed firefly on the ground. Lucinda looked down to the firefly and tightened her grip around his mother.

"It went to sleep." Kari answered simply. "A very deep sleep. It's very peaceful, and very soft." She felt Lucinda's grip tighten on her, and in return Kari gave her a soft squeeze. "When he wakes up... He'll be somewhere much nicer. A big field where it's always nighttime. Always warm. Where the stars can reach down and play with him. It's called Summerland." It was all very romantic, she knew, and strange and sad. Describing death to children.

"Summerland is where we all go in the end. And one day, it'll always be bright for us and we will run through the Fields of Green together."

Venser grabbed a metal tankard, then walked over to a barrel filled with neon blue liquid. He dipped it in and passed the girl the tankard.

"Blue Lagoon. Strongest thing we have." He said handing her a key too. "Right hall, fourth room on the right."

Soarin opened his hands a little, looking to the small fireflies in his hands and blinking his big, grass green eyes.

"When's it gonna wake up?" Lucinda asked looking up to Kari, blinking the same icy blues she shared with her mother.

"It's already awake somewhere else. In the place where the stars play." The star fly glowed weakly before its light went out, the tiny shape disappearing into the darkness without the light it provided to catch the eye. "It's a complicated sort of thing," she said simply. "Like, it's easier to understand when you get a lot lot older."

"Is Grandma Lucia there?" Soarin asked looking up to Kari as fireflies swarmed around them, lighting up his grass green eyes. "We haven't seen grandmommy in a long time." Lucinda said.

She knelt down in the grass, hugging Lucinda close to her side as she pulled Soarin in as well, pressing a kiss to his temple. "No, loves... Grandma hasn't gone there. Just because... You haven't seen someone in a long time doesn't mean they're gone forever."

SQUEAK SQUEAK!

Two louds squeaks were heard behind them, and Venser stood there holding Lord Bowler in one hand. "Hey. Trying to catch fireflies?" He asked with a smile. The twins didn't say anything and had sober expressions on their faces. "Uh, kids? Kari?"

Silca darted into a chaos portal before stumbling out of another in front of two children and a woman, thick fur now covered in dust and dirt.

Kari, too, was a bit too sober. What had once been a super sleepover had come to something... Much more serious. At Venser's bidding, she shook the more dire thoughts from her head. Tonight they needed to have fun. "That's right," she answered, pecking Lucinda's cheek and Soarin's hair. She pepped up her tone a bit, trying to enthuse them with her words. "And now we know where they come from! Right?"

"Where what comes from?" Venser asked as both twins took notice of the little furball. "Kitty!" They exclaimed at the same time, prompting Soarin to run for it.

Little Silca didn't know what was coming her way as she sat up and dusted herself off, rubbing her eyes free of the dust. Emitting several unhappy hrrs and mrrs as she cleaned herself up.

"Starflies." The white haired girl answered. She hadn't noticed the furry little creature before, but as both twins screeched and Soarin darted after it, she let Lucinda go so she could join in the fray. "We.. We need to talk," she murmured, once the twins were out of earshot. Kari cast her eyes down to the grass, where the dead firefly lay. "Once they're in bed."

Soarin picked Silca up and began to stroke her fur roughly. "Kitty! I like kitty!" He said happily as Venser's daughter joined her brother. "It's soft!" Lucinda exclaimed, petting Silca's head, scratching her behind the ears. "Talk about what?" Venser asked, raising a brow looking at his oldest lover.

Little Silca's fur would begin to gather static as she was petted. Her ears wiggled about as she got scratches.

"... Me leaving." Kari answered simply. Softly. "At least for a little while." The knot in her stomach seemed to grow, as did the lump in her throat.

"... What? "Where are you going Kari?" Venser asked after several long seconds. Lucinda giggled, stroking Silca's tail before yanking on it as hard as she could.

Little Silca would suddenly give off a bright flash of light as she changed into her much older and bigger form. Her ears laying back as she stared the children down for a moment, booping each on the nose and saying.

"No pulling tails hrr."

"Well I mean not forever sweetie. I said it wrong." She paused, watching the twins play with the 'kitty' before it seemed to make a full-fledged tiger. Kari blinked, but it wasn't the most outrageous thing she'd ever seen. "It's just, as much as I love spending my time with you and our twins... Like, I just need a little break. To go on adventure too, honestly. And not just be the protector of my own village. Marvella and the locals can handle it for a while."

The for year old twins screamed at the transformation and that it spoke in a weird voice and booped the noises. "Daddy!" Lucinda exclaimed running over to Venser. He bent down and scooped up his daughter in his arms, standing up while Soarin ran in circles around Kari. "You can remember here." He said frowning.

She shook her head softly, still not looking to Venser. Her eyes were focused down on Soarin's running in circles.

"... I can't. There's like, a word but I kinda lost it. I just feel like I need a break. Some alone time sweetie. You know how full our house always is and it's growing and it's good but... I just... I can't even explain it. It'll only be for an extra week you'll have the kids. I know you got Sanna and your new daughter their own room in the tavern and you're still doing all you can to get the farm..."

Older Silca would give a maniacal grin before returning to her much smaller, innocent form, and giggled. Fixing her fur and her little as she messed around with the children.

"Mommy! Big kitty! Big kitty!" Soarin exclaimed, clinging to one of his mother's legs. Lucinda nuzzled Venser's chest as he looked to Kari. "And so you're just going to wander? Look for some bounties?"

"Big kitty, yes." She reached down to ruffle her son's white blonde hair, the same color they shared, watching the 'big kitty' turn back to its smaller form. "For a bit, yeah Ven." Kari confirmed, looking up to Venser who was a few inches taller than her. "Explore. Relax. Just... Some much needed alone time."

"I understand. I suppose we all need some at times. I just... I know exactly how you feel, and I'm guilty of doing that too" The bearded man rubbed Lucinda's back as she buried her head into his chest.

"Will we see you at home?"

Little Silca would give a confused squeak before sitting down in the grass and hugging her tail tightly.

She couldn't bear to be parted from the twins any longer than that, but Kari really needed some alone time after having such a full house lately and a lot of other things to deal with. She bent down to scoop Soarin up into her arms.

Lucinda let out a yawn as she rested against her father's chest, and after that Soarin let out and hugged her mother tight.

"I think we should get the twins to bed." Venser suggested.

"I think you're right." She hugged Soarin closely, pressing a kiss to his temple. She would lead the way back inside, nudging the door open with her hip and carrying one of the two sleepy twins upstairs, past the few patrons inside, on their way to the twins' bedroom.

Venser recently had the sheets to their bed switched. Soarin's bed now had royal green silk sheets, and Lucinda's were light purple silk sheets. He laid Lucinda down in her bed and tucked her in, brushing some of her raven black hair to the sides. He gave her a loving smile, and she returned it.

Silca curled up into a ball and rolled back into the tavern, making her way to a corner where no one would hopefully bother her.

Kari likewise did the same for Soarin, making sure he was tucked in tightly. As she did every night when the kids were with her, she took his hand and brought it to her lips so she could press a kiss to his palm. A kiss for him to keep, to use when he needed it... With their time together, each twin would have quite the collection.

"Goodnight, my little moonbeam." Venser said kissing Lucinda on her forehead. "Goodnight daddy. I love you." His daughter said in her tiny voice as Venser stood up and walked over to Soarin's bed. "Good night speedster... Wildheart."

And then to their mother. You should sing to them." He said to Kari, "And I'll go get my guitar."

He disappeared in a puff of thick red smoke, and then reappeared wielding his bine white guitar, taking a few seconds to tune it.

Having switched sides with Venser so that she could give Lucinda her Kiss-To-Keep, she flushed at Venser's suggestion. But, perhaps if it were her last night with the twins for a while.... She nodded. Settling down on the edge of Lucinda's bed, she knew just the song to sing. Soft and sweet, and surprisingly beautiful, her voice filled the room with a quiet lullaby.

"You must know, I'll be here waiting. Hoping, praying that this light will guide you home..." Her fingers combed softly through Lucinda's raven curls as she sang. "When you're feeling lost I'll leave my love... Hidden in the sun... For when the darkness comes...."

Venser and Soarin craned their heads to listen to their mother"s sweet singing, and Lucinda curled up under her blanket and smiled warmly at her while she sang

She repeated the song twice, each time slower and softer, until her words were nothing but a soft hum that would help to lull the children to sleep. Only once they had did she stand up from the bed, her cheeks wet with the few tears that had slipped free while she sang.

Venser tilted his head to the side, curious of the song's word choice. The twins found it beautiful, as did Venser.

She caught the gesture and shook her head softly. The song, like most of the memories from lives long passed, had become nothing but a slight blur in her mind. The source was unknown. She remembered it being sung to her, of course. She remembered, even though it seemed to be the oldest memory she possessed. Motioning for Venser to leave the room, she didn't want to talk and wake the twins. Kari kissed them both on the forehead, and then she stepped out into the hallway with their father.

"It's just..."

"So no more love." The bearded man said leaning down to kiss Kari sweetly. "You just... You enjoy your vacation."

Vacation. That was the word she was looking for! The white haired girl smiled brightly.

"Thank you Venser. I'll be home before you and our family knows it."

CHAPTER FOUR: THE BARMAID'S NEW BODY

The Dragon's Head Tavern and Inn, Vorland, 1437 ATC

It was about noon now, and the sky was quite gray as it poured droplets of gray from the atmosphere. Kira was standing next to a window close by the bar, wearing a white and blue robe. As she stood there gazing out at the world that was unknown to her, deep down she had the strangest feeling in her gut that something was off. Sure enough though, the door to the tavern swung violently open, causing the splat of rain to coat the entryway, and there stood a large burley black wolf with sharp yellow eyes and long fangs. The barmaid hurried over to the stairs to spot the wolf, and as their gazes met, it bounded towards her with such swiftness.

"H.. H... HUH?!" Kira gasped in surprise as she took a few steps back to avoid the beast, but ended up tripping over a barstool. "G... Get away from me!" She cried out in desperation as the wolf leaped on top of the girl with a loud bark. Then, suddenly... It spoke

"KIRA! Kira it is me! I finally found you!" The wolf nuzzled Kira's face lovingly, then he would gaze at his master once more who looked horrified. "What have they done to you?" Spot places a paw on Kira's forehead, "I can feel your soul in that body." Kira shook, looking indeed horrified at the situation at hand.

"What are you talking about?! Get off of me at once!" She reached to try and clap twice for a shadow tendril but the wolf placed his paw down on her arm. "Just listen to me. Please. At least look at this..." The wolf then got off of the pink haired elven barmaid, then would leap onto the bars countertop with much ease. Then, he would nuzzle his nose into his collar, to pull out an all white marble. Setting this down on the counter, he then lays down and whines. Kira, out of confusion, got up.. sat down on the bar stool and gazed at this marble. "... I don't get it." She spoke, until the marble began to glow. Then, it increased in size automatically and eventually formed into a full body of a girl who appeared in her teens with porcelain colored skin, long thick eyelashes and extremely long raven hair that dragged all the way down to the floor. On her forehead appeared to be a wing shaped mark, while on her ankles and wrists were shackles. Kira gasped at the sudden surprise and pointed, "What the void is that?! Why is there a doll woman on the bar?!" The wolf suddenly spoke up in a loud tone.

"That woman is you... Kira Kurai. You just don't recall... But I found you and you will be yourself once more." The little pink haired Kira shook her head back and forth, "I don't ever recall looking as such... how can you be so sure? I know who I am and where I come from.." The wolf interrupted, "Those are false memories.. and it is too late to fight this now." The body on the bar's countertop began to emit a dark energy that was thick and cold. Kira's own little form began to feel a tug, like her soul was being plucked straight from within and transferred into this pale woman.

Suddenly, like a switch, the eyes of the doll-like woman opened immediately while the pink haired girl fell straight to the floor and began to dissolve into nothing. Now, Kira Kurai laid gasping for air, and eventually sat up feeling a heavy weight on her body. "Go find me some clothes, Spot." she muttered to the wolf, who immediately hopped down from the bars countertop to do as told.

The front doors of the tavern swung open and Venser entered, not even wet from the rain as his hood blocked the wetness. "Owner came in after getting TOO stoned and kicked me out. Who runs a tavern like that?" He wore a black traveler's cloak and hood over his head, the cape trailing behind him, along with his usual turquoise and crimson entertainer's tunic with bright red boots.

"I'm home!" He called from downstairs, walking into the kitchen. "Eh? Kira?"

Those eyes of the girl were extremely dark, but lovely and suited her face very well. She was a bit taller than that other blasted form, about five six now, and a lot stronger. Raising her bare hands in front of her face, she examined her body carefully to make sure nothing was out of place. "That body was horrible." she muttered lightly with a sigh, then tilted her head to the side as she gazed at her assets, all very well curved in the right places to where it seemed unreal.

"But I almost feel bad about sitting naked on top of this bar's counter top, though Ven does so from time to time."

Sweeping part of her long raven black hair over her ear, she then crosses her legs and comfortably waits while Spot went to find her some close. Sure enough though, he came back carrying a male's shirt that was not at all Kira's. It was bright red in color with long sleeves. "That is not mine.." Kira muttered, but took the shirt anyways as the door suddenly flung open and a loud familiar voice rang through the tavern.

"I'm up here at the bar." she called out lightly. Even her voice was a bit different.. it was soft, smooth and youthful, but unlike the pink haired Kira, her voice sounded more controlled and relaxed. "I may need your help with something."

Light footsteps was heard coming up the stairs, and Venser emerged from the top, biting into a green apple. He stopped right at the top and gawked at Kira as she sat on the bar. Naked. And she looked so different. Paler, black hair. More... Gothic. But she had one nice chest. "Uhhh... Ack!" He choked on a big chunk of apple and fell to his knees, holding his throat.

A woman called Koneko ran through the rain quickly, her hands above her head as the water beat against the protective orb around herself that kept her from getting wet. Above all things, water was something she would not allow to touch her. It wouldn't kill, or injure her in any way but She just couldn't let it touch her body. She saw the tavern and hurried up, she could feel the protective orb weakening from how long she had held it up but just in time she threw herself through the tavern doors and let it disappear, doubled over and breathing heavily from her running and once she felt a bit better in the lungs shed make her way up to the bar and fall into a chair.

Holding up the red shirt as she studied it, her eyes would then shift towards the familiar figure and an easy smile would form on her lips. "You really should pay more attention to what you are doing." she spoke innocently, then hoped down from the bar's counter top and landed on her bare feet with a light thud and walked over to kneel before the bearded man. Then pointed her index finger towards Venser's throat to attempt to stop him from choking with her black magic. Then her gaze would follow towards the Tavern door as it opened to reveal a patron coming in, up the stairs and sat down into a chair.

"Welcome." she called out sweetly, not at all bothered with her appearance. Who could blame her? Everyone else in the tavern was sleeping in mostly after yesterday's cleanup.

A shadow tendrils appeared in front of Venser, formed a fist, and then punched him hard in the stomach, sending the apple chunk flying out of Venser's mouth. It then bounced harmlessly off of Koneko's head. He let out a loud gasp and scooted over to Kira, wrapping his arms around her naked form and pressing his face into her chest. "By the void that felt horrible! Thanks Kira..." He froze for a moment, knowing how different she was. "What the fuck Kira?" He said looking up at her, his serpent green ones boring into hers. "Did you... Shapeshift? Heh, now I guess... Yeah, you and Thorn no longer look like twins."

Koneko would flinch as something hit her in her dire need of an oxygen head and rubbed it, glancing at the man with a huff and a cross of her arms before waving at the woman that gave her a welcome. "Thank you."

As the shadow tendrils did the trick to get the chunk of apple out, the piece accidentally flew right at the woman patron's head. Kira clapped her hands together in apology, then those black eyes went wide as Venser hugged her. Keeping perfectly calm she then placed a hand on the side of Venser's face and spoke soothingly, "I suppose I have a lot of explaining to do hm?" She then faced the woman, "Have whatever you want, it is on me as an apology for the apple piece."

Kira then raised her wrist in front of Venser's gaze, "Think you can help me with these?" These shackles were made from the powers of a divine being, pure magic of which Kira herself could not remove herself, then paused as another patron made his way into the tavern, who eventually fell flat on his face with a back covered in arrows. Seems everyone needed some sort of help today. Rainy days are quite lovely.

Koneko's long ears twitched and shed move from her seat and her eyes widened a bit as she glanced over the railing at the man, She'd make her way down the stairs and looked at them before placing her hand out, she dried the area around the male where the injury was so she wouldn't touch anything wet." Now... this is gonna sting a little but..." She would take the arrow and hold her hand near the base, it would hurt a little but she messed with the wound in order to wiggle the arrow out nice and smoothly before tossing it to the side and went to pull out the next one in the same manner.

"The shadow tendrils can deal with these people. Seems like we get too many patrons who enter with a near death experience..." He murmured picking Kira up and slinging her over his shoulder as he carried her back to his room. He sighed and asked, "Dyed your hair? Fuck no. Your eyes..." He entered his room and laid Kira down on her back, closing the door behind them.

The bearded man crawled onto the bed and moved close to his barback, looking her deep in the eyes. "Are you possessed?"

The wolf of which is indeed Kira Kurai's companion, stared at the result in silence. As he watched his master being whisked away by the bearded barkeep. He simply trotted over and watched as a male patron was getting arrows pulled from his back.

"Such lively creatures." He commented inside of his wolfy mind. Meanwhile, Kira was now on her back gazing up at the familiar ceiling through her own original eyes. She was silent for a moment in spite of Venser's questions.

Finally she answered, "Possessed? Aha.. No." she answered, then frowned, her face extremely pretty even when she frowned, then cleared her throat.

"Dear, I am a demon. But I was trapped in that small elf body for some short time. She raised a hand very gently to touch his hair then dragged that finger down his jaw.

"This is who I really am, Venser." She then sits up to where she is but inches from his face, those dark eyes lingering in his for just a moment. That long raven hair pooling around her form, and that skin was incredibly smooth. "Believe it or not I was originally headed in an entirely different direction... When I was attacked by a winged divine. Being off guard, she shackled me and placed my soul in a different body which so happened to have been running towards this very tavern with a false memory." She frowned again then sighed, "Thankfully my wolf companion has saved my original body and carried it all the way here to transfer me back into it."

Venser stared at Kira silently listening to her story, sitting down on the bed looking at her. He opened his mouth to speak, then closed it. Processing everything she had told him. "Eh? How... What? It's call complicated, but I sort of understand."

Kira sat up to properly seat herself on the bed, her head tilting to the side while a smile formed upon her lips. "That elf you knew... Was nothing but a vessel, a prison. Venser, the girl you see right now, is the REAL Kira. It is mighty confusing, I know." she nods in understanding. Meanwhile, the wolf known as Spot began to wag his tail as the woman had noticed him, kneeled down and began to pet him. As her fingers combed and scratched behind the ears, he would thump his rear leg like a happy dog.

"You still are the elf though." He said turning his head to look at the pale woman with long, flowing black locks who sat a mere foot away from him. "Right? Not just the body. You're still Kira."

"In a way yes." Kira nodded once more, but with a more thoughtful look in her eyes. "I remember every detail ever since I first walked into the Dragon's Head. But, I really am a demon." she stretched out her arms then, observing her own body once more with comfort and more confidence. Meanwhile, Spot was still enjoying the attention like a wee puppy, and would give a happy lick to the woman's face.

"Demon or not, yeah. Do you have any idea how many demons we serve her from time to time?" Venser asked, rubbing his temples. He laid down in his bed and pulled Kira into him, resting his head down on one of his many pillows with furry gold throwovers. "So-" His voice was cut off by the loud yelling coming from the bar area. "What the fuck... The shadow tendrils should be serving. They have never failed to do their job when neither of us are on duty." He sighed and sat up, cracking his back. "Are you... No, I can run the bar. You should get dressed and... Used to your body, Kira." He said absent mindedly dragging one hand down the side of her pale, smooth body.

"We sure do serve many." Kira agreed with Venser about how many demons came into the Dragon's Head Tavern and Inn. Then, as she was pulled into him, she rests her head easily on another pillow. She was still short, but not so tiny like the Pink haired body of what she once was held into. Then, the loud yelling from the bar of the Tavern, caused Kira to shift her eyes to look at nothing in particular. As she heard Venser speak and sit up, she too eventually sat up once her skin was grazed by his hand. A light smile formed at her lips, "Perhaps you are right. I should get dressed and get used to my original body again. Though, it is kind of hard to do so with these shackles on."

Spot got very happy as he was getting even more attention from a particular patron, so much so that he sticks by her side until his master comes back from whatever she was doing. It had been a long adventure without her, and finding her was a pain in the ass. So, for now, he will enjoy the company of some lady currently petting him and relax.

"I'm pretty sure Angel and Ceirra's dresses are too big for you, Sanna's might. No, no. Kari's." Venser said, glancing at the wooden wardrobe against the wall. "I should put some smaller ones in there just in case I have more company in here.

Heh." He then disappeared in a puff of thick red smoke.

Getting up from the bed, she makes her way slowly over towards a mirror once Venser had departed with a puff of smoke left behind. She gazed at her own appearance, making sure once again that nothing was out of place. But as she gazed up at her forehead, she could see the mark had vanished. "Wonderful." she said lightly, bending over to examine the skin on her forehead much more closely. Then, she simply left Venser's room and made her way barefooted towards her shared room. She would doubt any of the dresses would fit now... She was slightly taller than before... Though, she figured Kari's actually might.

Spot would then eventually speak towards the woman in full fledged common language as if it was normal. Then again... Whatever was actually NORMAL in this tavern? It did sit close to a dimensional rift after all. "You are a very good petter." He perked up his black ears and looked upon a patron woman with those piercing yellow eyes.

Digging through the trunk that held many hand made dresses by her vessel's hand, she pulled a black one out that would fit her waist and bust just fine. But definitely needed some alterations. So with a quick wiggle of her fingers, the dress pulled into two parts. Once the alteration was done, she placed her attire on her body, put up her long hair and walked out into the bar area with ease. She paused though as she spotted her wolf companion enjoying the company of the female patron. "His name is Spot by the way." she spoke lightly with a bit of a laugh. Wearing heels, her feet would lightly tap against the wooden floor as she stepped closer. "Wanna see him as a puppy?"

A tiny little mouse with a toothpick sized sword sheathed to a belt on it's waist arrived at the tavern, as she opened the doors with her tiny paws as she looked around before walking up the bar, and smiles as she hops up on it. "Hi there, one glass of ale please." She asked in a high, but low voice. "Please."

Venser the bearded bartender appeared out of a puff of thick red smoke behind Kira, his right sleeve was rolled up and he had a belt around his bicep for some reason. "A shot glass for the strange mouse warrior." He said teleporting behind the bar, pouring ale into a shot glass and sliding it to her. "There ya go!" He looked to Kira and said, "I'll be back in a bit." He then disappeared in a puff of thick red smoke.

The wolf spun his head around as he heard his master speak, and his mouth would open in shock at what she said. "Oh no.. not this again... anything but..." He was cut off as Kira raised her index finger and suddenly dark magic shot out from the very tip and engulfed the wolf. At once, it began to shrink in size till it appeared to be a puppy... All fluff with short cute legs. Spot glared at his master for a moment and then with a feisty set of yips he shouted, "YOU FOWL WOMAN!" Kira laughed lightly and shrugged, "I could not help it." she then looked back at the woman. "My name is Kira by the way." Then her attention was drawn to another patron who requested a glass of ale. As Kira was about to get to it, Venser came back in his usual manner, providing the customer with the order. Then, off again he went.

Kira sniffed the air as the red smoke began to dissipate quickly. She sighed dreamingly, taking in the scent of wine and freshly cut roses before it quickly faded away.

CHAPTER FIVE: KIRA

The Dragon's Head Tavern and Inn, Vorland, 1437 ATC

Kira Kurai was in her shared room, her arms and ankles still bearing the divine shackles. Trying her best to grip the metal and rip it from her form, the mere touch caused a spark to fly through her body causing her to shutter. "This is stupid..." The girl murmured. "There has got to be a way to be immune to this sort of stuff." Sitting on her bed, she eventually laid upon it with her eyes tightly shut.

"Still haven't got it yet?" Venser, the bearded bartender asked walking into her room, a pair of bolt cutters over his shoulder. "This is going to take some time getting used to. I mean, for both of us Kira." He said, stopping in front of her, looking at the shackles. "Oh. Um..." He looked at his bolt cutters with a puzzled look, then tapped the end against the shackles. "Open sesame?"

Kira opened those dark eyes to peer at Venser who walked into her room with a pair of bolt cutters. Those would sure do the trick. Sitting up, she rose up her arms only for him to tap them and say open sesame.

"I don't think that will work.... But.." She paused as sure enough the damn things snapped open and fell to the floor. The look of disbelief was certainly on her features as she sat there. "Well then... Proves that I don't know a damn thing anymore."

Venser set down the bolt cutters. "Oh great. I was going to go get something else because those only work with chains... But oh well." He sat down beside Kira and took one of her hands, trailing his hand up her arm. "How do your wrists feel?"

As one of her hands were taken, her eyes lowered to gaze at her wrist as he touched her. "Light as a feather once more, thanks to you." Kira spoke lightly with a raised brow. She then tilted her head to the side, "How ever should I repay you? I would offer to give you eternal life... But nowadays that seems way overrated and boring." she muttered the last part with a shake of her head.

"What are you talking about?" Venser asked, raising a brow. "Oh right! Demon memories clashing with... Yeah." He waved her off and said, "Already... Eh, it's complicated." He made a gesture to his emerald, slitted inhuman eyes and let go of her hand and stood up.

"I want to give you something else though. A nice, relaxing bath. Why don't you gimme about ten minutes to run it for you? Sound good?"

"Fair enough." Kira nodded with a calm smile, then her smile would vanish to a blank expression as he spoke of wanting to give her a nice relaxing bath. Those eyes widened just a tad bit, and a kind smile formed by her sweet lips. " That sound's wonderful. Thank you, Venser."

A few minutes later... The handsome bearded barkeep poked his head into the door.

"It's ready. Come, Kira." He said with a soft smile.

For the short amount of time Kira had got to know and work with Venser at the Dragon's Head, she was never too sure what to exactly expect when it came to his generosity. But he never failed to make her curious. So, once he poked his head into the door and spoke to her, Kira got up from the bed and followed him into the bathing room.

A warm bath awaited Kira, a tub big enough for the both of them that was filled with warm, sweet smelling water with rose petals floating in it. On a chair beside the bath was a bucket of champagne and ice. "What do you think?" He asked holding the door open for her.

As Kira took a look inside of the bathing room, she could see a pretty decent sized tub filled with warm, sweet smelling water with rose petals floating upon the surface. A single chair sat beside the bath with a bucket of champagne and ice. "Wow." was Kira's first word used at such a site. "You really out done yourself." she spoke in surprise, stepping fully within the room and leaning over just a tad bit over the tub to brush an index finger against a rose petal.

"This is very glorious."

"I run the best baths. Plus, you deserve to feel relaxed being in such an awkward body for a short time." He said walking past her, pouring them both bubbly champagne.

"Awkward it was indeed..." She raised her hands to scratch the back of her head with a light blush to her cheeks. One could tell she was not one used to being.. 'cute' or 'pink'. Kira in her current form was still cute though. She had more composure now.

"Are you going to get in or just stand there admiring the water?" He asked looking at her, letting out a small laugh.

"I don't mind admiring." Kira spoke honestly, then began to undress starting with the top piece of her dark attire. At once her chest was free from the cloth as she would then fold it neatly and set it on a countertop. Next she would wiggle out of the skirt, and do the very same like the shirt. Eventually she stood there completely naked once more, letting loose that long raven hair which fell graciously down her back. Easing a leg in first, the warmth caressed her rather pale skin, causing her body to respond with a comforting vibe. Then eventually, she dipped herself within the waters into a sitting position.

Venser removed his belt and set it down by the chair, undoing his tunic and stripping out of his clothes, revealing his muscular naked body. He sat down in the tub opposite Kira and sighed blissfully, offering her a glass of champagne. "Feels great... Doesn't it?"

The sight of Venser even joining her was intriguing enough, it was actually quite nice to have a 'human' like companion to share this watery bliss with. Taking the champagne into her soft fine hands, she then nods with a thank you. "This feels amazing." she spoke, leaning back and letting the bath salts tickle and clean her already soft smooth skin. Sinking lower into the water with her knees slightly bent, she looked at the handsome barkeep for a moment and took a simple sip from the glass. "Venser..." She started, gazing away at nothing in particular now. "I feel like I owe you an apology for the weird turn of events today."

He waved Kira off, splashing her a bit with water. "It's all good. Weird things are abundant around here." Venser poured himself a glass of the wonderful champagne and took a sip, eying her. Mostly her chest as they bathed together.

As the water splashed against Kira's face, she naturally turned her upper body slightly to the side while she winced with a light smile. Then, she would retaliate by splashing him right on back as his gaze was wandering towards her chest. Laughing just a short bit, she raised the glass up towards her lips to finish the first glass of champagne.

"Whoa whoa whoa hey!" He gestured to his glass. "Champagne..." Venser took a sip, and mid sip he playfully splashed Kira with more water.

As Kira halted her motions while Venser was taking a sip, he then had successfully tricked her and began to splash. Kira's mouth fell out with a gasp as she immediately retaliated by splashing back. Rose petals went haywire while water sprinkled about the tub like child's play.

He sat his glass down and picked up a single rose petal, pressing it against Kira's forehead. And it stuck there. "Boop!"

As that single rose petal was stuck on her forehead, her eyes would gaze up, and then eventually fall on Venser. An innocent smile formed by her sweet lips as she would pick up a few rose petals and quickly place a row on his upper lip and chin. Once she was completed, she raised her upper body from the water with arms in the air while she spoke. "Hahaha Rose Beard and Mustache!" Kira then grinned happily.

Venser laughed and relaxed back, watching her. He picked two rose petals off his upper lip, then leaned Kira back a bit and placed them each on her nipples, covering them. "Erotic..."

Kira would glance down at the rose petals now on her nipples, then could not help but to laugh. "These would be fantastic pasties." she then shook her head and sat on her knees within the tub. Then she would simply lean over and place a single rose petal on each of his nipples in return. "Now we match." She laughs.

"That we do. Marvella once suggested I pierce my nipples... Was thinking about it as a joke..." Venser raised his hands up and grasped her wet breasts, squeezing them softly. "Wow these are so soft..." He said tugging on her nipples a bit.

As Kira sat there, a light gasps suddenly escaped her lips as Venser's hands touched her breasts and was squeezing them. "Careful." she spoke, her face unconsciously turning pink as she bit her lip, "Those are sensitive." As her nipples were tugged she could feel them harden.

"I know... How's this feel?" He asked going back to fondling them, Venser then leaned forward and took one of her nipples into his mouth, sucking on it, nibbling it a bit too.

"It makes me hungry." Kira admitted as her face became a little more exotic while he took one of her nipples into his mouth and began to suck and nibble on it. A light moan escaped her partially parted lips as the sensation was vibrant and even tickled against her smooth skin.

"And not for food." The girl admitted even more.

"Mhm..." Venser wrapped his arms around Kira and pulled her wet, naked body into his, eventually pulling her onto his lap as his back pressed into the ivory walls of the bath. Sanna had gone to Montpelier to visit their other loves and taken their baby with her for the next few days, and she knew and was fine with her lover sleeping around with other women.

As her bare naked form collided with his, she rested eventually upon his lap, with her plushy breasts pressed against his. Her heart picked up for the sudden motion, and she could feel the heat rise within her form, causing her hands resting against the ivory walls of the bath while those dark doll-like eyes looked into his.

"How do you feel?" He asked running his hands down her back, loving the feeling of her breasts squishing up against his chest.

"Bewitched by a bar keeper." Kira Kurai answered in a calm tone, even though it was plenty obvious on how her body reacted towards his caresses along her skin.

"After we get ourselves clean... Do you want to do it?" Venser asked slowly. "I mean..." He sputtered. "Fuck. Kira. You said you once wanted to sell your body, so, if you're gonna be selling your body I need to show you what it's all about. Even if it's just once... It'll be our little secret." Brushing his lips against hers.

"Lemme show you what it's all about..."

The demoness who sat upon Venser's lap, blinked as she and also forgot that in her previous form.. she had the plan of selling herself. A laugh would then surface with a hand covering her mouth. Then, as she gazed at Venser she would answer, "I can see why you have so many lovers..." Those black eyes slid to look away, but it was not long before she gave him her attention once more. "... Since I have regained my true form... sSlling myself would be horribly unnecessary." she laughed once more, her tone so sweet, smooth and youthful. "But I wasn't you to show me regardless." she spoke in a more exotic quiet tone as she leaned forward, just inches away from his mouth.

"Show me, everything, Venser..."

"Your wish is my command..." He asked sitting up in the warm, comfortable waters of the bath they shared, picking up a sponge to clean her with. "Heh..." Venser chuckled at the thought, and considered they'd need another one soon.

That long raven hair pooled around her body, serving as a wet curtain which clung to her surfaced shoulders and back. "Why not?" she rose an innocent eyebrow as she gazed up at him as she sat still while he picked up a sponge.

The bearded man smiled in response and continued to clean her, pressing his chest against hers as she sat on his lap. "Well then..." He said after a few minutes. "Shall we go to my room?"

A little smile formed at her lips while she simply planted a sweet succulent kiss on his right cheek while she felt the sponge scrub on her form. "Room or here, it does not matter... Does it?" she questioned lightly.

"It's much better in my bed..." Venser said, gripping her body. "Hold on." The two disappeared in a puff of thick red smoke and reappeared on top of Venser's silk, turquoise sheets. "Now," He said with a pause holding both of Kira's arms down, rubbing his hardened cock against her womanhood teasingly, "Are you ready for me?"

As Kira was about to say something, Venser had gripped on her body and immediately the two disappeared from the bathroom and reappeared upon the bed. The girl laid upon those silk, turquoise sheets gazing up at him now, her expression calm for the moment as her hair fanned out over the bed while her body was fully exposed. "That I am." she answered his question.

Venser sank her body down onto Kira's, pushing his stiff member slowly inside of her. He moaned in pleasure as he began to thrust in and out slowly, looking down to Kira. "How's that feel?" He asked in between breaths.

Those dark eyes gazed up towards his green as she laid there in silence. The last time she let a man touch her, was a long time ago. The very man that had made her happiness turn into absolute misfortune. But this experience, was definitely going to be different... Kira would hope.

Those delicate hands gripped into slight fists as she could feel his stiff member pressing against her flower, causing her body to slightly tense up. Shockingly, as a result, the powerful demoness indeed appeared nervous. Her cheeks were of a lovely shade of pink as she then heard herself moan while her chest rose while she arched. As his member entered, it felt like her flower lips were expanding and her insides clung to his shaft in a tight manner. A set of shivers would vibrate through her body as he began to thrust in and out slowly, and her body would naturally respond by becoming moist and heated.

"It... Ohhhhhhh Ven... It feels... So hot."

"You're fucking tight..." Venser said with a moan looking down to Kira, thrusting in and out of her picking up his pacing. He paused for a moment to wriggle his cock around against the inner walls of her wet flower.

"Mhm..." He flipped them over with his arms wrapped around Kira, so she was on top now. He pressed his lips against hers while holding her close, thrusting in and out of her as she laid on top of him now.

A much more exotic set of moans would surface past her lips as his pace picked up and his thrust where claiming her body for this moment in time. Her hands gripped tighter into fists while her body rocked with every push his hips gave. Then, as her arms became freed, there bodies entangled to where she was on top with her breasts squished against his chest while her bottom jiggled while Venser thrusted up into her wet flower. Her fingers gripped upon those silk sheets tightly as her eyes were narrowed, her face blushed and her moans a desirable tone.

The sounds of Kira's ass slapping against the bearded man's thighs filled the room, sweat built up on Venser's body as he pressed his lips to Kira's, kissing her softly as he had his way with her body. "Mhm! Mhm!" He slowed down and gave her two, hard slow thrusts before going back to his original speed.

This demoness who was usually very well composed and calm, was now indeed in a hot heated place while her body was being plunged into by the handsome barkeep With every slap and pull her moans filled the room, fluctuating in volume as each blow sent her in a deeper lustful fit. Gripping those turquoise sheets even tighter with her delicate soft hands, her mouth is captured with soft masculine lips.

Venser's tongue slid into Kira's mouth as he locked lips with her, his hands ran up the sides of her body, and then down slowly, resting on her ass as he slammed into it. With each thrust he delivered a playful smack to her right cheek.

As his lips moved against hers, Kira would follow his motions until his tongue slid in-between her mouth causing her to sensually moan. She never knew that

Venser tasted so good, in more ways than one. This particular demoness was able to harmlessly feed off of a person's essence by touching, kissing or having sexual intercourse. This would have no bad effect towards the person being touched, kissed or having sex with her, instead, he would feel even better as the sex progressed. And Kira? Would gain energy that went towards her abilities and physical well being in general. With every slam into her body, sent a more powerful sensation into her already aroused body. Her fingers would then move to seductively brush against Venser's raven hair as she kissed him back with a bit more of a lustful force.

Venser's tongue lolled around in Kira's mouth, playing a sort of tug of war with her own tongue.

"Nghh." He sat up against the back of his bed frame and arched her back, taking her nipples into his mouth and sucking on them as she bounced up and down on his cock. "Loving this?"

The kiss turned into a more playful session between the two, Kira was indeed breaking out of a virgin shyness while her mouth would open wider to accept his tongue and try to get it back into her mouth. Eventually, Venser had sat up and arched her so her bouncing breasts were more exposed for his view. As his mouth took ahold of one of her nipples and sucked, a pleasurable out cry seemed to answer his current question. Kira used her hands to grip onto his shoulders, using her leg muscles to continue bouncing up and down his stiff hard member.

Biting her bottom lip, Kira felt the smack upon her bottom which caused the roundness to jiggle upon contact. She then felt pushed onto all fours as she was still being entered into by Venser. Gripping the sheets within her hands once more, she lets out loud sets of moans as each slow thrust was a full pound. Her back was fluttered with kisses and her breasts were being fondled, causing her heated body to rise in temperature while she reaped these rewards.

"You liking this Kira?" The handsome barkeep asked in between moans penetrating her wet flower faster and harder, loving how nice it wrapped around his member like a warm blanket. He sucked and kissed her shoulder, leaving a dark love bite. His cock twitched inside of her and he groaned, he was close now.

Gripping those silk sheets even tighter, Kira Kurai was moaning out with a more powerful volume as he began to plunge into her heated body faster and harder with every powerful forceful thrust. She felt her own upper body coming closer to the bed, her breasts hard nipples barely brushing against the sheets, and her upper arms, wrists and hands became more flat. The more her upper body seemed to naturally lower, the more her pussy would tighten and the more she felt like she might explode. "Ah! Yes yes yes!" She cried out with barely open eyes and blushing vibrant colored cheeks.

"Oh yes!" Venser sped up to the point where his hard, thick cock was pounding in and out of Kira like a steam powered piston, he pulled out and fired glob after glob of hot, sticky cum all over her rear and back. "Oh... Mhm..." He slapped his cock against her bouncy, wonderfully round ass and sighed, flopping over in bed. "Good girl."

The speed up caused Kira Kurai's demonic body to go on an overpowering serge as an orgasm ripped through her body right as Venser had pounded inside of her wet pussy with his thick stiff cock. Her out cry was loud, exotic and rather sexually youthful as she gripped the crap out of his sheets and thankfully did not tear them while her body was unsettled. But once Venser pulled out, Kira relaxed her upper body onto the bed while white globs of cum would coat her ass and slender smooth back. Collapsing fully, she panted, clearly out of breath.

"How was that for your first time in this body?" Venser asked wrapping the soft silk sheets around them, kissing Kira on the cheek and placing one hand on her breast, circling his finger around her hardened nipple.

The sudden relaxing atmosphere was definitely needed at the moment as Kira was doing her best to calm her breath while she laid wrapped up in silken sheets. Feeling the kiss from Venser once more on her face and a hand on her breast, she answered lightly, "Much different than I thought it would be." her eyes rose to meet the side of his face, "It was.. it was.." she could not find the right words to explain her sexual experience at the moment.

"It was fantastic?" He asked with another soft kiss as he snuggled into Kira. Venser chuckled and continued to play with her nipples.

Lowering her gaze to think about the term he used, she decided to settle for that word and gave a quiet nod. Her hands rose to gently touch him, trailing her slender well crafted fingers down his chest almost as if she was exploring the male body. Being this close to another human being was surely exotic, and it was something she hoped to do again sometime soon. After one sexual encounter, she felt her energy increase ten times than kissing or touching. This... Could be addicting... Kira was fully aware of the man Venser was, always having women in his bedroom... And now, she fully understood.

"Wonderful? Addicting? I can see you're at a loss for words..." Venser said placing his hands over hers, dragging them down his barreled chest as she explored his naked body.

"I can see how this could be addicting for the average person." Kira spoke lightly, almost in a mutter as her cheeks blushed with an adorable pink hue. Her finger nails barely brushed over his slightly tougher skin as she trailed them now down his abs and stomach, leaning up to give him a kiss. "Venser." The demoness smiled a little bit and couldn't wait to go again with him.

"Thank you."

CHAPTER SIX: VENSER'S NIPPLE PIERCING SESSION

Montpelier, Vorland, 1437 ATC

The handsome bearded man took in his surroundings, sitting in the backroom of some blacksmith's shop who specialized in piercing a person's body with metal. The piercing business was a minority in the country, and very blacksmiths did it, as most just preferred to do it themselves with a needle. In the center of the room was a leathery looking chair that the blacksmith's assistant ushered the bearded man to take a seat in. Which, he did, undoing the front of his tunic and sliding it off, sitting there with only his bright red boots and baggy red pants on.

"Alright, just give me a second to get everything all prepared. Find the right size of needle and heat it... Get the rings..." The assistant began moving to the other side of the room, washing his hands in a basin first. "Rings, bars, or chains in your nipples?"

"Hmmm... Rings. Or, bars first and then the rings. Always wanted to have nipple rings, actually. First as a joke like, when I go swimming I just take off my shirt and hey everyone look at my nipples ha ha." Ven spoke with a chuckle, the blacksmith's assistant wasn't amused.

The assistant took his seat in the stool next to Venser's right. He had with him a plate holding a handful of items. A couple of needles, the silver nipple rings, nipple chains, some aloe rub, and bandages.

"Alright, hold still this won't hurt much" The assistant said heating one of the small needles over a candle, before leaning in close to Venser's barreled chest.

He pressed his body into the leathery back of the chair, wincing in pain a bit when the small, hot needle went through one nipple, and then the other.

"Done. There we go."

He blinked his emerald, snake like eyes. "Just like that?"

"Yup." The blacksmith's assistant answered. Carefully, the small holes in his nipples were widened as new silver bars were put through them and capped them with rings and then linked a long silver chain between them.

"Mhmph." Ven grunted a bit in pain, his back arching as he watched the man work.

"For the rings, chains, and bars since you couldn't decide so I went with all three, and the piercing, it's going to be thirty silver from ya."

Venser stood up to look in a nearby mirror, and his eyes practically lit up when he saw them in the mirror. "Wow... Nice."

They began to swell so later on he'd just have to switch to the simple rings and let the holes heal properly.

"Sit back down, you need aloe and bandages. Sounds like you really like them." He said to Ven, who was admiring himself in the mirror with pride and a hint of amusement.

"I do." Was Venser Karkaldwin's simple response. "My lovers are really going to like these..."

"Keep them clean, soak them, do not touch or let anyone else touch them for a few days. And wear the bandages and change em regularly and... Ya know, standard healing stuff."

CHAPTER SEVEN: ANGEL BRITTONY NIGHTENGALE

The Dragon's Head Tavern and Inn, Vorland, 1437 ATC

The young hybrid began to make her way back to the tavern, it was one of the few places she allowed herself to become familiar with, though it had been quite some time since her last visit. She had come across a few other packs along her travels and she had been wounded quite some time ago but that was all behind her now and she was on the mend after quite a scare from a bite of an original hybrid. She longed to return to a place she knew and somewhere she felt safe...

Angel Brittony Nightengale was very beautiful and slender, and moved with a strange grace and elegance, her hair was a sleek dark blonde, which framed her slightly round cheeks, and she had glittering blue-green eyes. She was a bit of a mess covered in scratches and the bitemark to her shoulder was still visible. The Dragon's Head Tavern and Inn was practically a home to her and she still had some of her things there which came in handy in these situations. Making her way to the door, hearing patrons upstairs she frowned slightly wondering how she'd get her weak mangled self to her room without drawing too much attention to herself. Her clothes were torn, covering not much of her wounded body as she silently snuck in the tavern door, looking around at a way to get to her room on the second floor, to the room she shared with her old lover.

The bearded bartender Venser removed a small, sponge cake from his pouch and bit into it, revealing pink filling inside. "Mhm." After he took a bite he then took a sip of his hot chocolate. "Want some of my Pinkie?" He asked, offering the treat to Rec. "Welcome to the Dragon's Head Tavern and Inn!" He called out hearing the front door open.

A brow rose as she glanced over to Ven and shrugged "Sure, why not. You've shared everything else with me thus far this evening." The woman chuckled and took a bite of the Pinkie before her face twisted in dislike. She handed it back to him and chased the horrible taste down with a swig of rum. "Ew... Thanks but no thanks next time... I can't even... What?"

Angel Nightingale sighed, hearing a familiar voice and swore under her breath, not wanting to be rude by ignoring Venser's welcome but at the same time not wishing to draw attention to herself.

"Son of a bitch"

Though the young hybrid meant to stay quiet, cursing under her breath was enough for most to hear her. Angel sighed and made her way up the stairs, seeming as it was her only option. "Apparently I'm too weak to even turn back to wolf form to rid me of this humiliation." Spoken softly as she reached the top of the stairs.

"Seriously?" Venser said, gulping down the rest of it, drinking down the rest of his green tea. "By the void." He set his mug down and disappeared in a puff of thick red smoke, reappearing next to Angel. He wrapped an arm around her and they both disappeared, reappearing in one of the rooms where they kept most injured patrons. They landed on the bed and Venser carefully spread her limbs apart. "What happened?"

Oblivious to all but the horrid smell of dog she sneezed and wrinkled her nose as she began to sip from her glass once more. Rec cocked her head slightly as she searched for the cause of the smell then shrugged it off and returned to her grooming.

"I came across a far stronger hybrid and his rather large pack and let's just say he was quite capable of slaughtering me where I stood. I'm fine now it's nothing major and I'm on the mend but for a while one of the bites I received from him was more or less killing me and turning me a bit rabid along the way... May have slaughtered a fair few people in that state." Angel paused for a moment and looked at him, letting out a sigh.

"Am I making any sense? Ugh..." The blonde hybrid held her hand to her head. "A bottle of rum would be great right about now, maybe whiskey."

"Yeah yeah you are..." Venser said walking over to a nearby chest, kicking it.. It popped open and he reached inside to grab some bandages. "Won't do for now..." He disappeared in a puff of thick red smoke and reappeared behind the bar, quickly grabbing a bottle of whiskey and rum. He looked to the shadow tendrils that pooled on the floor behind the bar. "Get a wet rag and tend to the woman in the healing room!" He quickly spun around and looked to the three in the tavern. "So sorry! Shadow tendrils will serve." He then disappeared in a puff of thick red smoke and reappeared in the room where Angel was, the snaky, shadowy hands were wiping the blood off her. "Here." He said offering Angel both bottles. "Which one do you want first?"

Rec shivered slightly as the evening breeze blew through the front door as two new patrons entered. Smiling slightly before wrapping her tail about herself she began to eye them suspiciously seeing how the last time she encountered a horned individual it didn't end well for them. She kept her thoughts to herself but made sure to keep an eye out in case one was up to something funny. Finishing off her drink she signaled a tendril for a refill and she waited patiently for it as she picked nervously at her tail-

Angel had a slight frown as the tendrils were tending to her before her old lover reappeared. She looked to him briefly with a smile not helping but laugh slightly before taking one of the bottles gently from him. "That'll do. And you do realize I'm not dying right? my wounds will heal eventually, they're just taking a little longer than intended, once my strength is back up they will heal in no time and what better way to do that than with some good strong alcohol. How have you been anyway, stranger?"

She then popped off the cork and began to down the bottle waiting for him to reply. she paused a moment. "And I will be more than capable to come out and socialize. I just needed some of my clothes."

"You're still hurt." Venser said setting the other bottle of whatever down on the nightstand. He sighed and walked back over to the medicine chest, grabbing some healing paste to apply to her wounds. "I've actually... Been meaning to look for you." He said ignoring her question.

"Why? Why not earlier? How long have I been gone?" Angel raised a brow and blinked her blue-green eyes, and had quite a concerned look upon her face. She sat back up, still looking at him as he rummaged through the medicine chest.

He shrugged. "Not sure I just need someone to teach me how to ride a horse." Venser said bandaging her wounds, patting them down a bit so they would stick in place. "I might take a job that requires it. Plus I'll have to teach my kids and ehh... I don't think chariot racing counts as actually being able to ride."

Angel Nightengale winced. "Treating them really isn't necessary and right, I was meant to teach you before I went all rabid dog with all the blood moon crap and everything else in between... When I'm healthy again, we'll start. there's nothing much to it. I mean, you ride a woman well enough..." She said, licking her lips in delight.

"On a completely different note. How long am I going to be sitting here practically nude before you allow me to get changed?"

Venser sighed and moved away from Angel. "Alright. You can change in front of me if you'd like. Or I can go back and tend the bar." He said.

"It's up to you, nothing you haven't seen before. If you man the bar I'll be out there shortly, and I promise not to kill anyone... Or feed on them or whatever else..." The young hybrid stood up, feeling a little dizzy from having downed a whole bottle of rum so quickly. "Downing that bottle may not have been the best idea I've ever had..." Angel put her hand to her head for a moment before scanning her shimmering blue-green eyes around the place.

"You know I still have all your dresses in my room." He said sitting down on the bed as they conversed in the healing room. "I mean... I gave a few away... Sort of. Uh, lent some out. Added some."

"Well that would be a start but isn't you room like, twenty or so steps in that direction?" She pointed down the hall in a somewhat drunken state already.

"Did you forget I can teleport?" Venser asked, taking Angel's cleaned hand as the two disappeared in a puff of thick red smoke, reappearing on the other side of the tavern in the bedroom the two once shared. He rolled off the bed and tapped the angel feather on the nightstand twice, illuminating the room in a beautiful, benevolent bluish white light. He marched over to the wooden wardrobe and opened it. Revealing Angel's outfits still in great condition along with a few others that weren't hers. "Here, I haven't done a thing to em. But..." He walked over to the bed and placed his hands on Angel's sides, running them down her body.

The blonde hybrid glanced at him as they were whisked off to what was now his room. Seeing him open the wardrobe that still contained some of her clothes. then as he whisked back over to her. closing her eyes as she felt his runs run down her body. she then opened them and looked at him. "But...?" Angel cocked a brow as she looked back at him-

Venser said nothing, but went back over to the wardrobe and pulled out a box

that wasn't originally in the wardrobe before. He began to sort through it before he stood up again. "Ah." He tossed a red thong to Angel, with the words "Venser's Property" stitched into the back in green. "You'll be needing those. Unless you wanna go commando."

Angel quickly caught them having a look at the writing. "Well that's very straight to the point." The blonde hybrid chuckled slightly. "So what's next? you seem to be enjoying this way too much"

"Well, you put that on and get dressed and I don't know." He shrugged. "We go have a drink or something." Venser sighed and walked around the bed, laying down while waiting for his old lover to get dressed.

"Well I suppose that could be a start, we do have a lot to catch up on." She'd put on a red gown that she hadn't worn in quite some time, and brushed through her hair slightly with her fingers to tidy herself up a bit before sitting on the side of the bed opposite to where Venser laid. "You grew a beard and kept it, I see."

"Yes I did. So, bar?" He asked sitting up. "I was actually having some green tea before you came here hurt."

"Never knew you drank the stuff. But the bar sounds fine to me. Also, Ven, you never answered my question." Angel stood back up and made her way to his side of the bed as he sat there. If I could find out, then I know how long I can torture the shit out of the bastard if I come across him again before I kill him. Or maybe the amount of weeks or months could be the amount of pack members I kill first."

"I'm confused." He said standing up. "What question? permission to kill whomever did this to you? Well granted, obviously."

"No... I don't need permission for that, I'll kill the bastard either way... I meant how long was I gone?" She began to make her way to the bar, her mind set on a different drink entirely.

"Like I said, I don't know exactly. About... Almost three years?" The bearded bartender said, closing the door as they left his room. He couldn't help but pull up Angel's gown and take a peek at her rear in the thong he had given her. "Venser's property..."

Angel rolled her eyes, chuckling slightly. It was Venser Karkaldwin after all, she regarded him as the biggest manwhore on the planet Laguna. Making her way to the bar she stepped behind it for a moment getting a rather old bottle off the shelf. Pulling off the cork it gave out quite a foul stench though it was rather sweet to her... Usually. "Please don't be stale." The blonde hybrid took a slight sniff before sipping the liquid slightly. "I suppose I've had worse. And I will pay for this, though it's not like there's usually anyone around here that drinks this shit anyway." She took another moment to examine the countertop carefully as if examining it's materials and craftsmanship.

He gave her rear a playfully smack and sat down beside her, tapping the bar twice. "What I had about a half hour ago." Venser told the shadow tendrils, waving Angel off. "It's fine, I'll cover you."

She then glanced at the being that made its way to sit at the end of the bar, trying very hard not to stare and she tilted her head slightly. Getting her mind off it she poured herself a glass of the foul smelling liquid. Bringing to her lips and having a decent swig.

"So tomorrow you can teach me to ride a horse, Angel?"

"If I'm feeling up to it, I'm sure I could. I have no doubts my noble steed will be around these parts somewhere munching on some poor defenseless creature out there." She chuckled."Though I must say he isn't the most comfortable ride in the world."

Venser was unsure how to answer Angel. "Better than nothing I guess..." He said after a few moments. "Do you happen to know anything about crops and livestock?"

"Crops no, livestock yes. Kind of." Angel continued to sip from her drink, listening in as the other two conversed with one another, smirking slightly. a lot of the patrons had gone to sleep as it was getting quite late. and as much as she really wanted to cause a stir she knew that wouldn't go down very well in the tavern. her wounds had finally started to heal themselves and she licked the remaining blood from her lips tuning out from the conversation. she had closed her eyes for a moment before opening them and briefly glancing over at Venser and smirking slightly. she placed her now empty glass back down upon the counter and stood up, standing behind the handsome barkeep. "You know, I could always create my own entertainment and feed upon a couple of the guests." She had been getting a little bored of their conversation but wasn't one to interrupt.

That was merely a cardboard cutout Venser had placed behind the bar for no reason. He cleared his throat. "I need to show you something in my room. Well, more like an opinion on something. Go lay in my bed while I go get ready." He flicked her nose playfully, exaggerating his voice. "Boop!" He then disappeared in a puff of thick red smoke.

Angel Nightengale sighed and began to walk down the hallway to his room. She sat on the side of his bed pondering over what he was up to. Slipping off her red dress and wincing slightly at the bite mark that was still visible on her shoulder blade. The rest of her wounds had healed; she guessed this was just going to take a little longer. She laid down and waited for him though being the highly strung being she was, patience wasn't one of her strong points.

"Da da da!" Venser slinked into the room, shaking his hands like a runner does before a race. He was wearing nothing but a leopard print thong and he began to sway his body slowly in front of his ex lover as she lay on the bed. He gripped the front of it and began to pump his body up and down, his right hand slipped down inside the waistband of it. "Like what you're seeing here?" He asked spinning around, wagging his ass at Angel, showing off his muscular body.

The blonde hybrid couldn't help but chuckle slightly. "Well, you've proven you are most certainly insane. but I can't say I have any complaints, though I have to say leave the ass wiggling to us dogs, we do it far better." Angel said teasingly, giving the bearded man an amused smirk.

Venser's erection was very prominent inside the leopard print thong as he growled seductively in her response to her talking. His fingers dipped further into his thong, slowly pulling them down inch after inch, very very slowly... He slid down over his thighs for a very brief moment as he pushed his hips forward. Climbing onto the bed he swung his hips from left to right making his penis sway back and forth as he hummed "The Stripper." He cleared his throat and said, "I might take a job as a stripper soon to help pay for the farm. You like, Angel?"

"A stripper? Well yes I suppose that would certainty rake in some coin. Especially with all the women you've managed to woo over the years. Similar to how I work as part vampire and how I tend to feed. Though instead of being in it for money, or sleeping with the man I end up well, I guess you can figure out where that's heading. And I was thinking of being the main stable girl here..." The blonde hybrid said lifting her legs in the air and running her hands down them to the thong gently placing each one at the sides and pulling it off and sliding it up her legs, throwing it to the side before placing her legs either side of him, letting out a soft aroused growl.

He sat on the bed now, showing off his muscular frame and barrel chest for Angel now and grinned, looking down to her as she slid her panties off before backing up. Venser hopped off the bed, rubbing his hands up and down his body, occasionally gripping himself squeezing slightly before rubbing over it and throwing his head back with a soft moan like he was going to have an orgasm while he teased her. "Easy money. Plus," He pulled down his thong, fully showing off his nude body for her, "I can see that you want me..."

"I suppose it would be..." Angel glanced down at his lovely package before glancing up at him. Before rolling over and lifting her ass into the air wiggling it before him. She'd then turn back over and glance up at him. "Out of all the women you've screwed, why me? I mean technically this could be classed as bestiality. Me being a able to shift into a wolf and all." She'd tease giving off her devious smirk, her fangs bared.

"Only when you decide to morph into one." Venser said watching her wiggle her ass at him. He hopped back on the bed and grabbed her ass with both hands, positioning his erect cock in the right place. "If I were to fuck you in wolf form... Yeah." He rubbed his member teasingly against her lips. "Gonna cost you extra..."

"Can't say that'd be the best idea, I'd probably try and unintentionally rip your head off. I tend to be quite a bitch in my canine form..." Angel would give a slight moan as he rubbed his length against her, pushing her hips back against him slightly, spreading her legs apart more. "Oh I missed you Ven... Mhm. Just... Just do it. Fuck me!"

"And now you're home..." The bearded bartender said plunging inside of her.

CHAPTER EIGHT: LUCINDA'S PAINTING

The Dragon's Head Tavern and Inn, Vorland, 1437 ATC

Kari gathered a blanket or two as she walked into the women's room and gently laid them over her and watched over here until Angel got there.

Ivy the elven merc would blink a few times before she wandered up to the second floor. Her bare feet patting against the wooden panels. Nibbling at her bottom lip as she reached the top of the stairs. Suddenly she'd let out a soft sneeze. She'd drop her hands to her sides as she listened in on the conversation held between the few people who were present. She'd lift her chin and wander to the furthest bar stool, placing her hands firmly against her lap, as her bangle made a clinking noise with their moment. Her eyes slowly looked up and out the windows of the tavern and at the open land, sitting quietly, feeling somewhat tired today and felt like people watching.

Angel retrieved what she needed to help a mother, both of which while came to the tavern seeking help. "You may get called several names, but as I said, you don't have to act like one. I know it's hard but the choice is always yours, you can't exactly choose what you are, but you can choose whether or not to live by what people call you, go around and kill, have the blood of others fall on your hands and show them they're right in calling you those things, or you can stand up for yourself and prove them all wrong." She walked back down the hallway with everything and made her way in the door where the boy's mother and Brea was.

The sandy haired barmaid smiled as she nodded to Angel and made her way back in the bar area. Kari walked up the stairs, her boots clicking on each step as she made her way over to a table and sat down, looking around at the others. Brea went and made the kid some sweet tea. "Don't worry about what others think, being hated is a double-edged sword. Trust me I know."

Venser appeared out of a puff of thick red smoke in the middle of the tavern area, holding the hands of his two small children who had just gotten out of play school. Soarin wore a little red leather jacket with dark blue pants and black shoes, while Lucinda wore a black button up jacket, light blue pants, and little black boots. "Afternoon everyone!" He said walking with them, the twins let go of his hand and began to run back to their room. "Hey Lu, have you seen Kari anywhere? We went to her house and she wasn't there." He said crossing his arms. Soarin hopped up and down. "Hi lady! Catch me daddy!"

Ivy would place her palm down against the counter of the bar, her nails would drum down in a row before lifting her leg and crossing it over the other as she blinked a few more times, as she glanced over her shoulder at the boy who poked at his strew. Her eyes then rolled back over to the area in front of her pulling her hood down and off her head as she reached her fingers under her ravenous locks, they stretched down her back, her fingers brushing down her bangs a bit, making sure they weren't a mess.

Brea looked at Ven,"Kari is sitting around her somewhere, just look for her white hair." She chuckled as she looked at the lady at the bar, "Hello dear, what can I get you?"

"Right... I mean we've been with each other for five years. I know her hair color.'" Venser said looking back at his young son. "Go play with your sister! I'll catch you soon." He turned to walk over to the railings and sighed. White hair. A lot of patrons with white hair came in all the time. "Mommy!" Soarin pipped looking through the railings, he then began to run down the stairs as fast as his little legs could carry him.

Ivy's eyes would glance up and over at the female who spoke to her, her cheeks lifted up into a smile. "Hello, May I have a ale, please?" Her voice was kind, soothing. Her body would lean up slightly as she places her forearms on the bar counter. Laying out the silver in which to pay with, along with a tip.

Brea Rowland nodded,"Of course coming right up." She put the silver coins way and brought the lady a mug of ale."Here you are ." She smiled as she walked near the boy. "Kid ignore what they tell you, there will always be one person out there that loves to hate others just because it makes them happy to see others suffer." ... Meanwhile Kari noticed Ven and the twins and smiled waiting to see how long it would take him to see her.

Ivy would smile as she would take the mug of ale, pulling the scarf from her face, raising the mug to her lips listening as the female wandered back to the boy. Sipping the ale, her eyes rolling closed a soft, "Mmh.." murmuring from her lips of the wonderful taste.

Angel walked out of the room placing everything down upon a table before walking back down the hallway to the bar. She'd place some coin upon the counter before helping herself to one of the bottles off the end of the shelf though having forgotten to restock it she found it was empty. She'd give a slight deep growl before placing the empty bottle upon the counter, making her way to the stairs.

Soarin brushed his messy hair so blonde it looked white out of his eyes as he hopped down the last step and ran across the wooden floorboards, wrapping his arms around one of his mother's legs. Venser appeared about a minute later holding Lucinda's hand, who in turn did the same thing as her brother after letting out a happy squeal. "How's life going, Kari?" Venser asked, approaching the white haired woman, giving her a soft kiss. Wearing his usual crimson and light blue tunic, with baggy red pants and bright red boots. He really needed a shave and a haircut again. "Mommy I painted a picture at pway school!" Their young daughter said looking up to Kari, waving around a paper folded in half.

Malla stood outside the tavern, staring at the closed wooden doors before her. She took a deep breath in and exhaled, patting down the now cloth dress she wore. It felt odd and itchy against her skin, but she wanted to try to close the gap between her and Shin by wearing regular clothes. She put her hand out before her and gave a push on the door, walking through slowly. The chains on her horns jingled softly against her black hair and her boots made soft ticks on the floor. The smell of the old familiar tavern washed over her and she smiled, looking up at the stairs. So much had happened here. The scent of familiar people reached her nose and she looked down at her hands, feeling comfortable. As she heads to the bar her thoughts are on her new mate.

Malla was a strange, rare hybrid of demoness and dragon. She stood a little over seven feet tall, with long raven locks and piercing orange eyes. Her twin horns branched from her head, curving upwards. Her legs, thick and powerful, had a reptilian design, as well as her exposed skin, a long tail with a spade on the tip grew from her ass. Plump feminine thighs and wide hips as she walked in.

Kari smiled as she picked up Soarin and accepted the paper from Lucinda. "Did you now? Oh sweetie I love it so much..." She cuddled her while she opened the paper up and looked at it. And smiled at Ven. "Life's been good, what about yours?"

Angel made her way down the stairs and out the door to go for a hunt, having to feed and restock her stashes around the tavern. She turned to her wolf form as she made her way to the door, prancing past the other patrons and Ven and his family, slipping through the door as it opened for another being to enter.

Brea sighed as she walked back behind the bar and drank some honey mead she poured earlier.

"Yeah!" It was a watercolor painting, childish, of course of Venser and Kari along with the twins holding hands. Venser and Kari stood beside each other, while a yellow woman with black hair stood on one side of Venser, holding his hand while Lucinda held hers. The background was a house with some trees and grass and a smiling sun. "It goes well. Tending the bar making coin... Looking at property, going out to explore." Venser said, pulling up a chair from a nearby table. "Daddy can we have some smoothies?" Soarin asked him. He nodded and said, "In a moment son."

Ivy would tense up with a bit of a jump as the boy slammed the door. She'd glance over her shoulder to the hallway which he stormed into. "Hmph.." She'd raise the ale to her lips against taking another sip. Her eyes then suddenly focused on the sounds of children's voices, Her lips curled into a small smile. She leaned forward as her long black hair slipped off her back and to the side of her.

Kari smiled at the picture and folded it back, setting it on the table. "It's lovely Lucinda, I'm proud of you for how good it was." She decided to tease Ven. "It sounds like you were busy with other stuff when you didn't have them."

"Well, I'm the head bartender you know. And an entertainer but... I don't know. I haven't been too happy, oddly enough. Just... A down feeling." Venser said as he reclined lazily in his seat. Lucinda smiled when her mother praised her painting. "Thank you mommy." She raised her arms to Kari. "Up?" Soarin moved past his sister and hugged Venser's leg. "Be happy daddy... Smoothies make me happy!" Even though Venser had mentioned running the bar about two minutes prior, he looked back to Kari and said, "Daddy makes money so he can buy toys for me and Lewcinda."

Angel made her way back to the tavern after having a decent feed, still in her wolf form as she walked. Her snow white pelt covered in blood. She had a small deer carcass that was pretty shredded in her jaws as she made her way back through the tavern doors.

Kari picked Lucinda up and put her on her other knee. "I'm thinking we all might want smoothies and I can understand that. All work and no play with kids makes boring times sometimes."

Malla the dragon demoness hybrid saw her old friend Venser with the twins and smiled, hoping to be that happy in the near future with her own recently acquired lover, Shin. She walked up the stairs and over to the bar, a gentle smile on her black lips for once. She sat down and folded her claw tipped hands on the bar top, waiting to get either his attention or the sandy haired barmaid.

Lucinda smiled and rested her head on Kari's arm. "Mommy I got bit at pway school today." She said holding out her left arm, a small bandaid near her elbow. Soarin climbed up on her other knee and said, "And I pawn gummed!" He said, making a punching motion in the air as Venser went to the kitchen to whip up some smoothies, not noticing Angel nor Malla. Speaking of which, when Angel came through the door with a deer in between her teeth, Lucinda began to cry at the sight of the bloody thing. While Soarin had his back to it.

Kari tried to calm Lucinda down and cover her eyes to keep her from looking at the heavily torn deer corpse again. Brea finished her honeymead and looked over at the commotion.

Angel lowered her head making her way into the kitchen with the deer. before placing it down and turning back to her human form. She wandered around getting some empty bottles as venser made smoothies, her eyes were a lighter blue than normal and her skin a paler complexion. Filling the bottles with the blood of her kill and paying no nevermind to everything around her.

The smell of blood hit Malla's sensitive nose and she turned to look at the stairs, her dragon side of her growing hungry. Her pupils dilated and she liked her lips, but then shook her head and turned back to the bar. "Excuse me? Can I have some ale with blood mixed in please? From the deer." She asks, her fingers tapping the bar top as her hunger increased.

Brea raised a brow and nodded as she made the lady a mix of blood and ale and handed it to her. "Here you go Miss. Three silvers please."

"Dead deer it looked so bad..." Lucinda murmured wiping the tears off her face. As Venser cranked ice in a machine he looked to Angel as she morphed into her human form, grimacing a bit watching the transformation before his eyes. "By the void, you know my kids are out there right? And they love animals." He sighed and watched as she filled the bottles with blood. "Mommy." Soarin said hugging Kari close.

Malla nodded back and clung to her strange drink, pulling it up to her lips and taking a small sip, breathing deeply as her hunger fades. She placed five silver coins on the bar without taking the cup from her lips, relishing in the taste.

Kari sighed. "It was dead." She cuddled her twins to try and keep them calm.

Ivy would rise from her seat, as she took her last sip of ale and wandered to the window next to the bar, leaning forward as her elbows were placed on the windowsill, looking out at nature as she exhaled slowly with a smile. Blinking a few times as she rolled her shoulders back as her smile rolled from her lips she turned her head looking to the door she sensing a great power lurking not far from the tavern.

"I do apologize for that, and I would rather not have them on my main diet but feeding on human blood doesn't exactly go down with myself or others either. I'm the complete opposite of what I used to be. I once helped animals and now I kill and feed upon them in order to survive. It's not exactly my ideal lifestyle. Starving myself gets me nowhere, it only tends to make me more hostile." The young hybrid would sigh, putting a cork on a couple of the bottles.

"Poor deerie..." Soarin said with a sigh, both twins fell silent as they were comforted by their mother's embrace. "We have a backdoor ya know but..." He shook his head. "You didn't know they were here." Venser clapped his hands twice and instructed the shadow tendrils to finish the smoothies. He walked over to the deer and kicked it lightly. "And I could have made you dinner. A nice, juicy steak... Or fish and chips. You name it Angel. But we'll get this out of sight and have some venison. The kids, they eat meat. They just don't like seeing... Ya know."

Kari got up with the kids in her hands and moved to a corner of the room where they could see any more dead animals that might be around.

"Poor deerie..." Soarin said with a sigh, both twins fell silent as they were comforted by their mother's embrace. "We have a backdoor ya know but..." He shook his head. "You didn't know they were here." Venser clapped his hands twice and instructed the shadow tendrils to finish the smoothies. He walked over to the deer and kicked it lightly. "And I could have made you dinner. A nice, juicy steak...

Or fish and chips. You name it Angel." He said as the shadow tendrils began to pour the smoothies into glasses. "Mommy why do my little ball things hurt when I squeeze them?" Soarin asked as Venser emerged from the kitchen with a tray of orange smoothies. "Oh. Jwa- What?" He blinked a few times hearing his son ask that.

Kari blinked her icy blue eyes for a moment, "That's something you would need to ask daddy about."

"Unfortunately that doesn't satisfy my hunger for very long anymore." Angel Nightengale would sigh again, as he walked back out looking back down at the deer. "Oh how I wish I would." She pondered a bit as to where to store the remains for later, giving a slight deep growl and frowning as she looked down at the severely mangled corpse.

"Because they aren't for squeezing. And you shouldn't touch them." Venser said walking over to the three, offering the tray of smoothies. The twins cheered and took a glass. "Thank you daddy." They both said in unison, sipping the orange smoothies through the straws. "Freshly made Kari. You're gonna love this." He said with a smile.

Malla looks over at the dead deer and shivers, having been hungry for fresh meat for a very long time. When she rests in the void, her hunger seems to be satisfied for quite a while as though it fulfilled her appetite somehow. Now that she spent more time out of the void she had to fight the hunger more, but it was getting harder and harder to ignore. Soon, if she didn't find a solution, she could revert to a feral form and eat anything within sight that has a heartbeat. The thought made her shake her head and curse herself, not wanting to think of herself as an evil creature like that. She knew it'd be fine to hunt for survival though.

Kari smiled as she took and sip and watched the twins sipping as well, "It is good."

"I know right?" Venser said setting the tray down, picking up the last glass and taking a sip. "Can you watch the kids while I go socialize?" He asked messing up Soarin's hair, he giggled and raised one hand up, messing it up too so that his hair was spiky now. "Let you have the kids for now."

Kari nodded,"Just don't get in too much trouble." She winked as she cuddled the twins.

"Ya know... We all need to do something together sometime. As a family, since you've been so busy with the village." He said wrapping his arms around their children and Kari, hugging them affectionately before teleporting away. "How's the lover?" Venser asked Malla appearing out of a puff of thick red smoke behind the bar.

Malla lets out a sigh and looks up to the spot Venser, her old flame was about to appear and smiles when she was right at he did. She takes another drink and relaxes. "He isn't just a lover Ven, we are going to be joined together as soon as we settle on where we will live." She chuckled and put her cup down."How is the family? I still haven't met them you know?" She said, tilting her head at him and giving a small toothy grin.

Angel sighed disposing of the remains in her own manner back in her wolf form before returning to her human form and cleaning up after herself. wiping the blood from her face and cleaning herself up before heading back out with bottles in hand and making her way up the stairs with them as she glanced around at the other patrons.

"Right right... Fiance!" He made awkward hand gestures and then gripped the bar with both hands, thrusting his pelvis into it. "I remember when you were looking for a mate. We mated a few times but never managed to knock ya up." He humped the bar several more times. "Mhm! Mhm! Mhm!" Venser ignored the part about his own family and went on for a bit longer, until Angel came into view. "Oh." He stopped and placed his hands on his hips, pretending it never happened. "Really? My kids are almost five, I have a baby daughter, named Rowena whose only a few months, and more kids on the way... and you've never met them in the years they've been alive?"

The sandy blonde barmaid Brea watched the two while also watching the chaos that was happening as well as she stood there,"I see now why you didn't want to come into the tavern. That would get messy." She smiled with her bright hazel eyes shining in an amused way.

The overwhelming presence made Malla stiffen a bit. She looked at Venser and faked a smile, trying to ignore the feeling outside as it made her skin crawl. "N-no, I have never met your family. And our labor bore no fruit because we did not bond. Dragons mate for life and I thought I wouldn't be affected being as I am only half. Alas, it did anyway. And we are fine, me and him." She looked genuinely happy, excluding what she was reacting to from outside. Her tail twitched around with aggravation.

"Tell that to my dragon lover Nivarah. Or any of my others... Like, Nivarah is fine with it. We're still going to be together always along with..." The bearded bartender looked over to the blonde hybrid woman.

"Oh don't stop on my behalf Ven, I know approximately how many women you've screwed around with, it doesn't bother me in the slightest. I'm a hybrid, literally a bitch, we come in heat every once in a while. I'm used to you sleeping around." Angel placed the bottles upon the counter, opening one and taking a sip. "And once again I have an emergency stash to hopefully prevent me going completely rabid dog again."

There were three women in his dojo right now. And he screwed with all three of them. He remembered Brea was in there too. "Oh!" He slammed his fist down on the bar and pointed up at the ceiling with his mouth open, ready to speak. But nothing came out.

"Uhhh... The kids are downstairs... Um... Er, smoke break!" He then disappeared in a puff of thick red smoke.

Angel rolled her eyes chuckling slightly as she licked the blood from her lovely lips. "Typical Venser" She got to her feet and placed a couple of the bottles upon the shelf behind the bar and was still thinking of places to store the others.

Malla chuckled as well and leaned back in her stool, watching the other female messing with the bottles. "So you are the one who brought that deer in?" She asks with a small smile on her lips, her head tilted curiously. "You must be a strong one. Hmmm... Werewolf, and a few other things, strangely."

She could easily tell from Angel's scent.

CHAPTER NINE: GALAXTEAH

1437 ATC

A battle seemingly took place last night in the dungeon, fought... He couldn't remember. Venser's slitted, emerald snake like eyes opened halfway on his fair face, smudged with dirt on his skin. The bearded man was still in a hazy state, almost feeling as if he was waking up from a dream. he found himself knocked out against the cold hard cement floor, the same floor as the woman who was now crying out for help he gathered herself up and rubbed his eyes with the palms of his hands. "W-what the fuuuck." He shifted and looked up, against the wall was an unusual, small black kukrin blade with unusual markings and pink coloring on the blade. "Yess...!" He reached out and grasped it, raising it to his nostrils. "Lovely..." Pheromones that covered the blade's edge that made most creatures of the night and hell into absolute sluts or raging horny beasts. And now he had claimed it. He had the place to himself now it seemed, remembering this was the very same place where he had met the God Queen Y'vonne. He mumbled to himself, tearing off the remains of his top, showing off his barreled chest as he approached a bath near a few torches, seemingly waiting for him. He blinked a few times hearing the sound of footsteps approaching, a strange, buxom, four armed demoness standing a few feet away from the bath. He matched her smile.

"Hello there." The handsome bearded man raised a brow looking to her chest, and noticed a second pair of breasts underneath her normal ones.

She kept her dark eyes to him as she slowly came closer, the smile small but confident. She was being careful but not seemingly intimidated by this strange person who seemed to be a bit dirty from a fight. A warrior. A very fit and handsome man... A hand to a jutted hip as her stance stopped her close enough that her perfume was obvious in swirls of flowers, but not close enough to be within reach. Four, large bat like wings lifting high to beat with a slow motion that made her hair swirl about her cheeks and neck in a wistful dance. " Greetings... How do you fair this eve?" The demoness's voice like music as she spoke, something soothing to the mind with simple words.

"Oh what a sight to wake up too..." Venser said, dropping the blade. It clattered against the floor as he began to circle around the demoness. He himself was in his mid thirties, his rich dark hair with a green tint to it that had tousled griminess which promised finesse. He had strong arched brows and eyelashes so thick it demanded confidence, strength. Attack eyebrows! A prominent jaw curved gracefully around and the strength of his neck showed in the twining cords of muscle that shaped him. "I'm... Better, now." He licked at his lips agap just a bit as he walked around her, taking in her scent. "Alluring... Very alluring..." He said softly, and aloud.

"Exotic..."

Galaxteah blinked slowly, pupils that glowed with auroras of dark red color following his walk to her side until he disappeared from view. Just to turn to catch his form back on her other side after he made a round. Her weight shifting to the side he was now on as if her body followed him without sight. The demoness tall, muscular, and laced with soft scales that showed through the openings of her dress, the patterns drawing the eye to the small design of her waist over sweeping curved hips, and below full more than ample breasts that swayed as she took even breathes. A giggle on pale glossed lips at his words. A hand reaching up to stroke red locks of hair across the darker black at her cheek. The motion is rather vain in its gesture.

"I am happy that you find me as such..." She said again running one pair of hands through her hair as the other slowly snaked its way down her sides and thighs

His head was starting to clear up now, albeit his vision still blurred here and there. Now, all he could do was ogle.

"Happy? Of course..." The man let out a low, seductive growl and pushed her into the stone wall nearby. He was just as tall, and wore nothing but a pair of partially baggy red pants and bright red boots, mostly to show off his lean, muscular body. The bearded man lightly traced his fingers along the scales on her thigh. "I must say... I've come across creatures from the depths of Coldwrought... But never a demoness like yourself..." He examined her large, bat like leather wings and smiled. "Beautiful..."

Her eyes turned to the far side of the room at hearing the clink of something metal. Wings folding up higher to curl forward a bit as if being defensive. The attention being momentarily being away from the man and his intention to move her against the wall was indeed a surprise. A breath to leave her lips in a puff, wings out and flat against the wall with the weight of her back against their stumps. Hands lifting about chest high and fingers curling as if to show off the long claw like nails, making the gesture to strike at him but ultimately not doing so. Arms lowering to her sides and palms to press to the wall beside her hips. Her expression from surprise to being intrigued by his forwardness. His eyes panning over her and words seeming to calm her and feed her obvious ego. "I am... Quite unique, that is true. " Galaxteah purred the words gently and bit her bottom lip with a sharp tooth. The scales on her thigh under his fingers slightly lifted at his touch. The skin upon them was so soft that it seemed made of silk.

"Hm?" He raised a brow and turned his head, looking around at the room, for the source of the metal clank. Not like it mattered, anyway. Maybe just his imagination... Or maybe a peeping tom. "Hmmm... Succubi?" He asked looking over her again, looking down to her scaled thigh after glancing at her chest, noting again her four supple breasts. He trailed his fingers softly over them again, before raising his fingers up toward the ones on her stomach.

The demoness Galaxteah kept her eyes to his face, the glow within pulsing lightly amongst the swirls of color. Body seeming to ebb with the slightest of motions from the wall, spine slipping a disk at a time to give a subtle dance that beckoned all the more to be touched. " Hmmm indeed, you assume correctly... A very special type, brood mother... I am looking for strong seeds..." She dropped the words, the tone a near reverberation that ran through the ears, so very pacifying in nature. Her chest filled with air to present itself as his eyes passed over the more than perfect mounds that pushed at the material over them, straining it so every curve could be seen through it. Her core fluttered with firm strong muscle as his fingers reached for the designs upon it. His touch to find how the scales curled so delicately at the edge of the dress and dipped below and lower to be hidden under the material. She gave a toothy full smile, teeth all sharp in nature but somehow curved elegantly so not to be so scary by design. Her own hand lifting, fingers reaching towards his side, hoping to make contact with the skin there below his ribs in her own inspection. "A breeder... And I only procreate to make the finest specimens..."

"And does this... Brood mother have a name?" He asked as his large palm stroked through the females long red and black hair. Upon closer inspection, there were several small scars all over his torso. An arrogant smirk slowly appeared across his face as he ran both hands up her sides now, feeling every curve of her body as he examined her. "Mhm..." His hands stopped at her wings, tracing up and down the edge of her wings. "And I wonder what brings you here..." He glanced at her teeth as she flashed him a toothy smile. "A meal and a consort for the night, and my seed, perhaps?"

"Exactly." Galaxteah gave a chuckle, a soft playful one as her body stretched under his searching palms. Hair having a life of its own and wrapping about his fingers when he stroked through it. She let her digits stroke every crease and scar upon his skin, fascinated by them. "Am I so obvious to what I seek?" She answers his question plainly, not hiding her intentions with her travels that night, taking in Venser's handsome form. "You are what I've been looking for... You may call me Galaxteah, charmed to meet you." She bowed her head and it seemed subservient in nature.

His left hand tracing her one of her wings, bringing it down to massage a joint beneath where the wing met her back. "Lucky guess..." He said with his face close to his, she could easily feel his hot breath against her lips. "Venser, The Mac Daddy of the Dragon's Head... Along with... Other titles." The tight materials of her outfit caressed her breasts as he moved his hands cupping his large, warm palms around her round rump and giving it a good squeeze. "And a pleasure to meet you, Galaxteah... Lovely name, for a lovely demoness..."

Galaxteah murred in her throat with a vibration of delight with his hand caressing the base of her wing. Her palms foundpurchase at his abdomen, nails curling at the muscles to trace the grooves of them about his slides and to his back. Digits inching his spine as her head tilted up, lips parting to catch his close breaths with her own inhales of air. A flash of her spine, pressing her rear into his hands and squeezed the ample curves of her backside into them. "Well... Venser... Of many titles... It pleases me that you are not afraid of what I am. And that you are willing to give me many strong broods..." She sways ever so lightly, a dance that turns her hips in small circles in opposite of her chest. Giving show and trying to be tantalizing so very subtly and making a suggestive moan.

"Quite the opposite, my dear Galaxteah..." He stopped caressing right at the base of her wing, and his fingers grasped the back of her head, his other hand taking hers and sliding it down his well toned stomach, stopping it right above the fabric outside of his crotch. "Mhmm..." He let out yet another seductive growl as his emerald eyes lowered, watching her sway ever so slightly as he had her against the wall. His lips parted more, he bent her head back and kissed her, softly at first, before locking his lips with her sand letting out a pleased moan, noting they both stood at five eleven.

The demoness continued her dance, even more so as he watched her move. Long red hair tangling about his fingers with his grip to it. The corner of her lip curling up, her fingers letting him guide her down his body. She takes delight in his strong abdomen, digits curling the instant they are close to the edge of his belt line, nails easing under the edge. A deep sound that resembles a purr to crest at the top of her throat that gets amplified as he tilts her head back. Lips parting while his mouth finds hers. Skin nearly flavored like it is minty as she returned the gentle kneads of his lips. Mouth opening to take his moan into her wantingly. Tongue, long, thin and forked as it slithered against his bottom lip. Fingers brazenly inching down lower behind his belt line.

His warm breath caressed her lips as he leaned ever more closely, his nose brushing against hers. A tingle ran through his body as his moist mouth closed slowly round hers, forcing her to inhale through her nose. He felt excited feeling her tongue against his bottom lip, even more so by her fingers slowly pulling down his pants at the belt like The kisses were now rough, insistent, passionate but dominant. He brought both hands up now, grasping the tight fabric on both sides beside her cleavage and giving them a hard enough tug to rip it open. "You aren't going to need these clothes anymore..." He growled between kisses.

She was insistent on pushing the material she hand at her fingers downward, exposing more of his skin in her eagerness to remove it from her way. Lips and tongue working to taste every inch of his mouth even as he had control of the motions making her take large slow breaths through her nostrils. Breasts falling free without much help while the scan material was opened. The scales concentric about her four swaying orbs, all to draw the eye to the darkened peaks of pointy nipples that rode high on those large mounds. Middle tightening as if to make her body all the more pleasing to the eye.

"Oh by the void..." He said ogling the demoness as her clothes full away, exposing the nude demoness to him. He licked at her lips, his rough hands trailing all over her body and then wrapping one arm around her, bending her back and taking one of her nipples into his mouth, sucking on it and occasionally nibbling it. Such an exotic creature, and he had a lot to play with...

Galaxteah wouldn't mind the exposing of her flesh to his hands and eyes. Frame lithe and arching about his arm as if draped like linen over it. She giggles under her breath, middle flexing and pushing her large breasts up and unto his lips and teeth at the hardened nub of her nipple. Her own fingers pulling and trying to make the material about his hips and bottom disappear in her tugs and pulls.

When his baggy red pants were pulled down his hardened, thick cock sprung free and hovered above her wet flower. "Oh..." He nibbled on her hard nipples more and took her hands in his, using them to run her fingernails through his messy black hair. He let out a pleasured groan and used both hands to spread her legs apart against the wall, then lowered himself down, rubbing the flaring head of his cock in circles around her opening, his lips pressed against hers and parted them.

She spread open without issue. Long legs parted and body resting back to the wall. Her claw like nails tugging down over his sides and lower back to leave red scores of skin. Stomach tightening to a pit while he was pressing against and into her soft lower folds. Hands up at his design to pull at his hair, her other pair to feel him up. The four armed demoness tugged hard, pushing her hips forward as the head of his length teased her wet throbbing nethers. Dark swirling eyes staring nearly through him.

"Dahhhh...!" Venser growled and shuddered in pleasure as her claw like nails scratched down his sides. "Actually like that... As well as being bitten... Uh!" When she pulled at his hair his left hand reached down, grasping her large, bouncy rear and his other hand reached up and gripped her neck. The man's huge cock twitched, oozing droplets of milky liquid that trail down his shaft. "Eager... Aren't we? Don't worry..." He let out a small, pleasured moan when she bit down on his lip. Then he thrusts into her, HARD. Plunging him into her welcoming hole, burying himself repeatedly into her, He thrusts fast and hard into her, pulling her back onto his cock and breathing heavily all while pressing down on her windpipe as he fucked the demoness.

Galaxteah snapped her teeth at him as he mentioned biting. Her nails gripped harder to pull at the skin across his spine. Scratching him to bleeding. Chest growling with his grip across her small throat. Still panting and snapping like a caged beast at him as much as she could. Rear filling his hand, hips tilting enough with it to make his upward thrust easy into her tight depths. Her middle flashing out with a firm peak of him inside her. The growl turned to moans that were muffled by his hard grip about her windpipe. Strong frame bulging out hard as he thrusts into her so hard he nearly breaks through her core. Body tugging and kneading every inch of his massive throbbing length. She was clawing at his hips fiercely pulling at him to urge on his hard treatment of her swollen and tight pussy about him.

"Uuuhh...!" Their lower halves connected with force, making him yell out in pleasure as the tip of his cock slammed into her cervix, the bearded man could feel her tight inner walls quivering and squeezing around his thickness. He glanced down, watching the demoness's dark, partially scaled breasts bouncing with the fast thrusts; her breath hot and heavy as their naked bodies were pressed right up against each other. "Yeah, yeahh..." Ven chuckled a bit watching her snap at him, and then craned his head to the side, giving her easy access to his neck.

"Thirsty?"

The four armed demoness shifted hard up and down as he plowed up and into her tight wanting form. Body arching at the center as it crunched over his cock. Abdomen flaring out to bump his middle with his depth inside her. Pussy dripping her juices about him. The splash of them covering his thighs and balls as he came flush up against her each time. Her claws against reaching up to grip at his hair, tugging his head as he leaned forward into her snarls. Galaxteah took the first opportunity to bite at his throat she could and didn't hold back. Snarling as she sank her teeth into the tender flesh of where his shoulder met his neck to drink from him. Turns her head as much as his grip on her that would allow as she refused to let the skin go from her sharp teeth. Hips grinding hard into his thrusts now, trying to make him find the depths of her most forbidden portions with his long hard cock.

His massive member stretched her wet pussy as he penetrated her. His rough hands molded her nice, perfectly round ass, pressing her into the wall of the dungeon more. "Gah! Uh!" He groaned in pain more and pressed his face into her neck now, his grunts muffled as a bit of blood pooled underneath them and the demoness bit down on his neck with all her might. Venser took her flesh into his mouth, sucking on it and biting it, though not as hard as her. Hard enough to leave visible dark marks on her already dark skin... "Mhm! Mhm! Yes!" He bucked his hips wildly, taking his hand off of her throat and grasping her ass with both hands now. "Ahhh...!" His cock made it pat her cervix and into her womb now, her most forbidden portion...

Galaxteah lifted her legs high and wide as he grips under her round ass. Hips bouncing back and against the wall with his thrusts into her. Depths his breaking through the defenses inside obvious as she howls into her bite at his throat. Head turning now to try to shred his skin like a thrashing shark. Her own skin rippling and scales shifting under his own bites the covering damaged and marked with his teeth. Her claws tugging at the bag of his neck as she was frenzied and diving at her throat over and over. Belly pounding into her center and all four breasts jumping against his chest with hard thumps. Insides not forgiving with tightness making him work to stay so deep. Trying to make sure that he indeed gave her everything if he was to claim that portion of her form. She just moaned like a beast, now completely primal in nature.

The bearded man sped up his pace again, making very short deep thrusts, and growls, slamming her body down on his thick rod. "Ah! Fuck yesss....! I'm going to fill your womb with so much cum you will bear an entire litter of my children..." He pressed down on her throat yet again and shouted as she continued to savagely chomp and now scratch his neck. His cock twitched as it went deep. on the verge of climax. "AH YES...! YOU WANT THAT!" He struck her across the face with one hand, his thrusts slowing, but becoming harder.

She hissed as he grips her throat again, and followed it up with an almost pleased growl. Head pushing back to the wall with a hard thump that doesn't stop the snap of teeth his direction. Her lips darkened with his blood that she had gnawed from his throat. Her nails taking to pulling hard down the sides of his spine. Curled dagger like points trying to gouge the skin from his bones. Body heaving like a doll up and down upon his length. Skin impacting skin with hard slaps of sound with every motion. His slap across her face making her head turns slightly in reaction to the impact. Teeth baring at him in response as her voice suddenly appears from her very core as a echoing rumble. "Do not disappoint from your boasts... I want to feel you fill me with your precious seed until I burst or I shall disembowel you...." Galaxteah wheezed it out strongly, tongue flicking at him while the muscles in her center ripples and tightened all the more. IT was trying to make him give her everything

Venser had lost count of the amount of times he felt his shaft suddenly slicked by the rush of her hot, sweet nectars. But each time she came on that monstrous rod it only became so much easier for him to ravage her gripping little tunnel! The demoness practically sucked at him as he pumped her spasming depths! His own howls of pleasure growing deeper, longer with every stroke. She could feel him pulsing so wildly inside of her. Throbbing against those clenching walls each time they spasmed around him.

"Argh... An entire litter or my children... Eh, brood mother?" He growled feeling her inner wall try to draw out his seed. "UGHHH...!" A hot eruption that flooded her womb clenching womb. Causing the walls of her depths to stretch even further... His head jerked back hard. His raven hair flipping back from those tawny eyes that now burned like flames in the flickering light of the nearby fire of the dungeon. His mouth hanging open only heated cries of pleasure had a hope of escaping his lips. "CUMMING!" He growled out, perhaps more a warning than an announcement... For the moment the first potent load of seed gushed into her belly, the bearded man's hips began hammering away like a steam powered piston! The sudden shock of climax, the pleasured tingles that run through the body... Glob after glob shot into the demoness, an ever flowing river of fertile seed!

The beautiful four armed demoness had indeed cum over him multiple times. Only her body giving it away with its flexing and dripping of rivers of desire. Her mind just went wild and only reacted like an animal in heat, clawing scratching and howling in a fake type of dominance that was more show than truth. The demon inside wanting nothing more than to feel her core ravaged and split about a mammoth throbbing length. Hips twisting about wildly, small frame hammering to the wall over and over as if he was nailing her to it. He didn't have to announce his intentions as her frame felt his throbbing length thickening and stretching her all the more seconds before the release. Her howl nearly inhuman as he sprays her womb with that hot juice. Belly bloating and expanding as she was overfilled. Her hands releasing his sides and back to claw at her own pulsing and rounding middle.

"Yessss... Give me many strong broods! Mhhph! So strong...!" Galaxteah commanded it but knew it was going to happen without her words.

His cum ran down her thighs, and mingled with her juices that soaked the floor beneath them. All the while... He was sure the demoness could begin to feel her lower stomach swell... More and more of his cum pouring into her aching womb with each thrust! Where was it all coming from? The handsome bearded man could barely utter anything but loud, primal howls as he came deep within her womb, pumping a flood into her with each savage slam of his hips. He saw her tremble violently with each pulse of his exploding cock within her, lips moving as if to try and produce some kind of ecstatic moan... Venser could feel the heat radiating off of her, the slight drip of sweat from his brow landing on her scaled breasts, half-expecting it to sizzle with the heat that was tearing through them and being pumped into her depths.

"Gah! Mine...!" His slick rod slowly expanded her pussy and womb clenched and kneaded the still-pounding cock within, as if to milk him of every single drop he could offer!

Galaxteah turned her dark eyes up to the ceiling, they inched back under the half lids that fluttered uncontrollably. Massive breasts jumping upwards with the jerks of his length up and into her core. She grunted with each motion. A hard impact of her frame to the wall, coupled with the splash of flesh against flesh. The cocktail of both their desires spewing out about his motions and splashing across them and the wall behind. the sheath that was wrapped about him convulsing in waves of muscles meant to hold every inch of him in that fertile and now enlarging womb. The once flat smooth plains of her stomach now a definite firm growing core filled with all he pumped deep. Her body was kneading him in its want to be completely covered internally with that sticky sweet cream. She was smiling as she panted out her growls, hips pushing forward and legs lifting all the more in welcome to his motions to push every drop as deep as it could set.

He groans again as she shifts and squeezes his meat in a euphoric chokehold, feeling her juices drip down his length and grinning at her words while he rolls his hips back against her best he can. He moves in an effort to slide his manhood around inside of every inch he can, shifting as he twitches, his cock painting her inner walls, her inner walls his canvas. "'Gahhh..." Wrapping his arms around her, Ven carefully lowered himself down, laying flat on his back with the demoness on top of him. He reached up, grabbing her large breasts and pushing his hips forward so that her cunt swallowed his cock completely as he kept unloading inside of her, nearly done.

Galaxteah was nearly weightless as he lowers and she goes with him. Body ebbing into him in an on stop dance to milk the bearded man for everything he had. Legs spread about his hips as he rests on his back. A heavy grunt of sound in her chest with his fingers gripping them firmly. Already rounded core on display below that heaves out with his upward motion. Her smile sly as she licks her lips. Head back and splaying her red hair about her shoulders and across her four manhandled breasts. Her body turning and making him stir every drop into the walls of her hungry innards. Her arms reaching back to grip his thighs wings spread out to hold her over him. Giving him a full view of that still pulsing and growing stomach that indeed looked as if she was carrying four broods that were ready to escape at a moment's notice. Though, they were already cultivating inside of her, for she was already now pregnant.

The handsome bearded man licked his lips as well as she laid on top of him, himself laying in a pool of his own blood and his wounds still bleeding. His vision blurred for only a moment, and he felt pure bliss after they mated. He was still inside of her. "Mhm..." He placed both hands on her cheeks, lifting her face up and pressing his lips against hers, parting them and kissing her roughly. "You belong to me now..."

Galaxteah was still arching and dancing. The motions of all the demoness that wanted to feel everything in every way. She seems a bit surprised at his gripping her face. Head canting side to side as he pulled her close. Her core rocking over his center with its firm swollen frame. While he kisses here she nips at his lips like an animal would. Deep swirling eyes to his handsome visage, the expression not giving away anything she was thinking. She gave no response to his words but continued to unconsciously rock her hips against him inside her.

He gripped her chin. "I'm taking you home..."

The four armed demoness was growling and murring, still moving about in a mad slither. Body accepting and pulling in its need for all that was pushed into its depths. Eyes narrowed and flashing at his words as he held her chin that in his grip. Teeth baring in snarls that showed who she was. "Not sure how you intend to... Keep me. I do bite and scratch..." She trailed off words saying nothing and body ebbing to a different tune over him. "Though mhmmmmphh... You feel so good..."

"Oh I can tell..." She had bitten and scratched him, his back was covered with long scratches and both his back and neck were bleeding, all of which pooled underneath them as he dominated her, and filled her with his hot, fertile seed... His green, serpent like eyes glanced down to her bulging stomach now. "Mhmm..." He trailed one hand over it, and then looked about the room, spotting a roll of rope on top of a crate. He raised his left hand up, trapping it in a green aura and pulling it over to them. He wrapped it around her neck, tight, pulling her close to him again and kissing her. "Just until I get a collar..." He muttered shifting, slowly pulling out of her, seed and her sweet nectar leaking out.

Galaxteah eyes found his hand on her firm full belly. it pulses lightly with what it housed inside. She reacts with a jerk of her head and a twist of her body with the sudden rope about her throat. claws again reaching to slash at him, maybe taking another bit of flesh at his arms as he holds the rope. A breath leaving and eyes widening with the tightness to her neck. Arms then out to the sides, eyes flashing at him in anger. The breathing deep and full of howling sound , body though again seeming opposite as he pulls free of her tight channel and it refused to let him go. The flared head popping free with an audible sound and opening gaped and throbbing as it spills out that seed from inside her. Slitted eyes staring at him. Body posturing as if angered but hips lifting and twisting as if missing the thing inside her.

"Ah!" There was another giant slash across his chest now that was going to leave yet another scar. The man now let out an angered growl and whipped his head back, effectively head butting the demoness after she slashed him. "Oh I know what I'm going to fucking do now..." He grabbed his cock which hardened again, shoving it inside the scaled demoness, and then closing the distance so that their bodies were embraced, her large breasts squashing up against his chest. And then the two suddenly disappeared in a puff of thick red smoke, reappearing on a grassy shore by a great blue lake, the moon full above them. For her it would feel as if she were flung at a thousand miles per hour, and then suddenly stopped.

Galaxteah barked and recoils at the head but. Hair haloing out about her head as it jerks in the noose of rope. Arms again sweeping in to claw at him like a wild beast. Her body crushing against his, howling out in a determined pain of being trapped, hips jerking up and over his length again inside her. The wiggles half trying to escape and half working his arousal back into her tight pulling channel. The sudden movement surprises her, breath lost to the rope and the sensation. Body freezing in his grasp as she was transported. The growls still in her throat but muted, pants from lips that trickle darkened blood for the corners as his head but as had her bite at her skin and lips. Eyes darting about and frame petrified to a stand still, trying to find her breath and figure out what happened.

"Uh!" They both fell down now, the demoness landing on top of him. "Uuhhhh...!" She was indeed crushing him now, and instinctively he began to thrust again while she was on top of him. The sounds of her ass slapping against his thighs loud. "Hoooo... Uhhh..." He was having trouble moving now, and his vision blurred. No no no this wasn't the right place... He glanced around at the lake around them now, his hands trailing up her body and resting on her sides, gripping them. "Close though."

Galaxteah arched and fell over him with a thud. It drives him into her all the more. Her howl loud and echoing through the nearby forest. Body wrapped in his arms and heaving over the unconscious thrusts he was doing into her. Wings springing free as his hands ran up her sides. Hips jerking and bucking uncontrollably, innards wrapped about him and pulling as if starved for more. She slithered against him, not seeming to think of escape, more interested in how his hips were smashing into her. Rounded middle seeming to beat into him as he thrust, breasts rubbing his chest as she writhing about. Arms finally reaching out to claw at the soil about him. Trying to gain leverage, maybe to pull away though she was howling each time he was deep inside that gripping depths.

His eyes widened as he gazed up at her, her wings fully spread now and in the path of the moon. "Ohh..." That was a sight of pure beauty as the four armed demoness bounced up and down on top of his cock, starved for more and made him cum again already. "Ah!" He spasmed and a river of his hot fertile seed shot up inside her. Her cunny was overflowing. Where was all this coming from? He writhed underneath her and growled, "I'll give you many broods... You will be birthing my children for eternity, sweet demoness..."

"Gahhhhhhh yesssss... Perfecttt..." Galaxteah rolled her eyes back into fluttering lids, letting out a shudder of pure delight. Seeming lost in sensation and having forgotten her earlier issues. Body arching up from him. Massive pierced breasts heaving over an already so very swollen stomach that was pounding out with his outline. Claws again to his flesh, but not to strike as so much to do as a creature like her does. Grip to his skin like talons of a hunting bird. Hair tangled about his neck and the rope about it. A yowl and convulsion of her frame. Back pumping her hips downward into him as he releases yet again into her already filled frame. Tongue to hang from her lips as her hips jerk and body thickens in the center with him packing her all the more with his viable seed. The warmth bursting out about him being sheathed tightly inside her. Wings out and up, body arched and positioned in a way that makes her perched on him as if she belongs there. A claw to her stomach feeling the ample roundness and undeniable truth that she was indeed filled with what was his.

"Gahhhahhh! Needy... Aren't you? Yes yes I'm going to keep you... Ah...!" When she gripped his sides as well, drawing more blood and just latching onto him he gripped her sides harder, and teleported them again. Still in the same position, the two reappeared in a simple cabin near the woods he had started to use as his private play room, as normally it was too tiring of a walk to have his family stay here rather than inside the tavern. On the bedposts were shackles he and his lovers used for bondage play. The man tried to reach for it as he stirred his semen around in her, panting heavily and his vision blurred more as the demoness was literally milking him dry.

The four armed demoness was lost in sensation, the full feeling and his pumping into her making her lethargic. The again teleports, making her woozy and a bit nauseous. Body against jerking over him with muscles just meant to suck the seed from him in any way. Her nails clawing her own middle as she pitches to the side as he reaches for the shackles. She doesn't seem to notice what he is doing as she lists to the side and howls softly in her chest.

"Hooo... Hooo... That's a good girl..." He said reaching around to give her dark, round ass a harsh slap, everything blurring and getting dark as he continued to pump inside her, slowly, slowly, more and more seed until placed the shackle on her wrist, passing out. His cock still hard inside of the demoness as he finished breeding her.

Galaxteah was stretched out and shivering. Half from the fullness that was still happening as he continues to spew into her wanting form. The other half a bit of sickness from the trip. She doesn't seem to even notice that she is now shackle. Curvy frame draped over him in a shivering pile of stuffed flesh. A bark and growl at the spank, a nip of teeth before she falls over him breathing hard and silent.

The man let out a sigh and shifted slightly as she fell on top of him, his cock going soft again as her inner walls wrapped around it like a warm and comforting blanket. Blood was still spilling out all over the floor as he and his new mate started to fall asleep together. Before he did, Venser slid out of bed to grab some aloe and some bandages, and thought it'd be best to hunt a deer or something.

When Galaxteah awoke he had the feeling she really wanted to tear into something and consume it, and it wasn't going to be him.

Not like that. The tearing and blood drinking was fine, just not the tearing his limbs off and actually eating him. He was totally not into being killed and eaten, and Venser Tybalt Karkaldwin was into a lot.

CHAPTER TEN: MARVELLA'S JOG

Montpelier, Vorland, 1437 ATC

It was a hot afternoon as Marvella panted as she jogged. Stopping she buckled over as she used her hands to prop herself up upon her knees. Sweat ran down her body and dripped from her nose and chin as she tried to catch her breath, looking to her left she saw a few townsfolk staring in her direction.

Giving them a wave she noticed they were entranced by her figure and what she chose to wear, just her panties and a utility belt and her bra thinking it would keep her cool as she jogged, at most she found it more troubling as she felt her breasts bouncing, jiggling, and at times almost falling out of her top. Marvella Fullbuster had a slender body and noticeably thick hips, fair skin, strange purple eyes, dark hair tied back, pink lips, and a pair of earrings consisting of white round with an orange border with silver chains.

Grabbing her water flask she sat down on a bench as she leaned back to take a sip. "They keep staring like that," Marvella whispered to herself as she faintly rubbed her thighs together as she let out a light groan, "I wonder which of them would." Raising a hand to wave them over, Marvella watched as they slowly turned around and began to walk away.

She sighed and did some shoulder circles. Feeling the sweat slowly ride down her neck and between her breasts, Marvella reached up with one hand as the other pressed into her stomach and slid down to her crotch.

Letting out a faint gasp she sat up and looked around, "Thank goodness no one saw that." Feeling how hard her nipples became she smiled as an idea slowly formed in her head, "Could I get away with that?" The village protector asked herself as she reached back to untie her top.

As her breasts hung from her chest she giggled while looking around, no one had come by since those townsfolk left making her tempt fate. Reaching for her panties she slowly pulled them off, her heart racing as they neared her knees.

"This is so relaxing..." She whispered to herself as she stepped out of her panties, standing up in shock as a cool breeze kissed her bare ass as she picked up her discarded clothing.

Nipples erect and bare, Marvella walked over to a set of trees and bushes just near one of the outer farms. Carefully she hid her clothing in the bushes as she planned on retrieving them later. Walking further into the brush she continued to look around to make sure no one would catch her, though she also hoped and wished to be seen by Venser or a very pretty maiden.

"No Marvella, no." Finding a nice secluded and shaded spot she laid down in the grass faintly moaning as she felt the cool prickly touch of the green blades, "I've needed this." She groaned as she slowly parted her legs feeling the warmth of the sun on her soaking wet thighs, "It's been nothing but work, work, work, and the twins..." She sighed as her right hand followed the curves of her breasts down her stomach and passed her naval. "Mhm Ven..." She gasped as her fingers lightly pressed into her labia, slowly her fingers made small light circles on her soft tender lips, while a third finger flicked her clit every so often making her gasp and moan.

Her voice faintly echoed among the trees, yet she cared little knowing no one would find her as deep as she was. Slowly Marvella moaned as her free hand began to grasp her breast and tease her nipple, rubbing it, pinching it, twisting it all as her fingers worked her tender womanhood.

"Oh Fuck," Marvella whispered as she lifted her hips to gyrate them while pressing her fingers into her pussy, "Venser..." She moaned his name while thinking about his amazing body "Oh Ven..." She gasped as she recalled the time she walked in on him and Kari going at it in the kitchen. "How big you are..." She fantasized him grinding his large throbbing member against her wet staring lips, teasing Marvella as Alex fondled and caressed her breasts, "Oh yes Ven." She called out in a mix of moaning and groaning as she recalled the captain's tight body dripping wet from her shower, how she flaunted her naked body in front of Marvella that day to make her feel jealous of her rather lovely curves.

Squeezing her own breast with her right hand, Marvella rubbed her nipple with her index finger as she moaned out the names of her lovers. Her legs began to shake as her body lightly convulsed with the building sensation of an orgasm. As the feeling continued to build within her, Marvella released her breast and dug her fingers into the ground.

"Oh sweet gods yes." She moaned as her hooves bucked her hips into the air, "Right there Ven," She gasped as the urge neared its climax making Marvella cry out in pleasure, "Yes Alex Bonneville, lick my clit while your lover fucks me senseless!" All at once Marvella cried in pleasure as a thick liquid shot out of her body, her hand, thighs, and the ground soaked with the thick fluid.

The protector felt satisfied for a short moment as she weakly brought her soaked hand into sight, only for a lonely and longing feeling to return as her cum drenched hand fell between her breasts.

"Marvella." A voice said in shock causing the naked woman to sit up and cover her body as best she could.

"Alex." Marvella nervously chuckled as she looked up at the ginger haired captain "W-what a s-surprise. I didn't expect to see you, what brings you... Uh..."

"Was feeling a bit lazy, decided to come find you to jog next to you, ya know, train.." Alex answered before Marvella could finish her question, "I found this in the bushes when I got here." Holding out Marvella's underwear she dangled it in front of the naked girl, "Though I was making an excuse because I wanted a chance to stare at that nice ass of yours." She was ginger haired, average complexion, hazel eyes, and dressed in a beige pants, barefoot, and a simple white shirt, her pregnant belly protruding a bit.

"Oh yeah we've never... Actually done it before, I mean we've all done it with Ven..." Marvella blushed as Alex slowly walked closer, dropping her underwear as she neared her target.

"This is going to be quite the story to tell." She replied towering over Marvella leaning over as though she were going to dominate the situation.

"Yes... Come here Alex..." Marvella started only to find herself being interrupted by the soft warm muscle of Alex's tongue.

The female captain took her time exploring the village protector's mouth, carefully and gently laying her back as she rubbed and caressed her tongue with her own. Marvella enjoyed the moment as her heart raced, both from the shock of being caught like she was and from sharing a kiss with her ginger haired captain.

Slowly Alex slid her hand down Marvella's neck, passing between her voluptuous breasts and down to the woman's crotch.

Pulling away she smiled at her fellow warrior woman, "We both needed this didn't we?"

Marvella smiled as she blushed at her new 'friend." She gasped and moaned as Alex feverishly worked the inner walls of Marvella''s pussy, "N-not f-fair." She moaned as she arched her back and dug her fingers into the dirt of the earth.

"I know we can." Alex whispered upon Marvella's erect nipple, "And that's what makes it so much fun." Using the tip of her tongue she made small circles around Marvella's nipple.

Alex lowered herself down to Marvella's midriff, "I admired you when Ven brought me to your home, and I've always wanted to be closer to you." Kissing Marvella just under her navel. With a smile she slowly parted Marvella's legs only to look up toward the village protector between her breasts, and then she slowly dragged her tongue across Marvella's labia.

She savored the taste of Marvella's cooling thick nectar as she lapped away at Marvella's womanhood, teasing her clit with the tip of her tongue with each slow pass.

"Alex," Marvella gasped as she crossed her legs around the head of the ginger haired captain, "For Summerland's sake, please don't stop." She begged as she reached down to run her fingers through the hair of the captain caressing her scalp as the feeling of cumming a second time began to build.

Slowly Alex stood up and began to remove her beige pants, "Sorry, but you already got to cum." Marvella gazed up at the woman and her lack of panties, or more so her lack of care to her lower hedge.

Marvella's eyes never left the thick patch sitting above the captain's clit, "But I'm so close." She whimpered as the captain lowered herself down to Marvella's face, exposing a hidden albeit shaved pair of drooling lips.

Alex smiled to see her bush just under Marvella's mouth, "I know, but it wouldn't be fair to me." Slowly she reached down to tease her labia for less than a second only to show the warrior woman how wet she had truly become, guiding Marvella's sight with her wet fingers she begged, "Please, I need your help." Her voice carried the tone of wanting need, but it wasn't how she said that got Marvella to plant a kiss on the captain's tender lower lips.

Slowly Marvella ran the tip of her tongue through the slit of Alex's labia back and forth, she could feel the lean back as she enjoyed Pinkie's experience with her tongue.

"Oh fuck."Alex moaned as her hips began to move on their own, trying to take in as much of the sensation as possible.

Slowly and carefully Alex turned over to lay on top of Marvella, the whole time she felt Marvella's tongue inside of herself. Moving in ways she never expected to feel something move within the depths of her pussy. Wanting to return the favor to the girl eating her tender depths, Alex found herself only able to pant and moan as she lay helpless staring at Marvella's folds.

Alex had often stared at her own love hole in the mirror from time to time when she masturbated, often imagining that she was watching some other girl being just as naughty as herself.

Marvella's labia appeared to bulge and fold over covering a lot of what she had grown used to seeing of her own, "Umhhmmm oh yeah..." She mumbled into Alex causing the ginger haired captain to dig her nails into Marvella's's thighs, "Not like that!" She shouted as her tongue whipped back into her mouth, "Here I'll sort of show you." She explained making the her wonder what Marvella meant by 'sort of', only to feel two fingers gently caressing her own loving lips, "Like this, start soft and tender..".

Marvella kissed Alex's inner thigh as she slowly began to apply pressure to the captain's labia, "That, and the time you and and Kari and Ven did it in the kitchen, making out beforehand...." Pinching Alex's clit Marvella gave a small twist, "Next time you guys, actually lock lips, I don't care how cute the two of you looked covered in each other's spit. Like a frenzy of tongues between the three of you."

"Wh-what d-did you expect?" Alex moaned as her head fell between Marvella's's legs, between moans as she felt Marvella working her up to an orgasm she had never felt on her own.

"I bet." Marvella giggled as she slowly shoved two of her fingers between Alex's soft tender lips, "But that's not how you do it." She said slowly rubbing her fingers into Alex, parting them as they moved one way and closing them as they went the other.

It wasn't long before Alex cried out in pleasure, her body twitching for a moment before going limp. Marvella giggled as she slipped out from under the exhausted captain, her face and mane matted and glistening in the sun with cum. Crawling over to Alex Bonneville, Marvella Fullbuster helped the captain out of her shirt.

She marveled at her nice mounds, how they made a perfect circle as they tried to flatten out on her chest above her baby belly. Lifting Alex's leg onto her own shoulder, Marvella pressed her folds against the lower lips of the woman.

"Next time you and her try something together, make sure she enjoys every tiny bit." Marvella whispered as she smiled down at the near exhausted captain, "Just like I've been doing to you." Slowly Marvella began to rub and grind her womanhood against Alex's, the two girls began to pant and moan as Marvella kept to a slow yet heavy pace.

"Marvella," Alex moaned as she tried to move her hips in tandem with the village protector, "please don't stop." She begged through pants as she grasped her own breasts, squeezing them as a rush of ecstasy overflowed within her body.

Looking at the shadows around them Marvella let out a sigh as she came to a very slow stop, "Well have to pick this up later, I promised Sanna I'd come by this afternoon to help her with something." Kissing Alex on the cheek she whispered into the captain's ear, ""I'll see you at home." Stepping away Marvella took her time putting her underwear back on, making sure Alex had a good long view of her ass and glistening pussy before she was somewhat clothed. With a wink she tossed Alex her beige pants before taking a few steps away only to turn back with a smile.

CHAPTER ELEVEN: SWEET CREAM

Venser's lakeside bungalow, Vorland, 1437 ATC

Venser Karkaldwin awoke with a wet warmth around his cock. His emerald eyes popped open and he stared at his crotch. Galaxteah the four armed demoness had wrapped herself around him like a cat, her head was busy licking at his thick member and holding it in place with two hands, while her rear was just to the left of his face. The sunlight was filtering through the nearby facing window. Ven took a deep longing breath as he felt just the edge of her sharp teeth press against his cock.

She shook her rump in his face before running her tongue up the length of his hardness. "Morning Venser..."Galaxteah said between lusty breaths, the warm breath tickling and evaporating the saliva she had just coated his crotch with.

"Oh yes... Mhm... Morning Galaxteah..." He let out in response as she winked at him, just before taking the head of his cock into her mouth. His hips tried to buck into her mouth only to be stopped by a pair of arms gently pressing him back down.

The four armed demoness let him out of her mouth. A pair of arms continued to stroke him as she dipped her head down below his cock to lay kisses on Venser's inner thighs.

"Aah!" The bearded man moaned as she lightly licked his testicles before pulling his sack into her warm mouth and waylaying it with licks. After a thorough washing of his balls she looked back at the handsome man and stared at him, her eyelids lowered. Between her hands rubbing his base and the air his head was beginning to flare up.

"I hope this is a good apology for biting you so hard last night." The four armed demoness said before dipping her mouth down on his cock, reaching the edge of her throat before pulling back. Staring him in the eyes the whole time. His left hand went over to start rubbing on her slit, his right hand came to rest on her hair. He slowly stroked her locks while she sucked Venser's cock, running her wet, velvety tongue over his shaft. Again she released him, merely stroking him with her pair of hands for a moment while kissing it while letting his cock press back against his stomach.

"I thought you'd like this better than breakfast... We will go hunting together, to feed the broods..." Galaxteah said before swallowing his cock once more. This time Ven could only moan as she pushed the flaring head of his cock past her mouth and into her tight, writhing throat.

"Aahhh yes." Venser gasped as the broodmother pressed her hot mouth against his base, before pulling back until only the head of his cock remained in her mouth. The next stroke down to the very base was wetter as her saliva began to leak from the edges of her mouth onto his crotch for what seemed like forever.

"Mhm!" He lost control when her smooth hands caressed his balls. The moment she felt the twitch of his cock she pulled back until the head was firmly in the middle of her mouth. Her hands didn't stop as he felt the first rope of cum splatter the inside of her mouth. Venser could see her smile as she watched his handsome visage contorted in pleasure and his hips tried in vain to buck further back into that tight throat of hers. Well, smile as best she could with a spasming cock still lodged in her pretty mouth. The third and fourth rope filled her, her dark eyes suddenly betrayed the fact she wasn't swallowing fast enough. Soon, she let go, even as her soft hands stroked up and down his now oversensitive shaft. A final huge rope fired itself across her face before she let the cock point down at Venser's own stomach.

The bearded man couldn't help but laugh as he watched her eyes cross trying to look at the line of sticky white that extended from the bottom of her lower lips all the way across the bridge of her nose, with a little dollop of cum hanging above her right eyebrow.

"Mhm, your seed tastes so good Venser..." Galaxteah said, displaying the cum inside her mouth before throwing her head back and swallowing the cream.

"You love it... Mhm." She climbed over the handsome bearded man to rest her head on his chest, the demoness's four, milk filled breasts squashing up against his chest, but not without taking the time to lick up the little bit of sweet cream that had spurted onto his stomach, her large bat like wings going limp. The bearded man let out a laugh when she stuck her tongue into his belly button to get the small amount that had ended up in there. The broodmother then laid her head on Venser's chest sideways, before sticking her tongue out at me and smiling, running a hand over his thigh and up to his stomach, reveling in the softness of his skin.

"Mhm, you milked me... Last night you drank some of my blood and I know you'll want to again. So..."

"Maybe we could help each other out more... Sit up."

The broodmother demoness obeyed, and the bearded man was staring at two pairs of engorged breasts. Nice, round, mounds of flesh, with tiny beads of milk already dripping out of her nipples that rode high on her mounds and rolling onto Venser's body and the bed. She was certainly going to enjoy being milked.

Venser leaned in, teasingly tracing the tip of his tongue along the very edge of one of her breasts, collecting the spilled droplets that had escaped.

Galaxteah's body was hot, he could feel the heat radiating off her as he was pressing slowly against it with the flat of his tongue, scraping it slowly along the side of her teat, completely comfortable. The moment his tongue's surface pressed down onto the four armed demoness"s soft, giving flesh, she gasped over him, sharply drawing breath between her teeth.

Too quickly he felt the edge of his tongue brush against one of Galaxteah's perky nipple, a tiny spurt of milk shooting out and splattering against his neck. Her quiet moan and the sweet creamy smell that now filled the air was enough to overpower him, and he quickly found his mouth clamped tight over the tip of her teat, letting the thin spurts his light touch prompted dribble down onto his waiting tongue. She tasted lovely, like the sweetest of nectars. The sort of flavor that could cause a man to fall in lust, were he not already.

Galaxteah's low moans died out as she grew used to the sensation, but he took it in his stride and began stronger measures, drinking down her sweet savory milk.

Venser continued his servicing of her, pushing his lips into her breast as if to meet it in a kiss, parting them slightly to let her nipple between his lips, before squeezing it tight. The bearded man ran his lips over her soft flesh, sending sparks of rough pleasure shooting though her skin. Tongue found a job wrapping around her nipple, flopping and twisting against her, changing direction often and becoming soaked in the stream of fresh, gorgeous milk.

And Galaxteah still had three more nipples on her chest that needed attention.

It was a good start to a great day.

CHAPTER TWELVE: PURCHASING THE VILLA

The Farmlands, Pryldahn, 1437 ATC

A cloudless afternoon sky hung over the farmlands of Pryldahn, just outside the nation's capital, Capital De Seraphim. Three figures walked down the road, having just teleported nearby and approached the villa and the farm they were looking to buy. The villa was a nice little slice of paradise, nestled in the shadow where Castle De Seraphim was. Inside, the thin beige curtains billowed lazily in the warm saltwater wind. A magnificent, two story structure built with polished stone, wood and brick. The typical Pryldahnian villa was a big square shaped building divided into several suites. Bedrooms for the family, guest rooms, storage rooms that could be turned into any kind of room. Around the central villa, there were also granaries, barns and small cabins where the slaves would stay. At the end of the property was a large stone barn that had four pointed spires at the corners of it's arched roof, making it look like a big castle.

As they stopped right in front of the twin doors, one of the figures was a man dressed in a turquoise and crimson tunic with baggy red pants and bright red boots, a satchel at his side. He had a neatly trimmed beard, slitted emerald eyes, strong attack eyebrows, and a smirk upon his lips.

One of the figures was a tall, black haired succubus with burnt golden eyes and full pink lips. Ceirra Dusk, dressed to emphasize that beauty. Her amazingly long legs were exposed as she wore a short black leather dress that ended just underneath her thighs.

Sanna, who was beside him holding their daughter on her hip, a brilliant green sari-style gown on her lithe body. It trailed to her ankles and she wore simple sandals, her hair pinned up carefully to keep it out of their baby's reach. She looked up at the beautiful sky, its lack of clouds making for a gorgeous warm day in the villa that they looked to purchase in Pryldahn. They were close to the capital, which gave her a good chance to get familiar with the region - as she had only visited a few times before, to her knowledge. Their cute little daughter, Rowena, was in a matching green baby's gown, her black curls laid against her small head as she babbled and waved her arms to try and touch her mother's dress.

Sanna looked over at Venser then as they stopped at the doors, beaming at him as they looked to be inspecting the place. All of them were so well dressed, it was as if they were royalty... And in truth, Sanna wondered exactly who she was a lover to at this point. Was there something he hadn't told her? She wouldn't care either way; she simply wanted to know what she was getting into. She was always a practical woman who appreciated these kinds of truths. Though for the sake of timing, she decided against asking those questions right at this moment. "Ven, Ceirra... This place is so vast. So close to the capital, too!"

"Exactly. See Castle De Seraphim up there?" He pointed far across the farmlands up at the giant grand castle atop a nearby mountain. "I've been wanting to get this place for a while... For all of us and all those adventures, bounty jobs and some people overpaying at the tavern... Yeah. I can get us this place. Oh. And I'm supposed to be giving the man this..." Venser muttered reaching into his satchel and removing a scroll with the De Seraphim family sigil on it, a regal looking dragon on it. They approached the twin doors and he knocked in it, stepping back to brush Rowena's hair and beam down at her next to Sanna. "Yes we're gonna get you a nice big nursery and a lot of servants to care for your brothers and sisters..." He cooed.

"That's an interesting sigil. I don't think I've seen it before," Sanna said with a nod as she heard him out and watched him reach into his satchel to withdraw the scroll. She grinned as the man spoke to their lovely daughter, who reached out to his face and cooed back as though having a conversation, a big smile on her tiny face. Sanna chuckled and stroked the little one's cheek with a gentle thumb, beaming back over at Venser. She always saw him as such a loving father, and that would never change. The way he was so gentle in his voice around her, how sweet his words were toward her...it was wonderful.

"It's a beautiful place, this area."

"You have. When we went to the castle and anytime in the capital. And you too Rowena." He babbled a bit and tickled her stomach, wrapping an arm around his tanned lover, and out stretching his other hand to take the tall temptress's hand as the door opened. A tall, dark haired Pryldahnian man with yellow, partially scaled skin and brown eyes with a goatee and a moustache opened the door. "Ah, you must be Master Venser. A messenger said you'd be here today." The property owner said, clasping his hands. "And your lovely family I assume?" The man owned many a property in the countryside and was clearly wealthy, by his long blue silks and the two mercenaries that accompanied him. "Yes. Venser Karkaldwin, and these are my lovers... Sanna Karkaldwin and Ceirra Dusk, and baby Rowena..." He smiled down at their daughter again.

"Ahhh, alright. That makes sense." Laughing softly as she watched him tickle their daughter, she settled against him gracefully as he wrapped his arm around her. The door opened and she bowed her head in respect, smiling as her beloved introduced their little group. Rowena even seemed social, giggling a bit as her name was said by her father.

A woman came up behind the property owner, dressed to the nines in plated armor that was heavily engraved. Chainmail peeked out from beneath a portion of the chest and abdomen, though it wasn't a vulnerability; there was thick cloth and plate beneath there, too. Silvery hair was braided back, making already pale skin much paler than it was. black lips were the only thing that stood out, other than piercing crimson eyes. She was silent and seemed to only mind the orders of the owner of the property, standing out of his way and looking ahead at the strangers that encroached the new territory.

"Ci'ane Koffer, property owner. For any smaller providence or county you'd normally have the steward handle property and public relationships but thankfully property is just another up and coming trade around here, and I'm just another humble, noble merchant." The Pryldahnian man said as his long, draconian tail swished about behind him. "And I assume that is the God Queen's so called discount then?"

Venser let go of Sanna and handed him the scroll. "Indeed. She said this one in particular would be cheaper than most since she said the last owner ran out on his debts and everything else here was sold." He said, looking at him at one of the particular hired bodyguards that really stood out. Hair and eyes especially . She was pretty, and wondered what she looked like underneath her armor.

"Yes, that's true." Ci'ane nodded as he gestured behind them. "And I know royalty can take any piece of land that suits their fancy, but we all have to make a profit yes? I have a family myself to feed and other properties to upkeep."

"And Y'vonne always did tell me being a queen isn't just all tea parties, spa days and ballroom dances, she has actual responsibilities and... Paperwork. For being a true dragon and supremely powerful." Venser said, clasping his hands together, beside him the six foot tall seductress in the short leather dress looking at Madalina Lupator with her own burnt orange eyes, smirking at her.

"So, a tour then?" Venser kissed Sanna on the cheek. "From the outside I like this already."

Madalina met the tall woman's gaze with her own, raising an eyebrow at her smirk. She wasn't sure of this one, and looked to the person who hired her, Ci'ane, with some concern. She leaned in and whispered, "Be careful, sir."

Sanna beamed and nodded at the man's introduction of himself, glancing over at the dark-lipped woman as well but otherwise respecting her apparent outward need to not be stared at. Ceirra didn't seem to catch that drift for a moment, but she wasn't about to mention it. She purred as she was let go for Venser to hand him the scroll, and then again when he kissed her on the cheek. "It's a beautiful castle, and there is a lot to be done in the way of papers. I'm sure my love here is eager to get started; a tour would be wondrous."

Upon hearing that, Madalina backed up to allow for Ci'ane to move out of their way and begin said tour, keeping careful eye on the people that were soon to own this place. It wasn't anything personal, she was simply doing her job that the man had hired her for. As far as she knew she was to be here for the duration of the exchange, but what she didn't know is that she would be one of the first established guards of the new Karkaldwin manor.

"This is lovely." Ceirra gave his hand a light squeeze. "I love the architecture..." Letting out a slight purr as they walked through the doors and into the villa. "Right." He nodded to the white haired woman in the heavy armor. The estate itself was a two story house made of elaborate marble decorations, inlaid marble paneling, door jambs and columns and blank walls built around a courtyard known as the atrium. The atrium had many rooms opening up off to the sides and there was no roof above, letting the sky shine down on them.

Their feet dragged along the concrete floor as they stopped in the atrium, where there was a small pool and a fountain in the middle surrounded by a few stone benches. "The villa is divided into several suites, these included rooms for family and guests and accommodation rooms for the slaves and staff. As well as many other empty rooms you can do with as you wish. And this," Ci'ane explained. "Is the atrium, where guests are entertained and introduced."

"It is two stories as you can see and bedrooms, the master one especially, is on the second floor."

Venser simply nodded and took Sanna and Ceirra's hands. she leaned over and pressed a kiss to his forehead. "I know I've been busy and away, we all travel a lot I know... But I have not slept around. I've been as pure as a virgin since I was away." The tall temptress's long beautiful legs on display with her shirt leather dress, reaching into her own satchel she pulled out a rather hefty coin purse. "All of those drunken fools helped with our down payment." She winked.

Sanna followed Ci'ane like the rest, and Madalina waited until everyone passed by before taking her place behind the group. It was to protect all of them, really, and it was also a matter of comfort for her. She was a quiet woman, not prone to conversation or social graces. She was often too blunt for it. As they were introduced to the different suites and rooms, Sanna felt Venser's hand wind in hers and gave a gentle squeeze, offering him a smile as he and Ceirra spoke. She blushed at Ceirra's words and the sight of the purse, chuckling quietly so as not to interrupt Ci'ane's talking.

Then, she heard the mention of slaves. She stopped dead in her tracks for a moment and looked to the man, pale as a ghost. "...There are slaves here? I thought slavery was illegal nowadays." Venser could tell this was quite an important aspect to her, though she wasn't sure she'd ever told him why. Perhaps when they had a moment alone...

Madalina spoke up for once, looking to the tan woman who seemed to be bothered. "Madam Sanna, they are not mistreated I can assure you. I have worked for this villa for a long time; they are anything but abused."

Sanna turned to her, concern still in her face. "That...is not my point, but...thank you for the reassurance. Perhaps I'll explain another time.

"Not in Pryldahn, no. The elves used to be imported a lot from the Alphonse Islands, though in recent years most are just families descended from the older ones." C'i'ane said with a shrug, his draconian tail swishing behind them as they stood in the courtyard near the fountain. The rooftops were sloped so rainwater could be funneled into the refreshing pools beneath the ceilings for drinking and bathing water, and often collected and stored for later use. "Now, the kitchens are just far behind the fountain, and outside of that the gardens..." The Pryldah-nian continued as they walked the large rectangle shaped villa and he kept point-ing out rooms. Venser nodded and stroked his beard, already planning on buying some slaves next. "The slaves are property, smarter than say a donkey or so, but even then no one should mistreat their animals, or their own property. Otherwise they don't deserve it."

"And, it's all expensive." C'iane added. Venser nodded again. "It makes sense, if they work in the fields and do the cooking and... Well, why mistreat them? We help them, take care of them, and they help us."

In a hushed voice, Sanna spoke with careful consideration of her words toward her lover. "My people, the Krimeakhetii, are often recruited as slaves. They are not treated well, and I was to be sent to the same fate had I not left my caravan as I did. That is why I was apprehensive at first...I am glad that you and the others here do not plan on mistreating those who work here."

Madalina seemed to raise a brow at the tan girl, realizing her reasons as she lis-tened in a bit. So, she was a gypsyi... It wasn't the first one she'd met, but her en-counters with them in the past had not been memorable. This one, though...there was something about her. She hoped she would have the chance to stay and learn more.

Sanna squeezed his hand gently as it was held, giving a comforting smile as she walked with them, listening to the Pryldahnian man speak of the different areas of the villa. Hearing him say that slaves were property...it struck a chord in her that she wasn't sure she'd expected out of him. "The people that become slaves are still human beings and deserve the same respect...they are vastly smarter than the common barn animal."

"It's a mutual agreement, as your husband said." Ci'ane said opening a door to one of the side rooms, which looked like it could be used for storage or something. "We'd like to see the upstairs, as that's where all of our family will be staying. Ehhhh, we still gotta figure out what to do with those rooms... I mean bedrooms kitchen, out here is the living room in a way..." Venser nodded to Sanna. "We will not be doing that to our slaves, no. We will take care of them as they do us. And I've been to the markets before, I hate how sickly the slavers keep some of them..." He spoke as they neared a flight of stairs up to the second floor.

"A normal wealthy Pryldahnian nobleman probably has about fifty or so slaves to serve him, his family and his home. Slaves cater to the master and his family's needs and did everything to keep the home clean, comfortable and exactly how the master wanted it. And," Ci'ane raised a finger, "You and your family do seem wealthy since you are friends with the God Queen."

Ceirra Dusk kept quiet, blinking her burnt orange eyes and admiring the home. It could certainly use some decorating once they moved in. Perhaps one of these rooms could be their playroom? She hoped there was a wine cellar, or perhaps one of these rooms could be their own personal little bar. She giggled a bit and pushed passed Sanna, Rowena, and Ven, as she climbed the stairs they got a good look up her short leather dress and the skinny black thong the succubus was wearing, she looked back and bit her lip at Madalina, her fangs very apparent. "It's going to be such a goodly home for us all."

"You present a fair point...I suppose I should worry less, in that case." Sanna smiled to the group and nodded as they were brought to the rooms where they'd be staying, listening to the culture of the Pryldahnian elite as it was presented to her. So slavery was common here, but it wasn't like the slavery she'd seen...that was a relief. She blushed at being seen as wealthy; she'd have to get used to that, she knew, but it was always so foreign. She'd grown up poor, suffering. She'd never known this side of life so close and personal before, and that was clear in the way she presented herself.

Madalina saw the other woman's fangs and perked a brow once more, discreetly biting her lip to display her own to Ceirra for a moment before returning to the stony expression she was used to. She gave a humble bow at the waist to the new owners of the villa; "I am glad to hear you like it. Master Ci'ane, might these kind folk benefit from a general, or do they yet possess the means for an army? Do they truly need such, if they are friends with the God Queen? They could at the very least use protection."

"Normally the wealthy hire their own guards." Ci'ane answered as they climbed the concrete stairs. "There are multiple rooms including quarters for the slaves, baths, pools, storage rooms, exercise rooms, and the garden behind the kitchen but we can't forget all of these." The Pryldahnian said as they all reached the top of the stairs, and Venser was looking to the room at the very end of the hall, and the dark eyed Pryldahnian stood beside him. "That is traditionally the office, or study. But it can be whatever you like once you and your family move in. Actually, come, all of you will want to see the master bedroom." The bearded man looked down to Rowena in Sanna's arms and tickled her stomach. "And right beside it we're gonna have a nursury for you and your siblings and future siblings!"

"Yes, sir. Understood." Madalina no longer spoke after that, nodding as she too followed all of them to the main area that the family would be sleeping. She couldn't help but smile a bit; this was her favorite part of the villa, personally speaking, and she found it the most beautiful.

Sanna beamed as Venser tickled their daughter at the prospect of a nursery, blushing at the idea of more children. Was he considering ensuring she had another, or multiple in the future? Or was he referring to his actual wedded wives, one of which she was not? They had not married, but rather had remained lovers in this time frame - despite her mothering his daughter. Surely society frowned on that, but she wasn't about to tell him how he should live. Besides, she was content with the way things were presently... She was happy. Even if they were poor and hungry, she'd be happy because she was with him. "I look forward to seeing what happens with these rooms," She said humbly, smiling.

"This is a truly fantastic place. And it will make a good home for all of us."

Ci'ane turned to Venser and clasped his hands together. "And a lot of farmland. So, what are you going to be farming?"

The bearded man thought for a moment, reaching for the metal tin on his belt which held his special cigars.

"Cannabis!"

CHAPTER THIRTEEN:
THE BROOM CLOSET

Castle De Seraphim, Pryldahn, 1437 ATC

It was another day inside Castle De Seraphim, the cool fall breeze rode the air outside. Inside the castle walls, down a particular hall, moans of pleasure could be heard from a solitary broom closet.

Though air was cool, and so too, was the youngest daughter of the Great God Emperor. She shivered in her large, overly cushioned chair as she hugged herself in an attempt to gather as much warmth for herself as possible. Then, a harsh cough vibrated in her throat, followed by a few others that echoed in the large room around her. Another violent shiver. It would appear this one was ill, though, if asked, would never admit it. No, the woman just wanted to sleep. To drown in a blanket of warmth, to which for reason she could not obtain herself, no matter what she tried. She turned, this way and that in the chair, hoping she would drift off into sleep but it avoided her, unlike the annoying cough that lingered in her throat. Voices, mumbling and groans kept catching her ear, disturbing her already unpeaceful night. She growled and stood with a heavy blanket the practically swallowed her form. Her face was annoyed and pale. She would find the source of that incessant noise...and end it. She made her way into the hallway, following the sounds, her once graceful movements now slow and slightly clumsy though her posture was still straight. She may be ill, but she was still royalty and she would not allow an illness to taint her image.

When she would open the door to the broom closet, she would find a short, chubby brown haired servant girl with soft features and submissive hazel eyes, with her dress hiked up, and the serpent eyed court jester behind her, with his suit around his ankles doing what they did. At the sight they both stopped and looked at her. The servant girl blushed in embarrassment and moved away from Venser. "M'lady." She bowed in respect to her before quickly exiting the broom closet. Venser didn't have much of a reaction as she stood in front of her. "Y'vonne." He gestured once more out the door, still pretty much naked in front of her. "Uh... Ya know you got some nice servants around here. Her name is Kimmy. She works in the kitchen and makes the best rolls you'll ever fucking taste."

"Kimmy Burnham, yes." The woman was not all surprised by the state she found the couple in. Her face was harsh and unamused and she merely blinked and stepped aside as the girl exited the closet. The blanket she held around her was hugged more tightly as a rather violent shiver of a cold wave washed up her spine. Y'vonne bit back a cough that tickled her throat as she stared at the half naked man. How irritating.

"I ask Venser," The regal draconic woman started with a cracked form. No doubt a side effect from all of her previous coughing. "That you do not... Distract the servants from their duties, yes?" She knew this was folly, but wanted to make it clear that we would never do such things again. She sounded irritated, more stuck-up than usual, which was hard to imagine honestly. But, what would one expect? She has been lacking sleep. One could tell just by looking at her lightly red-lined eyes and dark circles.

"Do dress yourself." She snapped. Though soon, she couldn't hold back the cough anymore, so she turned her head sharply to her right to cough. It came out scratchy and weak. When she found a break from her fit, she added. "I do find it pleasing that you enjoy the benefits of the servants," She sighed deeply. "And their cooking was one of the ONLY things I hoped you'd indulge in."

The bearded man nodded in affirmation and pulled up the leopard print thong he wore beneath his baggy red pants. "The food is good and the servant girls are lovely." He cocked his head to the side, looking at her. "Are you alright? You look tired. And sick."

The obnoxiously thin woman all but rolled her electric blue eyes at his comment about the servant girls. Of course he would think so. She turned fully now to allow him to dress himself, her back now to him. Once he finished and he inquired about her health and huffed and stood straighter. "Of course I am alright." She practically hissed. She held her nose in the air, but in her throat threatened another cough.

"Oh c'mon. No you aren't." Venser said pointing to the bags beneath her reddened eyes. "Either that or you've been smoking too many cigars. Happens to me occasionally." He looked around. "Shall we walk? Go back to wherever you were sitting or laying down rather than chatting in a broom closet."

She now glared at the man. "I do not smoke cigars... Often." She said slowly as she soon found her feet moving down the hallways, her blanket trailing behind her like a long veil. Rest... Yes... Rest is what she wanted. Her eyelids grew so heavy so wobbled a bit on her feet, one hand reaching out to reach for balance on a wall. Summerland, her head was spinning, her vision blurring. But, she fought it. She squeezed her eyes shut, willing the foggy cloud that draped over her mind away. "A-... Are you well tonight?" She needed to talk, to stay awake. "You and your family looked at that piece of property I recommended, yes?"

"Oh yes, pretty damn well actually." Venser said as they walked, he watched Y'vonne stumble down the hall, having to use the wall for support. He sighed knowing she could barely stand up right, he took her arm and put it around himself, helping her walk. "I just got back to the castle yesterday. After being away on a family vacation for a little more than a week. How about yourself, Y'vonne? I know, I've been around less and less... Doing my duties of entertaining you and everyone else, and spent the summer trying to get everything move into the villa and set everything up."

She hummed to herself, leaning against him once the bearded man had reached out and settled her arm around himself. A few servants passing by gasped at the sight of someone outwardly touching one of the daughters as such but made no noise or effort to object. "Vacation? How lovely..." She coughed now again, and a few more times after that. She breathing now came slow and steady, her mind now half asleep already. "Me?... I've...been busy." And that was it. Her vision went out, the woman now dead weight to the man as she now lay collapsed in his arms.

"Well hello beautiful..." Venser said a brunette female servant with a thin hourglass figure. She blushed seeing how nicely he cleaned up, his crimson and turquoise tunic was nice and smooth and he was well groomed. Not to mention his pretty green eyes. He was oblivious to the reason why they were gasping.

"Yup! Took my twins and their mom and Sanna and our new baby Rowena and a few other lovers to Crown City Grigwald. We really have to go to the city of Gideonice when they have Carnival, several days of partying wearing masks and just dancing in the streets..." He stopped at the chair that Y'vonne had originally sat in prior to discovering Venser and Kimmy. "So what have you-" He set her down and stopped talking once he realized she was out cold.

"Y'vonne!" He said, raising his voice, clapping his hands together.

"Oh great..." Scooping the God Queen up in his arms he sighed and began to walk Y'vonne to her room, concerned about her paperwork load now. Hopefully he could somehow help her with it when she awoke.

CHAPTER FOURTEEN: TROUBLED CHILD

The Dragon's Head Tavern and Inn, Vorland, 1437 ATC

The sandy haired barmaid snacked on a sweet roll in the corner; one of the last few. It was fluffy and sweet, with little crumbs being few and far between. Brea Rowland was quite content with her progress as a new and upcoming baker, but she could see ways to improve. For instance, this roll was rather dense and doughy. All in all she was content, though, and she smirked to herself as she ate.

"How's the baking going?" Venser asked from beside her, as if he had been there the whole time. He had an annoying habit of appearing and disappearing at random. He held a sketchbook in one hand, and upon closer inspection he had drawn a particular curved helmet with a frill on top.

Brea jumped, dropping her sweet roll on the dusty floor. "Oh, hello." She said, quickly catching her breath, then frowning at her toppled pastry. "I suppose it was going very well up until I dropped the baked goods." She added with a chuckle. "How's the hunt for the perfect home going?"

"It ended, actually. We have a big lovely villa with a lot of land to grow crops in and... Eh, we've been in. the process of moving and shopping for furnishings." He said, shrugging. "Half hour rule." He said raising his left hand, his mark glowed greenish white and emitted steam as the sweet roll was trapped in a green aura, floating into his hand. He handed it back to Brea and asked, "How do ya feel about your boss fighting in an arena? Or doing chariot racing? I know it's like a national pastime, sort of."

The sandy haired barmaid chuckled as she let the roll fall back into her hands. "Thank you. And I guess I feel like my healing skills need polishing if that were to be the case." Although he said it was fine to eat, she didn't fully believe him, as she saw specks of dirt and dust in the butter. She put it on the table. "Why are you hypothetically going to an arena?"

"For money and to entertain the masses. Why else would anyone fight to the death in an arena in front of hundreds of people?" Venser asked, clapping his hands twice. "Water!" A shadow tendril brought him a cold glass, and he picked it up with his scarred hand. "Grigwald has jousting so does many places since it came from there, chariot racing, so much. So why not partake?"

"... But are you aware you could die?" She said slowly, making sure he understood every syllable. "It's usually a fight... To the death. Death." She stressed.

"Yeah. So what?" Venser asked, still unphased as if he didn't quite hear what she had said. "And these fighters are slaves and prisoners."

"You seem very... Okay with the idea of murder. Or being the murder-ee." She said, getting up and tossing the sweet roll away. "Think of your children Ven!"

"I honestly... I do enjoy it sometimes, the challenge and the rush of it, for those who deserve it. Sometime in the capital since that's where a lot of people live, and it gets plenty of travelers..." He shrugged, "Sometime in Capital De Seraphim in Pryldahn, up North over the border ya know." He sipped his water and pushed aside his sketchbook. "Not the first time it's happened. Though, I gave chariot riding a try only once and would like to do it again." Hearing a local farmer call for a tankard of ale and watching his barmaid fetch it.

"Er... You, chariot race?" Brea said, turning and finding a tankard while filling it with ale. "So, sometimes, I've only heard about it, they kill people for sport? I'm lost, I feel." She said, passing the mug to the guest and taking his coin.

"Thank you ma'am." He took the mug and chugged the ale down, sighing a sign of great approval.

"Yeah. Exactly." He clasped his hands together and stated, "People love violence. So why not? Do you think I'd do no good or something?'"

"Well, you did run through a bunch of mannequins in here the other day... And you told me about those brigands you took down to help pay for your home." She said with a nod. "I think you'd hold your own just fine, sir."

Rauri the islandic elf needed alcohol, and soon. Alcohol could help, it always had, why would it stop now? She lifted her head from where it was laying on the countertop, only enough to where she could speak without being muffled. "Someone get me something to drink, please." She asked quietly. Seeing as how she hasn't spoken in a good few hours, it was a bit surprising to hear her own voice, to hear how incredibly bitter she was.

The sun began to set over the trees, cool evening air blowing through the underbrush. The soft sound of foot falls sounds in the twilight as a large yellow creature moves slowly through the wood. The creature's dark eyes glance around quickly as it moves, towering over most of the animals. Its large stinger tipped tail drooped behind it in a curl only inches from the grass below and its small insect-like wings sit folded against its back. The physique of the creature is mostly female, the yellow on its skin interrupted by brown belly and leg pattern. A long thin forked tongue flicks from between the reptilian lips to taste the air. The smell of treated wood, food, and humans wafts on the breeze. She tilted her large head and moved in the smell, a tavern coming into her line of view through the trees. She walks up to the doors, cautiously, then pushes them open gently. She has to bend over to walk in and then straighten up again, glancing around the wooden building.

Brea Rowland went behind the bar and then stopped in front of Rauri. "I like the tune, but it's down in the doldrums as they say." She said, offering a half smile.

"Something wrong, Rauri?" Venser asked, grabbing a bottle of his favorite brand of cider, setting it down in front of her. "You're drinking a lot. And I can tell you aren't having fun."

"What about tunes?" She asked with a muffled voice, her face squished against the counter. She didn't bother lifting her head. "A stupid letter, is all." She mumbled. She reached up and out to grab the cider, not bothering to pour a glass as she sat up and drank straight from the bottle. The short elven girl was dressed similar to a belly dancer, her outfit consisted of baggy red pants, a red sleeveless top that matched, and black red boots with a rapier strapped to her side. She had a relatively thin figure with a nice rear, and she had tanned olive sunkissed skin with eyes the color of the sea and long dark red hair that was semi curly.

Brea leaned against the counter and crossed her arms. "We won't pry if you don't want to talk about it. Right Venser?" She said pointedly, raising her eyebrow at him.

The sound of voices reaches her and she glances up, seeing that there seems to be a bar atop the second floor. She moves up the stairs quietly and peers over at the people seated at the bar curiously. She kneels down on her haunches and watches, her head tilted to the left.

"Naw c'mon." Venser said, crossing his arms. "I have a saying, people go to healers for physical wounds, while people go to bars for the wounds of the soul." He gestured to Rauri. "Clearly her soul is hurt. Right?"

"No, no, go ahead, pry all you want! I would rather get it over with now than later. Ask away!" She gestures wildly, like only a drunk can. She leaned back in her chair, waiting for a question to be asked.

The bearded man leaned forward and asked, "What has you troubled, friend?"

Emikolet's forked lounge flicks out again as she watches them from a comfortable distance, her tail now resting comfortably on the ground around her feet.

"My clan got sick of me being their 'Trouble Child' so they cut me loose. That's it." She spat, taking another swig from the bottle in her hand. "I am such a long way from the Alphonse Islands."

"Well they're all missing out." Brea mumbled her support, always afraid of over-stepping boundaries. She never knew where she truly stood while working here, since her boss and frequent guests were always raunchy. But she wanted to help however she could, especially to one of her favorite patrons.

Emikolet stood up and walked cautiously to the bar, looking over it curiously. Her three fingered, claw tipped hand glides across the top gently. Ignoring the others, she explores the upstairs area. Towering above the tables she wonders if she will even fit in any of these chairs.

Ruari gave off a snort of laughter. "Are you kidding? They think--They know I'm no good, magic nor brute strength!" Her ears flicker a bit in annoyance not at the question, but at everything in general. "Gods, they had to put power runes on me once they found out I was magically inclined because I was just that weak! Why would they want me?" She grumbles, looking down into the bottle to see how much of the cider was left.

"Ya' know... I probably wouldn't be nearly as mad as I am if they had let me back on the island... Fuck the clan, I just want to return to Koneroi." She sniffles as tears begin to roll down her face. "Why can't I just go home?"

"Can you not return to your island at all?" The sandy haired barmaid asked, engulfed in her tragic story. It was truly heartbreaking. "I can't go home, either. But I'm sure these are two completely different worlds."

"N-no..." She tried to control her sobbing. "They control t-the island. They'll most likely kill me." Rauri stopped her crying enough to where she's no longer making a mess of herself. "Why can't you go home?" She looked up at Brea through teardamp eyelashes, concern written all over her face.

Brea shook her head. "No, this isn't about me right now." Whilst abandoning her place behind the bar to comfort her. She took the small woman in her arms, holding her albeit not too close, just enough to be soothing. "But I know that losing the one place that you thought you would always have can shatter your world. Picking up the pieces will cut and hurt. But it is inevitable."

Ruari's bottom lip began quivering as she tried to hold back a fresh wave of tears. She nodded, unsure if in agreement or acceptance, and pulled Brea into a tight hug. "Thanks."

Venser, after staring off into space for what seemed like forever, finally said, "Homos naked." He sputtered and shook his head, speaking clearly, "Home is where ya make it." A nod of his head and a quiet sigh, thinking of his own little family he had now.

The sandy haired barmaid nodded, hugging her back. "Home is where you make it. And I guess it's time to start over." She said, taking the advice that she gave. "I could have used that advice myself. And here I am."

The islandic elf smiled at the duo's words. "Then I guess here is my home. Until I get another job, at least. Doing... Something. I did practice belly dancing for a few years." She laughed at her own little joke.

"Oh that's perfect! And I can play guitar or something, get the shadow tendrils to play something and yeah. Patrons can give you coin for dancing. My lover Sanna is a dancer, the best, in fact." The bearded man shrugged. "I live here at the tavern. This place is my life. I have other homes, in Pryldahn, places you've never heard of.. But... I work here. I spend almost every day here. I've met so many people here, my friends and family are here. Though it may change eventually."

"I will have to consider it again... Yeah."

"Well, that seems cause to celebrate!" Brea chirped, squeezing her close one last time before releasing her and going back behind the bar, pulling out a tankard and filling it with mead, raising it in the air. "To the new member of the family." She said, smiling kindly at Ruari.

Venser hopped atop the bar, sticking a large stick of pepperoni in-between his legs. "I'm sexy! Imma sexy boy!" He waved it around "Ding dong! Ding dong! Ding dong! Ding dong! Ding dong! Ding dong!" He proceeded to slap his employee in the face with his big sausage.

Brea put her tankard down and protected her face. "What? No-Venser..." Instead of protesting, she just groaned and pushed the stick away.

The islandic elf just stared blankly for a few moments. Ruari looked down at the bottle in her hand and then raised it. "To me, I guess." She raised it to her lips to take a swig. "And thanks... Jester."

"To Ruari." The sandy haired barmaid tried to toast as she was slapped in the face with the promiscuous meat.

"To Ruari!" The handsome bearded man said, raising a bottle of cider, somehow the pepperoni was replaced with it. He disappeared in a puff of thick red smoke and reappeared beside her. "Oh, and you know, I actually am employed as a jester. Sometimes."

The elf girl tilted it back a bit more to finish off the bottle, but she ended up leaning too far back and tipped the chair over, landing on her back with a heavy thud. Though she didn't seem to react much to the impact.

Her attention returned to the people at the bar as they seemed to toast to the girl. Her head tilts to the left and then to the right, not understanding. She approaches slowly, smelling food and drink. Her tongue flicks out and her mouth begins to water as she realized she was hungry.

"Brea?" Venser asked blinking a few times, craning his head to her before jumping back at the sight of the tall scaly scorpion thing. Now just noticing it. Somehow. "What the?!" He grabbed his bladeless sword from his belt and twirled it around, allowing the short blade to extend. "As, well you're... Close to a dragon?"

Emikolet jumped back at his actions, a hiss escaping her throat and the fin atop her head raising. She scoots back a few paces and stares down at him cautiously.

Having been one to typically avoid the sun these days, Arys had managed to sleep all day and found something to keep herself occupied for the start of the evening. When it was late, she ventured back to, as it was unofficially dubbed, Ven's Tavern in hopes to get a drink. Instead, she walked in on a scene she could have done without seeing. Aquatic, reptilian creatures of any sorts managed to leave her on somewhat of an edge... Whatever it was, Arys found herself navigating the opposite side of the room until she found a corner of the bar to mind her own business.

Brea Rowland jumped. And yelped. And grabbed her skirts. "I'm really not that much of a fighter, sir."

"Ooh! A dee dee! A dee dee!" Venser yelled, waving his short sword around. "Not the first time I've tangled with scorpion reptile people! Once cleared out a whole cave of them!" He continued to wave his sword around to scare the creature, slowly moving towards it. "A dee dee! A dee dee!"

Emikolet bared her rows of large sharp teeth, her tail raising over her head very much like a scorpion. "What did you call me?!?" She yelled, her two fangs swinging down from the roof of her mouth out from behind her teeth as her mouth opened. She growled low, trying to understand why he was acting this way. He acted like he knew what she was but she wasn't even from this realm. She snorted, getting up and jumping out a nearby window, much to everyone's surprise.

Seriously, what the fuck was this? It looked so... Beastial. Way more than a majority of patrons that came here, even the occasional furries. "Umm... So you can spea-" He jumped back again when she just decided to leave just like that. "Holy fuck!" Did Venser take acid? He didn't know? Was he.... Oh what the heck..

"Should have known... How did I not notice? I mean..." Awkward squeezing gestures. "I acted kinda like, I shouldn't have..."

"We know." Said Brea and Ruari at the same time.

CHAPTER FIFTEEN: BREA

The Dragon's Head Tavern and Inn, Vorland, 1437 ATC

It was an ordinary, quiet fall day at the Dragon's Head, and it had started to rain recently. The rain poured lightly outside while the clouds blocked out the blue skies above, but rays of sunlight broke through them. A very beautiful display. Meanwhile, Venser Karkaldwin cleaned his room of any clothes and junk lying about, both to take with him to his new villa, and to prepare for the two ladies he planned to invite to the privacy of his room soon enough.

Brea Rowland had caught herself staring outside at the rain, the constant blur of movement entrancing in it's own right. It was peaceful; the tavern was empty and she could afford this moment's solace. Just a few more weeks and they'd get snow most likely.

Ruari the tanned Islandic elf opened the door to the tavern just enough to wiggle herself through and not get any wind or rain into the tavern. She pulled down her black cloak's hood and made her way to her usual spot at the bar. "Rather dreary day, huh." She said with a soft voice, trying not to scare anyone.

A sudden clap was heard from behind Brea. "What a lovely day, right?" He smiled and looked out the window. "I mean, in between the rain and the sun breaking through the clouds occasionally." He sighed and turned around, calling his usual line, "Welcome to the Dragon's Head Tavern and Inn!"

If Ruari's little greeting didn't startle her, Venser's outburst suddenly did. She grabbed a fistful of her green skirts and cringed, taking some calming breaths as Venser greeted the tavern and it's furniture. "Hello." She said flatly, eyebrows furrowed. Her demeanor changed when she saw there was a guest present, and she smoothed her skirts and plastered on a smile.

"Glad to be here, sir." Ro nodded towards Venser. "I seem to recall you talking about real vintage... Mind showing me?" She asked with a tilt of the head and a smirk.

"Sorry for scaring you Brea." Venser said backing up a bit. "You were really in the mood, ya know?" He turned around and clapped again, plastering a smile as well. "Yes, I was talking about vintage drinks. And a rare one from home, Apple Street Brandy." Venser began to walk back to his room, motioning the two to follow. "Come! Come!"

The sandy haired barmaid sighed and followed, heart still racing from the scare earlier. Brea made sure to wait for Ruari to walk first, not wanting to leave a guest trailing behind like a caboose.

Ruari stood and followed Venser to his room, swaying her hips as she walked. "It better be as good as you say it is." She gave a deep chuckle.

Venser's room was fairly big. A queen sized bed lay by the windows, and it was covered in turquoise silk sheets and he had about a dozen pillows all with furry gold throwovers. The royal colors of his homeland. Off to the left was a wardrobe with a few dresses hanging out, some spilt onto the floor. To the right of the bed was a desk with a bag of silver in it, a mirror, and some makeup. Right beside it was various papers and pieces of art. Above Venser's bed was a multicolored painting of a woman's vagina, and below that his signature double bladed sword, the Dual Personality. In front of the bed, was a wine rack, which held wine alike and a variety of other bottles of a design of which neither Brea and Ruari would have seen, one of which contained a reddish brown liquid. Venser led them down the hall, to the sixth door on the right, and opened it for them. "Eh? What do ya think?"

"Holy shit..." The elf muttered, leaving her mouth gaping at the sight of such extravagance. What really drew her attention were the sheets, their blue-green hue reminding her of the more expensive things one would find back in the Alphonse Islands i and their soft look adding on to their appeal. "How did you afford it?"

Once she crossed the threshold into Venser's room, her whole demeanor changed from pouty to amazed. It was nothing like she had ever imagined for Venser, infact, she thought he'd have a surprisingly plain room. But the painting of a vagina on the wall proved just how wrong her theories were. Oh, and there was alcohol.

"A lot of odd jobs. Different exchange rates..." Venser moving into the room with them, crossing the room to grab a tray of glasses. "Why don't you two make yourselves comfortable on the bed?" He said moving the tray onto the desk, moving over to the wine rack. "In one country, one ounce of gold is about... Four hundred coin? That's if it's pure. There's been a shortage of purity. And here at the tavern, we get paid occasionally in pure gold."

"Not to mention gems and pure silver, which fetch a pretty price too..."

Brea nodded, walking around to the wine rack and glancing at all of the bottles in scripts she couldn't read. Each of them was like a different masterpiece in the way the bottles looked and the way they were crafted. It was interesting, so she knelt by the rack to continue.

"Pure gold? Now that is unbelievable. Back home I got paid in clan favor and powdered herbs. And the occasional silver, if I did a job for a foreigner, and we get a lot of those, mostly pirates." She removed her cloak, wrapping it around her arms as she sat down on the bed. She fell back and nearly drowned herself in the sheets she could probably never have afforded on her homeland. "We had to get the majority of our goods from the surrounding isles. And sometimes the mainland, but we don't really trust mainlanders- And then when we got the goods they were overpriced. To the clan, at least. The foreigners had enough gold or silver to purchase them." She began to go on a tangent about how corrupt her homeland was, not seeming like she would stop anytime soon.

After glancing over the majority of the bottles, Brea took a seat on the edge of the bed, looking over her shoulder at the now cocooned Ruari. She chuckled. "Someone looks comfortable."

"Very." Ro turned to shove her face into the sheets.

"Where I'm from coins are part gold, and then they mix them with other metals." Venser said choosing the bottle full of burgundy brown liquid. Pouring them each a glass, he glanced over and said, "Why wouldn't she? It's the best silk money can buy." He set the tray down on the bed and sat Indian style, picking up one of them. "Apple Street Brandy. Nicely aged brandy with rare spices, and a drop of cannabis oil. Enjoy." He took a swig and smiled warmly.

Brea swirled it in the glass and looked at it carefully. Not wanting to be rude, she looked away and took a sip. "Oh my." She said, followed by a short cough and her cheeks turning a little pink

"Let me just die surrounded in these sheets first." The elf joked, lifting herself up from the cocoon she had made for herself. She took the drink and immediately swallowed the entire glassfull down, not realizing how strong it was. She only winced a little at the burn it left in her throat. "Pretty good, pretty good." She nodded, a flushed look of contentment taking over her features. "I still say that islandic vintage is better."

"Considering this came from the Isle of-" He stopped himself, not sure where he was going with it. Venser shrugged and drank down his glass quickly. "Lemme get you a refill." He poured them each another drink and said, "Guess that's something we have in common. We both come from islands, originally. Though I do... I should start saying I'm from Timberline, a small town in Pryldahn right near the border of that and Vorland..."

The sandy haired barmaid now had two almost full drinks in her hands. "Ehrm, thank you." She said, sipping at her first one a little faster, the pink deepening as it burned the back of her throat.

"Oh, that's right, this is an islandic vintage... Well, I ment the alcohol I grew up with." Ruari corrected herself as she swiftly drank down that glass, too.

"Getting greedy?" Venser asked jokingly downing another drink.

Several drinks later... The man in the crimson and light blue tunic swayed back and forth on the bed, abysmally deep philosophical debate on the subject of the connotations of love and beauty, the likes of which had not been known for centuries since the natural philosophers and thinkers from his homeland. Alas, our myopic, unsophisticated comprehension of linguistics and subtlety could only perceive these groundbreaking revelations as the following: "Yer sexy." Venser slurred with a laugh, nuzzling his co-worker and flopping over next to Ruari. "You too... Both of ya are sexy... Reminds me of... Sex!"

Brea set the now empty tankards down on a nearby bookshelf, and kept herself seated upright although he leaned on her. Her face felt warm and flush, and she was very occupied playing with her apron. Brea didn't drink often, so she was working extra hard to not do anything that'd embarrass her.

Ruari swayed as she set her glass down on the floor. "Pshhh... I hiiighly doubt you would after.... Eheh..." She gave a spinning gesture to her head as if she were trying to find the words to convey whatever was on her mind. She gave up once she forgot what she was trying to tell.

The beard poked Ruari's brown chest and sat back up pouring another glass. "Ah fuck I feel wasted... Hic! Mhmmm...!" He got on his knees in bed and wrapped his arms around Brea from behind, kissing her neck. "I think... Hic! Yer the sexy one...

And Rory is.... hic! The sexy one second! Hic!"

"And yet he pours." Brea joked, laughing with a short, high pitched hiccup. "Well, thank you, sir. I do appreciate it." She said, patting the top of his hand before trying to unravel it. She recognized that this was a place where she could potentially put her foot in her mouth, so she made sure to not say much, for fear of saying the wrong thing.

Ruari rolled her eyes, looking the two up and down with something akin to lust blossoming in her chest. Yeah, she was definitely starting to feel the effects of the alcohol.

"I might be able to... Hic! Trust ya with the secret of Pink Footed Booby..." Venser said running his hands up and down Brea's body, hiccing a bit more. "Should I- Hic! Tell you?" He pulled the sandy haired barmaid into him, looking to Ruari while feeling her up. "Yer- Hic! Missin' out... Hic!"

Ro gave a huff of laughter, crawling over the bed to place herself in Brea's lap. "Please do tell me..." She said with a purr in her voice, raising her head to look Venser in the eye.

This time when Brea blushed, blinking her bright hazel eyes, it certainly wasn't because of the alcohol. "Someone is quite touchy feely..." She said with a snicker, pulling her skirts close to her and helping her be sure she was covered. "And you really should..." she said, trailing off. "Probably would be good for b-buisiness."

The bearded man ignored the question and let out a seductive growl. Lowering one hand, it trailed down Brea's stomach and then rested on her thigh. "It's something that makes ya warm..." He said looking up, smirking at Ruari. "Hic!"

Ro bit down on her lower lip, her blush spreading and becoming more vivid. "I'll show you 'warm'." She reached up with one hand and dragged the handsome bearded man into a kiss.

Brea Rowland giggled at the two of them. "Never would've seen that coming, honestly." She said, laughing again. "Whatever is in your country's alcohol has it's re-recipients feeling frisky. Hic." She was making light of the events surrounding her, and quite literally on top of her.

"Mhm..." Venser moaned into the kiss, using his free hand to trail up Brea's stomach, fondling on of her breasts. He suckled on her lower lip before breaking the kiss, letting go of the sandy haired barmaid and scooting over a bit, undoing his tunic and throwing it off in a random direction, revealing his muscular barreled chest. "Oh I'll show you and her warm..."

Ro pulled back with a smirk, turning her attention to Brea. "Oh, sweetheart... the alcohol isn't making me do this..." She muttered before turning her head just enough to place an open-mouth kiss on her neck, suckling at the spot.

"Oh...Oh dear..." She said breathily. Brea raised her arm to move Venser's hand away, but before she could, she was distracted by Ruari's kiss on her neck. She could feel her lower back arch ever so slightly as the softest gasp escaped from her lips. The pink on her cheeks crossed the border into red.

The bearded barkeep then hopped off the bed and slid his pants down, leaving him in a leather thong as he moved behind Ruari, giving her rear a nice, hard smack. Then placed both hands on her hips and thrusted into her rear. "Yeah... This is going to be nice..." He said leaning forward to kiss the tanned elf girl on the neck. "Why don't we get out of these clothes..." He whispered softly into her ear, nibbling on her lobe a bit.

Ro gave a gasp when he thrusted, her thighs beginning to shiver with excitement. But these clothes f-feel so nice..." she whined, moving her arms to wrap around Brea's neck. She nuzzled her face in between the breasts in front of her with a smile as she arched her back, giving Venser a better look at her round, covered ass.

Brea smirked and looked down at Ruari, her fingertips lightly tracing the curvature of her spine. "I wonder how long you've waited to do that." She teased, moving her chest slightly as if to shake her around a bit. Once her fingertips had reached the base of her spine, she gave Ruari's behind a quick pinch with a giggle.

"Well clothes are a- Hic! Prison..." Venser said hiking up Ruari's dress so that her rear was uncovered. He slowly pulled his thong down, allowing his hardened member to spring free. He slapped it against the fabric covering her rear and said,"Anticipation always makes sex better." He then placed both hands on her panties, slowly pulling them down her legs.

Ruari swiftly brought her hand down on Venser's wrist before he could get too far. "Wait a minute..." She huffed, turning herself around so that her back was pressed against Brea's chest. "I would prefer that we don't get that friendly just yet." She gave a smirk as she beckoned Venser to come closer, keeping her hand locked around his wrist.

Now Brea felt like an uncomfortable piece of wet bread. All of this action was happening on top of her as if she were the mattress herself. "Ehrm, I think I'll go grab something from upstairs. Excuse me." She said, trying to wriggle out from underneath Ruari.

Venser gave the elf a quick, pelvic thrust. "Oh c'mon... Hic! We're already getting friendly..." He said moving to the side a bit, taking one of Brea's free hands, placing it on his shaft, rubbing it up and down slowly.

"Oh no, you don't." Ro purred, bringing her free hand under the skirt of her dress to rub at her opening through her panties.

Brea gasped as multiple hands felt around for ways to stop her from leaving. She was frozen, one hand grasping around at her skirts for Ruari's hand, while the other was doing as it was told, or better yet, shown.

"Hic! Shy? Haven't... Fucking- Hic! How ya feel?" Venser asked as he used Brea's hand to rub him off. "Anticipation..."

Ruari chuckled softly as she flipped the skirts over her head to go down on her. Once she got her underclothes off she immediately began running her tongue up and down her opening, humming in delight.

The sandy haired barmaid's knees buckled, but she remained upright. The hand that was initially going to swat Ruari away was now lifting her own skirts to grant her easier access. Her moans were few and far between, but they were always quiet and breathy. Her other hand continued to please Venser, and she looked up at him briefly from behind her fringe. She thought about it for a few seconds, but enjoying the two, she gave into her lust, and theirs.

"Let's take it all off..."

Once it was clear what they all wanted, all three of them rushed into position in a quick blur. The bearded bartender suddenly found himself staring at two upturned rumps, an incredible sight from the two naked women in his bed. Ro's was firm, but still had a good bounce to it, while Brea's was not only big and had a bounce like Ro's, but looked softer. He watched with a sly smirk as he watched the redheaded elf and his sandy haired co-worker kiss each other with no end in stopping soon.

"Oh yes..."

Ro's legs shuffled impatiently, arching her back and spreading her legs open a little wider, to the point where her pussy began to spread open as well and show a tiny sliver of pink in the middle of her nice tanned body.

"Ven! Just hurry up and stick it in us!"

CHAPTER SIXTEEN: RUARI

Venser's Bedroom, The Dragon's Head Tavern and Inn, Vorland, 1437 ATC

Ruari leaned back in her seat at the bar, flipping through a small book. Today hadn't been particularly exciting, considering she hadn't been called up to heal anyone and her new friend Gale was out on her own mission. So she sat, alone at the bar, just reading elven text and drinking what was given to her earlier in the day.

Venser walked down from the hall wearing absolutely nothing. Showing off his nude, muscular form. He was unshaved, his bearded looking a bit scraggly and raven black hair that needed to be cut. His expression was bored as he walked to the bar, drinking from a bottle of cider. He drank down the last of it and tossed it aside on the floor, sitting down beside Rauri at the bar.

Ro glanced to the side, immediately noting that he was in a public area without clothes. She looked him in the eye, expression unchanged save for a blush spreading across her face and reaching the tips of her ears. "Venser, why are you naked out in the bar area?" She asked.

"'Because I am." Venser said, pulling another bottle of cider off the shelf to him, catching it in his left hand. He popped it open and sighed, shifting a bit. Then wrapped his free arm around Rauri and began to fondle one side of her small chest while he drank. "Clothes are a prison." He said almost as a matter of fact.

"I guess I quite like prison, then." The islandic elf huffed, letting Venser do as he pleased. "What I'm saying is that my clothes, my dress, does not come off while I'm in public." She leaned against him, placing a hand against his thigh and continuing to 'read' her book.

"Then I guess you've never been to a nude beach." Venser said, setting his bottle down, taking Rauri's hand off of his thigh and sliding it up to his member.

"No? In the Alphonse Islands a lot of elves wear next to nothing though with the year long heat." She kept her blue eyes glued to the pages as she gripped him lightly, moving her hand up and down slowly, apparently disinterested enough not to look away. "Beaches are fun and all but I don't really see the appeal of nude beaches where pirates could sail by anytime. Besides, sand being able to get into even more areas than usual is something that I never liked to experience."

The bearded man wasn't even listening to Ruari as she explained why she didn't see the appeal of it. He set his bottle down, then slapped the book away from Ruari. Not too long afterwards he picked her up, slung Rauri over his shoulder, and then began to walk towards his room. "Coarse, rough, and gets everywhere. Yeah."

"Hey! I was reading that, you prick!" Ro pouted, giving him a soft kick in the leg. She tried to huff but it slowly turned into a giggle. "At least I have a nice view." She let herself hang from his shoulder with a smile.

"Exactly. It'll be there when we come back." Venser said, kicking the door to his room open, laying Ruari down in the soft, silk turquoise sheets of his queen sized bed. He made a backhand motion at the door and a gust of wind slammed it shut. He hopped into bed and quickly curled up with Ruari. "Just wanna cuddle..."

"Just cuddle?" The tan elf gave him a skeptical look, raising an eyebrow. "Why do I feel like 'cuddling' is going to turn to 'fucking'?" She asked with a smirk, making no move to curl up or push away.

"Because we've fucked before?" Venser said in an almost whining tone running one hand up the side of her body. Giving her rear a hard smack. "Why? Do you wanna have a go right now? It'd sure beat reading..."

"Nothing beats reading, Venser, dear" She stated, giving a small, disapproving shake of her head. "But I wouldn't object to having something else to do. Or someone." She pushed herself up to sit, dragging a hand down his body to rest next to his cock. "Since you so rudely interrupted my reading session, I think it's only fair that I get to use you as my new source of entertainment." Ruari smiled, her ocean eyes flickering down to where her hand was placed.

"Well then," Venser said with a pause laying out on the bed, stretching out his body as his cock stiffened up before Rauri, "Show me what you can do..."

With a chuckle, she closed her eyes and went to work, grabbing hold of the base and licking a long stripe from where her hand held him to the tip. She gave a kiss to the head of his cock and took it between her lips to suck on it, using her tongue lap at the slit. She brought the hand holding the base up to pump the shaft as her mouth worked at the head. As she began to take more of his cock into her mouth, bobbing her head up and down at an irritatingly slow pace, she then used her other hand to play with his balls.

"Yeah..." Venser said, licking his lips, watching the small elvish woman go down on him. He moaned as her lips formed a certain suction while his balls and shaft were massaged. He sat up and ran his fingers through her hair gently, before pushing down on it, making Ro go deeper.

She pulled off momentarily, taking a breath and moving her hands to grip his base. When she returned she opened her mouth up wide and swallowed him down in one go, moaning around him once his dick hit the back of her throat.

"Yeah. Gag on it." Venser said as her head bobbed up and down on his member. He moaned and shifted again, peeking a glance at her ass. He leaned forward and pulled her dress up, so that he could see her black thong. "We need to get these clothes off..."

When Ro resurfaced again, it was with a smirk gracing her spit-coated lips and a heaving chest. "You know what, I change my mind." She brought the skirt of her dress up and over her head, sliding right out of it and sending it to the floor. Underneath lay her nearly flat, completely tattooed chest and inner thighs and her black thong. "I guess I don't like prison after all." She said, moving forward to take him down again.

Venser blinked a few times when Ro took off her dress, blinking a few times and not minding her small, petite chest. "So what was I feeling?" He asked aloud before clearing his throat, rubbing his cock up and down in front of her. "And now all that's left are those." He said pointing to her thong underwear.

"Just having too much fun sucking me off?" Venser asked with a chuckle, it was followed by a hiss. "Fuck..." He slowly thrusted his cock in and out her mouth as she went down on him. "Just... Anticipation... I'm gonna give you a nice, hard dicking...."

Ro looked up at Venser through her eyelashes, letting him fuck her mouth while he went on about fucking her. With a small and soft chuckle, she reached a hand up to play with one of her nipples at the thought, moaning loudly from the stimulation.

There wasn't much Venser could do for now as he gripped her head tightly, fucking her mouth, his dick sliding against her cheek in the most beautiful friction. "That's a good girl..."

The tan elf pulled off yet again, taking deep breaths in and out, using the hand that wasn't playing with herself to work at his dick in place of her mouth. She licked her slick lips and moved her other hand from her chest to slip under her underclothes to rub at what lay underneath the fabric, moving her hands at the same pace, sighing at the attention she was giving herself and moving her hands faster.

He pushed her head back as his pelvic thrusts went deeper and deeper, his cock twitched a bit. "No." Venser thought holding back his orgasm. He was going to get her naked and fuck her before that happened. He groaned loudly and shook.

Knowing that he was nearing his climax, she took him down to the root, choking herself on his dick. She used her throat to coax him to release and tightly gripped his balls, creating near torturous pressure.

"Ohh! Mhm!" Venser's cock twitched more and spurted several drops of hot, sticky cum down her throat as she choked and gagged on his cock. "Ahhh... Fuck!"

When he was done shooting his seed down her throat, she pulled off with a smile and a giggle, keeping one of her hands on his cock to keep pumping it. "Too much?" She asked innocently, her voice sounding just as sweet as before.

"Squeezed the balls too hard..." Venser said with a heavy sigh, his breathing was heavy as well. He fell back onto the bed and stretched his body out again.

"Aww... I'm so sorry... Here, let me make it up to you." The short elf who stood at five two crawled up the bed to face Venser up close, wrapping her arms around his neck and giving him a quick kiss. "How about this? You getting to do whatever you want to me as an apology."

Venser smiled and kissed her back, wrapping his arms around her waist and flipping them over with surprising strength so that she was on the bottom now. He growled seductively and kissed down her jaw, biting and nipping his way down her neck. His cock was still stiff despite the fact he already blew his load. "Deal." He said with a pause before trailing down her chest with kisses,, sliding down her panties with both hands.

She whimpered at the sudden motion and again when he removed her underclothes, revealing her soft lower lips. "What were you thinking of doing?" She asked, breathless and nervous.

"Heh..." Venser was a very sexual person, everyone knew. And one patron in particular claiming he fucked more women than one can imagine. Venser gave her folds a long lick and smacked his lips a few times. It tasted odd, but he knew pleasure would come from this. He placed one hand on his cock, and began to rub it up and down slowly.

Ro gasped at the sudden wet heat that ran up her body shivering from the pleasure. "I t-though we were going to move on to more- Ah! Interesting things..." She muttered, a little disappointed.

"Like what?" Venser asked leaning forward, playfully licking at her lips before moving to the side, whispering into her ear. "Tell me what you want..." He whispered before he went onto sucking on her earlobe.

"Mhn..." The islandic elf whined, squirming impatiently and grabbing hold of the sheets below her. "I would greatly appreciate it if you put something, wether it be a cock or toy, up pussy and fuck me until I forget how to think, please and thank you." She huffed.

Venser flipped her over roughly and grabbed her sides, pulling her ass into him. "Yeah... I'm gonna fuck you hard..." He slapped his hard cock against her rear a few times, spreading her cheeks apart and teasing her. "Tight. Really tight..." Adjusting himself on the bed and pushing the tip in. As soon as she felt it Venser pushed all the way in.

A loud moan was ripped from her when she finally had what she had asked for. She bit into the back of her hand to muffle any more overly loud noises from escaping and buried her face into a pillow to hide her full-face blush, whimpering and moaning softly into her hand.

"Fuck... You're so tight..." Despite that he had lubed himself up he found it very difficult to keep fucking her like this. Venser took himself out and fell onto his side, then pulled Rauri on her side too and lifted up her leg, then shoved himself back in and started to thrust again. "'Ah! Mhm!

Ruari gasped when she was suddenly flipped on her side, suddenly feeling much more exposed than before. She braced her arms on the bed, removing the hand that she was using to muffle herself with, and pressed her forehead against the sheets. "More..." She moaned out, gripping the sheets hard enough to turn her knuckles white.

Now that he had full control over Rauri he closed her legs feeling the tightness, he shivered and wriggled his cock around in her ass, feeling how tightly it hugged him. Then he lifted her leg again and felt the ease. "With your legs like this and my thickness..." He groaned breathing in pleasure as he rocked his hips back and forth.

She gave a yelp at the slap, clenching around his cock tightly. Her moans were increasing in volume and frequency with each passing second, her expression showing nothing but pure pleasure.

Driving his hips forward, the bearded man entombed the first third of her shaft into his partner. The warm, welcoming embrace of Ro's depths was fantastic. Hot, wet, and sublimely snug, the womanhood clenched around him, as if drawing him deeper. He sighed, giving them each a moment to savor the sensation, before slowly starting to move.

Bucking up to meet his thrusts, Ro writhed in place. The feeling of being so abjectly full was incredible. Deeper and deeper the head barkeep plunged, stretching Ro's sex with each drive forward. One hand crept downward, intent on playing with her clit, but he paused.

Seeing Ro's heaving chest, he was filled with a sudden compulsion. Reaching up, twisting one nipple in each hand, he grinned up at his elf friend.

Pinned beneath the larger man, with her face pressed against his barreled chest now, there wasn't much Ruari could do but enjoy herself. While she certainly didn't mind being used in such a forceful fashion, she would be remiss for not reciprocating in some degree. Yes, her body was utterly at Ven's disposal for now, though she still had a trick or two up her sleeve.

Squeezing her womanhood on the backstrokes, while relaxing on the thrusts, she milked her friend's length. Squirming her head to the side, questing for something, she found what she was looking for. No sooner did her lips graze the hard bud of flesh than she latched onto one of Venser's pierced nipples.

"Mhmn..." Ven bit his lip, as his nipple was suckled upon, an odd but wonderful feeling. On some subconscious level, something clicked. Hammering his length into the elf, feeling his nuts slap against the cheeks of her rump, his body went into overdrive.

Moaning around the teat, Ro screwed her eyes shut. She could feel a cocktail of her juices and Ven's pre-cum leaking down the crack of her body moistening the sheets below. With a particularly forceful plunge, her cervix suffered a direct impact; to the uninitiated, it would have been jarring or uncomfortable, yet she felt nothing but bliss.

Pulling out all the stops, vehemently plowing Ruari, Ven jackhammered his friend's succulent cunny. The velvety confines around his tool, the muffled sounds of carnal pleasure, they were perfect.

Pinned under Ven, Ro suffered the full wrath of the nigh unstoppable muscular handsome bartender man. The steady, inexorable heat of approaching release burned within her. Every part of her canal was packed with Venser's heavenly member, causing a warmth to seep into her abdomen.

Taking note of the vice-like grip on her length, Ven reared back. On the brink, feeling his cock twitch inside her again. "Getting' close!"

He was so close, so very close to reaching his limit. The strong body atop her, the steady slapping noises of her cunt being pounded, how exquisitely stretched she was around Ven's tool, it was all just perfect. Before Ro knew it, her thighs were trembling wildly and her heart was going a mile a minute, signalling her imminent release.

Hilting himself, cramming every last inch of her shaft into the elf, Venser peaked. Gritting his teeth, he felt the tip of his manhood expand outward, locking itself against Ro's inner walls. His dick throbbed violently, as cum surged through its length and into her partner.

The monumental influx of scalding seed erupting into Ro broke her, leaving her to moan like a woman possessed. Her sex spasmed wildly, as it was packed to the brim with Venser's potent spunk. Being cummed in, claimed in such a primal way, pushed her over the edge. Howling loud enough for the entire tavern and inn to hear her.

Between the screams of ecstasy and nectar squelching from Ruari's snatch, Venser had no doubt that the tanned elf had a monstrous orgasm. The velvety walls around his cock constricted, struggling to contain every drop of jizz he had to offer, but to no avail. While the overwhelming majority of his load was pumped directly into his friend's cunny, some of the gooey substance squirted from around his dick.

Bodies pressed against one another, the two rode out their ecstasy. Awash with bliss, covered in sweat, they took a moment to bask in the post-coitus euphoria and simply breath. It had been intense.

Venser was the first to move, pushing himself away and dragging his marginally softened member from Ro's sex. A miniature deluge of seed followed his escaping length, spilling forth and oozing onto the sheets as he rolled over beside the short tanned elf.

"Oof fuck that was amazing Ven..." Ro said stretching out on the bed and letting out a relaxed sigh. "You have a bottle of after sex rum in here for me, right?"

"I do... Yeah." The sweaty man reached over his side of the bed and handed her the bottle. "Hey it's... Wanna go to The Witch's Wiggle later?"

Ro sat up on the bed for a few seconds, frozen in confusion, before getting up and taking the bottle from him. "Wait, wait, you're just gonna take me out? Why so suddenly? What game are you playing?" She asked, opening the bottle and taking a swig.

"I mean, why not? Fuck around like we just did less than thirty seconds ago."

"...That's it? Wait, does 'fuck around' mean sex or get into trouble and be obnoxious?" She swirled the contents of the bottle around, awaiting the answer.

"Obnoxious how?" Venser asked, scratching his chin. He sighed and took the bottle from her, taking a heavy swig.

"Being naked at the bar. Fucking around like you do when you have kids and other lovers... Not that it's bad, having many lovers, I mean. Ahem. So this is a sex-venture, is it? Well, it I could use it... In an hour or so." She let him take the bottle, only complaining a little. "I was drinking that."

Venser sat down on his bed beside Rauri and shoved the bottle into her hands, reaching out to grip one of her nipples and tug on it a bit, a lewd grin on his face.

The islandic elf sighed dramatically before flopping back onto silk sheets. "Fine, just give time and I'll throw on something."

Venser flopped back on the bed with her. "Or we could get a prostitute or one of my lovers... and bring her here rather than going over there. Galaxteah is often out hunting, Nivarah resting somewhere out in the forest, Sanna is at my new villa with the baby along with some other lovers..."

" ...I like that idea better. Be sure not to take too long." Her long ears flicking slightly, then Ruari turned over to give him a kiss on the cheek.

Returning a kiss to her cheek, he said, "I don't know if you prefer a bigger or smaller crowd but... It's around that time of three months again."

"Hey, I'm up for anything." Ro rolled over onto Venser, wrapping her arms around him in a hug.

"Well we could get like four and bring em here... At The Witch's Wiggle they'll have all sorts of people just doing whatever." He said.

"Men and women alike, clearly."

"Hmm... well, not that I particularly oppose that idea, I was thinking that maybe we could save it for later..." Ro sat up, looking down at him with a smirk. "There's something else I would like to try."

"What do you wanna try? Cause if we don't go tonight we have to wait three months." He said crossing his arms.

"...What?! Three months? Why?" She got off of him, moving off to the side so he could sit up.

Venser sighed and rubbed his temples, laying back down again. "I don't know. But that's when they organize all of the big orgy parties, every three months. I suppose one every night would... Yeah. Dunno." He said before muttering to himself. "Did have a fling with the owner briefly..."

Ro huffed out a sigh. "O course... All right, I guess it can wait. I'll get my cover up and we can go down to Witch's Wiggle." She stood up from the bed and looked around the room's floor. "...That's if I can find it."

"You ever been to No Name Port?" Venser asked scooting up on his bed and laying his head down on a pillow, nuzzling into it. He wore what he always wore, and actually cleaned his boots. Clearly he was ready, well, he was always ready unless he decided to tend the bar barefoot, or wearing nothing at all.

"Not that I know of. Even if I did, I don't really pay attention to the towns I visit, so I wouldn't know anything about it." She shuffled around discarded clothes.

"...Gods above, where did I leave that overglorified robe?" She muttered to herself after an unsuccessful attempt at finding her coverup.

"Naw." Venser just wrapped his arms around Rauri from behind and pulled her into him. "Why don't you just wear nothing?"

"You know very well why." She shoved lightly at his chest, not really trying to push him away. "That and these nightclothes are really cute. Maybe I want to show off how cute I look in them."

"Ha, well Ro, I think you look your cutest in nothing at all..."

CHAPTER SEVENTEEN: SNOW

Montpelier, Vorland, 1437 ATC

Sunlight shone brightly off the fresh layer of snow, sending the sharp beams into the large house. Dark brown curtains helped keep the master bedroom semi-dark. Resting peacefully in the large bed were three women and one man, all cuddled into each other. Their hair were sprawled over the pillows, intermixing the white, dark, and red strands.

There was a crisp stillness to the new winter air. Something that was shattered by a high pitched shout. Everyone on the bed jerked at the sound before going still, trying to identify what was going on. Another shout, closer to their bedroom, along with two sets of little feet moving rapidly, signaled approaching visitors.

"Ugh... Mornin! Kids!" Venser's tired exclamation forced a hearty chuckle from his lovers. When the man shifted however, Kari pouted cutely and pulled the man closer.

"Nooooo....!" The woman smirked when her plea worked for a brief second. "The twins are old enough to deal with it themselves surely... Stay in bed with me...?"

"Asher isn't. I'll be back soon." Alexis Bonneville said, giving all of them a kiss before sliding out of bed and slipping on a robe, leaving the room.

The man sighed through his nose but didn't move away. He moved back into place, grasping her Marvella and Kari close once again, while they both smiled with satisfaction.

Just as they relaxed, the door started to creak open. Two bright green eyes peeked around the door frame on each side. The boy's short white locks hung over his face as he brushed them back, his eyes were followed by a very similar pair that belonged to a girl his own age with long raven locks.

"Told you! They're still asleep!" Soarin scolded in a whisper, glaring at his twin sister. "You can't come with me!"

The bearded man exhaled and sat up more. Limbs loose, the beard man shuffled even closer to his lovers, silently signaling her non-involvement. Kari situated her mouth to the top of the bearded man's head to speak clearly as she kept her eyes closed.

"Kids, where do you think you're going?"

The siblings in the doorway froze, eyes wide.

"We were going to have a snowball fight…" The lad inched forward, opening the door further with his lanky shoulders.

His sister, hunched close to the ground, edged out from around the boy's hands. "And I want to go!" Lucinda exclaimed.

Kari silently laughed at the feeling before complying. "Okay then kids, make sure to bundle up and stay around the house!"

The two children let out a whoop of excitement and ran down the hall respectively. Venser murmured once more, forming another name. Marvella rolled her eyes with a bemused grin, then looked to Kari, reaching out to poke her white haired sister in arms.

Two shouts agreed as the children raced downstairs. The lovers listened to the front door open when the bearded man sat up in bed, he shouted to the excited young twins.

"You two had better be wearing your winter clothes and not running around naked! Especially you Soarin!"

The lovers waited, noting the several long seconds of silence, before they heard their children yell once more as they left. "We are!"

"Ugh again, morning everyone…" Venser said, moving into a hug with all of the girls in his bed, when a happy gurgle from the door to the master bedroom distracted them. Looking over, they saw Alex carrying their newest baby, Asher, who had auburn hair and grass green eyes, cooing gleefully to his mother, other mothers, and his father from Alex's arms. Kari, mother to the twins, started making baby noises just as happily back, though she stayed in the bed. Venser watched with a wide grin for another minute before moving past the girls and out of bed.

"Alright loves, gotta make sure we've got plenty of firewood and check on the food storage." The man gave them all a loving kiss. Standing up with a half stretch, he walked up to the Alex and their newborn son, giving the tiny baby a nose nuzzle. "Behave for your mother and other mothers, you hear little Asher?"

Kari, Marvella, and Alex watched with a sweet gaze as their mate walked out. Asher continued to make the same burbling noises back as they walked downstairs. The living room was strewn with garland along the tops of the walls, ribbons decoratively placed and a medium sized pine tree with miniature candles placed among the branches.

Kari picked up some leftover dishes into the sink and reached out to the cabinets near the fridge. Once she selected an appropriate meal for the baby, she began to pull out ingredients for herself and the other adults of the house. While the meal was underway, Alex washed the dishes as they dirtied, trying to save time and effort for the holiday.

The baby Asher scooted along the ground, heading for the family room where more shiny things awaited a curious, chubby hand. Two golden hands took her small form and lifted her up into the air. The captain picked him up and set him down in his high chair. He looked over his new domain, tapping both hands against the oak tray.

Alex smiled at the happy Asher and pulled over her chore list for the day, letting out a soft sigh. Unfolding the long paper shared amongst the family with bullet points detailing each item, she looked over her notes as she set the food on low while absent-mindedly trying to feed the baby.

"We have a lot to do today, don't we?" Kari nodded to herself, barely glancing to the frying eggs and bacon cooking or the spoon of mashed peas and celery.

Alex tsked to herself. It was the smell of eggs almost turning too overdone that distracted her from the self-made list. The little baby laughed at the funny face her mother made as she rushed to save the meal. Two seconds later, she found the sink was getting close to full and about to overflow with bubbly suds. Asher leaned back with a laugh at the high pitched half-shriek of distress.

The front door opened just after the noise, showing the bearded man with a half-uncertain face, snow on his bright red boots as he began to wipe his feet on the mat. Spotting the source of the issue, Venser released the nervousness in favor of amusement.

"All of you doing alright?"

"Yes, just fine. Have you finished sweetie?" Kari asked.

"Thanks love." Venser grabbed a cloth and began to clean off his tunic. "I think I might need some backup if... I'll ask Marvella. Though, I know you would love to swing an axe, or a sword, Alex."

The auburn haired captain laughed as she wiped the dribble from the young boy's chin. She shook her head with a disappointed smile. "Remember, we still have to finish this evening's meal and I wanted to plan for us moving into the villa, and helping decorate too I guess.

Venser shrugged and watched as his lovers cleaned the house, Marvella was coming down the stairs, dressed in winter furs now. "The place looks plenty clean. You sure ya don't want to come play outside?"

"No no, it's fine ," Alex waved a hand as she brought the adults' meal to the table. She waved for Venser and Kari to sit as she took her own place beside them. "We'll be nice and warm in here as I get the last few things done."

"Alright. I'll be finishin' up and check on the kids."

"If you wish sweetie." Kari gave them a light-hearted grin, certain of what would truly happen if they stepped one foot outside.

It wasn't long before the family finished their meals. The white haired cryomancer grabbed the plates and immediately washed them. Venser gave Kari a smooch while she did the dishes and put on a scarf. Kissing Kari and Marvella, and brushing baby Asher's hair and giving him a kiss on the forehead as he passed, the bearded man opened the door, tilting his head down rapidly as five snowballs were shot right at him.

"Ah!" Quickly, he made a backhand motion with his left hand, mark flashing greenish white as he obliterated the snowballs with a strong gust of wind.

"That was close." Closing the door and stepping outside, he scooped up some of the white powder in his bare hands. Licking his lips, he shot the projectiles in a straight line forward. There was an explosion of laughter along with several sounds of pelting snowballs.

Alex wiped the rest of the mess from her child's mouth and put away feeding time supplies. She lifted Asher up from her chair and nuzzled his face as he reached both hands to his mom.

"Come along my little monkey, let's start getting ready for your first winter." The auburn haired captain walked up the stairs to the upper levels of the house. Once there, she set the Asher in his crib while she began to clean up each of the rooms.

"Here it comes!" Venser exclaimed grabbing a chunk of snow, quickly packing it into a cube rather than a ball

"Take that!" Venser yelled, tossing the snow cube right at Marvella's head who decided to join them, moving back a bit and making more snowballs. "Eh!" Lucinda tossed a small snowball at Marvella as well, but it only went a mere few feet in front of her. She threw several more, but few of them made it even close to the girl in the combat uniform and furs.. "Kablamo!" Soarin said from behind slapping Marvella's rear with a large chunk of snow in his hand, which also contained a bit of ice.

As Marvella was frantically trying to pick up snow to make a snowball, she was getting bombarded with snow from Venser, Lucinda and Soarin. She squealed lightly, but could not escape the bits of laughter coming from between her lips. She then simply ran her hands against the snow, brushing it up to cause a light wave of snow to rush towards Venser and Lucinda. Then she wiggled the snow down on Soarin. "Hahahaha!" she cried out and started to run.

The children laughed happily. "Noooo...!" Soarin covered his hands with both arms to block the snow, only to get it all over his bare arms. Nevertheless, he didn't mind. "Eh!" He punched Marvella in the rear as she took off running. "Son, don't hit her." Venser said walking over to him. He bent down and put his leather red jacket on. "Thanks daddy!" Venser ruffled his hair and handed him a big snowball. "Go get her!" Lucinda wore a crystal bracelet around her right wrist, with a small tag that read 'Do Not Remove' on it. She did and flicked her wrist in front of her, giggling and accidently freezing the ground in front of them into a slippery field. '

Marvella yipped as she was punched on the bottom, and then ended up slipping on some ice and fell with a good thud.

"HEY, you used magic!" She spoke out poorly. "Alright, since you wanna cheat." she got up from the ice carefully, threw off her gloves and created a few small orange portals that caught the snowballs, and then shot them all back at the twins and Venser.

Lucinda opened her mouth to protest but was smacked in the face by the perfectly round snowball. "Ow! Owwwiie...! You knocked my eye out!" Lucinda squealed falling face first into the snow, circling up a bit. "Lewcinda!" Soarin called running over to help his sister, slipping on the ice too and landing on his back. "Ow!"

Marvella lowered her hands to place them on her hips, "Yeah, falling on ice did not feel very good now did it?" She spoke lightly, then offered both of her hands to help both of them up with a light smile.

"No it didn't poop head!" Lucinda yelled flipping over, slinging a snowball up into her face. Afterwards Venser spoke up, standing right behind Marvella with a snow shovel full of snow in hand. "Yeah! Poop head." He then proceeded to dump it all on her head.

Marvella did not have anyone in her side at this moment as she was again bombarded with snow all over her from. So much so, she had to sit down on another snow heap so she could wipe the snow from her face to see better.

"Ah!" Venser was hit in the head by some snow. "Bullseye! Ha!" Soarin ran past his father and got behind his sister. Now the two began to pelt snowballs at Venser. He teleported back and began to punch the snowballs out of the air.

Marvella smiled and watched as the kids then turned onto there father, throwing those snow balls like a team while Venser was bunching them. Watching in slight amazement, her eyes went from one person to the other.

After a few minutes the twins began to make snow angels in the snow. "By the void how do they not get tired after running around so much?" Venser asked, sitting next to Marvella.

"I have no idea.. but I am exhausted." Marvella spoke honestly, watching as the twins were making snow angels. "Hoo boy... Part of me feels like this is going to be a short winter."

CHAPTER EIGHTEEN: ELANAEA

Great Blue Lake, Vorland, 1438 ATC

Spring. A time for the ice to melt. A time of rebirth.

Spot glanced around the area while sniffing about in interest. Then, he watched as Sedna produced a pillowcase from Venser's bedroom and knelt down with it. Perking up his pointed ears, he gave a yip and moved to give it a few sniffs. After a few seconds of sniffing, Spot gave another bark to affirm Vensers sent and turned about to sniff the air, a tree, some grass to catch the familiar scent. Meanwhile, Kira was now fully dressed, walking into the bar area while fighting with her long black hair.

Sedna the huntress breathed in the scent of the forest, and grasped her bow firmly. She recalled in the dream she'd had, that she walked straight into the forest, and Venser had appeared to her from out of nowhere. But surely there was more to finding him than that.. She watched as Spot ran from tree to tree, trying to catch Venser's smell. "Soon, my darling," she murmured to their newborn daughter, a sleeping girl with long black curls Elanaea. "Soon we'll find your daddy, and you'll get to meet the man who started it all."

Surrounding the lake were a wide variety of beautiful trees, the water while calm had so many different hues of blue, reflecting the bright blue sky, near the shore it was pale blue, nearly translucent, as it got deeper it changed from pale blue to deeper color. Birds called overhead and a figure in a black cloak stood on the cliff-side, the breeze blowing the cloak softly along with the vibrant green grass that swayed barely in the wind.

Spot halted in his track as he picked up the scent and gave a bark that was not so strong.. last thing he wanted to do was to alert any beasts or... Scare an infant. He then began to tread lightly on the trail, following it as far as it would go. Meanwhile in the Tavern, Kira Kurai walked into the bar area to greet any patron around. "Good afternoon." She spoke aloud, and at the same time a Patron had ordered something, and immediately a shadow tendril did the beck and call to give the strongest 'stuff' the tavern had to offer. It did not take long for a pint to be filled up, and slid over to the patron who gave the request. Kira stood there baffled.

At the bar, Ruari didn't look up from her book, too engrossed in what was written to pay attention to her surroundings.

Kira finally made her way around the bar's counter top to smile politely. Ruari was engrossed with a book currently, while the other Patron was appearing more than ready to get trashed for the day.

Sedna looked back at Spot at the sound of his bark and began to follow him, drawing an arrow from her quiver and nocking it to her bow, her steps soundless as she followed the huge wolf further into the forest. Looking around, she recognized some of the landmarks from the previous time she had been in this forest. She and Venser were hunting, and she'd wanted to impress him by bringing down the first deer. But when she'd brought down the pregnant doe and rescued the fawns, she'd made an idiot of herself in front of him. He seemed to resent her ever since that trip, he never treated her the same way again. Whether that was because he'd gotten what he wanted or if it was from other causes, she had no idea how to approach him since. A bird startled her out of her reverie, and she drew her arrow and shot it down without thinking. She retrieved the arrow and placed the bird in her cloak, not wanting to waste a kill if she had to.

Pristine, with a blue mirror of which the clouds reflected off of. The hooded figure let out an audible sigh and continued staring off at it while on the cliffside.

Spot continued to chase the scent, picking up his pace as the scent was growing stronger and more fresh by each pawed step he took. He gave another few barks after he witnessed the huntress shooting down a bird which seemed to have startled her. They were drawing near, he could tell.

Holding Elanaea still with one hand and gripping her bow with the other, Sedna lengthened her stride and soon caught up to Spot, her mind whirling with insecurities and things that she wished she would see when she saw Venser, but she knew he was going to be distant. He might hold Elanaea if she was lucky, he might want to be part of her life, but she doubted it. She wanted so much, but knew the things she wanted were never going to come true because of how Venser was.

The big black wolf patted over the green grass, getting closer and closer to what seemed to be a cliffside.. The beast rose his nose up to have a few more sniffs before using those sharp yellow eyes to spot a figure up ahead. That must be him... it smelled like him... So, Spot simply sat down on his bottom and gave a powerful bark. Meanwhile in the Dragon's Head Tavern, Kira was quietly cleaning glasses with a fresh white moist rag. Her blue eyes would once in a while look up toward Ruari the islandic elf to see her reading, then glance back down to continue cleaning. Until the sound of the Tavern doors came to an open and a male patron approached the bar. "Good afternoon, What can I help you with today?" she questioned lightly, then gazed back in the direction of the front door as another Patron came inside. "Good afternoon, welcome to the Dragons head tavern." she spoke out in greeting. Ill be with you in a moment."

As Sedna reached the edge of the forest, Spot sitting down, gazing at the cliff. Looking in what she hoped was the same direction as Spot, she saw a cloaked figure, standing on the edge of the cliff, staring out at the pale blue sky. Sedna placed her bow back onto her shoulder, thanked Spot for all his help and began to slowly walk towards the figure, recognizing the crimson and turquoise tunic beneath the cloak, holding Elanaea firmly against her. When she was about two meters away from the figure, she spoke to the figure.

"Venser? Is it really you?"

It was warm, finally the performer didn't have to freeze to die from starvation in her travels. Jingling the coins in the tiny pouch, Lace pursed her marred lips, furrowing a single brow as she stared it down. How can we go through so much gold, so fast!? "We ate a large meal, and found boarding instead of a barrel. It is pricey." We need to put on another show, but we have no stage. "Forget the stage, look ahead of you FOOL!"

Thunk!

The traveling jester woman ran right into the doors, staggering back and delicately rubbing her nose. Where had that come from? Her head tilted back, dark orange hair lightly flopping against her back as one hand pushed them open, allowing Lace's entrance. It came out of nowhere! "No, you just do not pay attention... This is all."

Kira gave a light smile towards a female patron who requested a warm meal and some milk. "Hmmm I believe we have some delicious selection of fine cut meats, a pot of chicken crème soup on the stove along with an assortment of veggies including corn on the cob. Anything specific you desire?" Kira asked politely, this would give the demon girl something to do. Getting away to cook in the kitchen for a tad bit was something she felt that she needed to do at the moment. Meanwhile, Spot continued to sit, watching as Sedna and her child moved towards the 'possible' Venser.

The cloaked figure turned around slowly, the hood casting shadows over its face. It only took a few seconds for him to pull it down, revealing the man himself. Sporting a black beard that needed to be cut, and a dulled, but surprised look on his face when he saw the baby girl Sedna held in her arms. He opened his mouth to speak, but nothing came out. He closed his mouth and just stared at them silently.

"Oh we sure do Miss. Plenty in fact. I'll get working on your order... Would you like anything else with it? Some corn on the cob? Sweat bread and a small bowl of broccoli and cheese soup?" Kira asked as she moved about helping the people in the tavern.

"Uh huh. Right away Miss." Kira spoke lightly with a smile, and hurried off into the kitchens to work on the meal. Sure, the Shadow Tendrils could do the job, but... Kira felt that it would be best if she kept herself busy. For some reason she was beginning to feel a bit nervous, something was definitely pulling on her mind today. While in the kitchen, Kira plucked a fresh loaf of the bread from a shelf, and began to neatly get it into slices. Then, clapped her hands together twice to summon a few shadow tendrils, "Be sweet lovey tendrils and get cooking on that roast beef? Meanwhile I'll go get the cheese." she hurried about the kitchen gathering things while the shadow tendrils followed the kind order.

She lumbered up the steps, resting her arms across her chest with a grotesque smile. It smelled kind of nice in here, now that she thought about it, going to take up a stool at the bar. Oh, people! Hi other people! "Do not make eye contact, do not interact.... We are just here to eat and rest." Party pooper... Lace giggled and waved wildly to the other patrons with both hands, appearing quite innocent in nature.

After a bit of time, Kira could hear the doors of the tavern come to an open and foot steps making its way up towards the bar area. She could definitely hear the voice of a female patron greeting people with such energy. This honestly made Kira giggle, for some reason.. Seeing people in high spirits was a genuine good thing. But to be back on the task at hand, the Shadow Tendrils had accomplished the roast beef in remarkable time and had placed it neatly on a wooden platter. Kira had found a good triangle of cheese, placed some corn on the cob on the plate as well, then proceeded to put the bread slices on a separate place along with a small cup of butter and a knife. "Thank you shadow tendrils for your help." she smiled warmly, and gracefully made her way out of the kitchen with the meal on a serving tray. Kira set the tray down carefully before the female patron who had requested it, and a shadow tendril not too far behind, placed a fresh glass of cold milk next to the food. "There you are miss. If you need anything please let me know." she smiled warmly, then moved back up the stairs to assist the next patron. "Hello, how may I help you today?"

"I wanna' say surprise me! "Please no actual surprises, however. I could not take that kind of burden..." This is why we never get invited to fancy parties. "No, we do not get invited because we look like shit!" Aww... I don't look like poopy, do I?" Lace pouted at the counter, laying her chin on it with a saddened expression.

Kira innocently stood behind the bar as the patron spoke of wanting to be surprised. But then she said she did not want any actual surprises. Hmmmmmmm. So what did the patron exactly want? Food? and Drink? Kira then could not help but asked, "Have you ever had.. a cherry.. soda? We still have a tiny bit left." She raised an eyebrow. "Unless you are requiring food... then we have a delicious pot of chicken crème soup... Got a selection of meats... Anything really." She laughed.

"Cherries? I like cherries! "Just give us some food. I grow weary of these bland exchanges..." Lace huffed, setting the pouch of silver onto the bar top with a thunk rather unceremoniously. It was a tad annoying sometimes, literally being half-and-half on almost everything that she did. Stupid people and their stupid magic things. "Cherries still sound good..."

"Alright, so, I can get you a bowl of cherries... And to add to things... Some whipped cream in a separate bowl?" She then hurried away from the bar and went to go fetch a bowl of cherries. Eventually, the black haired demon girl would be making her way back up those wooden stairs with some delicious beautiful cherries and a smaller bowl of whipped cream in case she wanted to add more sweetness. "Here you are."

The cloaked figure turned around slowly, the hood casting shadow's over it's face. It only took a few seconds for him to pull it down, revealing the man himself. Sporting a black beard that needed to be cut, and a contemplative, but surprised look on his face when he saw the baby Sedna held in her arms. He opened his mouth to speak, but nothing came out. He closed his mouth and just stared at them silently.

Cradling the infant in her arms, Sedna watched as her off and on bearded lover lowered his hood to see them both, and watched the surprised look in his eyes grow with every passing second. She stepped a little closer and offered him the infant who lay in her arms, transfixed by the big man in front of her, whose eyes were so like her own, yet so very different. For she was born with his natural grass green eyes, before Venser had been cursed with his inhuman serpent like ones.

Kira's usual burst of energy was dying down, dramatically. Just as things were picking up, Kira slouched, feeling more than tired with running around. Those blue eyes lowered to look at nothing in particular... She honestly was not paying much attention to her surroundings until the Tavern door kept opening and one after another she would say a gentle greeting, "Welcome to the Dragons Head Tavern, please make yourselves comfortable." She smiled sweetly, then leaned on the bar table.

The bearded man opened his arms out to the baby that Sedna held, waiting for her to hand the little girl off to him. Still silent, and his face spoke for how surprised and unsure he was, with a mix of sadness in it.

Sedna placed the infant in her father's outstretched arms and stepped back, biting her lip in uncertainty. The baby was tiny still, her head rested in the crook of Sedna's arm and her tiny feet were normally suspended over her palm. She hoped that Venser would take a liking to her, and come home to the tavern to raise her. "Venser... I'd like you to meet your daughter, Elanaea."

Venser took Elanaea in his arms and gazed down to her tiny form. Carefully holding her in one hand he brushed aside some of her hair, and sighed. His expression was almost blank as he held his child. Today was the anniversary of the day his daughter, Viviana and her mother Laven had died. But, he never liked to talk about them. Or think about them without sinking into sadness, and so, he often pushed them out of his mind altogether as terrible as it was. And now this. It felt like he was going crazy. He simply stared at his daughter in his arms.

Sedna watched on, feeling helpless as Venser held their daughter with the utmost sadness, she was amazed Elanaea didn't start crying then and there. Their daughter lay in her father's arms, her tiny arms waving her chubby fists in Venser's face, trying to catch a fistful of his black beard.

"Ven, please say something. I thought I was afraid to show her to you, but now that you're holding her, it scares me that you have nothing to say about her. Please, say something..."

Venser was at a loss for words as Elanaea's arms waved in front of her, trying to grab some of his beard. He laughed and held her close, letting her grab his beard. He kissed her forehead as his cloak swayed in the wind and said, "I'm going to take care of you."

The huntress felt tears well up in her eyes and had to look away from Venser and their daughter while they played. She quickly blinked back the tears and looked at Venser as he held their daughter close and let her grab his beard. "I didn't realize you were such a softie, Venser. If I'd known you looked this cute around kids, I would have let you impregnate me long before now" As Sedna was speaking, Elanaea let go of her father's beard, screwed her tiny face up and began to cry.

"That was weirdly worded. But I mean... Almost every woman I've ever been with. Ha." Venser said looking up to Sedna for a brief moment as his daughter began to cry. "Shhh, shhh." He began to rock her back and forth in his arms.

"She.. Uhh... She might be hungry, Ven.." Sedna blushed as she thought of feeding their daughter in front of Venser, but it's not like he hadn't seen everything before. She began to unbutton the front of her dress, but thought better of it. "You should know by now Venser, I'm a strange person, therefore it will be my tendency to speak strangely. If you're happy to hold her, would you mind checking her wrappings? I brought extra clothes for her, but I hoped I wouldn't have to use them." She smiled as Venser rocked Elanaea, thinking about how much her daughter looked like her father.

"Looks good to me." The bearded man said walking over to Sedna, offering Elanaea to her so she could feed.

The huntress swiftly unbuttoned her dress and took their baby daughter, who was squirming in her arms in order to get to her breast faster. She placed her breast right near her daughter's mouth, but Elanaea didn't latch on like she usually did. "You really are being difficult today, my lovely. I know you're hungry, but you need to reach for it, not just lay there and cry."

Venser just crossed his arms and watched, still unsure what to say, or ask. All he could do really was watch. And wonder how the rest of this day was going to go.

Sedna laughed as her off and on lover watched, sensing his discomfort, raising a finely shaped brow thinking of him and his lovers and kids he already had. "You should be used to fussy babies and breastfeeding Ven." Elanaea finally latched on and her cries were finally silenced.

The bearded man smiled and nodded a bit, holding the baby girl in his arms close and tight, keeping her safe and warm, his black cape fluttering in the nippy early spring wind. "Let's go back to the tavern and get settled in, yeah? Then we'll introduce you to the rest of your family... Your siblings Soarin, Lucinda, Rowena, Asher..."

The baby in his arms looked up at him and giggled, waving her hands and cooing happily.

"Sedna. We'll have a drink or two, catch up, spend the rest of the day together?"

The huntress smiled happily and stood beside Venser and their baby girl as they took their first walk together as a new little family.

CHAPTER NINETEEN: FLOPPY

The Dragon's Head Tavern and Inn, Vorland, 1438 ATC

"Feed her some lunch... Uh huh. Give her plenty of nap time? Yup while I'm working the bar... Change diapers when necessary? Ugh, did that doing that."

Venser looked over the list before him several times, slowly nodding to himself as he looked over everything as Sedna had left for him before she went out to hunt for tonight's dinner at the tavern. He noted how intricate and yet legible her handwriting was. After a while, he was satisfied that he'd covered just about everything, and so took on a slightly prideful smile.

And it was only about two in the afternoon

Elanaea was there beside him, happily giggling to herself as she played with her favorite toy, a stuffed raven, Floppy. She was the very picture of happiness right now, content and smiling as she played. Naturally, Venser himself couldn't help but smile back to her, as he set his scroll aside and took a step closer. Getting to his knees he leaned in towards her.

"Hey there Elanaea. Having fun?"

The infant looked up to her carer for the day, gurgling in-between her laughs.

"Ba! Ba-ba-boo!"

Her father chuckled.

"Yeah, I think I've done alright here too. I mean, I do have experience with your siblings..."

He sat down earnestly, sighing to himself before again looking at the baby girl beside him. She happily continued to bounce her stuffed raven up and down on the floor, eliciting another smile from Venser, who started to look around. After a while, he'd found what he was looking for, a stuffed deer. Besides Floppy, they were definitely Elanaea's favorite toys, and so the bearded man reached over and picked it up. He thought for a moment, then looked back to the young infant.

"Hey there Elanaea!"

The small black haired baby looked up, just in time to see Venser use the deer as a sort of mask, hiding his face behind it so as to give the "illusion" of having the deer itself speak.

"I'm Deary the Deer, and you're my very best friend!"

With one hand, Venser took hold of the toy's arm, willing it around to make it look like he was waving at her. Elanaea, of course, was very entertained by this, and so giggled loudly, before reaching up for the talking stuffed deer. Her father chuckled behind the stuffed animal before continuing to do this.

"Say, would you like to play with me?"

The baby Elanaea giggled even louder than before, making it clear that, yes, she very much did want to play. The bearded man began to move backwards, taking the deer with him while continuing to mimic its voice.

"Look at me, baby! I'm a flying deer!"

Elanaea babbled, eagerly trying to get to her deer, while Venser for his part, did his best not to make things too exciting, lest his daughter get over-excited and do something unexpected. For a second, he pondered how much of her mother's magical talent she had inherited, and just how powerful she was, or would be. On and on this went, for quite a few minutes, him lowering the deer and making it gallop around her until finally Venser had decided that they'd had enough.

"Wow Elanaea! You're really fast! You win!" he said, again from behind the deer.

She reached out, carefully taking the stuffed deer from her father. Granted, it could hardly have escaped her notice that her stuffed animal was now no longer speaking to her, but she didn't really care. She was just happy and satisfied that she had him, and so hugged him tightly while continuing to merrily gurgle with every breath. Venser, on his side of things, chuckled, both amused and endeared by the baby's antics, sitting on his rear and reaching over, gently patting her on the head.

He looked down to the baby, continuing to smile at her.

"Have you had fun here today?"

Baby Elanaea giggled again, nodding enthusiastically, leading to an even wider smile on her father's part.

"Glad to hear it. I know you probably miss your mom but she'll be back soon..."

He sat down properly, reaching forward and taking hold of her. He held her carefully, while she looked up to him wide-eyed as usual.

"I've enjoyed being with you today. It's been nice."

Elanaea blinked to him with her big grass green eyes. Venser didn't quite know if she truly understood everything he'd been saying to her, but as she started to smile at him again, he at least knew that she understood the sentiment behind his words. In a slightly absent-minded manner, Elanaea dropped her deer to the ground, using her now-free chubby hand to reach out, booping her father on the nose and tugging on his beard. She of course giggled to this, and Venser himself let out a dry chuckle.

"Ha... I love you too Elanaea."

The bearded man watched as she herself moved closer to him, resting her head against his chest and holding him close, in much the same way that she would with one of her cuddle toys while sleeping in her crib. And speaking of sleep, that was what she now started to do, continuing to lovingly rest her head against her father as her eyes slowly closed, and babbled and squeaked.

Venser slowly smiled down to her, lifting his hands and holding her close, cradling her gently as she drifted off into what he hoped would be a restful sleep full of sweet dreams.

CHAPTER TWENTY: CUDDLE WOLF

The Dragon's Head Tavern and Inn, Vorland, 1438 ATC

It was a rather quiet evening at the Dragon's Head. And a rather peaceful one at most. The rain outside pattered against the windows softly and the night was still. As was the tavern. The sole woman at the bar enjoying her solitude with a tankard in hand was interrupted by heavy footsteps.

"Well what do we have here?" Venser asked, leaning up against the nearby wall. He only wore a pair of baggy red pants and nothing else. Showing off his barreled chest as he approached her. "We met once, fun night... Angel's sister... Ermm... Seline, right?" Yawning as he spoke and enjoying a much needed night of not having to deal with his kids for now, and mentally tired after coming up with schemes to sell the cannabis he had started growing back on his farm.

"Mhmmm..." The handsome barkeep closed his eyes and sucked in his breath. "I love spring."

The woman glanced up. "A familiar voice" She'd place her drink upon the counter before turning in her seat to face the familiar voice. "Been a while. long time no see stranger, and close enough, it's Selina. Ah. But I'll let it slide." She gave a devious smirk as her eyes faded from a crimson red back to a beautiful greenish blue.

Rain. At least it wasn't sticky and humid like her last destination. A short woman with an orange bobcut appeared right by the bar, holding a bowl a friend of hers had stolen once in a rush to leave. She wished to return it and get a look of the place herself. Not what she had in mind. A frown graced her petite features and the bowl was slid into place on the bar and left there. "Err what is there to eat here." She asked the only two that she could see at the moment.

Glancing up not having heard the newcomer come in she could only assume she possibly appeared with the use of magic perhaps, turning to face them for a moment. Selina was a relatively tall woman, five eleven same as Venser with fair skin, scarred in a few places, with dark brown shoulder length hair. "The tendrils can make just about anything you desire, if you want recommendations ask Venser here, I'm sure he could assist you." Selina gave off a wicked smile before returning to her drink and taking another swig.

"I could swear it was Seline... Aaaaa... Close enough.'" The handsome bearded man said looking her over, a smile coming across his face. "Yeah. Didn't see you the morning after..." He looked to the girl and nodded his head, glancing at the bowl. "What do ya need, miss?" He patted his chest. "Venser head bartender."

And the tendrils were going to get a VERY disapproving stare. "Something warm?" Nadine lifted an orange brow and walked over to the two. Each got a stare though the nature of her look was neutral. She held no ill will toward them. "Perhaps spicy? Maybe with fish, and broth and bread?" A hand was offered to the man, upon closer inspection she wore a shiny silver bracelet with a smooth polished blue stone on the top. "Nadine, traveler. I work for the Explorer's Guild, and I specialize in artifacts."

"You have to be specific with the shadow tendrils, as do you with bartenders. Anyone you want anything from." He said extending his scarred right hand out to shake hers. "And what brings you here this evening?" Venser looked over to Selina. "Her I know why."

"To return the bowl that my friend stole." A thumb was pointed at it. Thankfully it had been cleaned, through probably not even missed. "That's really it." Her eyes shifted to the two then the tendrils. Nadine didn't really didn't even want anything, just wanted to see what would come of it. Shrug. he scooted up onto the bar to sit. "Just bread then." May as well buy something out of courtesy.

"Uh? Who? Right, doesn't matter I suppose... Since you returned it." He asked, blinking his green, snake like eyes at her. A snakey, shadowy hand popped out from behind the bar and set some bread down in front of her. "You can buy one of my cigars then. If you smoke."

"Was in here a while back. Got weirded out by a whorish princess and a giant cat man. I doubt she lasted long." She picked up the bread and inspected it thoroughly. "Cigars? What kind?" Nadine didn't smoke. But plenty of those around her did.

"Only the finest!" The shirtless man exclaimed, stepping back and showing her a red and yellow poster on the wall of his handsome mug looking quite confident, a sharp glimmer in his eyes. The poster was advertising "Karkaldwin's Fine Cigars". "The best is this little beauty right here." He said moving towards her, removing a small silver tin from his pockets. He opened it and handed her a light green cigar that had an earthly scent to it with a hint of citrus. "So, even though I only have a small amount on my farm up in Pryldahn... When the rest grows, I am going to be selling this allllll over Laguna!"

Nadine gave it a sniff and made a face, squinting her bright hazel eyes. Blech. That was something she never smelled before. "What... Is it?" She munched from the bread, still seeming paranoid it was going to bite back or something.

"Cannabis. The best in the world!" Venser said. "This after sex, or with a glass of wine... Or if you wanna lay around and do jack shit and relax... Oh! Especially after a long hard day of dealing with people or finding someone to do your posters... It's... What's the word..." He said scratching his head, glancing out the window as the rain pattered against it. "Bliss..."

"Relaxing, eh?" She rubbed her chin and narrowed her eyes at it. Unfamiliar... Should he be trusted? But... If it worked she could try to give it to an acquaintance... Who could always chill the hell out at any time. "How much for one?" After digging in her sash she found a coin bag.

"Heh." He fumbled around in his pants looking for a match or something. "For you... Fifteen silver." Venser, still with his hand in his pocket, moved his other hand over to Selina and snapped his fingers a few times. "Maybe she's had too much cannabis staring off into space."

Well that was much more expensive than she was expected. Highway robbery! Though she had no idea what she was buying. The coins were laid on the bar and she too looked at Selina, assuming she had just been drunk. "I might just come back in a few minutes... Gonna go check on my horse." She held out the cigar and a snakey shadowy hand held up a match, lighting it for the orange haired girl.

Seeing Venser snapping his fingers at her out the corner of her eye she glanced up for a moment, having been glancing out the window and not paying much attention to what was going on around her. "I gather you want my attention?" The hybrid glanced back at Venser for a moment.

Venser sighed and dumped the coins into his pocket, watching the woman light up the cigar and leave. Leaving the two alone in the tavern. He turned to Selina and asked in the bluntest way humanly possible, "Wanna fuck?"

She raised a brow at him, a displeased expression on her face. "Could you be any more forward? Few women take to that sort of pick up line calmly." The hybrid smirked slightly and sat herself up atop the bar.

The bearded man shrugged his shoulders. "Worked last time." He cleared his throat and sat down at the bar looking at her. "Allow me to be less blunt..."

"So, let's get down to business."

The hybrid couldn't help but chuckle giving out a slight huff. "Well being in heat I suppose it won't take much to persuade me." She glared at him with a lustful, almost predatory look in her eyes.

"Sex!"

A short moment later he made awkward hand gestures. "Ya know, business. Sex. Yeah..."

"I know what you mean you crazy fool." Selina smiled slightly, trying to hold back some laughter before appearing behind him and running her hands firmly down his shoulders.

The bearded man took her hands and dragged it all over his barreled chest, down to his stomach and back up. For a brief second he thought of Angel. Did she know she slept with her sister? And that talk not too long ago... Though, the last time he was super drunk. Her sitting in his lap after a long, sweaty session of love making... Talking about pretty much being together forever. They split. But she always came back to him. For Selina, Venser was just staring off into space.

The hybrid girl chuckled slightly, bending down and gently kissing the side of his neck and lightly biting it for a moment before appearing back on the counter in front of him. "Hmm? Something troubling you?" Her eyes flickered almost black for a moment as she looked down at him from on the bar.

Venser let out another sigh. "Honestly not in the mood for sex... I don't know why but I feel like either cuddling or going out for a walk in the rain..." It was dark but in his mind he thought he could just lay in bed with Selina and listen to the rain. Relax.

She raised her eyebrow slightly. "You're a very hard many to keep up with, very well, how about a drink?" She crossed her legs, her too giving out a sigh. "I doubt this will last long..."

"Let's bring a few drinks to bed, shall we?" He asked.

She smirked, still slightly confused. "Alright." Selina grabbed her bottle off the counter taking a swig before getting to her feet, licking her stained lips. She'd hop down off the counter and elegantly make her way to her room.

"What's that you're drinking?" Venser asked as they walked down the hall, watching her go off. "Where are you going?" He stopped at a door on the right and opened it, his queen bed with turquoise and gold silk sheets visible. A rather inviting bed... "My room is here. Remember?"

Selina glanced back at him for a moment. "You don't want to know" She then turned around and followed him to his room, sitting on the end of his bed and taking another swig from the bottle "So first you want to fuck as you put it, and now you're more than happy to just lay in bed listening to the rain? You really are a difficult man to follow." She took another sip a little of the liquid dripping from her lips before she licked them.

"Were you serious about the fucking? Because I swear last time we had a one night stand that's exactly what happened." He said, pulling down his baggy red pants, kicking it aside and hopping into the middle of his bed nude. "I recall you called me charming..."

"Or was it today? Maybe both."

"Me calling you charming was more or less sarcastic." She watched him as he removed his baggy pants and hop into the bed nude, standing and slipping her dress off from over her shoulders to reveal her lacey black lingerie.

"I think you look better wearing nothing at all." The bearded man said getting underneath the covers, raising his left hand and trapping the door handle in a green aura, closing it behind her. "Take it off, and c'mere... With the bottle..."

Placing the bottle down for a moment knowing removing her lingerie would be a little harder than removing her gown, she then ran her hands down her body to pull down her lacey pants, revealing her nude body, her hair covering her breasts. she then picked the bottle back up and sat at the edge of the bed beside him.

"Come," He patted the space next to him and scooted over.

The hybrid woman took another decent swig and placed the bottle down beside the bed and scooted herself into the bed, glancing over at him for a moment after her red eyes shifted back to their usual green blue.

He wrapped his arms around Selina and pulled her naked body into his, pressing tightly into her. Venser leaned over her and picked up the bottle, taking a heavy swig of it. "Gah... Mhm..." He blinked a few times and set it back, falling back in bed. "What is that? Seriously."

The hybrid woman gasped for a moment trying to stop him. "I wouldn't drink that." She paused for a moment as he drank it, unable to warn him fast enough. "Um, uh, yeah I gathered you wouldn't enjoy that... That would be one of my secret stash bottles, so I don't have to constantly go out on a hunt to satisfy my thirst. Though I may sometimes enjoy drinking whiskey or rum, it's not exactly my prefered beverage."

The handsome bearded man spat it out and held out his tongue, combing through it with his fingers. "Blood... Human?" He grumbled to himself and moved his face close to hers. "Yeah... I know you enjoy the taste more than I..."

Selina chuckled slightly, a smile forming on her face. "I have some vampire in me, what did you expect? I can't exactly live off the same drinks and food source as you do, if I tried I'd go more insane than yourself and probably kill someone. Though I did kill someone to produce enough blood to fill that bottle." She paused a moment.

Venser leaned forward and pressed his lips to Seline's, kissing her a few times to get the blood off of his lips. "And half werewolf?"

She gently licked his lips before licking hers and then looked at him with darkened eyes. "Hybrid... Yes, though I understand it can get confusing." She then gently bit his lower lip before kissing him gently.

"Weird half this and a little bit of that..." Venser said with a yawn, pulling Selina on top of him, running his hands down her body and resting them on her ass after giving it a squeeze. "You know what the best feeling is?"

Selina raised a brow slightly before looking down at him. "And what is that?" Smirking slightly as his hands rested on her ass.

"This." He said pressing his body into hers as she laid on top of him. "Cuddling naked... Feeling the warmth of someone's body against yours..."

The hybrid woman gave out a slight gasp as he pressed his body firmly against hers, her hot body up against his. "Some warmer than others. I must say it's quite the experience, something so simple yet satisfying, though I must admit, resisting the urge to bite you right now is proving difficult." She bit her lower lip for a moment as her body grew hotter.

He turned his head to the side molding her ass with his hands, fondling it. Squeezing it. Giving it a hard slap here and there. "Do it..."

Her eyes widened slightly as he encouraged her, glancing away for a moment barely able to resist the urge. Her lips closed in at his neck, her hot breath against his skin before sinking her teeth into his flesh.

"Ahhhhhhhh...!"

About two minutes later...

Selina gave out a loud lustful moan as he pressed her down upon his shaft, leaning forward on top of him, biting gently at his lip before beginning to kiss him back rather passionately. Clawing down his back before parting from his lips for a moment. "I have to say it's been quite some time since I've been screwed by a man."

'Mhm... Yeah..." Venser moaned into the kiss as he bucked his hips up and down as Selina rode him, shivering as she clawed his back and pretty much wrapped herself around him. "Feels so great doesn't it?" The handsome bearded man asked, moving his head to the side, sucking at biting one particular spot of her neck.

The hybrid moaned louder, giving out a soft lustful growl as her body became tense, her arms gripping firmly to his back as her cunt gripped tightly around his length. "Can't... Mhmpf... Disagree with you on that one. Ahhh!" She began to pant as he wildly thrusted in and out, her eyes closed and herself filling with lust as he sucked and bit at her neck whilst giving her quite the wild ride.

He leaned forward and pressed his chest up against hers, leaving a bruise on her neck and locking his lips with hers as lust and pleasure coursed through their bodies. Venser gave her ass a hard slap as she bounced up and down on his cock, the sounds of her rear slapping against his thighs really loud.

Selina gasped giving out a bit of a growl as he firmly slapped her ass, her glowing eyes opening for a moment. Parting from his lips and kissing down the side of his neck, her steaming body pressing firmly against his, her moans becoming louder and more frequent as her juices began to flow out. Firmly biting a tender spot along the side of his neck.

Venser loved the feeling of her breasts being squashed up against his muscular chest. And moaned at his neck being bitten. "That's my sensitive spot!" He exclaimed, giving her rear another hard smack. "Alright... Get on all fours..." He said slowing down his thrust as she still sat on top of him.

Selina Nightengale gently slid off and positioned herself on her hands and knees, arching her back slightly and wiggling her ass from side to side in a teasing manner. Brushing her dark brown hair off to the side and lowering her eyes at the sight of him.

Venser got off the bed and walked over to his wardrobe, looking through a box for a few seconds before pulling out a leather spiked leash with a chain. He licked his lips watching the feisty hybrid woman wiggle her ass from side to side in a teasing manner, watching it jiggle a bit as he walked back over to the bed. He set the collar on the bed and then mounted her, wrapping his arms around her waist before shoving himself in.

"Mhm, yes!" Venser moaned locking his legs with hers penetrating her from behind in the true doggystyle fashion.

She gave out a rather loud lustful squeal as he firmly shoved his length inside her again, pressing herself back against him firmly as she got a firm grip of the bedsheets. her body steaming hot and panting heavily, moans and squeals coming from her as they experienced a great round of hardcore sex.

Venser began to sweat heavily as he had his way with Selina's body, slapping the collar around her neck and pulling back on the chain while he fucked her. "Yeah, you like that don't you bitch?" He asked giving her one hard thrust before going back to his fast paced speed.

The hybrid gave out a loud growl as he placed the collar around her, her whole body tensing and her juices flowing frantically out of her. panting heavily and biting her lower lip slightly, she pushed herself even firmer against him so his shaft went in deeper, letting out continuous lustful moans as he pounded her firmly. Her moans and squeals became louder and more high pitched as she reached her climax, squirting juices everywhere as her body began to relax slightly.

"Arghhh I'm a bitch!"

Venser held back on the chain more, the collar pulling her head back as he gave her a hard pounding. "Mhm! Mhm! Mhmm...!" Her juices splashed all over his cock as it went as deep into Selina as it could. Actually managing to hit her G-spot as his love juice spurted deep inside her. "Ahhh fuckk..." He moaned, taking himself out, slapping his soaked member against her soft, round ass.

The hybrid continued to pant, slowly getting her breath back. "I'll let it slide this once, but if you put a collar on me again, I'll kill you. On a completely different note, I can see why my sister screwed you." She smirked slightly before sitting back and grabbing the chain off him. She then turned over and laid down on the bed still panting.

"That was fast but... Excellent. Would have been better if it lasted longer." Venser said laying beside Selina, pressing his naked body into hers, cuddling her close. "Ohhhh by the void I needed that I am so tired... It's been a rough... Couple of sleepless weeks..."

She gave a slight chuckle looking over to him, her eyes not glowing quite as much. seeing the slight bite mark to his neck and shifting her eyes gently as she bites her lower lip before smirking slightly. "It certainly was a good round, and you really know how to give it hard to a bitch, as I recall you calling me."

"You sure you don't like the collar on during sex?" Venser asked again at her comment about being a bitch.

Selina smirked a bit, licking at his neck.

"Try putting it on again in a few minutes and I'll show you how rough I can really be... No holding back..."

CHAPTER TWENTY ONE: TURNDOWN

The Dragon's Head Tavern and Inn, Vorland, 1438 ATC

Brea Rowland hummed to herself as she continued to clean the same spot on the counter. Her rag made a wet trail of a figure eight as she sipped from a tankard with her free hand. She was a little tipsy, that much was true, but she wasn't drinking for any reason in particular. No celebration, no mourning... Just a nice little night where she could actually enjoy herself by herself. It seemed like everybody was out working, on an adventure, or spending time with their loved ones. Most of the people who stayed here were asleep. So, she simply enjoyed the peace and quiet whilst alone at the bar in the middle of the night, wearing a simple green work dress.

A familiar figure lay on the floor in the middle of the bar, face down and wearing nothing but a leopard print thong.

She stepped over him and deposited the rag in the sink. With a slight prod of her foot, she nudged her boss's side and calmly said, "Hey, sleepy. Try a bed."

A loud groan was heard and Venser flipped over, gasping heavily. "Brea! Mhmm...!" He sat up and got on his knees, grabbing her leg. "I was sucked in a way I've never been sucked before!" His raven hair brushed back and his beard neatly trimmed. Venser looked very presentable tonight.

She stumbled a little, but caught herself on the counter.

"Ugh. Was it a dream or somethin''? Wait, er, no. Just no..." She asked, words the tiniest bit slurred. Her brown eyes shot daggers down at him, and from gritted teeth she asked: "Did you get on that powder shit again? I heard... Grey Amber was it? And you spent so much time trying to kick your addiction."

"No! No... You got it all wrong. Grey Amber... No. No more. Ahem... Hic! When my kids were born... That's when I put that powder SHIT down for good. Theyyyy-y...Hic! Saved me." Venser rambled shaking his head, snapping it a bit and looking right up at her. "Are you drunk?"

Brea blinked and looked to both of her sides slowly. "No...?" She said, phrasing it almost as a question.

Venser stood up and took the tankard from the barmaid. "Then what's this?" He asked before taking a heavy swig. "Mu- Erp! Must I ask?"

"Mead." The sandy haired barmaid said with a shrug. "Sometimes a person enjoys a little nip now and again..." She tried to defend herself, but she looked at her feet to avoid eye contact. "Some more than others, clearly."

"I'll show you clearly..." Venser grabbed Breas's cheeks and locked his lips with hers, allowing the mead in his mouth to flow into hers.

Brea wasn't prepared for that in the slightest, so the mead dribbled out of her mouth briefly, and down onto her dress. Soon she was able to catch onto his game, and once he was out of mead, she pulled herself away and wiped the corner of her mouth. "That was warm." She said, irritated at her fairly nutty boss. He certainly had his moments.

"I know right?" The bearded man asked, cracking his joints, stretching out his back. "Wanna go back to my room and continue drinking? Not sure how long-ggg you've been in here." He looked around at the empty tavern, the moonlight pooled in through the windows, their shadows flickering along the wall from the single candle atop the bar.

She shrugged. "I think the weirdest thing that could've happened just did, so why not." The sandy haired barmaid said, grabbing her tankard and starting the route to his room.

"Oh? It could have been more weird." Venser said as he walked behind her, catching a glance at her fat rear. "Speaking of which," He said with a pause lifting up her dress and letting out a goofy laugh. "Mashed potatoes with a molten lava center."

"Delicious."

She swatted his hand away. "Quit it, you." She said, turning her head back over her shoulders to glare at him, but it was followed with a quick smile.

"Pfft. You love your boss." Venser said moving past her, pushing the door to his room open. He then flopped over into his queen sized bed and stretched out his back, it cracked. "Ah void... I feel so lazy today... It's been GREAT like... Like, it feels great and weird... Time to myself sorta."

"Nobody's asking you to do anything, Ven." She said, drinking the last from her mead cup. She looked at his almost-nude figure on the bed and chuckled. "And aren't you cold at all?"

"Naw. You get used to it. And besides," He patted the silk turquoise sheets before getting under it. "Warm. Come here."

Warm did sound nice, but she also didn't think it'd be that smart to crawl under the covers with her boss, again. "I'll just take this blanket here." She said, pulling a tawny knit off from the back of a chair.

"Naw c'mon. You've been in my bed before." He said sitting up. "Is it the beard? I can go shave right now. Ehhh but actually... Naw. I've grown to enjoy it. Women enjoy it."

Brea blushed, remembering that random time with him and Ruari the islandic elf. "Nah, this is fine." She said, wrapping it around her and moving her ponytail to the outside.

"Do you remember?" Venser asked, looking to her. "A really fun night of drinking... Threesome..."

She blushed and nodded. "Yeah, I remember." Damn, if she had more mead...

"Ya good on mead or do I need to get you more drink? Well," He paused and clapped his hands together twice. "Water!" A snakey, shadowy hand set a glass of cold water down on his nightstand right beside a glowing feather on his night-stand he often used as a source of light. An odd artifact from a previous lover, he simply needed to tap it once and it would glow, and then another tap would make it glow even brighter, and then a third tap would simply make the light fade into a perfectly normal feather, though one imbued with divine beauty and benevo-lence.

Brea traded her empty tankard for the glass of water, sipping at it gingerly. "Thank you, kindly." She said, her words less slurred this time around.

"That was my water actually." He sighed and clapped his hands together twice, ordering another glass of water and a bottle of whiskey. "We could share some of this." Venser said leaning over and picking up the bottle, shaking it in front of him. "Haven't had it in a while... Whiskey makes me frisky... Oohh! Specially, okay... This. Mixed with lemons and limes and syrup... And wham! You have the best drinkkkkk- Hic! Drink, for getting smashed!"

Brea laughed a little. "Sorry, didn't mean to steal your water." She drank it until it was around halfway full. "No thanks, that wasn't my first tankard of mead, if you catch my drift." She giggled briefly before folding her hands in her lap.

"In a good mood? Celebrating?" Venser asked, sipping his water. "You sure you don't wanna join me in bed?"

Brea nodded. "Positive, thanks. And not really. Just kind of drinking to drink."

Venser flailed his arms and laid back on his fluffy pillows with furry gold throwovers, staring up at the ceiling. "Drinking is always fun." He yawned and rubbed his eyes, drinking down the last of his water and accidently getting some on his face. "Don't make me beg now. It's what, past midnight? And I've had a long dayyyy-Hic! I'm sure you have to."

She sighed, walking over and sitting on the edge of the bed, still wrapped in her blanket. "I suppose." With that, she kicked her legs up and scooted into the bed. He was right, it was warm.

"Are you really going to sleep in that thing? Why not just sleep in the nude?" Venser asked, making a backhand motion at the door. His mark flashed greenish white and a gust of wind closed the door with a small slam. "It'd get wayyyy too hot for you. Trust me, I used to wear that suit over there to bed." He said gesturing to a mannequin wearing his signature red rubber suit with rubber nipples and an over-sized codpiece along with a white comedy mask.

"Mhmh." The bearded man mumbled to himself and sat up, extending his left hand and trapping the mask in a green aura, pulling it over to him, his fingers gliding over the porcelain thing.

She chuckled as she looked at the mannequin. "I suppose." She said again, undoing the corset and removing her green tavern dress. Underneath was a slim fitting nightgown, and Brea wrapped herself up like a burrito again before getting into the bed.

"Eh." Venser waved her off. "I think you'd better wearing nothing at all. I mean, you do... And your ass...! Mhmph."

Brea giggled. "Thank you, and you wish." She said, tugging the blanket around her tighter.

"Hey," He leaned in close to the sandy haired barmaid. "Clothes are a prison. I mean... Why?" Venser slid his thong down and tossed it over Brea, it landed on the floor in front of his dresser.

"Whoop!" Almost losing grip on the theater mask in his other hand.

"Because I like them, and we already have... Had relations once, so why bother doing it again?" She said, grabbing her blanket and entwining her legs in it more.

"Well one," Venser said with a pause laying on his side and counting on his fingers, "It feels good. Two, it feels great. And three, it feels nice. I mean... You had fun with me and Ro, right?"

The sandy haired barmaid scoffed, sitting up again and taking the mask from Venser's loosened grip.

"I did." She said slipping the mask over his face, and the bearded man allowed her, watching Brea slightly amused the entire time. She leaned in, pressing her soft pomegranate colored lips against the wide smile of the mask.

"It will be another time, maybe. You really should sleep, Ven." Brea said, turning Venser down, gently pushing her palm against the center of his barreled chest, and the bearded man simply laid on his back when she pushed back against him, mumbling nonsense before letting out a yawn.

"Your teeth look so good..." More drunken gibberish as he laid on his side, feeling heavy eyed.

"Mrrrmm... No one loves you more than The Ven... That's... I... Like, always been my biggest problem... I just love too much and too fast... Here you are loved... Stay with me... Please... Hic! Hic."

Brea sighed softly, standing up to collect her dress and corset, quietly sneaking out of her boss's bedroom and now planned to enjoy a tankard of mead in her own room while Venser lay on his side for several long minutes, recanting all of the various women in his life, and the ones from his past life, the mysterious life he had before he ever set foot on the planet Laguna.

CHAPTER TWENTY TWO: CANNABIS

The Dragon's Head Tavern and Inn, Vorland, 1438 ATC

Ruari slammed open the door to the tavern as the day began to fade away, causing it to put a small scuff in the wall behind it. She marched up the stairs and swiftly made her way to the bar, giving anyone whe so much as looked at her for a second too long a glare that could cut steel. With a small, annoyed sigh, she sat on the stool, leaning onto the counter and directing her sights outside the window while she waited for a drink to be placed in front of her.

"Hiya Rauri." Venser said slowly with a wave sitting at the end of the bar. He was wearing his usual entertainer outfit and seemed fairly relaxed. His eyes were red and glazed over and he held one of his usual light green cigars in one hand. He swayed back and forth singing some obscure song.

"Feel the arms of the ocean as it breaks into the skin, of the waves of the motion open wide and spread open, so closeee and so farrr awayyyy from something somethingggg reality…!'"

He took a puff of cannabis cigar and stood up, walking over to the seat where Rauri sat and sat down beside her. Glancing over at the sandy haired barmaid in the green dress who was ignoring him for the past three days and helping a few other patrons who ignored him too.

He kissed her tanned cheek close to her lips and then asked, "Wanna get high? Brea doesn't… Actually probably best not to talk to her tonight."

"No, I don't." Ruari grumbled, gritting her teeth. "The only thing I want to do right now is kill someone." She turned her head too look him in the eyes with the same glare she had given the others. "And if you don't want to be that 'someone', I suggest you make me the strongest drink you can."

Venser stared into his eyes with his reddened, lazy ones and blinked once. "Okay. Best I do it and not.... Eh." He said simply standing up, grabbing a random tankard from off the shelf. He slammed it down into the barrel of Blue Lagoon but it was stopped by the cover that he had forgotten to take off, making a thud sound. "Oops." He pushed it off and got Rauri a drink, bring the neon blue drink over to her.

"Free for you..." The handsome bearded bartender said setting it down in front of her. He brushed back some of her crimson hair and said, "I can be that someone... I don't mind... If it will make you feel better."

"Thank you," She brought the drink to her lips and took a long draw. She looked down at the liquid in the tankard, swirling it around and thinking. "... Why is it free?" The islandic elf glanced up at him, her gaze still cold and her grip on the cup tight enough to turn her knuckles white, one of her long pointy ears twitching.

"Just take the free drink dear..." Venser said stroking her hair gently, before disappearing in a puff of thick red smoke and reappearing right beside Rauri. He draped an arm around her and took another drag, breathing out greenish white smoke slowly. "I'm soo good, this is like, my sixth or seventh one tonight."

Selina had walked out of her room hearing all the commotion going on and groggily made her way to the bar, having heard their conversation. Selina Nightengale was a was a relatively tall woman, five eleven same as Venser with fair skin, scarred in a few places, an athlete's body, with dark brown shoulder length hair and blue green eyes and wore a long black leather coat that reached her knees and was belted in the front.

"Kill someone huh? Well, don't let me stop you" She gave a wicked smirk before making her way to a stool and placing her rough frame upon it. "Had a shit time have we?" Her head slowly started to spin, remembering she had gotten into quite a fight previously, a slight cut across her cheek just beneath her eye but she had cleaned it up earlier."I suggest if you plan to kill someone, don't go up against a large pack of rival lycans, doesn't end too well."

With a grumble and an ever-tightening grip, the tan islandic elf took another large gulp of her drink. "Trust me when I say I will not be doing that." She called out to the woman, not bothering to look away from her drink. "If I'm fighting anyone it's going to be those damned merchants..."

"Hey hey Selina..." He gestured to the seat next to him, nuzzling Rauri's head.

"C'mere..." Venser took yet another puff of his joint and blew out more greenish white smoke that seemed to hang in the air around them. "What merchants hun..."

She slammed her tankard onto the bar, turning to face both Venser and Angel. "Is it legal to prevent someone from buying goods because of your race?" She asked, her glare becoming even more fierce. "I've heard things about this continent and I hoped it wouldn't be true..."

Selina looked up at Venser for a moment. "I'm fine here thank you, though I could use something to take the edge off." Eying the cigar and inhaling some of the smoke, she then turned to face the light brown elf in the dark blue dress. "Aye unfortunately this day and age it is, though not everyone agrees with it. With more and more free Alphonse island elves running about."

"Sellers have the right to refuse service... Not smart since you need as many customers as possible..." Venser said slowly inhaling more of the fantastic relaxant he held in one hand. "I might..." He shut his eyes and nearly fell asleep in his seat before sitting up and sighing slowly. "Mhm. Selina, I can help you take the edge off. And so can Ro here..."

"Gods damn it all!" She cursed, growling and crossing her arms, clawing at them. "Not even one potion-- He wouldn't let me buy not one damned potion because I was an elf. You know what happened? Wait, how can I... Oh I know..."

"I mean, up North in Pryldahn a few other places... I know the elves from the Alphonse Islands were slaves but, stick with me Ro and I'll get you whatever potions you want. Fuck em."

"I get it. Fuck me." Ro said with a heavy sigh, moving past the two and grabbing Venser's hand, tugging him down the hall. "I'm so mad right now I just want to feel better..."

The bearded man gave her a smirk and gladly followed, quickly reaching out to grab the hybrid woman's hand to tug her along as well.

"Let's go then! Selina Nightengale, Ro of the Alphonse Islands. Ro, Selina. Bam."

Once in his bedroom, Venser kicked off his bright red boots and undid the front of his tunic, opening it to show off his barreled chest.

"So, shall we get started?"

Ro looked at him, indignation rising in her chest as she raised one of the light green cigars to her lips, inhaling the smoke and let it slowly fill her lungs before exhaling it. "Of course, let's do it."

Passing it to the taller hybrid woman who also took a puff.

"I'm not used to this..." Selina admitted, taking longer drags than Ruari.

"Very well then," He gestured elegantly to the bed and moved behind them again, closing the door. "Firstly, sit. Both of you, next to each other."

They did so. Venser walked around, looking at them from multiple angles.

"Now, you've kissed before of course?"

They both nodded. "Of course... And bit..." Selina muttered as they casually passed the cannabis between each other.

"Good. Show me. Both of you" He gave a little wave of her hand to indicate that they should start.

Ruari felt a little rushed by the austerity of the command. She looked at Selina, who looked back at her. With a second of unspoken communication, only a shrug from the hybrid woman, they both leaned in and locked lips. The handsome bearded barkeep continued to walk around them, tracing her lip again with one finger.

"Good, good. Move in a little more as you go. Keep up an even pace with each other... Let's see a little love between you two."

Selina had to admit that she felt a little uncomfortable with Venser watching them. But she kept her eyes closed as she felt the islandic elvish woman's lips part at the tentative urging of the hybrid's questing tongue.

"Mmm," Venser hummed, gently taking the cigar from them and placing it on the nightstand so neither of them accidently dropped it. "Keep going, pay no attention to what I'm doing."

That set off a few warning bells for Selina at least. She felt the bed dip, and could tell without seeing that Venser had sat down behind Ruari.

"Why so tense?"

Up until that point Ruari had been fairly engrossed in the kiss, her hands feeling up Selina's side and the back of her neck. As soon as Venser finished speaking however, Ruari let out a little gasp of surprise. Selina felt Ruari's hot breath inside her mouth and her hands suddenly tense a little, prompting Selina's green blue eyes to open a little. Ruari's crystal blues were pressed firmly shut.

"What's with these shoulders?" Venser whispered sensually, his rough fingers gently massaging at Ruari's's neck and back.

Within seconds the islandic elf's kissing became all the more engaged, the movements of her hands freer and more questing. Selina closed her eyes again, and after a few moments Venser stood up again.

"Oh come on," He chided playfully. "The scene... Both of you are lovers locked in a romantic embrace. A little closeness wouldn't be uncalled for."

Ruari felt one of Venser's hands push against the small of her back. She moved around a little and felt Selina do the same, pressing their bodies together. Selina set her arms to close around Ruari's waist, and Ro gripped into Selina's brown hair.

"That's better," The bearded man murmured. "I don't believe for a moment that you two haven't kissed before. Ah ha!" He chuckled, sitting down behind Selina and began working her massage upon her as well. She still moaned into her continuing kiss as Venser sent electricity running down her back.

Transports of pleasure may be a little overwhelming when first they steal upon one, but Selina was acclimatising well to the new sensations. Ro's taste filled her mouth, her smell penetrated her nostrils as she breathed deeply. Her slender body ran underneath the hybrid's fingers, and she was overtaken with a sudden urge to seize a hold of Ro's small breasts. One curious hand lifted tentatively upwards to the spot, when suddenly another hand took her wrist.

"Go on Selina, explore..."

As her hand probed the tender areas of Ruari's nearly flat chest, her kissing became a little more erratic. Suddenly she broke the kiss and bit suddenly at the nape of Selina's neck. Selina's athletic body shuddered in response, and she let out a another pleased growl as the two girls explored each other.

Selina felt Venser lean in behind her, felt him insinuate his strong arms underneath her arm pits, and then felt gentle hands take a hold of her chest. The touch was sensual. Firm yet not overly forceful. Between this, the proximity of Ruari, and the trail of bites and kisses on her neck, the heat in Selina's face seemed to be overriding her brain functions. What was more, a familiar tenseness was building down beneath her gut. A pressure or gnawing sensation like a sleeping creature being roused within a confined space. The hybrid couldn't help the little gasps and moans the two of them were forcing from her straining throat.

"Very nice as ever... Just Ro do her thing... Relax and try not to go berserk..." Venser whispered admiringly as he gave Selina's breasts a squeeze, his voice richer and deeper than most humans.

Selina didn't know whether it was this comment that made Ruari do it, or whether she was merely feeling the same sense of build up as Selina was, but Ruari suddenly took the offensive again, and pushed the hybrid girl onto her back.

"Clothes. Off."

Venser didn't interfere for now, but returned to his pacing, watching Ruari pull undo Selina's long black leather coat, exposing her black bra and the faint red claw marks on her shoulder and neck. Ruari pulled her dark blue dress off, revealing her frilly red undergarments, and returned to work. Selina had to fight a certain degree of surprise at Ruari's aggressive behavior. Both of her hands were closed over Selina's wrists, pinning her to the bed as her mouth traced her chin up to her mouth and locked them both into another kiss. Once their lips met Selina let out a pleased, animalistic growl, biting at her lip. Before breaking the kiss and playfully biting Ro's neck.

"A lot of people underestimate the importance of foreplay, as much as I love to just jump into it." Venser said thoughtfully, puffing a few clouds of smoke from his cannabis cigar. Selina noticed out of the corner of her half closed eye Venser biting at her index finger a little as her other hand gently groped her own chest. Her heavy lidded eyes were fixed hungrily upon them, and Selina could only imagine what might be going through the tan elf's mind at the moment.

"Don't forget the pacing," He reminded them. "It's important to understand what your partner is communicating. You both have needs. Feel them out."

Obediently, Selina's hands began moving further around. Reaching Ruari's panties and brushing her hand against the front of it.

Ruari's body was so warm, her mouth hot and eager, the feel of her body pressed against her own was doing wonders to drive Selina's mind out of control. Ro's stunning new boldness showed itself again as she suddenly abandoned the hybrid's mouth and slid downwards. Selina looked down with some curiosity, and saw Ro eying her right breast with a predatory gleam in her eye, much to the hybrid's pleasure. Lifting her bra away from it, she gave it an experimental lick that filled Selina's face and neck with fire.

"Are we sure we haven't done this before?" Venser asked, smirking. "Exploration."

Ruari, entirely engrossed in massaging and licking Selina's breasts didn't seem quite as aware until Venser kneeled on the bed behind her, sitting up directly behind the short islandic elf, his chest brushing against her back.

"Let's see how honest we've been," Venser whispered, towering over the pair of them. He reached a hand forward, and slipped it down the front of Ruari's flat stomach, right down into the lining of her panties. Ro gave a little jump at the touch, and seemed caught between surprise and a lustful desire to continue worshipping Selina's ample chest. Venser felt around for a moment or two, eliciting little grunts and gasps from Ruari as she hummed thoughtfully.

"Here we go..."

The bearded man pulled back his hand, which glistened with a stickiness that caught Selina's immediate interest. Her eyes followed those fingers as Venser inspected them with the detached air of the connoisseur. And then apparently as an afterthought, opened her mouth and sucked on her individual fingers with an almost obscene degree of relish, following it up with a puff of his cigar before he set it down again. The dominant part of Selina's mind had a sudden curiosity to know what the stickiness had tasted like.

Venser's left hand moving to brush the front of Ro's neck, and the other returning to her panty line. "This is very telling," she said, thrusting her fingers back into Ruari's womanhood. She shuddered, the glow in her face growing. "See? All intact. And so ready." He held up her fingers again to show Ro what she meant.

Without quite meaning to, Selina sat up, staring at the juice on Venser's hand. The handsome bearded man grinned and held the hand out.

"Go on," He murmured seductively. "There's nothing to be embarrassed about. She's giving it to you, after all."

Selina leant forward, honestly divided about whether or not to actually do it. But the gnawing in her loins was drowning her thoughts out, and she found herself sliding her lips down the fingers, her tongue wrapping itself around the soft skin. The taste was utterly new to her, a strange combination of sweetness and saltiness as the lycan hybrid was not used to laying with women.

Although the taste itself was, to Selina;s's mind anyway, unremarkable, the effect it had upon her was like a drug. She grabbed a hold of Venser's wrist to stop him from pulling away, and sucked lovingly at the fingers as though they were coated in nectar. Ruari watched her, biting hard on her own finger as though trying to hold herself back. Venser's free hand moved from her neck, and took a hold of the top of Ro's free hand.

He directed Ruari's hand down to Selina's thong, and the girl raised a red brow noting that it did not match her bra. It was red and green.

Ro pushed her slightly trembling fingers down into them. Taking hold of the forefinger, she maneuvered it expertly between Selina's lips, dragging a prolonged moan from the nicely tone werewolf woman.

"Feel that?"

Selina abandoned the dry well of her fingers and was beginning to feel the tight knot beneath her gut burn. She grasped her own breast and began to massage it desperately.

"Oh gods.."

"She seems to like that, doesn't she?" Venser remarked to Ruari the islandic elf. "Let's be rid of these, shall we?" He said, unhooking the back of Ruari's red bra and allowing it to fall away. He gave Ro's small chest an approving grope as she continued to finger Selina.

"Mm," Venser said, thoughtfully kissing Ro on the cheek. "Not bad love, but I think we can do better. Selina, could you roll over please? Ro is going to treat you to something special."

Selina did as she was bidden like a good submissive mutt, lying back on the bed and revealing that her thong had the words "Venser's Property" stitched into the back. Without preamble, Venser leaned forward, passed Ruari, and pulled Selina's thong down her legs and over her feet, casting them lazily aside. Selina felt an agreeable sense of unfamiliar helplessness for once before the two kneeling over her. Ruari was staring down at Selina's tall beautiful body in a lust filled trance, whilst Venser just behind her appeared like a ghostly conscience made manifest, whispering suggestions of lust and desire into the girl's ears, everything in a misty dream like state.

The handsome bearded barkeep gestured with a hand. "Would you mind spreading your legs a little?" Selina did, shivering a little at the sudden slight surge of coldness.

"Now," Venser began, "We're going to have to be a little more technical here, Ro. Reach down there and gently pull apart the lips. Yes, that's it. Be gentle now," He reminded her, light greenish white smoke filled the room as Selina tensed up at Ro's touch. "You're entering a sacred temple, remember. You have to tread carefully, or the mistress of the temple might not let you back in."

The hybrid could tell that Venser was enjoying himself immensely despite not being able to have his hands on fun yet. His every word, spoken in a hushed and sultry tone had just the faintest tint of satisfaction peppering his instructions. He gazed down at Selina's exposed womanhood with as much greed as Ruari's expression had.

"Ahh, there we are," The bearded man exhaled, running his hands up and down Ro's front as she worked. Ruari had succeeded in finding Selina's most intimate treasure. "I'm sure you know what power that little button has," Venser whispered to Ruari, who stared down at it in glowing interest. "With every woman, if you figure out how exactly that button works and how to work it, you can make her do..." He let the sentence hang for a fraction longer than he needed to, holding both of his girls in breath-stopping suspense.

"Anything"

There was a moment or two of complete and utter silence. Selina brushed her brown hair over her shoulder and gazed up at the two with lust filled, lowered eyes that began to darken, whilst Venser's slitted emerald eyes looked over the tan elf girl's shoulder like the serpent in the garden, tempting her to seize the forbidden fruit.

"Well?" Venser asked with a slightly amused inflection. "Come on Ro, what are you waiting for? Remember our fun time with Brea?"

The question seemed to echo Selina's own mind. What would Ruari do? And when would she do it? She needed to be taken, she needed Ro or Venser to take her. She needed them to do something!

"Oh, the anticipation is killing her... But, some things are worth waiting for..." Venser began licking his lips a bit. Then abruptly, Ro leaned forward, and before Selina could utter a sound, lowered her head. The bearded man smiled more, and Selina pushed herself up slightly, only to instantly fall back again as she felt Ro's breath on her womanhood.

Ruari was not to be outdone, nor underestimated. The islandic elf was now asserting command of herself. She wouldn't be told what to do by Venser. She knew what to do, and she knew what she wanted, and she was going to have it. But not too fast. She didn't want it over too quickly. Eyeing the little mound of pink flesh, she extended her tongue just far enough to give it the briefest of contact. Selina's body gave a little quiver. Despite herself, Ruari grinned, and ran her tongue all the way up Selina's exposed slit. The stifled moan this action elicited was like a stimulant, fuelling her confidence.

The tan elf braced the hybrid woman's legs apart with her hands, enjoying the feeling of power she had over her as she provoked every little moan of pleasure and gasped with the merest of touches. But then it wasn't as though she was free from allurement; everything about Selina. The feel of her skin, the moans, the warmth of her, the smell, and the taste, the sight of her nicely toned, somewhat scarred body of a hunter warrior was sending great surges of hormones and longing pulsing through her blood.

Unable to take any more teasing, Selina's hand shot forward and pushed Ruari's head further in, gripping her curly dark red hair. Ruari tried to pull back in alarm, but stopped when she saw the pained expression on Selina's sweating face.

Venser licked his lips and slid a hand down his baggy red pants, rubbing his shaft up and down slowly as he watched the two. She watched Selina's breathing become more shallow, watched her furiously fondling herself as Ruari pressed her tongue deeper and deeper inside. With a slightly crooked smile and roll of her eyes, Venser leaned down over Selina, running a hand over her searing cheek. The beautiful hybrid woman looked back up at him, eyes dark and mouth agape.

"Isn't this wonderful? Letting everyone else do everything for you for once..."

Taking advantage of Selina's open mouth, she slid her tongue down into her throat, and pushed her hand away from her breast.

Perhaps this was unfair to Selina, or perhaps a gift beyond all others, but Ruari suddenly felt the spectre of jealousy rise up again, and so redoubled her efforts to please. Venser meanwhile was not letting up in the least. She could feel the pressure building in Selina, could read the signs even as she intertwined her tongue around Selina's own. She felt it in the spasms of her back, in the heightened moans and whimpers escaping her throat.

"Keep going, Ro,"The handsome bearded man urged, breaking the kiss momentarily as Selina let out a genuine scream of pleasure. Ro reached down and planted her index and middle finger over the hybrid's clitoris, knowing full well how to use it to its fullest effect.

"Don't you dare stop now!"

"H- Ahhh. H-" The hybrid gasped.

"What was that?"

"H-Hold me down..." The lycan hybrid pleaded. Venser's eyebrows raised in genuine surprise. "Please, hold m-me down! Hold me down before I rip your throat out! NOW."

Unable to prevent herself grinning, Venser pulled Ro's hand up to take over her position on Selina's pearl. He stared down at Selina contemplatively for a moment or two, and then with surprising strength took hold of Selina's right arm and pressed it down above her head. Leering down at her, Ven gave a low, ominous laugh.

"So you really do like to be dominated, then. Deep down I always knew... Very much like a dog." He said to the rough lycan woman who seemed to be in a world of her own now, hooking his thumbs into the top of his baggy red pants and pulling them down, allowing his hard length to spring free, revealing he was going commando the entire time.

"How naughty. Exploration, something I'm sure you've never had... Not like this."

Selina had never been so turned on as she was right then. As she felt Sonata's tongue lapping inside her, her own arm twisted above her head, she felt the pressure in her loins pulse.

Venser finally leaned down and licked Selina's cheek, then pulled her into a full-blown kiss. She was a bit more aggressive with her tongue than Venser, pushing past his teeth and wrestling her own tongue playfully, biting his lower lip and tugging back. Breaking the kiss and now aggressively biting his neck in multiple spots. The bearded man gave an appreciative groan, just to help him speed things along, then gestured for Ro to move and shifted back on the bed so that he was atop of Selina now.

Ruari started to suck on her earlobe now and Ven reached out with a hand and gently ran his fingertips up one of the islandic elve's thighs still locking lips with Selina, he followed Ro's leg up to her groin. As Venser began to lightly stroke Ruari's nethers, the girl squeaked and bit down on Selina's earlobe for only a moment.

She felt Venser's manhood pressing against her thigh, and shifted to allow him to rub it against the surface of her sex. Venser moaned into her mouth, and he reached down with a hand to guide it inside her.

"Wait," Selina gasped, breaking their kiss.

Venser drew back and raised a brow. "What?"

The lycan hybrid woman wiggled and shifted under him, flipping herself onto her belly. She thrust her ass into the air and waggled her rear from side to side. "Like this! Like the bitch I am..."

"You'll never change, Selina." The bearded man hastened to follow orders, and Selina shuddered and stretched her arms over the edge of the bed as he mounted her.

Penetration came upon her the way it always did. One moment she was warm, wet, and wanting, and the next moment nothing existed but Venser"s rock solid shaft, pressing against her inner walls, drenched in her juices, stretching her cunt in the nicest way possible.

"Ahhh! Mhmm...!" Selina Nightengale moaned out, clamping her eyes shut and shuddering more. Every one of his thrusts was accompanied by one of her rough cries of pleasure all while Ruari peered over Ven's shoulders, and then moved around him on the bed.

There was a reason Selina wanted him to take her on her belly and not her back, and it wasn't due to her werewolf nature. She looked back at the red haired elf and flashed her a devious grin, then cocked her head to one side, raising a brow.

Selina grabbed Ruari by the hips, and they both worked to re-position her so that her legs spread to the side of the lycan hybrid's face. Selina looked at her glistening folds, inches away from her face, then up at Selina, who brushed back her hair with a smile, before reaching over to the night stand and picking up one of the lit cannabis cigars, taking yet another slow drag.

She lowered her mouth and dove into Ruari's sex tongue-first, and the islandic elf groaned as her back arched. Ruari tasted like spring water and coconut mixed with sex, and Selina devoured her with enthusiasm. It helped that Venser was plowing her like she was his toy all the while.

"'Rrrrrrrrrrrr..." Selina Nightengale's dark eyes rolled into the back of her head, and she squeezed them shut as she moaned again into Ruari's tender pussy. Venser was certainly making it difficult to focus, and the gentle, pressing motion of Ro's hips accompanied by her soft cries of pleasure weren't helping either. The lycan hybrid already felt an orgasm coming on.

That was okay, she thought as she leaned into Venser's thrusting. Orgasms were like dessert, and Selina's couldn't come quickly enough. What a truly unexpected night this was.

Selina felt Venser pull himself closer until he was right on top of her and breathing in her ear. The pace of his hips changed, and the athletic hybrid shuddered as he thrust himself into her with deliberate slowness, drawing himself all the way out of her before pushing himself back into the hilt. "You know... Mmph." The bearded man said through labored pants and grunts of pleasure. "I really do love the way your thighs start to shake when you're about to cum... Ahh."

His thrust was accompanied by a wave of heat and pleasure. "And I love how when I do this..." He bit down on her ear, then drew the tip through his teeth.

"Ammph!" Selina groaned into Ruari once again. "Rrrrrrr don't make me draw blood form you..."

"You always make that sound." Ven finished. Ro's hips were rolling against her face, and Selina felt a slender press down on the top of her head as Ro let out a deep groan once again. She wedged her shut even more tightly as Venser penetrated her over and over again,

She was close. The hybrid woman used her lips to push back the folds guarding her tender nub and sucked it into her mouth.

"Ah!" The red haired islandic elf cried in a high pitch. Apparently Selina had surprised her. She didn't slow down or soften the force of her tongue, intent on pushing Ruari over the edge as quickly as possible.

It didn't take long. Ruari fell back into the sheets and splayed her hands out on some pillows beneath her as she began to cry out loudly with every panting exhale. She ground her sex into Selina's face, and she let the flowing juices run down her mouth and neck.

"Ahhhhhh…!"

Eventually, Ruari collapsed limply onto the bed with a satisfied sigh. Selina slowly raised her mouth out of the girl's drooling womanhood, and juices drizzled off her face and onto the sheets beneath them her tongue lolling out of her mouth.

"Make her cum," Ro said to Ven. She locked eyes with Selina once again, his emerald greens staring into her darkened reds.

"Make her scream."

Sweat had caused several locks of Selina's lustrous, shiny brown hair to plaster against her face, and her mouth was filled with Ruari's overwhelming taste. She could feel Venser panting hard in her ear, and more importantly, feel him pressing against her inner walls as he slid in and out of her. He'd taken it slowly, keeping her on the brink, and now she wanted it so bad it was like an ache inside her.

And then he started plowing her like she was his shameless little bitch. Deep, penetrating thrusts as fast as he could manage, his bed creaking a bit beneath them. The three of them could hear the sound of their flesh slapping together, and could feel the sweat gathering between Selina's back and Venser's belly as he leaned over her. Her heartbeat sounded in her ears, and the edges of her vision blurred as he beat away inside her. She was going to cum, she was going to cum HARD.

"Aaaahhhh!" Selina screamed as she threw her head back. "Aoohhhhhhhhhhhhhhh! Rrrrrrrrrrrrr!"

Her voice was muffled as Ruari locked lips with her and aggressively thrust her tongue into her mouth. Selina responded with her own tongue, her eyes half-lidded as pleasure overtook her body in waves, wriggling on the bed. She heard Venser begin to groan as her orgasm finally subsided.

Immediately, the lycan woman growled and broke away from Ro"s mouth. "Cum in my mouth." She demanded. "Cum on my face! I want the whole Venser Experience!"

"Yes! Venser Experience? Do women actually call it that?" Ro asked, blinking her crystal blue eyes a few times, smiling in amusement. "The Venser Experience..."

Venser pulled out, and Selina flipped onto her back. He brought his throbbing manhood still slick with her own juices, to rest in front of her face, and the rough lycan woman eagerly closed her eyes and opened her mouth wide.

"Ohhh...! Ahhhh...!" The bearded man moaned as he rubbed his shaft up and down as fast as he could.

The first spurt of creamy spunk landed on her forehead, then strung over her closed eye, across her tongue, and finally streamed down her chin. Selina let out an excited exhale as it touched her tongue. She felt it land against her face, on her throat. When he was done, both Selina and Ven collapsed back onto the bed with Ruari in-between them.

Immediately, Selina felt the soft, wet surface of Ro's tongue drag itself across her eyelid and down her face. She shuddered as Ruari reached her mouth and pulled her into a soft kiss that was laden with Venser's sweet cream.

Eventually, Ro broke away, letting a thin string of fluid to break between their tongues. She continued to clean Selina's face. The ends of her legs were still tingling.

"We're not done yet..." Ro sat up a bit and brushed back her curly dark red hair, leaning over Selina's body to grab for the light green cigar, taking a few puffs from it while Venser sat up with her, running both hands up her stomach and chest, and the islandic tanned elf leaned back into him.

"Here, try some of this Selina..." She said handing her the cigar before turning back on the bed to face the handsome bearded barkeep.

"Good," Ro said. She grabbed him by the front and tossed him onto his back. "Because I need to be obliged." Selina watched as Ro straddled him, slowly guiding his still erect cock into herself. Ro groaned, her crystal blue eyes half-lidded as she placed both hand on Venser's barreled chest and then leaned toward him, rolling her hips against his.

"Mmmmm," She groaned, letting her head fall back, her fingers playing with one of his nipple rings now.

Selina's eyes traced the curve of Ro's arched back. She was very thin and barely had a trace of muscle, but the islandic elf did have a rather nice rear end. The girl's dark red hair was behind her, and lips were barely parted as she moaned.

Her thrusts were slow and powerful, and while Venser was moving happily in time with her, there could be no doubt that Ro was in control for now. A burning need overtook Selina as she watched them.

Venser let out his signature, low seductive growl as Ruari began to ride his cock. "What are you waiting for, Selina? Come here."

Selina scooted up beside him and began to give him kisses. Venser smiled against her mouth, nuzzling her head. With her close to them now, presenting her naked toned body to them. The bearded man grabbed her around the waist with one arm, gently guiding her downward. His tongue slid along the wet lips of her cunny as soon as she was properly positioned.

"Mmph," Selina moaned as Venser's tongue explored all her tenderest places.

Ro's head rolled forward, and her eyes shot open, as though she were noticing Selina for the first time. As she ground herself against Venser, she gave Selina an intense stare. Drool gathered at the corner of her open mouth and trickled down her chin.

She leaned forward, slowly so as not to interrupt Venser's work. Ro leaned forward as well, and they met halfway. Selina slowly drew her tongue up to the corner of her mouth before eagerly plunging her tongue into her mouth. Ro, like always, took things slowly, and their tongues tangled together in a gradual dance.

Selina's eyes rolled into the back of her head as she brought an arm up to wrap around Ruari's head. She felt Venser's tongue working against her clit furiously, and realized that her next orgasm was not far off.

She felt Ro trembling under her as their tongues and lips slid over one another without regard for which was which. She tasted Ro's need, and pulled the hybrid woman closer as her body tightened. She smelled sweat, sweet nectar and sweet cream and felt Venser writhing beneath them through her aching legs. A high pitched, slightly muffled moan reached her ears, and she realized that the sound was her own voice.

She was cumming for a second time.

As her body was once again wracked with pleasure, Ro began to lightly suck on Selina's tongue, and she was once again left to moan into her mouth. Venser did not slow down despite her shaking. He locked his lips around her nub and pulled it against his tongue. Between the two of them, Selina trembled as she tried to contain herself.

When it subsided, she pulled herself onto Venser's barreled chest and wrapped her arms tightly around Ruari. She broke away from their case. "Thanks, Ven!" she called back. His response was a groan. "Hmm," Selina whispered into Ro's ear. "I think he's close again... Amazing."

Ro's response was to take Selina's earlobe into her mouth and gently bite down on it. She let out a tight little moan. "You too, huh?"

"Aaahhhhh!" Ruari screamed as she released Venser's nipples and threw her head back. Beneath her, Vensers back arched. Selinai pressed her forehead against Ro's and rode every one of her convulsions with her. She felt the islandic elf's hot breath on her face and trembled.

Eventually, both Ruari and Venser stopped. Ro pulled herself off of the handsome barkeep, fluids drizzled out of her womanhood and onto the handsome bearded barkeep. Selina fell back to lay beside him on the bed, and Ruari followed suit pulling the silk covers around them, nuzzling his neck and allowing him to be in the middle. It was his bed, his room after all.

"Mmmmmm, What a perfect night..." Ruari sighed, Selina gave a tired yawn, biting Venser's shoulder once, her eyes returning to their normal greenish blue as she closed them again and began to drift off to sleep.

"Mhmm," Venser said, nodding. "Making my lovers happy is what makes me happy. And what better way to make someone happy than sex? Maybe a nice cannabis cigar before AND after sex..." He said reaching out again, grabbing one of his still lit cigars and puffing on it, letting out a calm, relaxed and pleased sigh.

"You know I'm going to be selling a ton of these soon..." He mumbled quietly, before staying quiet all together so they could all rest.

Finishing it and wrapping his strong arms around the women on each side of him, Venser soon joined them both in the land of sleep.

CHAPTER TWENTY THREE: THE FORGOTTEN GLADE

The Dragon's Head Tavern and Inn, Vorland, 1438 ATC

Sleeping in-between two gorgeous women, the handsome bearded barkeep had an odd dream. A memory.

In the shadow of the forgotten glade, a lone figure sat up against one of the stone obelisks inside the glade, unmoving with his eyes closed and a cannabis cigar in between his lips. The man's facial features were hidden by a black hood draped over his head, and he wore a crimson and turquoise tunic with baggy red pants and bright red boots caked with mud. He exhaled smoke and shifted slightly, rubbing his head before giving it a shake. He had no idea how long he had been here as a pair of snake-like eyes surveyed the area. He was surrounded by cherry blossom trees and their petals fell slowly inside the peaceful area in the forest, the particular obelisk he was up against seemed to be made of a hard, white porcelain material. The hooded man made a lazy attempt to rise to his feet, only to let out an audible grunting noise and slide back down a large white obelisk. In the same sitting position he was in prior.

A wandering female elf walked through a forest she had stumbled upon in her journey. She walked slowly, looking at her surroundings and taking in all of the beauty nature provided her. As her sky blue eyes scanned around the trees, she noticed a small opening and picked up her pace to investigate. as she entered the area, the moonlight that now bled through the trees illuminated her yellow blonde hair, and her white feathers on her boots seemed to glow in the moonlight. The closer she came to the center, she could see a lone figure in the distance. She grew weary, not sure if it was friendly or not. Nuikia Pollux figured it best to announce her presence, just in case the lone man didn't take kindly to people sneaking up on him. "Greetings. I do hope I am not intruding on your meditation."

"Beautiful place, isn't it?" Venser's voice called out to her, followed by several coughs and greenish white smoke being turned out into the air.

"Ahek! Ahek! Yeah... I come here to think and just... Just think really. I mean it was the one time a while back and I was putting it off, but yeah. Erp, I meant to say yeah."

The man in the entertainer outfit shifted again, trying to stand up. "C'mere for a minute, lemme have a look at ya." He said gazing to the blonde elvish woman, more smoke coming out of the shadows of the hood.

Nuikia smiled, approaching him. Her body relaxed though she did keep a close eye on the male who seemed to be having a coughing fit from his cigar. "Thank you. I have been walking for awhile and was curious as to how thick this part of the forest was. Little did I know something like this was hidden within. Yes sir, it is very beautiful here. There's a sort of.... Calm air that just seems to melt all the tension from my aching muscles."

There was nothing but crickets and the night wind as the man inhaled slowly, then exhaling just as slowly. "Want a hit?" The man asked the woman, trying to stand up again, his back pressed up against the obelisk. A small tearing noise was heard as he fell back down on his rear again. "Think that was the cloak..." He muttered, lifting his free hand up to scratch his face, still holding the lit cigar out to her.

The blonde elf girl lifted an eyebrow at the man's peculiar behavior, shaking her head in a 'no' fashion "No thank you, sir. Are...you sure you don't require any assistance? I could go find you a decently thick branch to lean upon so you can stand."

"No no, I'm good." Venser said inhaling more of the cigar again. He grunted and then hopped up with his back pressed to the stone obelisk again. His good caught on it and fell down, revealing the face of a man nearing his mid thirties, with messy raven black hair, fair skin, a black beard that was starting to grow out, and unnatural emerald eyes that looked like they were plucked from the skull of a snake. "Ta da!" He said with a smile throwing his arms to the side, before coughing a bit and falling to his knees right in front of the woman he was speaking to. "Oh by the Void what a day..." He gasped and looked up at her.

"Haven't I served you before? Think I... Not sure... I do get a lot of, ya know..." He babbled smacking the side of his head a bit with his free hand. "Thought process is kinda slowed right now."

Nuikia Pollux took a small step back as the man fell to his knees before crouching down carefully. Her pointy nose crinkled a bit at a smell she couldn't really identify. Was it from whatever herb he was smoking? It had to be. Or perhaps the man had drunk a form of liquor she wasn't familiar with. Maybe both. "Sir, you can't stand on your own. You are either seriously injured, have some sort of mind illness, or you are intoxicated."

"No seriously. Haven't I seen you in my dojo before?" Ven asked, scratching his beard, looking up to her with his reddened, serpent like eyes. "Forgot to mention this helps me think." The man muttered whist enjoying his spliff, which emitted an earthy smell with a hint of citrus to it. Despite the fact that not two minutes ago he admitted to the use slowing his thought process down. "You will not believe the day I've had today before I came here, miss... Miss... What's your name?" He asked with another cough.

She rolled her eyes at the man and shook her head "I have never set foot in a... Dojo? Or met you before in my life. You may call me Nuikia. Nuikia Pollux. And I can't really help you with whatever your issue is if you don't tell me. It obviously has something to do with 'the day you've had." "She stood back up and exhaled sharply.

A couple hours earlier... Several miles from here laid a very desolate place, much like this but... Dead in contrast to the glade. Venser, the lone adventurer made his way through a lonely, crumbling tower seemingly devoid of any life. However... "'Too late for what?" He asked aloud moving to the center of the room, besides the broken chandelier. Whatever entity, or entities hovered around him, he assumed they were tied to the tower. If it fell apart, then they would vanish. "Too late for you too..." He said raising his left hand, and the mark on the back of it glowed greenish white, emitting steam. He moved back sharply when something touched his face and backhanded the air in front of him, blasting it with a powerful gust of wind. The wind did nothing and once she got the okay for the feed she smirked widely. She also felt it funny that this man assumed they were bound to this tower, thinking it was too late for them. Yes she supposed it was too late for them, they died and turned into something less than a spirit. Something much more terrible. But they were not bound to this tower. This tower acted as their headquarters for many years. Floating behind the man she placed her two index fingers into his temples. She would not make him a host, only a surrogate until she found a proper host to feed from. He was her snack. Her index black fingers slipped into his temples, it would not hurt but he would feel a cold caress against his temples, and as she did this suddenly his darkest fears would come up to his mind staring him right in the face. She began to whisper in his ear, the eerie voice of a dead girl speaking, "I warned you..." She spoke softly. "Oh by the void!" Some adventure this was. Here Venser had recently kicked his heroine and Grey Amber addiction and was getting out of his usual dojo to travel and this went south fast. Then again, he knew the risks of adventuring. He nearly vomited at the sight that looked him in the face. He tore away from it, only for limbs to reach out of the floor and grab his legs. "Oof!" He tripped backwards and quickly disappeared in a puff of thick red smoke, reappearing against the wall. "Still think something here is of any value?" No. He had to- Everything froze and went cold. And his back arched and he heard a snapping noise as his mind fell away to the things he feared most.

And there they stood in the dark halls of The Veil Tower. Venser's short sword crackled with unstable magical green lightning, while The Revenant approached with a glowing orange claymore, steaming and red hot as if it had just been pulled from a forge. The resurrected foe approached and swung, the handsome man did the same to meet his blade. A clash ensured, sending sparks everywhere within the ancient tower.

In the present... "And once you see that shit," He said with a pause making awkward hand gestures, "It'll fuck you up for life. Like, what... Mhm. The work of evil spirits. It... Saw into my mind, and made... All that real."

"You really did have an interesting day. No wonder you can't stand up."

"Don't really wanna think about that damned place." The bearded man said after telling his story to her. Venser raised his fingers to his mouth and sputtered a bit.

"What did I do with..." He placed his scarred hands down in the grass and began to feel around. "What did you say your name was? I apologize, it's rude to forget a lady's name."

"I apologize for asking about your day, then. And again, my name is Nuikia Pollux." The blonde elf looked at the ground around the man "Have you misplaced something?"

"No, no. It's fine. It was a while back and I got plenty- No no, not that one." The man in the cloak stood up again before Nuiika, revealing that he was about several inches taller than her. He fumbled about with the many pouches of his belt, before pulling out a thin, silver tin and opening it. "Outta matches..." He sighed and shook his head, slamming the tin shut and putting it back into his belt.

"Venser Karkaldwin." He said holding out a scarred hand to her. "Or Venny. Or Ven. Or VenVen. Or Handsome VenVen. Or My Little Vensie. Whatever you want. You sure you've never been in my tavern before?"

Nuikia cautiously held her hand out to the man, but mentally said 'Screw it' and grasped his hand firmly. "Pleased to meet you, Venser. Now before you asked if I had been in your dojo. That was a definite no. However, I did used to frequent a tavern, however it was ran by a Pryldahnian woman named Sud'lina."

"Sud's Tavern? I've heard of it but never been in." He laughed a bit and began pacing around in circles, enjoying the falling cherry blossom petals around them, head down. Venser held onto a tre with one hand and stares off into the woods. "You should visit my tavern sooner or later. Never a dull day in the Dragon's Head I always say. Oh! I can mix the best drinks like... No drink you've ever had in your life."

Nuikia faced the man once more a chuckle a bit "Now that, I'd like to see. It's been awhile since I've been to one. I might take you up on your offer later."

She smiled at the man, thinking back on the days where she spent most of her time going tavern to tavern providing game for them. Her smile would fade slightly as she remembered the curse that had been placed on her at birth, but her smile quickly returned again as she realized that if not for her curse she would not have been able to hold a job there. Perhaps as a hunter for the tavern, as hunting and trapping was her current occupation. Though, she never did stay long.

"Never a dull day at the Dragon's Head." He repeated blinking his reddened, snake like eyes staring off into the distance. "What brings you- Whoop!" Venser lost his grip on the tree and fell over on his side, hitting the soft grass of the glade floor.

"See you soon." He waved to her before disappearing in a puff of thick red smoke.

Her short, slender pointy ears that stuck straight curled a bit at the scene before her, falling to the ground and feeling it up, fanning away some of the thick red smoke that quickly disappaited, noticing he had left his cigar behind.

"Venser?"

Two later, Venser awoke in between Selina and Ruari, the sheets around his crotch looking like a pitched tent, blinking a few times recalling the dream.

"What the mhmhpbuba... Eh."

The morning was quite pleasant, waking up in a warm, shared bed with two beautiful naked women sleeping at his side. Both of them pleasantly asleep... And heavily flushed, with Venser's hands working beneath the sheets of the bed now, he smiled, exhaling through his nose and shaking his head. The caramel skinned elf to the left of him cuddled closer.

"Hmmmm... I think I sense a new lover coming around the Dragon's Head... What else could that dream have meant?"

CHAPTER TWENTY FOUR: THE NUBILE WILD ELF

The Dragon's Head Tavern and Inn, Vorland, 1438 ATC

Ruari kept her hand on her cutlass as she walked towards the lake for her and Venser's spar session. Seeing as she tended to spend her days dodging swords or using them, she gave him a bit of an advantage and decided to let him go first "Alright. You can try and hit me first, since you're the one who hasn't spent the past months fighting for a living. At least as far as I know." She told him, keeping her back to him as she began to walk around the lake.

Once Ro awoke earlier, she decided to slip into the first outfit she wore when she had first sailed to the continent of Posiil. A navy blue tunic that basically looked like a swimsuit with a flap of material at the front and back. Her green and red thong that read 'Venser's Property' visible when jumped or made quick movements. A red scarf around her right bicep, black boots that came beneath her knees, and a leather pauldron on her left shoulder. The islandic elf was a little over five feet, had long pointed ears, crystal blue eyes, and a thin, belly dancer's figure.

As they stood on the edge of the great blue lake under a clear, spring sky Venser grabbed his bladeless sword from his belt and held it in his right hand. "Letting me take a free hit huh?" He asked twirling the hilt around, allowing a short, ivory colored blade to pop out once it made it's round. He entered a defensive stance with both hands on it before fluidly stepping to the side, and to the side again in front of Rauri, swinging his short sword at her and dealing the opening blow of their spar.

Ro swiftly moved to the side, narrowly missing the hit before drawing her cutlass. She held her sword pointed to the ground, and her stance was not one someone would use in a real battle; a hand at her waist and standing at her full height. She raised her blade in challenge. "Once more, and try not to miss this time." She teased with a smirk.

As the cool breeze flowed through the air, so did the sounds of their blades cutting through it. Swish. Wish. Clashing and chiming of blades that met in the duel.

Venser stepped back and thrusted the blade of his sword, aiming to hit Rauri in the chest. His strike was fast and ferocious.

Before he could land a hit on her, she yet again simply moved aside. "Come on, what did I say about missing!" She laughed, bringing her sword up to swing at his lower body so she wouldn't damage anything important.

Before he could land a hit on her, she yet again simply moved aside. "Come on, what did I say about missing!" Ro laughed, bringing her cutlass up to swing at his lower body so she wouldn't damage anything important. "Mhm!" The bearded man jumped back and the cutlass barely caught his pants, not actually doing any damage but Venser could feel how close it was. He sidestepped with her and brought his sword underneath hers, moving forward and turning his sword that clashed up against hers, attempting to disarm Rauri and toss her sword away.

She slid her blade away, once she caught onto what he was trying to do. She, instead of going for his sword, slashed at the arm holding it in her own attempt to disarm him.

Venser swung his sword to the side to deflect her strike but she swung too quickly and cut the underside of his arm. "Gah!" He growled and swung his sword at Rauri's neck from the left with oen hand.

Ro ducked quickly, successfully dodging the strike. She grabbed at his wrist and held him in place only to deliver a swift kick to the side of his chest to try and send him to the ground.

"Ah!" Venser held his stomach and dropped his sword in the sand. "That's cheating!" He made a backhand motion at Rauri and his mark glowed greenish white, blasting her with a powerful gust of wind strong enough to send her flying back into the waters of the lake.

Very surprised, Ruari was sent flying into the lake. She gave a gurgled scream and flailed in the water before realizing that it was only waist deep where she landed. She stood, embarrassed and shivering from the cold, to flick her hand over to Venscr. Immediately, a shadow-like spell appeared to 'punch' him in the face. "So was that!"

"Ow! What the fuuuuu...!" Venser held his nose and fell back down again. "Some spar... Fun while it, ya know."

With a sigh, Ruari trudged her way out of the lake. Ro gripped her sopping wet and algae stained dress to wring the water from it. "I have to admit, I didn't expect you to use magic outside of conjuring those helping hands at the bar and teleporting. Good job on surprising me." She said bitterly, taking a step and cringing at both the sound and feel of whatever the hell had gotten into her boots. Her good boots, too. With an exasperated groan, she sat on the ground and took off her boots, shaking them around and watching a rush of water come out of both shoes, along with some aquatic plant life. "Gross..." She complained.

"By the void you're wet." Duh. He shook her head at Rauri and said, "We need to get you out of those clothes."

"Aha... No. Let's just go back to the tavern, I have some clothes there I can change into." She took her boots in one hand and stood up, turning towards the direction they came and walking forward, barefoot and leaving a trail of water.

"I'm not done sparring with you." Venser said, tackling Rauri to the ground, wrapping his arms around her waist and giving her a few pelvic thrusts from behind.

The islandic elf gave a yelp when she was tackled and manhandled. With a dramatic and annoyed sigh, she rolled over onto her back, pinning him to the ground, and squirmed in his grip. She tilted her head forwards only to swing it back in a sort-of headbutt against his collarbone. "Venser, If you don't let go of me this instant then I will make sure to leave extra early!" She threatened.

He grunted in pain but still held the short olive skinned elf close, brushing his lips against hers gently. "C'mon Ro..." Venser said with a seductive growl. "Let's perform an experiment of our own right now... Let's just do it right here..."

"Enough!" Ruari yelled, grabbing his arm roughly and sending extremely painful shocks down it. "Can we please just go to the tavern?!" She asked him, anger very present in her expression.

"Arghhh...!" He fell back and held his arms close to his chest, breathing heavily. "Yeah... Yeah... Let's get going..." Venser let out a few coughs and sat up. "You'll have to do that to me again sometime."

She gave a loud noise of disgust, getting up from where she was held and marching back to the tavern, leaving her boots behind. "...Can't believe you..."

Venser appeared out of a puff of thick red smoke beside Rauri, walking beside her carrying her boots in one hand, his sword back on his belt. "C'mon. You love me."

"Not right now, I don't!" She exclaimed, not acknowledging him past responding verbally. "Right now I'm pretty damn pissed at you, actually."

"Right, right. Sorry for supposedly cheating." Venser said as they walked. "We didn't exactly establish a no magic rule right before the duel."

"Mhm." She glared forward, shivering and hunched over. "And I'm assuming you still would've used magic even if we did set that rule, correct?"

"Only if I got desperate. Which I kinda did." Venser said lifting up his arm, showing Rauri the sliced fabric and the small cut. "I'm sure you would have used magic too to escalate the fighting."

She sighed, bringing her arms to her chest and crossing them. "I don't bring magic into FAIR swordfights. Unlike some people... Ahem."

"Next time it won't happen." Venser said, clearing his throat. "What can I do to make ya feel better?"

"Make yourself useful and get me to the tavern. Now, preferably." She uncrossed her arms and stopped walking, looking up at Venser with the most venomous glare she could muster.

He sighed and held out a scarred hand to Rauri. "Fine. Bedroom or bar?"

"Bedroom, but as soon as we're there, you leave." She took his hand in her own.

Venser took Rauri's hand and the two disappeared in a puff of thick red smoke. For her, it felt like she was being thrown very fast and then stopped abruptly. They slammed down in the silk sheets of his bed and Venser hopped off, walking out the door. He turned and asked, "You sure you want me to leave? I can stay and watch you change if you'd like."

"Out, you pervert!" She threw a pillow from off the bed at his face.

"Hey wait but-" He raised a hand up and caught a pillow with a furry golden throwover in a green aura, and then tossed it back at Rauri, closing the door. "Right. I gotta piss." Venser said with a sigh walking off towards the bathroom.

She groaned into the comfy sheets, shoving herself off them and, unknowingly, rolling off the bed and onto the floor. Her yelp was loud enough that it could be heard by anyone in the tavern. She got up uneasily and walked around the room, looking at the furniture. "Where did I put it... That's not my dress... So many dresses... Rahda, Kail, and motherfucking Marilla..." Ro muttered, swearing to the Island Gods.

After some fumbling around with drawers and through the wardrobe, she eventually found her other change of clothes that she hid away in Venser's room. She quickly took off her skimpy pirate outfit, dried herself off with some of Ven's clothing, and put on a sky blue dress, grabbing a good book she went outside to sit at the bar, bare feet pattering against the wood.

A few minutes later... Venser emerged from the bathroom, revealing that he had trimmed his beard and his hair a bit as he wandered back over to the bar. "Ro?" He asked, looking about the room scratching his stomach. "Oh pussy... Um. Everyone! Shadow tendrils will serve. I gotta go restock." He said taking a few steps onwards the stairs, before looking down to his boots. He sat down and removed them, setting them on top of the table before walking downstairs, and down another set of stairs to the basement.

A female elf of average height with long blonde hair bound up in a braid approached the building. Nuikia Pollux stopped just a short distance outside and took in her surroundings, trying to ensure that she had come to the right place before entering. Her nose crinkled a bit, as the definite smell of alcohol wafted past her on the breeze. "I suppose this is the right place. If I remember the name right. Dragon's Egg, Dragon's Kneecap, Dragon's Body, a lot of taverns with dragon in the name..." She mumbled softly to herself as she walked forward and pushed open the doors. she was welcomed with a rather warm setting. Her felt shoes pattered on the wooden floor as she took a few steps in and sighed, looking around her once more for any people that may be inside

"Welcome to the Dragon's Head Tavern and Inn!" Venser yelled popping up from behind like in a cartoon. He grunted and set a wooden box down on the bar, turning around to restock the bar. "Wait a minute." He said, holding a bottle of wine in one hand, looking to the elven woman. "Well hello beautiful... I've seen you before..."

Nuikia rolled her eyes a bit at the comment, recognizing the man instantly as she began to walk up the steps to join the two gentlemen she could now see at the bar. "So wonderful to see you again, Venser. After all this time." She opted to sit directly in front of Venser. "It did take some asking around to find the place. You left without giving any clue at all as to where it was located. And this is a big continent." Upon closer inspection, she wore a brown hide top that only covered the chest and a waistcloth with slits over the hips, leaving her midriffs and belly uncovered. Along with this, she also wore simple felt shoes, and iron armor plates on her shoulders as well as a bandoleer with many pouches and a quiver and longbow.

"Wonderful to see you too." Venser said with a smile, laying his head and elbows on the bar looking at her. He chuckled and stood up. "Yeah... Um, work called me." He cleared his throat and grabbed a silver cocktail mixer from behind him, setting it down on the bar. He clapped his hands twice and two snakey, shadowy hands popped out from behind the bar. "Restock the bar." He ordered them.

The blonde elf gave him a half-smile back, an eyebrow raising slightly as she watched the two shadow figures appear behind the bar. "So, you told me you'd fix me a real drink if I ever saw you again. Well... Here I am."

"Yeah... Yeah... Really love the outfit you're wearing..." Venser said ogling her body, taking a bottle of vodka from the shadow tendrils. "Grand Marnier and Whiskey Sour Mix." He told the shadow tendrils again pouring some of the vodka into the cocktail mixer, followed by an orange liquid and the whiskey sour mix. "Ice." A third shadowy hand dumped a fistful of ice into it and Venser finished it off with a drop of glowing pink liquid from a vial he kept on his belt. He hummed something to himself shaking it up for about a minute, then poured her a glass of glowing pink liquid. "I present to you... The Pink Footed Booby!" He aid clasping his hands together, setting the drink before Nuikia. When she would taste it she would find it tasted exactly like a strawberry starburst. Only liquid.

Nuikia Pollux smirked a bit, but it didn't last long as she giggled a bit at the hilarious name of the drink she was given. Her left hand grabbed the drink carefully from the counter, bringing it close to her face as her nose crinkled again from the smell of alcohol that greeted her. She had a rather good tolerance to the stuff and did enjoy a good drink, with her heightened sense of smell she normally tended to chug her drinks to get them away from her as quickly as possible. However, wanting to appreciate the drink for what it was, she took a decent sip from the glass, humming in approval as her mouth burst with a lovely taste of strawberry. "I must say, Venser. You do make a nice drink. This may even be a new favorite of mine. Who knew a..."Pink Footed Booby" could taste so good?"

"I know right? I love boobies!" He said grabbing a glass for himself, pouring himself some of the drink. "It should be the house special. It's my signature drink. But the owner has her own signature drink that's the house special."

Nuikia nodded in understanding, and downs the rest of the glass, her nose wrinkling as the liquid nears her face again "Well, I can't agree with you until I've tried more than just this drink. And I must concur, there's nothing wrong with a nice "booby.""

"I think pairs of boobies are better." Venser said, peeking a quick glance at her chest as she sat before him. He picked up his glass and took a sip, some of the glowing pink liquid dribbling down his beard. Upon closer inspection, part of his left sleeve was cut and he was bleeding. "I mean, two are better than one right?"

The blonde elf propped her elbow up on the counter near her empty glass and placed her cheek upon her raised hand as her other hand drew circles on the wood with a slender finger. "Well, I have been with some species that only have one, but pairs do tend to be more pleasing to the eye." Her eyes look around the bar a bit and she notices it's a bit bare when it comes to decorations, but it is still a very cozy place. Her blue eyes landed back on the man's face in front of her. Nuikia observed his emerald eyes, and the tiny slits of pupils inside of them. Eyes have always been her favorite part of a being.

"Ya know, in all the years I've worked here not one like that has walked through this door." Venser said, refilling his drink, looking past her trying to remember. "Maybe... I don't remember." He chuckled. "I have a tendency to get drunk on duty. But I still do one void of a job when I am drunk on duty!" He matched his gaze with Nuikia's, staring back into her eyes. He caught her on this and asked, "Like what ya see here?"

She smiled, breaking her gaze to just look at his entire face instead. "I apologize. I always try to look at a person's eyes when getting to know them. Some people say they are gateways to the soul. That may be true. I feel that eyes can tell a lot more about a person than what they might reveal themselves." Nuikia did notice they barely reflected, as if the snake-like eyes were simply an illusion.

"True, true, very true." He said nodding his head with a smile. "We are getting to know each other." Venser opened his mouth to speak, but then closed it. "Hmm... What can you tell me about yourself? Where do you come from? What's your favorite food? What's your best friend's name? What shoe size are you?"

Nuikia ponders to herself for a moment. "Well, I don't much have a best friend. Not anymore, really. I am not sure where exactly it is I came from, as most of my memories have been...taken from me, I assume. I know not much about myself, as my memory only goes back a few years. Everything else is blank. My favorite food is just about anything with meat. As long as it's juicy. And my shoe size? Small."

"I should make you my blackened alligator sometime. Or... If you'd like to stay the night I can make it for you pretty soon." He said tapping his fingers against the bar as the two conversed. "Did something happen? Hit your noggin and forgot several years of your life? It happens to me all the time, no seriously true story! Along with getting drunk a lot, yeah."

Nuikia looked down at the counter and sighed softly, short pointed ears twitching a bit. "I honestly don't know. The only thing I know about my past.... Is that I live with a curse? Or at least I assume it's one. I wouldn't know how else to describe it..."

"What can you tell me of this curse if you can't describe it?" The handsome barkeep asked, taking a sip of his Pink Footed Booby. "Surely something."

Nuikia chuckled a bit and looked back up at the man. "I can describe what happens to me... But I'm not sure if it was mean to be a curse, or if maybe it is something that..."runs in the family" or something, since I don't know who they are..." She stopped for a moment, thinking to herself how best to say it, and decided to just be rather blunt with it. "I don't know when it will happen or why, but... Every so often my body... Shifts into the opposite gender. It never lasts the same amount of time. For a long while, maybe about a year or so, I never changed back. I was afraid I never would. You see, when I am... A male, I am literally a totally different person. It's as though I live inside his head and can't do anything but scream to no avail. While I am myself, I do not know if he is a "voice" inside my head, fighting to get out like I am, since I don't hear anything... But it is quite terrifying..." Her voice trails off a bit, not sure of what else to say, so she opts for silence.

"That shit sounds serious." Was all Venser said, kinda weirded out by it. "Well, let's just hope it doesn't happen again soon. We have something... Well where I come from originally... Eh it's complicated. Less than yours."

Nuikia's blue eyes showed a hint of sadness, as she was used to people not really.... Having a true reaction to her story. most people never believed her until it happened before their own eyes. "Mhmm...Quite serious." Was all she could say. The air was thick with tension around her, and she wasn't sure how to move on to a different topic. Her mind was now elsewhere, wondering when she might lose herself again.

"No really. I mean it must be... Hard, and confusing for you." Venser said, clear empathy in his voice. He sighed and said, "Why don't I make ya some of my famous blackened alligator? I can tell you're troubled from thinking about it. Oh but I will have to run to the market..." He ran out from behind the bar and began to run towards the stairs, spinning around to face Nuikia while he ran. "Sit tight and don't go anywhere!" He did a front flip over the railing from the second floor and yelled, "Up up and away!" A few seconds later a thud followed by a howl of pain was heard.

She smiled half-heartedly at Venser, his effort at trying to cheer her up starting to work. she tried to shout after him as he dashed off. "You really don't have to go through all that trouble, I'd be happy with another Pink Footed Booby."

Ruari sat at the bar, reading the book she had, thankfully, left at the tavern. She didn't look particularly happy as she flipped through its pages, quiet and lost in the background.

The blonde elf sighed as she realized he was already out of earshot, but as her eyes circle around back to the counter, she spotted the mixer that Venser had made her original drink in. her hand was just about to reach for it when she heard a new voice shout to her right about the drink, so she retracted it and stayed silent. Her eyes peered up from the book, and she couldn't help but notice the drink that Ven had left on the bar. It looked lonely.

Nuikia shook her head, a smile growing across her face as she turned to the other female. "It's okay, between Venser and I, we have already drunk about half of it. I'm happy to share it.

Venser's head popped out from behind the bar, looking at them. "Of course you do. It's practically addicting." He looked at Nuiika and said, "Gimme a bit to cook. I'm also doing sides." He glanced at Ruari and clicked his tongue. "Ruari." He then lowered his head out of sight, disappearing completely.

Nuikia smiled at her and carefully lifted her glass to her lips, her nose crinkling as it always does before downing the drink, but not before thanking the lady for being so kind. "You really didn't have to do that. But thank you, nonetheless."

"Ven is kinda an idiot, isn't he?" Ro asked. A shrug and half a nod from Nuiika.

"Wanna get out of here?"

Venser appeared out of a puff of thick red smoke in the middle of the bar pushing a trolly with a big platter in the morning. "Nuikia! I have blackened alligators for everyone! Oh." He stopped abruptly and looked around for his elven friend. "Where did she go? Uh, Ro? Ro go..."

The young hybrid would make her way back to the tavern a little hunting in the woods. Having been satisfied with her hunt she had decided to return to the tavern which had become somewhat of a second home. Her pelt was black which helped her to lurk amongst the shadows of the night, though it tended to stand out in a crowd in broad daylight. Her eyes still bluish green whilst in her wolf form. Old claw marks stretched across the side of her face and right shoulder and chest. As she approached the tavern, she would nudge the doors open and skulk her way inside before turning back to her human form completely in the nude. Her long brown hair cascading down her back and covering her breasts as her shimmering eyes scanned the area and those already situated within the tavern. Making her way for the stairs and ducking down the hall to Venser's room to retrieve her long black leather coat.

"Lovely!" So far no one else asked for the meal of luxury he had spent a lot of time and effort into so Venser went back over to the trolly and scrounge up a plate of a big piece of blackened alligator, with a side of mashed potatoes with butter and a molten lava center and collard greens.

He glanced over to Rauri and asked, "You hungry? Ohhh...!" He clasped his hands together and rubbed them together. "Selina... Hey. Just in time. Still hungry?"

She was standing up against the wall now, belting the front and looking to the meal before her, pondering for a second.

Venser disappeared in a puff of thick red smoke and appeared pressed up against the wall beside Selina. "Hey good lookin." The bearded man leaned close and asked with a hushed whisper. "Feeling slutty? There was... Where'd she go. A pretty blonde elf I think we could invite to my room together..."

Selina glanced up for a moment as the man appeared before her- "I may have been a bit... Slutty, back in my day, made it far easier to prey upon mankind that way." She licked her lips slightly as she looked directly into his eyes.

"So-" He whispered before straightening up and raising his voice, looking to the rest of the unnamed, uninteresting patrons. "Glad ya love it Ro! Everyone," He pointed to the trolley and platter on it, "Blackened alligator, potatoes, collared greens for everyone! Help yourselves!" He turned back to the rough hybrid and whispered again, "So yes or no?"

Selina raised a brow unsatisfied. "I bite, remember. Although judging by your appearance and vulgarity, I knew you'd probably like that the first time I saw you."

"Mhmmm you know it... So how about a drink? Or a cigar?"

"This early? I suppose after such a rough day a drink would be nice." She gave a slight chuckle nudging him for a brief moment.

"Well it's a good thing I live here most of the time. I only bought a proper home only recently, but I've been leaving it for my other loves and some workers to properly... Cultivate it." Venser said, gesturing to the bar. "So, shall we?"

"We shall" Selina made her way over to the bar and placed her slender frame down upon an empty stool, an eyebrow raised as she continued to judge him with a slight smirk, her eyes glancing around at the other patrons every now and again. Her fingers lightly tapping upon the counter.

Venser wore his usual red and turquoise entertainer outfit with baggy red pants and he was barefoot as he walked around the tavern. His beard was trimmed along with his hair, but it was still somewhat long, and he was stuffing his face with one hand. "So, what'll it be?" He asked as he looked down at her from behind the bar. wiping his chin.

"Anything that's as feisty as myself will do just fine." Selina Nightengalde gave off a wicked grin baring her fangs.

Venser picked up the neglected cocktail mixer filled with a glowing pink liquid and poured her a glass, passing it to her. "Free of charge." When she would taste it, she would find it tasted exactly like a strawberry starburst.

"Thank you." Selina glanced down at the strange liquid for a moment studying it within the glass before bringing it to her lips and taking a small sip, she paused for a moment with a blank expression upon her face. "Well uh, that is certainly an interesting taste."

"Fruity with a kick, with a kick." Venser said, raising a finger up. "So, I really don't think we've talked a lot about ourselves, really. Both of us being more... Ahem. Speaking more, physically." He waggled his thick eyebrows.

"Taverns. the easiest way to get a quick meal, so many easy targets for a start. I tend to be rather nomadic, always going from place to place and never really staying in the one place too long. Human is my main diet though I have fed on other species and some animals if desperate for a good feed. Both my sister and I were turned by a very strong and far older hybrid in attempts to create his own pack, I became an alpha female but was then later exiled after having quite a brawl with the original alpha who turned us. I received many wounds in the outcome, though in turn, so did he and that didn't sit too well with him."

She was Angel's sister indeed, who disappeared often much like Selina. He listened to her life story closely, blinking, nodding here and there and grunting 'Uh huh' every now and then. When she was done, there was a silence for about a minute. "Right. Hot." Venser then leaned forward and pressed his lips against hers.

The rough hybrid woman gave out a deep growl for a moment, pulling away within an instant, getting to her feet and pinning him down on the counter. "I have to say I'd prefer the drink." She'd tease with her lips just before his. "You have to earn this..."

"You sure about that?" Venser asked, licking at her lips when she teased her lips on his, despite being pinned to the bar.

The hybrid woman narrowed her eyes slightly as she looked down at him for a moment before biting his tongue as he licked her lips, her eyes glowing a dark red color giving out another deep growl before letting go and sitting up. "Weak. You'll have to do far better than that." She gave a smirk and got up off of him and off the counter and began to walk away.

"Oh...!" Venser let out a seductive growl and leapt over the bar, running up behind Selina and tackling her to the wooden floor. "How far we talking?" He asked, licking at the side of her neck while he laid on top of her, his crotch pressing into her rear from behind.

Selina gave out a slight roar as he tackled her to the floor, giving out a bit of a chuckle. "You're lucky I have wolf in me and tend to like a little rough play, most women would kill you if you did that to them." She got her arm free, grabbing his and pulling him off her and to the ground before rolling over and ending up on top of him. She'd gently bite his neck playfully before whispering in his ear. "That would depend on what you're willing to offer, a single pink drink isn't exactly going to cut it. Nor a cigar... Not like last night." Selina Nightengale would give off her famous devious smirk.

He moaned more and shook feeling the bite in his neck, wrapping his arms around the hybrid. "Why don't we go back to my room and I can show you what else I've to offer..."

"Are most women you meet usually that easy to get into bed, Venser?" She'd chuckle slightly, sitting upright, pressing herself slightly against his crotch as she looked at the handsome bearded man.

"What do you think?" Ven asked nuzzling her back, his hands running up her sides and her stomach. "You're loving this..."

"Am I just?" She raised her eyebrow slightly at him. "And what makes you say that? For all you know I could just merely be plotting another feed all this time..."

"Well, the fact we're still in this position when you could have gotten up and walked away." He did have her on all fours after all and she was pressing up against his crotch. Venser placed his hands on her hips and gave her rear a few pelvic thrusts to prove the point.

Selina gave a slight gasp before pulling away and turning to face him. "Alright you've made your point, though part of me is still tempted to rip your head off." She laid on the floor for a moment glaring up at him before getting to her feet again.

Venser stood up and offered his hand to her. "Maybe you'll get rough and rip my head off during our fun." He said with a smile.

"I wouldn't count yourself that lucky." Not taking his hand she stood up and began to walk away again, making her way past the bar for a moment and downing the rest of her drink and placing the empty glass upon the center before continuing to walk off. "And I know you are, were my sister's lover. Have you no conscience? Are you a strumpet?"'

"Uh, nnnneehhh. Ahem. My dear. I love everybody. Every woman I come across. Why can't we all just love each other? The world would be a better place if we all did. " Venser appeared beside her, walking along Selina. "Admit it. You enjoyed it." He wrapped his arms around her from behind again. "And you want it... This is you we're talking about... Your own natural desires..."

"Sounds like a strumpet to me." Selina grabbed him, pinning him against the wall. "Don't for one second think you know me that well, and if I go through with this again, don't go thinking we'll be making a regular habit of it. Having wolf in my blood there are times where our sexual desires are heightened..." Her eyes continued to glow as she looked at him with quite an intense, almost predatory stare.

"Even better... Heightened." Venser said with a smirk staring back at her intense stare. He dragged a finger down her finger and said, "We all have an itch that needs scratching sometime."

The hybrid ran her leg slightly up along his, leaning in to pretend to kiss him, her lips only just before his in a teasing manner before parting ways again and making her way to what she assumed was his room, judging by the overall appearance. Leaning against the door as she stared at him with a playful smirk upon her face and a more lustful look in her eyes, hands on the front of her long leather coat.

"Come on Ven. Come earn it..."

CHAPTER TWENTY FIVE: A DREAM OF TEMPERANCE

Several years ago...

A man in his early thirties wearing a red and black suit with a crimson velvet coat appeared out of a puff of thick red smoke behind the bar, with his back to everyone and carrying a burlap bag over one shoulder, a cane with a neatly carved whale handle top in the other. "Goooooood evvvvvvvvvvening patrons! Can I get anyone anything?" He asked taking a few clinking coins from the tavern's payment jar and dumping them in the bag, tossing the cane away in a comical way and completely forgetting about it.

Rec's eyes shifted up towards the man she had seen plenty of times before and she was shocked to see him dressed for once. And like a fancy aristocrat or something. "Evening... A grapefruit beer will do, thanks."

"Gimme a second..." He mumbled, filling up the bag with a variety of coins. Once he was done he set the bag down on the bar and poured the woman a glass of grapefruit beer straight from the tap, then he slid it to her. "Fourrrrr universal silver if ya please." He said as he crossed his arms and awaited the payment. After a few seconds he grabbed a silver cocktail mixer from off the shelf and set it on the bar, then disappeared in a cloud of thick red smoke that quickly disappointed.

As she passed through the human town, most just stared at the rather large structure of the passerby covered in armor. Most assumed it was a man based only on height and she never removed her hood to let them see otherwise. In her experience the humans of Vorland did not tend to like out of the ordinary individuals, but they were even more puzzled when nothing seemed out of place except the woman's height. Temperance continued her long stride hurriedly through the streets and towards the forest where she hoped she could find the tavern and get herself a drink. Her horse was trotting alongside her, the reins in her hand as they maneuvered through the forest. A sigh of relief escaped her lips as she spotted the tavern. She unharnessed her weapons and left them with her horse, Titan. The armored giant gave the beast one long stroke against it's soft neck before pushing open the tavern doors and stepping in. The smell of liquor in the air made her chest already so warm. She still remained completely covered, she preferred to get a feel for the environment before showing her face. And her face currently wore no emotion, even as she requested a good bourbon and sat down at the bar, struggling to adjust and sitting a bit awkwardly once settled.

Rec rummaged through her belongings and slid over the payment to the man before grabbing at the cup and bringing it to her lips. "Thank you"

"Welcome to the Dragon's Head Tavern and Inn!" Venser called from the kitchen. He always seemed to know when someone new entered. He reappeared behind the bar holding a bottle of rosewater in one hand and a bottle of grapefruit juice in his other. "Oh you're a tall one. Ordinary bourbon? Coming right up." He said to the hooded woman in the banded metal armor glancing right in her face for a second. Her hood reminded him of the one he once wore. Heh. "Three silver." He said to the woman passing her a glass of bourbon, he then snatched up the payment from Rec and tossed it into the tavern's payment jar.

The half giantess preferred her bourbon 'ordinary' she never had much of a test for anything mixed. She was strong like that. Temperance only nodded when he confirmed her order and reached into her pouch to pull out five silver and set it on the bartop and pushed it his way in exchange for her booze. She says nothing until it is in her hands, "Thank you." Those were the only words she said and her face remained expressionless. A light amount of sweat covering her apparently fit body, the parts of flesh actually visible.

Leaning her elbow onto the other side of the bar bar, Rec traced the rim of her glass with her index finger, a soft hum erupting from the touch. Biting her lip, she would turn her attention towards the window and the few stars that could be seen from where she sat.

The sharp dressed bartender passed two silver back to the hooded woman. "And there's your change." He looked over to the payment jar, then slipped one of the gold coins into his coat pocket. "Two for Roselie... One for me..." He tossed them lazily into the payment jar and still made it in.

"Yes!" He mumbled to himself making a fist pump movement.

Temperance had just noted the two coins still in front of her. She had been told it was not wise to leave out a tip, otherwise things could be tampered with. "Excuse me," her words were smooth as they left her expressionless face. "I did not mistake my payment. I always leave a tip." She stated it in the most simplest of terms before pushing the coins back and then returning to her brown colored liquid.

He cocked his head at the hooded woman, then glanced down at the coins. "Very well then. I have kids to feed anyways." He replied holding up his left hand, his mark glowed bright greenish white and the clinkey coins were trapped in a green aura. He then pulled the coins towards him and caught them. "Need anything else?" He asked as the shadow tendrils set down a cup of black tea in front of a timid woman patron.

"One more thing, if you don't mind." Again, nervous. "A large piece of meat, raw and very bloody" She gave the biggest smile she could muster.

"Very very rare. Bloody." Several seconds later the shadow tendrils manifested themselves in the form of a snakey, shadowy hand and dropped a plate of very rare meat in front of her. "Three silver, two for the tea one for the meat." The man blinked a few times then leaned in. "Hey, don't be nervous. You're in good company here. I'm handsome. See?"

Rec picked up the glass and downed its entire contents in two large gulps before placing it back on the bartop, pushing it forward towards the barkeep. She rummaged through her coin purse once more and slid over another twelve silver for the drinks and six as tip before turning her gaze to Ven. "Keep them coming dear, for it's going to be a long evening."

The half giantess enjoyed the mindless chatter around in the tavern that didn't matter much, her face would not show it but she did very much enjoy it. She turned her head to now study the others that were in the tavern as she had always been an observant individual. She felt no threat which eased her mind and relaxed her shoulders. Even when sitting she seemed tall when she stood she was seven feet tall. She tried to hide her awkwardness but it could not be consumed behind the hood. Temperance could feel the nerves of the woman beside her and she wasn't certain what she was even nervous for. She shrugged to herself and finished her amber liquid pushing the empty tankard away from her. "Another please, when you have a moment."

"Easy pay tonight..." He muttered grabbing the coins, stuffing half into his pocket and the other half into the payment jar. Then the six coins into his pocket, and the other six into the payment jar. "I agree stranger. It's a quiet night, and a slow one as well. I could be in No Name Port right now watching a show or getting fucked." He passed another glass of grapefruit beer to an old familiar patron of his. "Here. That'll make things easier." Venser turned his attention back to the neglected bottles he was going to use. He filled the silver cocktail mixer half full of Grand Marnier, and the other half full of grapefruit juice. He added to dashes of rosewater and then began to shake up the contents while watching the timid woman eat.

Rec snatched up the glass among her empty ones on her insistence and hogged them like a fat kid would hog a cookie jar. Her mouth widened in a large grin as she thanked Ven before guzzling the sweet liquid.

Temperance was getting overheated in her wears. She used both of her hands to remove her brown cloaked hood and finally relax enough to fully show her face. "If I could get another drink when you have a moment, it would be most appreciated." She asked for a refill on her drink. Her face wore strange markings, and her hair was a deep brown short pixie cut. Her eyes were wide and noticeably different colors as well, one green and one blue. Confident and mature, her body spectacularly muscular and athletic while not sacrificing a single drop of femininity, despite being mostly covered in armor.

"Coming right up." Venser said pouring the dark orange purple drink into a martini glass, he set it aside for himself then refilled the hooded woman's glass of bourbon. "Got a name, miss?" He asked, looking her over. She had such a pretty face. Despite the scars and overall roughness of the tall, armored woman.

"Temperance Dathuer, though I do not have much." The name was given to her by her father and she often was referred to as Tempey or Temperance. She offered a small smile and then placed her dues on the bartop for the bourbon and took a long and slow sip of her strong liquor. "And your name?"

"Temperance, lovely name." He replied leaning up against the bar, holding his martini glass full of dark orange purple liquid. He sipped it and said, "Venser. Karr-rrkaldwin. Sometimes Venny, Ven, My Little Vensie, VenVen. Whichever you may prefer. That's mah name don't dragggggg it out."

The half giantess only smiled softly, again taking another swig, hand reaching up to push back her shaggy, unbrushed hair. "It's a pleasure to meet you Venser." She stated, "You can call me Tempey, most do. Especially in taverns when speech gets lazy and my name seems long." She smirks.

"Alright then. Tempey. What brings you to our cozy little tavern tonight?" He asked with a half bored half tired look on his face. Then again, this look was stuck on his face for some time lately. After a few seconds a small smile began to appear on his handsome visage.

Rec placed her cup upon the table and sheepishly smiled up at one of her friends, her dull green eyes twinkling in the light of the tavern. It was apparent the grapefruit beer was making its way to her head and she leaned lazily onto the table with a sigh. More background chatter.

"For the same reason anyone walks into a tavern," Temperance began, "my particular poison is bourbon. So I suppose I am here for bourbon." She lets a small smile sketch it's way upon her lips. "I ended up here after not having much luck in town just a ways down the road. They don't take kindly to women of my height it seems. I know I'm intimidating."

"What exactly are you, Tempey?" Venser asked, leaning forward a bit. He appeared to be any ordinary human, early thirties, grass green eyes, coal black hair that was brushed off onto the side, and fair skin. If one looked close enough, there were faint lines running from his lips to his ears in the form of a smile and he was clean shaven. As if he had scars that were being covered up. On the back of his left hand he had the black mark of some cultist symbol, and on the back of his right hand he had a brand burnt into his skin of the letters, "RG" with several scars running through it. Indicating he tried to erase the brand.

The half giantess smirked, speaking up a bit more, "An abomination if you ask most." She laughs lightly. "I am only certain of the giantism, as that was what my father was." She only remembers her father fondly, "My mother I know nothing of. Most assume human, and others have many many stories of her." She explained. It was unlikely her mother was human, she had too many non-physical features that didn't seem human or giant. "And you? You are human, yes?"

"I am indeed very human. Mother was a human, father was a human. I think, yeahhh." Venser replied, examining Tempey's unique features. The unnatural features of him he usually hid via makeup and trickery. The mark and his brand, he did not typically hide, as the alien mark was the source of all his magic. "Maybe I am. Maybe not. Maybe more."

"By the void, where I come from giants, dragons, those things are merely myth. And magic, looked down upon. Few use it. And those who do are always persecuted."

"Well a very extraordinary human then." Tempey stated and again turned to her amber liquid swirling it around before lifting it to her lips and she smiled as she pulled the glass away from her lips. "So I am only a myth then."

"If you were in the Isles people would just assume you have gigantism, some genetic disorder. But the marks on your face... They'd be skeptical of those." He replied. "They'd mistake you for some sort of witch. If you were in Pantia though, they wouldn't care."

"Well you come from some intriguing places, I might have to visit these Isles some time, " The half giant laughs lightly but only jokes. She knew what she was, and witnessed what her father was for the longest time. "Most places tend to just stare at the large humanoid woman in clanking armor."

"They always do. They also stare at men who have a large smile carved into their face and eyes that looked like they plucked from the skull of a snake." He chuckled and took a sip of his cider he had set aside for himself

Temperance nodded, "Anything that is slightly out of the ordinary." She finished what was left of her straight bourbon and grabbed payment for another, "Another, when you have a moment." She pushed her glass away.

"On the double." He grabbed a metal tankard from off the shelf then dunked it into a barrel full of the glowing blue liquid, then teleported over to a man he knew as James and set a Blue Lagoon down on the bar. He then poofed in a cloud of thick red smoke and reappeared in his original spot. A dim low watt bulb went off inside Venser's head. "Ah ha!" He exclaimed, snapping his fingers, he trapped a bottle in a green aura and pulled it towards him, then set it on the bar in front of Tempey. "Where do you come from, Tempey?"

She pulls her bourbon into her hands and lifts it to her lips to take a slow sip, enjoying every bit of flavor the liquid had. Her ears slightly twitched at the question. "Well that is not a question that I can answer," she began, "My father and I never stayed in one place too long and most of them I do not remember." She stated and bit her lower lip slightly as she often did in thought. "You see my father was a giant, and giants love money and royals like to pay giants to be a part of their army. So wherever there was coin is wherever we went. He never swore loyalty to anyone."

"Just another traveler huh?" Venser said. "A soldier's daughter, so no wonder you moved around so much. Well, mercenary... I know what the merc life is like."

"Not just a daughter of a soldier, a soldier myself." She states. "Now I was nowhere near the size of my father, but where he lacked in strategy I made up for it. I've followed maps, planned attacks, and even fought when kingdoms and countries will allow women to do so." She explained. "Nonetheless yes very much of a traveller. Now that it is just me and I do not have my father's hunger for money I am a wanderer."

"Brilliant, not just one to charge in without a plan." Venser drank down the rest of his cider and set down the martini glass. He set it next to all the other dirty glasses then grabbed a clean one, and a bottle full of sparkling green liquid. "Just a wanderer with no particular goal in mind?"

The half giantess smiles, "Well it was all for my father because he would just march in at the front lines where they kept him. My way for keeping him as long as I could." She laughs lightly, "Yes I suppose, I learn much from wandering."

"Heh. I never knew my father here." Venser replied, sloshing his drink around in his glass. "Can I interest you in a glass of Elksback Cider, Tempey? You'll love it, I'm sure."

"Well certainly you must have known someone important to you, at some point, where you would do whatever you could to protect them." She stated and then tilts her head slightly at his question. "I usually just drink whiskey, mostly bourbon, cider is mostly fruity. Are you certain I'll love it?" She smirks.

Venser couldn't help but let out a half insane cackle, similar to the way he used to laugh. It was very brief and he smiled widely, glancing down at the RG on the back of his right hand. "Once. Heh heh... I have two babies, Soarin and Lucinda. And they mean the multiverse to me." He grabbed a second glass and poured Tempey some Elksback Cider, smirking as well. "If you aren't a fan, you will be. On the house."

Temperance noted the woman who plopped back into a bar seat and offered her a smile. "Why are you so certain that I will like this?" She smirks holding up the glass, questioning whether or not she even wanted to taste it.

"Are you not a fan of fruity drinks? If not I can offer you my favorite drink. Which I know you will most certainly like." Venser turned his head to Rec and said, "Need a refill or anything, miss?"

"I despise fruit flavors in drinks," She smirked lightly. "I wouldn't want to be rude and turn down this cider but I assure you I cannot control my foul face if I do not like it." She explains to him.

"Foul face? Very well then." He took the glass back and set it off to the side, then grabbed a dark red bottle from beneath the bar, hidden next to Winter's secret stash of her personal Dragonfire whiskey. He held the bottle in front of Tempey and explained what it was. "Kupid Red. Nicely aged brandy, rare Pantian spices... Interested?" He showed off the bottle to the timid woman as well. "Actually, I got something special from my personal collection... No no." He put it back and disappeared, only to appear once again holding a different bottle.

"Marchant's Steller Bourbon. Never opened, and I usually just save it to show off.'"

Pop!

He popped the cork and refilled her empty tankard, the rich scent of nicely aged bourbon with hints of sweet vanilla, charred oak, and smooth tobacco filled the air before Temperance Datheur, causing her to give a rare, genuine smile and feel truly special.

The half giantess now had rum in front of her, she did so enjoy bourbon more than any drink. However she did not have the tolerance of a giant for liquor just the tolerance of a soldier who drank heavily. She only gave a chuckle, "Well thank you kindly, Venser, all these drink offers and I may not be able to stand if it continues." Taking a swig, her smile only widened.

"Enjoy that slowly, along with other drinks? Switch on and off?" Ven suggested, trying to make it last the entire night.

"This is wonderful bourbon. Never had anything like it... Thank you." The half giantess smirked with the fine liquor to her lips and nods. "Sure that I will try." She smiled sweeter now. She was way more relaxed then when she first came in, though that was surely due to the drinks she had been drinking or given.

Venser poured Tempey a tall glass and slid it to her. "This is pretty expensive stuff too. Worth every coin though! "On the house. I'm in a generous mood.

"Well I certainly hope it is, if it is as expensive as you say." She smirked before lifting it to her lips and taking a long and slow swig. She let it sit in her mouth for a moment as she swished it around to really taste the flavor. She swallows and her belly warms. "This is quite exquisite."

"Indeed. After a day of work, fucking about, I often enjoy sitting in my smoking room just reading, drinking a bottle of Elksback, and smoking a Kullero cigar." He turned back to a patron who called for red wine and smiled.

"Right, and yes, my name is Venser." The handsome barkeep looked over to the stairs and called out, "Welcome to the Dragon's Head Tavern and Inn!" Once the man had reached the bar he nodded and poured the man a glass of red wine, then set it down in front of him. "That'll be three silver... Alright, thankie doodles."

"It does not sound like a bad end to a day's work." Tempey said. She then turns to the woman next to her and tilts her head slightly, "So is Rec short for something?"

Venser pocketed half the coins and the other half went into the tavern's payment jar. "Thank you kindly. Excuse me for a second." He grabbed his bag of coins from off the bar, which included his weekly pay and everything he had tonight then disappeared in a puff of thick red smoke.

The regular patron politely told the woman "Yes Rec is short for Alirec, however I found it too formal and preferred to go by Rec instead, giving my tom-boyish behavior." At this she gulped again from her glass, coming to its end once more.

"Ah yes Rec, you are much like myself I see." She noted her wears and the short sword at her side. Temperance always carried at least some form of weaponry just the heavier stuff she left outside.

Back in his room inside the tavern, he made his way past the mannequin which held his old red rubber suit with rubber nipples and a comically oversized codpiece, past his bed, past the twin's cribs, and set his loot of coin down on his desk. Intending to sort them out later. He took note of the many dresses that littered the floor near his wardrobe, they were beginning to collect a thin coat dust. Venser really needed to put away the dresses. He then teleported out of his room and back behind the bar. "And done! Back just like that!" The handsome barkeep looked down at his mark, the stranger symbol glowed greenish white and emitted steam. "So helpful... I've heard that the teleportation spell is the hardest to learn on Laguna. But for me, it just comes naturally. Just like my charm!"

Temperance jumped slightly startled by his sudden appearance behind the bar again. She only smirked at how ridiculous she must have looked, and how most of the patrons just kept to their own little groups as if him poofing around was a regulated occurrence. She slowly sipped on the bourbon realizing that she had lost count of which drink she was on. This was not a new circumstance for her.

Rec chuckled before raising her glass to the woman and sipping gracefully.

"The glass is easily replicable. Not like it's Roselie's fine porcelain... Or the time I got drunk and decided to hammer nails right into the bar for no reason." He said with a small laugh recalling the memory. Oh, he was... Wild when drunk. He recalled the time he had he was serenading Ione, a billion year old shadow demon and mother to one of the barmaids at the tavern, naked with a guitar covering his crotch. Which ended with Ione smashing the guitar, splinters in Venser's crotch, shocked looks from the fellow patrons, and the shadow demoness storming off.

"Very true but you are the one who spoke of your tom-boyish behavior. That is all I am comparing." She also raises her glass and takes a long slow sip only to realize that her mug was once again empty. She sat there in debate on whether or not to order another drink, and noticing the unremarkable red wine patron try to flirt with the Rec, offering to buy her a glass of wine too.

"Trying to get laid?" He asked, noticing the red wine patron offer to buy Rec a drink.

Tempey looked up from the bartop shocked that yet another person had ordered her a drink. She only smiled when Rec slid the bottle her way and she held up her mug, "Well thank you much," She was now a lot more smiles and giggles, although she did still try to contain them. However as soon as she had the sip in her mouth she spit it out in laughter at Venser's commentary on the woman's generosity to the gentleman.

"Want me to wet your whistle huh?" Venser asked, taking a random woman's cup. "Not a sexual thing by the way. Unless you wish it. Right right... What'd you have again?"

"Hhppht!"

Bourbon. Everywhere.

"May I get a rag or something, it seems I've made a mess of my laughter." Tempey explained looking to Venser and then to the spewed brown liquid on the bartop.

The handsome barkeep held his hand out behind him, trapping a rag in a green aura and pulling it over to him, and then set it on Tempey's head. Then poked her nose. "Boop!"

Her mismatched eyes would cross as she tried to follow the finger that poked her nose and she scrunched her nose. "I just asked for a rag, no need for that." She stuck out her tongue before wiping the bartop in front of her.

"And a rag you got." Venser decided he wanted to get roaring drunk. He wasn't watching Soarin and Lucinda. So he felt he could do as he pleased. It had been rather complicated to learn to care for children, being quite new to it he preferred to get away for now and go to them when he was ready.

"I'll have another of your... Merchant Steller Bourbon?" Tempey asked and then turns her attention to Rec, "I did not think that was something you'd give up so easily?" She smiled playfully.

Rec smiled sheepishly and she brought the rum back to herself. "Normally it isn't. But I'm quite buzzed myself however seeing that no one is talking to me I suppose I'll go back to my greedy and selfish ways and keep these for myself." At this she would snatch up the bottles and wander back to the table in the far right corner

"Marchant! Guy who made it. A merchant named Marchant? Ha!" The handsome barkeep was quick to snag up several empty tankards and glasses, quickly filling them all up in a swift manner, with a helping hand from the shadow tendrils. "Bam, bam, and bam kablamo!"

The half giantess smirked lightly, adjusting in her seat. "Well I never said to leave my side by any means," she called over to her with a playful pout that she had wandered away. She then looked to Venser's rapid refillment and clapped her hands lightly, "Impressive barkeep."

He smiled at Tempey. "I'm the best barkeep here. Been working for about five years now. Started as a barback, now I run it most of the time."

A small smirk played delicately on her lips, "Well it shows," she smiled at him before sipping the exquisite brandy. "So what made you decide to work here in the first place?"

"My dear friend Thorn, who is like a sister to me. A hot sister!" Venser replied tethering a dirty glass over to him and a cloth, he then began to clean the glass while looking at Tempey. "I've been coming here for sometime, drinking away, being social. Sometimes it was just Thorn running the bar all alone, and Roselie would work the poor girl to death. So I started off helping her, then as her substitute so she could relax more. Now it's full time.."

Tempey was starting to struggle to focus but she listened and she listened well. "Oh, right... Well what a good friend you were." She smiles softly before taking another sip of her drink. "Are you happy in this establishment then?"

"Oh yes, very." Venser smiled and leaned forward against the bar. "This is my favorite place. Pretty much home to me. Seconded by The Hole In The Stall. Well. Lately it's been a tie between The Hole In The Stall and The Witch's Wiggle... But I'd say, ya know, the first one. Been going there for years and years and years."

"I'm not sure I know of those places, or if I want to know." Tempey chuckled lightly and smiles at him, her mismatched eyes glittering with interest. "Well this place here though is a fine establishment." Her upper body swayed in her seat slightly using the bartop to catch herself, laughing.

"I'm sure you can guess what those places are." The handsome barkeep chuckled as well then disappeared in a puff of thick red smoke and reappeared next to Tempey. "If you'd like I can rent you out a room, give you a place to rest after a long night of drinking."

"You can sleep in my room." Ven blurted out without thinking. Maybe he did think for a second. Yeah, totally.

Temperance very well knew what those places were by the names of them, being rather on the nose. She jumped again as he disappeared and reappeared it follows with a fit of laughter. "Oh my, there you go again startling me. I've never actually seen that before today, despite how well traveled I am." The half giantess couldn't help but laugh more with him, listening to his offer of a room and then his room. It had been such a long time since she had laughed, and even longer since someone had asked to be alone with her. "I suppose staying would be the responsible thing to do..." Her voice trailed off, "And both of those offers sound favorable." She gave a playful wink.

"I'm down the left hallway... Sixth door on the right." He said with an arrogant smirk and a low, seductive growl. Venser then drank down his cider and started another. "Drinking on the job... Oh fuck my cock I meannn... Yeah! Too much temptation Tempey baby."

"Well now." Temperance said in response to his seductive growl and she shook her head lightly as her scarred face deeply reddened. "Though I may be sleeping right here, I'm not sure my feet will carry me, and I'm not yet done." She laughed lightly and finished another drink. She waves her empty glass in front of the Venser's face. "Ohhhhhhh bar wench," She teased requesting another.

"I'm not done either. And I'll gladly carry you if I have too." Venser laughed a few more times and took the empty glass from her, then grabbed the bottle of Marchant's Steller Bourbon and filled it to the rim. "Let's just get completely smashed..." He raised his own glass of brandy. "So here's to it!"

The armored giantess smiled wickedly at his toast. "I cannot think of any better way to spend my eve then completely smashed with a dashing barkeep." Towering over him in her seat, she sipped her dark liquid still enjoying it's flavor.

"A wickedly handsome- Hic! Barkeep." Venser said, raising his voice, starting to feel a little bit tipsy. "Let's just get ourselves another bottle of the regular..." He muttered grabbing one from behind the bar and setting it down. "Whoop!" It nearly fell over but it was caught just in time and kept in place. "Ughhghghgh fuck my ass with a loaf of bread... AHEM! The shadow tendrils will serve while I... Ya know, with this fly honey."

A few patrons rolled their eyes, and shook their heads and Venser's foolishness as the shadows manifested themselves into physical shades that resembled the man himself, watching over the patrons of The Dragon's Head and expecting them to order.

Temperance giggled at his obvious signs of being drunk but she only smiled to herself as she tried to keep her posture straight. However she was failing miserably as she swayed in her bar seat. "Oh how could I leave that part out? Foolish me." She smirks

"And what other better way would a wickedly handsome barkeep be spending the evening with a tipsy, beautiful brave strong traveler woman? Hic!" Venser asked, almost accidentally knocking over the bottle again, he lifted up his right hand and began to trail his pointer finger down the side of Tempey's face. He always did have a thing for women taller than him, especially the strong ones. He did so admire strength. His eyes taking in her features, her heterochromatic eyes, broad, clear forehead, firm chin, and a kind smile despite the scarring on her face. Ritualistic, he assumed by how some of them were patterned.

"And you have scars, I have scars... So..."

"Well aren't you charming as well," The half giantess said with a smirk, taking another sip she rested a large hand on the bartop to keep from swaying. When he touched her she jumps lightly at first but then smiles as his finger trails down the side of her face.

"I get that often..." Venser said scooting a bit closer to Tempey, brushing back some of her hair so he could fully see her face. "Handsome, thoughtful and considerate. A little good, a little bad... Bit of both. Very desirable..." He gave out another seductive growl and asked, "Do- Hic! People often compliment you regarding your- Hic! Your- Hic! Shexiness... Yeah this... Routine.."

Tempey studied him with both of her eyes, one which was green and the other a soft pale blue. She only smirked at his drunken mannerisms. She laughed very much amused as he pulled back her hair and was talking about his desirable self. "I'm usually seen as freakish, in the areas that I have been. Though, not so much in open battle..."

"If only they could see what I see right now..." Venser said, lowering his voice a tad, he raised his left hand and grasped her head with both hands, stroking the other side of her face with his other pointer finger. His grass green eyes locked onto Tempey's mismatched eyes and he gazed into them longingly for several long seconds.

She was not used to all of this touching, it was an oddity to her but then again she didn't seem to mind it even as he stared at her for a moment. "You are much too sweet." She smirks and raises up her mug once more, "To getting smashed."

The handsome barkeep arrogantly smirked back and raised his half full glass. "To getting smashed. And to this lovely day and lovely night." He clinked his glass against Tempey's then took a heavy swig.

When their glasses clinked, Tempey managed to spill most of hers and she looked slightly distraught that it had fallen out. "The sadness of the good liquid on the bartop, and parts of my outfit, and the floor." She looked to all of these places. "Perhaps we drink something cheaper after this bottle." She giggles swaying a bit too far, she had to catch herself with her hand on Venser's shoulder. "Oops." She smiled at him.

"Heh heh whoa there- Hic! Hic!" He draped an arm around Tempey's waist and pulled her close to him, noticing his arm barely went around her. "Don't want you- Hic! Falling out of your seat now... What shall we drink next? This shit used to burn the shit out of my throat when I was younger... Ooh! How about the tavern's strongest drink? Like, whoa."

The half giantess giggled as he wrapped his arm around her waist and pulled her close to him. "I was going to be just..fine." She smiled brightly. "That sounds like the best worst idea ever. Let's drink the strongest. Hit me with your best shot, oh bar wench."

"Still." Venser disappeared in a puff of thick red smoke and reappeared next to a barrel beside the bar. He held up his left hand and his mark glowed bright green-ish white, then began to emit steam. Two tankards floated over to him in a green aura and hovered in the air, he made them hover closer together then dunked all of them at the same time into the barrel full of glowing blue liquid. "Here we are. Blue Lagoons.."

"Oh my it sounds fruity." Tempey scrunched her nose as she accepted one of the drinks. "I suppose I'll hardly taste it at this point anywho." She shrugs lightly and throws the drink back only to realize she had drank it all in so few sips.

"Mhm!" Terribly fruity, though it did hit her harder than straight bourbon. She curled a fist and slammed it down with a loud thud into the wooden bartop.

"It is fruity... I'm not such a big fan of this either... Toooooooo fruity! But still, damn strong." He took a heavy swig and let out a deep sigh. "Kinda- Hic! In this drunken state... If ya don't drink it. Then- Hic! I'll make ya Tempey..."

The half giantess smiled sweetly down at the five ten bartender, "I'd like to see you try, but it seems I've already finished it."

"Like to- Hic! Like to- Hic! See me try huh? Very well then..." The handsome bar-keep drank some of the Blue Lagoon, got up and knelt in his seat, and then locked his lips with Tempey's, then allowed the strong, fruity drink to flow into her mouth.

Temperance Datheur was startled to say the least, her mismatched eyes widened and once she sipped it all down she was more shocked than anything. "Oh my..." Was all she managed to say, she was very awkward in these situations.

"What do you think?" Venser asked with a smile, holding his tankard in one hand.

Surprised, clearly. He took notice of her clothes, some parts were stained with the drinks she had spilt. Drinks had been spilled on the bar as well, Venser was gonna have to clean it when he could.

"It's not terrible." She confessed. She follows his gaze and also realizes the messes that have been made. She only giggles, "Look what you've done bar wench!" She exclaimed and held her long arms out wide at the mess before them.

Venser shook his head and gibbered slightly. "The shadow tendrils can clean it." Upon hearing it, a snakey shadowy hand shot out from behind the bar, grabbed a cloth, and began to wipe down the bar. "Now... Look what we've done to your armor and those cloth parts. I think we should get you out of them... And get you a good rest after a long day of travel..."

"I'm sure you do, but you see I do not have any other clothes. I left them on my horse and I'm not sure walking down the stairs is the best idea right now, oh bar wench." Eyes glancing over at the shadow thing clean up the bar's mess.

"Oh Tempey. Clothes are a prison. That banded metal, metal bars. You don't need em..." Venser said leaning forward, slurring now. He nuzzled his head against hers.

She leaned part of her weight against his head trying to still hold herself up. "Then I suppose you won't be needing yours either?"

"Fuck no!" He laughed a bit and put his arm around her waist again. "Oh... You would not believe the times Roselie has yelled at- Hic! Me for bartending naked. Or getting drunk and expsosing myself to the patrons... Hic! Sides... I'm not the one who spilt, all that ya know, over her outfit."

The half giantess smirked yet again, "Well you kept serving me so you are partially to blame." She giggled and shivered lightly as his hand kept feeling her up. She pushed her forehead against his lightly nudging her nose against his cheek.

"Welcome to the Dragon' Head Tavern and Inn..." He mumbled hearing the front door open. Venser moved his head to the side and buried his face in her neck, then with one tried to grab his nearly empty tankard of Blue Lagoon.

Tempey watched closely as he reached for the nearly empty tankard and she nudged it just right so that what's left of it spills onto bits of his clothing. "Oops, look what you've done now." She laughs.

"This suit was made by the Royal Dressmaker of... Urp! Sugablahblahomsi-yahanna... Gonna have to get out of it and something clean..." He mumbled before he began to kiss and suck on Tempey's neck, letting out another low seductive growl and nipping just a bit.

Unusual for herself, the armored traveling warrior, Tempey giggled and squirmed at the kisses on her neck and smiled as he spoke. She leaned towards his ear and whispers, "I don't feel bad if that's what you're trying to go for."

"The opposite my dear, shexy Tempey... Trying to make you feel good now... Real good!" The handsome barkeep whispered back leaving a small bruise on the left side of her neck. His vision began to blur and he slurred more. "Hic!"

Tempey smiled again, and glared at him when she realized he had left a mark. "You rarely behave, don't you?"

"No... Hic! I don't..." He gazed at Tempey longingly, examining her body, all it's curves. Perfect breasts. Well, judging by the way she carried herself and the armor she wore, she had to be strong and healthy. And the height... Tall women were the best. "Ya know... I think some of Angel's old dresses will fit you... She was a pretty tall girl too. Well like... Eh they'll be short but like... Yeah!"

The half giantess swayed in her chair smiling at him. "What are we still doing at this bar? You said you live in one of these rooms?"

"Indeed." Venser stood up and offered his hand to Tempey. "Allow me- Hic! Allow me to show you to my quarters."

Tempey stumbled off of the chair but luckily had his hand to grab lightly enough not to drag him down on accident with her inhuman strength. Though soon she grabbed his entire arm to feel more structured, "Please do."

"You gonna be able to walk? Bah... Lemme save the walking... Hold on..." Both of them disappeared in a quick cloud of thick red smoke and reappeared down the left hall in front of a door with a crude replica of his curved, pointed helmet kept around for an outfit he planned to put together, but instead became a mere decoration. Some parts of the door were discolored, due to Venser getting drunk too many times and throwing various bottles of liquor at his door. He pushed the door open with one hand and the helmet fell onto the floor. "Gonna have to renail that later..." He mumbled stepping over it and into his room.

Tempey wasn't sure she liked his methods of transportation but she couldn't help but giggle with all the smoke. She grasped the wall to walk in and she smiled softly, "You're messy." She turned to him with a bright smile drawn upon her lips and her eyes lit up. She swayed again and caught herself on the wall giggling again. "You should have cut me off bar wench.."

Venser's room was fairly big. A queen sized bed lay by the windows, and it was covered in turquoise silk sheets and he had about a dozen pillows all with furry gold throwovers. The royal colors of his homeland. Off to the left was a wardrobe with a few dresses hanging out, some spilt onto the floor. Beside that was a mannequin with Venser's original outfit. To the right of the bed was a desk with a bag of gold in it, a mirror, and a few pieces of jewelry and some small boxes. Right beside it was various papers and pieces of art. Above Venser's bed was a multicolored painting of a woman's vagina, and below that his signature double bladed sword, the Dual Personality that he had just retired, seeing as cool as it was to fight with a double bladed sword, he needed one hand free for magic.

"Oh come on... People are a lot more fun when drunk! Ha ha!" He took Tempey's arm and pulled her into the room with him, using more strength than usual due to Temperance being one mighty glacier.

She studied the room and some of it was very comical to her, other parts of it seemed slightly dark but she wouldn't speak of any of it. She was surprised to be pulled into his room so rapidly, she swayed and stumbled in catching herself on him once more. "So sorry." She smirked and studied his face again, knowing she would never forget it soon enough.

A cocky smile on his face, he brushed his hair back and teleported around the half giantess again, using one foot to slam his door shut and then making a back hand motion at Tempey, hitting her with a gust of wind and pushing her back, and she voluntarily fell onto her back in his bed, the frame creaking just a bit, climbing atop her and letting out a moan. "Excited?"

The blood was pumping at twice it's rate through the half giantess's body as she could only give him a nod of affirmation. This was the kind of touch she had not been used to for a long time now. She smiled up at him as her back laid against his bed.

Venser smiled back and removed his tie and his coat, tossing them near his mannequin, noting he would wash them later. Beneath his shirt he was muscular, and barrel chested. With slight claw marks running up and down his chest. Directly to the left of Venser's bed, stood a nightstand. And on that nightstand was a long white feather that glowed whitish blue, illuminating the room in a beautiful light. Venser walked forward and bent down by Tempey, then locked lips with her yet again.

The alcohol, the lighting, and the handsome barkeep were all so intoxicating she felt overwhelmed but she still wore a truly happy smile. Was this a dream? She watched and studied him as he removed his coat and tie, she said nothing, just watched, mouth slightly agape seeing his barreled chest. When he bent down by her and pressed his lips against hers once more she smiled again before pressing her lips back firmly against his.

Venser planted kiss after kiss onto Tempey's rosy lips, each one ranging from soft and gentle to rough and quick. He wore a very happy smile as well, his hands running across her tall body, undoing the cloth fittings of her armor to remove it.

Temperance Datheur shivered underneath him, she felt his hand run over her hot body. Her lips remained locked with his as she matched each of his kisses, the smile never leaving her lips.

CHAPTER TWENTY SIX: GETTIN' DOWN SOLID

Venser's bedroom, The Dragon's Head Tavern and Inn, Vorland, 1438 ATC

Ruari lounged around on silk sheets, reading one of her many books she collected while traveling. The particular book she was reading wasn't one of her favorites, as it was about religion of the world, and it was boring her to tears. Somehow.

"All right, I think I'm done with this..." She muttered to herself before tossing it over her shoulder and letting it smack against the wall and fall to the ground with a thud as she spread her legs out.

As Rauri lounged about in Venser's bed, the door to his room opened and the man himself saunted in holding the hand of a very tall woman with very long black hair and demonic orange eyes. "So we did miss it..." He said to her before squeezing the woman's hand. "But... Ceirra?" He moved behind her and wrapped his arms around her waist and stood on the tips of her toes, kissing her on the cheek from behind. "Are you up for some fun?" He looked around her and to Ro.

"Are you? My succubus lover has come all this way to retrieve me so... I'm talking about gettin' down solid before we head out baby!'"

The tall temptress smirked when Venser held her from behind and laughed. "What in Laguna are you dragging me into now? I enjoyed the surprise but...." Her voice trails off when she sees the tanned woman. "Woah. You didn't tell me she was gorgeous. You're forgetting things again."

The olive skinned elf giggled at the compliment, her freckled cheeks lighting up with a fierce blush, taking note just how high pitched the other woman's voice was. "Well, I'm not all that but..." Ro grinned happily, the gap in-between her teeth clearly visible now, her voice now trailing off. "All right, I'll join. Just... Promise me we will not do anything towards religion."

Venser let go of Ceirra and hopped onto the bed beside Rauri, giving her a quick kiss on the cheek. "Of course you'll join..." He nuzzled her head and looked to the succubus while he undid his entertainer tunic, sliding it off to reveal his barreled chest and toned stomach. "Ceirra, now she's... Words can't describe." He said, his voice trailing off as he looked over her body, admiring her long lustrous legs and the bright red dress she wore that exposed the navel. "Better than any woman at The Witch's Wiggle..."

The tall temptress smirked walking over to the two. "Gorgeous elf. What more could a basic sex demoness like me ask for? Words don't need to describe, let her actions tell me all I need to know." She winked at the elf. "Didn't get your name, sweetheart."

"Aha... Ruari. Just Ruari... What's yours?" She grinned widely, the blush on her cheeks spreading and becoming more vibrant, brushing back her curly burgundy hair. "And I would be more than happy to prove my worth, ma'am..." The islandic elf kept her tone respectful, if laced with joy.

"Why don't we start by getting these clothes off?" Venser asked, moving behind Rauri, sliding down the straps of her night dress, patting a spot on the bed. "C'mere Legs... Legs, fun little nickname for her."

"Ceirra Dusk. Legs as he calls me like now... Ahem. Ma'am? Ven... I swear if you told her my status... I'll kill you and keep her and all your other lovers to myself. Ruari. Ro-ohhhh reeee." She chuckled softly sitting on the bed watching him strip Ruari.

Ruari let him undress her as he wished until she was nude, keeping still on the bed. "I assure you, he's done nothing of the sort." She slid out of her dress easily enough, exposing her new, elaborate and beautifully colored tattoos.

Ceirra leaned over and traced the designs, her burnt orange eyes looking over them. "Beautiful. Your body is simply beautiful." She smiled trying to resist the overwhelming urge to trace the lines with her tongue. For now...

"C'mon. All three of us can share with each other. I mean, wouldn't be the first of course..." The handsome bearded barkeep said scooting over to the six foot succubus. He locked his lips with hers and kissed her gently, raising his hands up to undo the front of her outfit. After planting a few kisses he moved around behind her and latched onto her neck, sucking and kissing on it while getting Ceirra out of her red dress.

The islandic elf moved behind the woman, helping Venser rid her of her clothing and suck marks into her neck. "If I'm beautiful then you, my dear, are a goddess."

Ceirra shrugged her shoulders letting the soft fabric fall down to her waist revealing her plump breasts. "You know how that gets me going." She eyed Ruari seductively and gave into need. She gripped her hair and pulled her into a deep kiss.

"Oh yeah... That's hot..." Venser said, sliding out of bed, slowly licking the side of the succubi's cheek behind her now as she and Rauri kissed deeply. He inhaled sharply and grasped her plump breasts, fondling them while his groin rubbed up against her rear. Ceirra would feel something stiff and familiar poke her from behind as Venser tugged on her nipples and continued to suck on her neck, leaving dark spots in certain places.

Ruari relaxed into the kiss soon enough, giving as good as she got, moaning into the kiss and grabbing ahold of the other woman's hair for something to hold on to. When she broke the kiss to regain her breath she took hold of Ceirra's hand and moved to rest on her small chest. "You can touch me, ya' know. In fact, I rather encourage it." She told the woman, moving forward to go in for another kiss.

The tall temptress welcomed the second kiss with passion. She gripped her breasts massaging the globes as she grinded her ass into Venser moaning softly.

The handsome bearded man slid down her dress and was careful sliding it down her legs, lifting them up a bit and tossing the dress aside on the floor. He put his hands on Ceirra's's sides and thrusted against her black silk panties, his baggy red pants had an obvious bulge to them. "Hmmm..." Venser stood up and moved in front of them, to be in between them and began to slide his pants down, allowing his throbbing, rock hard member to spring free. "Ro, should I be on the bottom or the top?"

"Hmm... I'm good with either, sir." She spoke, her voice filled with giddy laughter. "You can choose for me... Unless Legs has something in mind, of course." The islandic elf brought a heavily tattooed hand down to touch herself, not bothering to be gentle at all. "Do you have anything in mind, dear?"

"Which do you prefer?" Ceirra smiled sweetly, dipping her hand down to touch Rauri's womanhood, using her fingers to stroke her crotch. "Guess it's good I have more than one hole then... I don't think Ven has ever stuck it in my ass."

"I'll have one of you ride me then." Venser said, licking his lips, before quickly leaning forward to lick at Ceirra's and Ruari's. "Me on the bottom..." He looked to his succubus companion. "You riding me." He turned his attention to Rauri. 'You sitting on my face, this is going to be fantastic. Bam. I have spoken."

"Ah!-- Mnh..." Ro moaned softly at the stimulation, thrusting shallowly and slowly into the hand currently giving her pleasure. "I like that idea, Ven..." She responded, biting into her lower lip. She reluctantly pulled away from her hand, instead moving behind the woman, prompting the handsome bearded man to trade places with her, sitting up in the middle of his bed and watching them both.

The tall temptress rose up and pushed Ven onto his back before crawling over him. She was soaked already and had a feeling she wouldn't last long. She never did when she was as full as she knew she was about to be. She bit Ven's neck as she grinded her wet pussy over his cock.

"Ah...!" Venser groaned in pain and chuckled, smiling as he raised his left hand and trapped her black panties in a green aura, swiftly pulling them down as her bare, wet pussy rubbed up against his cock, gently teasing the lips.

"Get these off... Gonna bone you like a chicken cutlet..." Venser mumbled.

He pulled Ceirra Dusk down on top of him and kissed the spot right beside her lips, looking back to Rauri before looking back to the orange eyed succubus. "You two ready?" He asked with an arrogant smirk slowly pushing himself in.

"Nnngnn...!" Impaling herself upon him, burying every glorious inch of his fat dick into her cunt, she gyrated upon him. not caring about taking it slow and bringing her ass downwards, causing Venser to take off and start plowing the tall temptress hard, the sounds of her thighs slapping against his pelvis filling the air.

"Oh yes, sir..." Ro watched as the two fucked in front of her, rubbing herself to the sight. The islandic elf swiped two fingers around her lower lips, using the wetness to slick her fingers.

Ceirra moaned arching her back as he pushed inside of her.

"Mmm." She looks back at the elf. then back to Ven. "Fill me completely..." She leaned forward exposing her ass to Rauri. She bites her bottom lip waiting a bit impatiently.

"Tsk... So impatient. Maybe I should just sit off to the side and watch you two the entire time, instead..." Ro joked, shoving the slicked fingers into her asshole. "But then again, I wouldn't get to have any fun, then, would I?" She began thrusting the fingers in and out, watching with a hungry gaze.

Venser ran his hands up and down Ceirra's body as he kissed her softly as she bounced up and down on his dick. "C'mon Ro... Quit teasing the girl and come sit on my face already..." He said with a soft moan slowly tracing a scar on her side.

Ceirra moaned arching her back, letting out a high pitched squeal. "Fuck.....Mmm. More. Gods it feels so good actually." She dropped her head and placed her hands on Venser's toned stomach for support, clenching around his shaft.

"Ah... Gods above, woman..." Ruari cursed as she thrusted completely into her. She brought a hand around her body to rub at the woman's clit as she fucked her, adding to the pleasure while watching from behind.

Impatient, Ven just moaned out again, "RO just sit on my face already. Gods, fuck me..."

"Alright," Ruari rolled her azure eyes whilst playing with Ceirra from behind, "since you asked soooooo nicely..."

The islandic elf moved around on the bed and hovered her dripping snatch to his mouth, making herself comfortable and looking at the tall succubus across from her, her breasts bouncing up and down in front of her. Ro gasped as Venser began to eat her out. She wriggled and ground her cunt against her friend's mouth, her breath coming hard and fast as she felt Venser's tongue enter her.

Ceirra smiled at the islandic elf and leaned over to kiss her hard on the mouth. "Mhm you're lovely..." She kissed down her neck, her tongue gliding over Ruari's small chest and stomach, enjoying her soft, light brown skin.

Ruari smiled back at the succubus with burnt orange eyes and nuzzled her face against hers, before kissing her deeply, pressing her hips down and smearing her wet cunny over Venser's face, covering it.

Ceirra gasped and moaned into Ro's mouth as she felt her pussy being stretched open. Oh how he had many, many points of stamina in the bedroom and actually kept up with the succubus. Once Venser had worked himself all the way inside of her he began to pump in and out of her again. In tune with this thrusts, he plowed Ceirra with reckless abandon for what seemed like forever. Though, it was moments like these where time didn't seem to matter. Only the here and now.

The tall succubus was getting close to popping already as Venser continued his work beneath her. Ro was leaning on his shoulders making out with Ceirra and moaning into her mouth as the tall temptress bounced up and down on his lap. Ruari was getting so turned on at the moment that she even briefly considered letting him fuck her rather than simple oral pleasure, but she quickly pushed that thought out of her mind. For now, she ground herself harder onto the handsome barkeep's face and continued to wriggle about.

At last, the islandic elf felt herself peak, screaming in pleasure as her whole body tensed up and the flood gates opened into Venser's waiting mouth. He greedily drank the offered liquid, even as his face became drenched in Ruari's fluids. The sight of the pretty elf cumming on his face after he ate her out nicely was enough to push him over the edge as he pumped his load into Ceirra's cunny.

"Mhmmm...!" Painting the succubi's interior with his hot, sticky baby batter before going still underneath the two girls, finally worn out by his lover's efforts. Though, the previous night had been a rather fun one. And the one before that. Nearly every hour maybe. Ro rolled off of Venser's face, and the three spent a moment collecting their collective breaths in silence, the handsome bearded man had a girl on each side of him and admired them with his emerald slitted eyes.

Wordlessly, they all cuddled up together in bed not minding the dampness coating each other's bodies, rather, basking in each other's sweatiness...

They could clean the love juices off later, for now a nice nap sounded wonderful. As he dozed off in the loving embrace of Ruari and Ceirra, Venser sighed in contentment. When they awoke, all he really had to do was lot up all the coin he had and then... He considered a simple carriage ride, but he'd just teleport all of them back home so he could see the rest of his family after about a week or so.

Actually, maybe a carriage would be fine. So they could all be wildly screwing one another, like rabid animals in heat on the road to Villa De Karkaldwin.

Or maybe teleportation so they could meet up with all the other women he lived with on his farm?

Tough choice, as much as he loved choices.

CHAPTER TWENTY SEVEN: PRYLDAHNIAN ICE CREAM

The Dragon's Head Tavern, Vorland, 1438 ATC

Sanna held Rowena in her arms as she babbled and waved her arms, giggling up a storm as she tickled her as they sat at a table at the Dragon's Head. Happy to visit the place where they had met again.

"Gotcha, gotcha!"

Sanna laughed along with her as she waited for her lover, grinning as she was excited about the love of her life taking them for ice cream for a little family outing. Not the whole family, as Ceirra insisted she stay with Alex and baby Asher who was feeling under the weather. The twins were with their mother Kari, and her sister in arms Marvella.

The door to their room opened and Venser himself stepped in wearing a long crimson jacket, a waistcoat, a cravat and black pinstriped pants with fancy riding boots. It was nearing the end of the afternoon and getting into the evening for them and the weather was fair. "Sorry about having to teleport you and Rowena all over the damn place... When we were home in Pryldahn we could have just taken a carriage into the city. I'm sorry I insisted we come back for this old suit and a few other things..." He sighed and adjusted his tie, walking over to them and kissing Sanna on the lips, and then their baby daughter on the forehead. "Ready to teleport?"

"You don't have to be sorry beloved. I don't mind the teleporting, I think it's fun!" She chuckled as she kissed him back, Rowena making a kissy face at him as he kissed her on the forehead. "Mhmm. All ready." She straightened Rowena in her arms and held tight, taking his hand.

"Rowena... Not too sure now that she's fully awake now." He nuzzled Sanna's head and sighed, squeezing her hand and wrapping his arms around them. All three of them disappeared in a puff of thick red smoke and reappeared in the Ten Traders district. There certainly were shops, but bars and eateries abounded and most importantly of all, a creamery that the rich, nobles from all different parts of the world and even the God Queen herself fancied. "I always teleport us to this alley..." He muttered looking out of it. Not too busy today.

"Have you ever had ice cream before, Sanna?" He asked tugging on her hand as they walked. "Common where I come from... Other places have never heard of it. And here, they used to send runners up to the mountains until they figured out how to make it with cryomancy became a big thing. Good for business..."

"Like, imagine having the capability to use and learn magic... And you use it to make frozen treats rather than use it for healing or battle." He rambled.

Rowena squealed, eyes as big as dinner plates and clung to them both as they teleported, whimpering a little but settling down with a gentle shushing from Sanna. Soon she settled and they both looked around, seeing the alley and she tilted her head a bit at the question. "Honestly no, I haven't," she answered as they walked, holding his hand. "I've heard of it before you told me about it back home." The golden gypsy was wearing a simple black gown and their baby was playing with the lace on the front of it.

The handsome bearded man stopped for a minute to admire a poster of himself on the wall of the right of the alleyway, his handsome, confident mug on the front of it and above the words, "Karkaldwin's Fine Cannabis" above it.

"Heh. As I said, aside from my home everywhere else it's either non-existent or luxury for the elite. He led them out of the alleyway into the streets of Capital De Seraphim.

"I was going to bring Soarin and Lucinda but their mom wanted to take them training with her and Marvella. Already..." Venser cleared his throat and said, "Little nice family outing... Ya know? Lucinda has cryomancy like her mom... She would make a killing here., especially from the tourists."

"Ah, I see... Why training? They're still so young..." She asked, frowning a little in worry. Rowena babbled some more and played with the lace of her mother's dress, nuzzling against it and pulling on it. She chuckled and gently unhooked her hand from her long black hair, cooing gently to her that it was nothing to play with. She looked at the poster and tilted her head, reading slowly. "Can... Canna...bis? What in the world? Selling this to the whole world?"

"Just in case... Not kidding. She's the protector of the village and all..." He sighed and shook his head. "I don't want them to grow up to be warriors. I want them to be whatever they'd like... Though I suppose, yeah the exercise is fantastic. Let them be athletes for the Grand Games maybe. Good place to sell..." The handsome barkeep looked back to the two and smiled warmly watching Rowena play with her mother's dress.

"And we want the same for our little girl, don't we?"

"I know. That's what I would want for them too. Of course! I don't want her forced into a fate she doesn't want... She should be happy." Sanna smiled softly and kissed her little girl on the head. The little baby grabbed her mother's face and gave a sloppy kiss to her nose, causing her mother to laugh.

"Reef restaurant, best in town uh huh..." He said, glancing to a rather large building across the street. At the creamery they stopped at several other merchants and their own families, all wealthy were sitting out on the balcony chatting amongst themselves.

"Why don't you take a seat, I'll go in and order?" He asked. "Dunno if you have a..." He stopped himself there and sighed.

"If I have a?" She asked, tilting her head.

"Preference for flavor... Compared to home, the stuff they have here is... Lacking." He cleared his throat. "Variety. But... Here ice cream is in its infancy."

"Oh, I see. Well, what flavor do you like?" She asked. "Maybe I'll like it too."

"Vanilla, custard, lemon, honey, hazelnut... And that's pretty much it. And then topped with fruit like cherries." Venser answered. "If I were to list all of the flavors from back from... Ya know, we'd be standing here all day."

Sanna laughed softly and nodded in understanding. "Honey sounds lovely."

Venser leaned in and kissed Sanna softly again, nuzzling her head, his beard brushing up against her face, and reached out to give their baby's tummy a little tickle. "Be back soon..." He entered the building fumbling about for his purse.

The golden gypsy blushed darkly and kissed him back, nuzzling him in return and placing a quick kiss on his cheek before he left, while Rowena giggled and waved her arms out for her father. "Take your time."

It actually wasn't even five minutes before Venser returned with a metal tray with three metal bowls atop it. He sat down at the table and set the tray in the middle, setting Sanna's ice cream in front of her. Which was nothing but vanilla ice cream drizzled in honey and rose water with a few slices of apricot. Venser himself got custard. "Pretty much all the same thing. Just eggs... More expensive..." He rambled, tipping a spoon into Sanna's ice cream, though, only the tip and some of the back of the spoon. "I know Rowena hasn't had ice cream. But what about you, my love?"

Sanna chuckled and shook her head. "Never before." Sanna looked at her bowl and grinned, dipping her spoon in and taking a little into it, lifting it to his lips. "Want a bite?"

"First, I think Rowena should have her first ice cream." Ven said, offering the spoon to their baby daughter, a bit of the honey and vanilla standing at the tip.

She nodded in agreement as Rowena opened her mouth and ate the small spoonful, making a face at the temperature at first but then grinning like crazy at the flavor going "mmmm, mmm" in a babble.

"She loves it!" The handsome bearded man smiled and looked up to Sanna, then back down to Rowena as she babbled and wiggled her little arms out at the spoon.

Sanna grinned and nodded, laughing as Rowena tried to eat the bowl now, babbling and squeaking.

Venser laughed heartily with Sanna and dipped the spoon back into the ice cream, offering the tip of it to Rowena again. The sun shined down upon them and it was a rather nice peaceful day in the city. Not too busy, not too loud. Just... Rather peaceful.

She ate the ice cream at the end of the spoon as Sanna tried some herself, moaning softly at the taste and grinning. "It's so cold, but so sweet."

"That's the idea. When I was young I got cravings all the time... And can you believe some places ice cream doesn't even exist?" His smile weakened for a split second, but strengthened again seeing Sanna have her first taste of ice cream as well. He leaned across the table and pressed his lips to hers, whispering softly, "Not as sweet as you."

"I wish they knew that it existed. This is fantastic!" Sanna grinned, pressing her lips to his in return and nuzzling him gently.

"Venser... Would you marry me?"

Those four words hit Venser like a train. He froze for a few seconds and smiled weakly, nuzzling her head. "Shouldn't I be the one asking you?" Venser loved Sanna, that was true. But he had other matters to discuss with her before marriage. Even though it had been on his mind for some time...

She flushed and chuckled softly. "Sorry, love...it just... Kind of came out..." She was red in the face, biting on her lip and she nuzzled him softly. Either way, officially married before the gods, ceremony or night when Sanna was with Venser she was happy. So happy it almost hurt

"I love you."

Venser kissed her on the forehead and wrapped his arm around Sanna. "I love you too Sanna. So so much... I'm sorry we haven't been able to spend much time together lately on account of me traveling for business and running the tavern and spending time with all our other loves and kids... And yeah."

She snuggled into his arm and kissed his cheek. "You know I don't mind, my love. I may miss you, but I know you'll always come home. I know you're always with me, and I know that you love us both very much. You work so hard to provide for us, and I can never repay that my love."

"You do with love and affection." He said snuggling into Sanna closing his eyes. "And that is all I ask for..."

Rowena snuggled against them both and cooed, and Sanna smiled warmly snuggling into him. "Thank you. You both are my world... And I'd love to keep broadening our family, to be your wife officially... It's honestly what I dream of."

"Sanna?" Her lover asked with a hint of concern, opening his snake like eyes to look at her, his eyebrows lowered.

"Yes?" Sanna asked, tilting her head.

The bearded man let out yet another sigh and spoke slowly with a more serious tone. "You know I love you. And I can't imagine how perfect our wedding would be but..." Venser paused and swallowed before he spoke, speaking more clearly. "You know I have other children with other women... So... By the void this is hard..." He rubbed his temples and took a few more bites of his ice cream. "What if I married you and other women too? How would you feel?"

Sanna smiled warmly. "I would love them as much as I love you, even to the point of considering them my sisters or even wives if they like that. As I already do you know... I would consider them a mother to our children just the same, and I would love you even more for having so big of a heart. You truly amaze me." She kissed his cheek as she took another bite.

"You would even though to other's it sounds almost despicable? I mean I told you multiple marriages is common in Pryldahn..." Venser said eating more of the ice cream too, offering another bite for their little girl. But at the same time not making eye contact with either of them. "You know... With sex, and love and ..." With his free hand he made awkward hand gestures and he wasn't too sure where he was going. "I think in the end it's all about love and family. Like," He paused and put on a mocking voice, "These women are stuck loving this one person who has several other women loving him too when they could be loving someone else."

Their baby daughter took another bite and cooed again at the taste as Sanna listened and chuckled at the mocking voice, nodding in understanding. "I don't care what others think of us. I consider it an honor, a treasure to be with you. Whomever you choose to be with, I will love with all of my heart."

"Even if I were married to three or four girls along with you like all at once?" He asked, his smile growing a bit more as he wiped honey off of Rowena's face.

"Yes." She smiled warmly as Rowena babbled in agreement, or so it seemed.

That was true love right there. Venser held his face to Sanna's and looked into her bright, intense green eyes with his own emerald slitted ones, looking over her beautiful features. He set down his spoon and raised his scarred hand, placing it on her cheek. He tilted his head to the side and felt her breath against his, before kissing her as softly and sweetly as the night they had met.

Sanna of Krimeakhet felt the same as she looked into his slitted eyes with her own intense bright green ones, resting a hand on his cheek as she returned his kiss while a happy tear slid down her cheek. She remembered how they had kissed the night they met and smiled warmly against his lips, sighing contently as she snuggled them close.

"It'll be a full house soon..." He chuckled as their lips collided, biting her lower lip.

Sanna blushed with a soft moan and grinned at him evilly. "Yes, yes it will... But I'm going to enjoy that."

"Not mentioning the servants or the... Hired guards who watch over the fields." Venser added. "And there was something else I was going to mention... But... Eh."

"What's that, love?" She chuckled, tilting her head.

"I travel a lot between the tavern and Pryldahn and the farm, which isn't too far from here, and Wicked Port but... I've been wanting to travel more. Explore, adventure, raid tombs! Travel time and space. Ya know? But... Family obligations and business... And I mean, Brea and Kira the tavern when I'm not there." It almost sounded like he was rambling now.

She listened as he talked and Rowena began babbling back as if speaking to him too, causing her to chuckle a little at their daughter. "How about your up and coming business?"

"Yeah and... Hire more, need to find more coin... Part of the time, or handle things in Wicked Port like warehouses and such when I'm not there." Venser replied, he finished his ice cream and held his hands out. "May I hold Rowena?"

The golden gypsy grinned and happily handed him their daughter, who proceeded to reach out to hug his neck with a squeal.

"There's a happy baby." Venser said holding Rowena close on his chest, rubbing her back. He sighed and said, "I wonder..." He looked to Sanna and said, "Living in an estate as opposed to living in a gypsy carriage, or a tent with your gypsy family. And with a few other siblings and servants and other mothers..."

The golden gypsy smiled warmly at the thought, nodding gently. "I think that would be wonderful," she answered as Rowena cooed and rested her head on his chest, eyes drooping.

"What do you think she'll grow up to be? Being raised way differently than either of us." Venser said, rubbing her back still.

She tilted her head. "If we have our say, anything she wants to be. I'd love for her to dance, though." She chuckled softly as Rowena fell asleep on her father's chest.

"Yeah... A dancer like her mother... That would be nice." Venser said holding their daughter close. "Shall we go home now? Well, I mean the tavern since the bedroom and the nursery is still being renovated at the estate..."

She nodded with a grin and stood, setting up her empty bowl next to Venser's as their daughter slept soundly. "That would be very nice. What would you like to do once we get home and get her put down?"

"Just lay in bed and enjoy each other's company? Just... Embrace it for as long as possible before I have to run the bar or speak to the Guild of Merchants again here in the southern part of the city. I'm out on my own right now with a cart and posters and that's it but... Taxes and advertising and all." He suggested.

"I would love that. It's been so long." She said softly as she kissed his cheek, relaxing as she stood in front of him. "Sorry for blurting out that question. I know you probably wanted to ask when you were ready, it just...came out. But everything I said, I meant. I love you no matter what."

"I love you too, Sanna." He said looking down to kiss Rowena on the forehead. "And our child too... So so much..." Venser extended his right hand for Sanna, getting ready to teleport.

The golden gypsy smiled warmly again, taking his hand, and in response he leaned in and kissed her.

Not a hard kiss, not a rough kiss or a hungry kiss. Just a simple loving one. He started off slow and gentle, brushing his lips against hers, their hearts beating rapidly as they sat with their lips locked together.

CHAPTER TWENTY EIGHT: CEIRRA'S BITE

Venser's Villa, The Farmlands, Pryldahn, 1438 ATC

It was a beautiful day in Pryldahn.

Not that this surprised him in the slightest. Just about every day in this world was nice.

The villa and farmland Venser had bought was quite grand as it was built from fine stones and marble. The long painted white columns decorated the entrance's exterior and a long white stone staircase led to the double door entrance to the massive house. Inside the villa had a waiting room at the entrance which had a fountain of a large breasted naked woman with dragon-like features holding a large, world shaped egg above her head, this being Seyr, the fertility goddess and one of The Trinity, and a few stone benches open to the air. Upon further exploration there was a closed parlor with luxurious seats and other comfortable blankets the family shared and behind the estate a rather large hedged off private family garden.

The second floor contained more parlors and bedrooms for everyone, as well as Venser's study where he collected various items. A grand balcony overlooked the private garden as well.

It was rare for Venser Karkaldwin to still be sleeping at almost noon. Even if he was drinking heavily the previous night or having fun he always seemed to be up at ten AM at the latest. Despite the last few days were rather relaxing, discounting him trying to do paperwork for the Merchant's Guild, with God Queen Y'vonne, and talking to various farmers for advice.

The handsome bearded man wandered around the property, dressed in nothing but his baggy dark red pants and bare feet as he watched the sun reach its full height and the birds flying high and mighty through the clear blue sky. He sighed and leaned up against the wall of the villa, scanning the horizon of the tall cannabis plants that grew in the field. He had hired a few mercenaries to patrol as well as a few local laborers and he had planned to buy a few elven slaves later on. He sighed and smiled a bit, looking over all the land he had bought so far. The farm, the massive house was his, and would be passed on to his lovers one day, and their children, and their children's children and beyond.

Then a familiar, high pitched female voice rang out.

"Good morning, love." Ceirra Dusk chirped, choosing to wear a cloak and hood over a simple black gown to protect her face from the sun.

"Good morning Legs." Venser replied. "Close to afternoon... But still morning, yeah."

He stretched out his arms and yawned, rotating his shoulders. "Sedna is due to come up here by carriage and bring Elanaea with her to meet all of her other siblings and see the place. Ugh... Gotta clean up and figure out what to do before fall and winter... Gotta use up as much cannabis as we can... Like, make as many cigars as we can and store them properly and hmm... Make some snuffs. Snuffs will sell well. Yeah."

A cool breeze blew the tall succubus's long, straight black hair around her face as she stood before him and listened to Venser ramble. She was not in love with him but drawn to him in a way she could not explain. Or was it truly love? Ceirra wasn't honestly sure. But she did know for sure this man stirred something inside her. She needed to feed from him, entice him, be with him. And the rest of his family, the other women he slept with and lived with, she just felt so... Comfortable.

Then he leaned up a bit to get face to face meet the succubus's lips. The two shared a gentle kiss, followed by a couple more and Venser reaching both hands around to grab her rear, in response she stifled a giggle. While Ven was five eleven, she was six foot exactly. Not much of a height difference but it was still there.

"Such an excellent kisser..." The tall temptress uttered. "Your lips are some of the softest mine have ever touched."

Sanna and Kari passed by with the children and also looked quite happy at her acquiescence. Not quite as happy as the kissing king that was walking around showing off his nipple rings, but happy nonetheless.

"Come on sweeties, lunch time!" Kari spoke up, wearing a rather large sun hat on her head while holding Soarin and Lucinda's hands, the little black haired girl bounding as they all walked.

"Eats! Yay!" Exclaimed the little white haired boy Soarin as he took off running to inside the family villa. Venser chuckled looking past the succubus to his wives and children as they went inside. Baby Rowena babbled in her mother's arms and seeing her father she waved her arms out to him, and Sanna kissed their little girl on the forehead and turned to face her beloved, offering him a simple, loving smile before following Kari and the little twins. Alex and her baby son Asher were already inside.

"Come come love. Your father will join us soon..."

He leaned forward again, ever so slightly and pursed his lips, eyes closed. He could feel the warmth on his mouth, obviously Ceirra's breath, and then a set of puckered lips made contact with his.

Despite being a blood sucking demoness, she was quite gentle with him and his other loves. The softness of her lips made him so pleased. For a brief second there was a stronger gust of wind, Ceirra's long raven hair billowing about her like some wild halo.

As the succubi race are meant to dine on love, to seduce men and women to sustain themselves from their life energy, though Ceirra had no malicious intent towards The Karkaldwins and genuinely enjoyed being with Venser. Especially for kissing. Of course their various body parts would likely be better evolved for sappiness. The perfect romantic predators, made for intimacy and affection.

"Mwah!"

The exaggerated noise that Ceirra made beneath the hood caused the bearded man's cheeks to color brighter, yet brighter as her kiss tugged at his lips.

The succubus let out a low growl and her canines began to sharpen supernaturally, biting his power lip a bit to barely draw blood.

Then, before he knew it, she pulled away, leaving you with the faint phantom feeling of her addicting lips still on his. Ceirra only looked down to him with a wide smirk, a mixture of pride and joy on her face, bright orange eyes looking him over, and she couldn't help but grab one of his nipple rings and giving it a light tug.

"So?" Ceirra Dusk asked with her signature high pitched voice. "What did you think? More? After lunch we can do it right outside in the fields..." The shadows beneath her hood made her burnt orange eyes seemingly glow as she stared at a spot on his neck. "I will want some of your blood soon..."

"You know I'm always up for it. Every square inch of the property, in every room..." He said, taking notice of the tall temptress's gaze at his neck, craning his head so she could get a better view. "After all... Isn't that the goal?"

"Yes it is Ven... And thank you, for all of this. For letting me live and love you and your family." Ceirra replied. Then she gave him a genuine one. Truly, she was honored. It wasn't often people opened up to her and let her into their lives, let alone into their family.

"Our family." He corrected me.

"Our family... Mhm." She responded, giving him a wink. "I've barely woken up, after all. Just like you."

"So, before lunch... Go ahead and drink me. A little appetizer right?"

A soft moan escaped Ven when he felt her lips brush against his jawline now. Ceirra's lips descended his neck, leaving soft kisses, and chills when her fangs sometimes brushed against his willing neck, looking for the sweet spot.

A tiny drop of blood trickling down Venser's lip, an intended cut caused by having been lost to the kisses of a succubus who had four sharp fangs. Ceirra admired her own work for a few short seconds.

"Well, what are you waiting for, Legs? Just take a bite... You know I like being bitten." His arms tightening around her waist.

Ceirra paused for a few more seconds, and then leaned down and bit down on Venser's neck, her fangs sinking as her own demonic magic began to work on him. He had been a magnet for her. And now just like a moth to the flame she would follow him.

A tidal wave of pleasure and pain that collided into the handsome bearded man. He could feel the succubi's hands holding onto him in return, and the pain in his neck was a very vivid effect he had on anyone she bit.

"Ahaha... Mhmfph that's good Ceirra..." Ven mumbled as they stood there near the fields and she gently sucked his blood, savoring his sweetness.

After several long moments her fangs extracted themselves from her lover's neck, and emerald slitted eyes met her glowing orange ones. Oh how she adored his lovely greens.

"I'll see you inside, Ceirra? I'm gonna have a bit of a walk around before I go and eat."

The six foot tall succubus nodded and smiled, grasping the bottom of her cape with both hands and using it to wipe the blood off of her mouth and chin.

"Before I do, we need to clean you up." She said wiping off his neck with the bottom of her cape.

"Hold on..."

Keeping him in place just as her lips found the four fang marks she'd left on the bearded man's neck. She smacked her lips and worked up a lot of saliva, licking at the bloody holes and they began to heal back up.

"Ahhh... Amazing. This is why you should come along with me when I decide to go out and adventure, Legs. You can be the healer and the uhhhh, ya know. Fight when you can."

Ceirra shook her head and stepped back.

"Yes, my saliva can heal small cuts and bits. And I'm not much of a head on fighter you know. Maybe I'll consider it one day... I'll think about it over lunch."

And with another smirk, the succubus kissed Venser on the check and began to saunter off towards the family dining room. eventually wandering out of sight.

CHAPTER TWENTY NINE: ABOUT THE ROSARIANS

The Nursery, Villa De Karkaldwin, Pryldahn, 1438 ATC

"... I think it's because I was pregnant for two years, Venser. That's fifteen months of extra development. I'm not surprised that she's extra bright, and can use magic already. Plus, I had been travelling for almost half the pregnancy, so I had to take medicines that would make me impervious to seasickness, and my family's blood allows us to fully control our metabolism." Sedna Rosarian tied her ebony hair back in a simple braid and looked at Elanaea playing with her baby half sister Rowena and half brother Asher. The daughter Sedna had with Venser had bright, grass green eyes and long black hair, and wore a crystal bracelet on one wrist that blocked her from using her unstable baby magic, the Rosarian bloodline was strong with Elanaea.

"Venser, what is it that makes your children so happy?"

"Musta been really shitty... Carrying her for over a year whilst hunting for the Dragon's Head and a few other places. And I didn't know for a while, kinda... Well, it's complicated." Venser Karkaldwin said relaxing lazily where he sat on the floor, legs crossed.

"Lots of love, getting out and doing stuff, not letting any tempers come to me or anything, teaching them about life. Ahem, I know it's kinda frustrating... Having them here, and then in Montpelier, and then the tavern... Just moving all around."

"Venser, I carried her even after I gave birth. All mothers do. And no, I didn't even know I was pregnant until I got morning sickness, which was about... I can't remember." Sedna sighed and looked at their daughter.

"I don't know what to do. I thought she was happy with me, but now that she's with you and her other siblings... I'm not sure she can go back to living with me alone anymore. How are we going to raise her if you are the only one who can make her truly happy?"

Venser's head shot over to her, and he rose up and sat beside her on the couch. "What? You make her happy, you're her mother! Her brother and sisters make her happy. Ya know," He paused and let out a sigh, turning around in his seat to point at an intricate red and yellow advertisement with Venser's handsome mug on it. The words, "Karkaldwin's Fine Cannabis" in the text above it. Plastered in his own home, pretty much every room, of all places.

"Venser, it's not the same and you know it. I just feel like if I let her stay with you for a while, she'll have a well-rounded childhood. I just want what is best for her, you know? I know it's hard to believe, but we have a child together, so maybe we need to nut out how we are going to raise her. Together. Not, 'she lives with one of us while the other just visits.' She needs a home where both of us are present." Sedna looks over at the advertisement. "Are you serious? Your chin doesn't look like that. Why'd they make it look so squared? Why do you have that in here and I hope to god your children don't know what cannabis actually does."

"Sort of. I've told them never to chew on the crops or anything. And well... It's good enough." Venser shrugged and then held up a finger, shaking it a bit.

"Yes that's exactly right! Which is why both of you should move up north and live with me and the rest of the family on uhhh... Here. Villa De Karkaldwin! Yeah, that's what I'm calling it now."

Elanaea turned her attention away from her baby siblings to her parents seated nearby, and she attempted to stand and walk towards them, but knelt down and began to crawl towards them, babbling happily.

"Allow me, Sedna." Venser got up again and picked up baby Elanaea, sitting back down beside Sedna. He lifted their daughter to his shoulder, patting her back gently. "Hey there... That's a good baby... Happy baby." Slowly, she rested her head on Venser's shoulder, hiccuping every few seconds, one of her tiny hands trying to grab at his beard.

Sedna leaned over and kissed Elanaea right on her cheek. "Mommy loves you, my darling. You be a good baby for your father and... Your extended family."

Venser nodded and nuzzled her little cheek. "You're going to be so happy here with us. Both of you."

Elanaea closed her eyes with a content coo as her parents watched over her.

"Yes. I've been meaning to speak to you about that..." Sedna said letting out a sigh, sitting up and adjusting the light hunter's tunic she wore. "As well as... When I get it all sorted out." She did not like the idea of Venser sleeping around like a man strumpet, having many wives and many other children.

She blinked her azure blue eyes and sighed, giving Venser a cold, silent look, before it warmed up again looking to their little girl. Meanwhile Venser peered past them and watched Rowena and Asher roll a ball back and forth to each other on the floor.

They heard Elanaea suddenly give a small snore and chuckled, lifting her up into a nearby crib and covering her with a thin blanket.

"Nap time... Sleep well, my little love." She kissed her cheek again before she suddenly opened her big, grass green eyes and yawned, wiggling a bit.

She then sat up and started happily gurgling with her right hand up, the magic negating bracelet slipping off somehow and a ball of blue light forming in her palms. Venser moved past Sedna and walked over to her crib and booped Elanaea's nose, startling her enough for the light to fade away and for Sedna to bend over and retrieve the bracelet, sliding it back over her wrist and tightening it.

"No, no, love. You need to keep this on. Magic is not a toy."

Elanaea sniffled, looking up at her parents who smiled lifting her from her cot. "Maybe when you're older I'll teach you how to properly use it. But, for now, let's get some milk into you before your nap, hmm?"

Elanaea squealed at that idea happily, her stomach rumbling.

After a long day of relaxing with the family. A motherly warmth spread through Elanaea's chest as she looked upon her slumbering child in the crib, all tuckered out after exploring all she could of her new home. It didn't take long for the little girl to descend serenely into dreamland. The child's eyelids stayed closed save for the occasional flicker, her little black locks falling softly against her head and onto the pillow.

A smile curved the exiled princess's lips, and she held a hand to her chest, tilting her head as she just silently stood there, admiring her own little bundle of joy as she slept. Elanaea's chest rose and fell gently, a small contented smile still on her face. She had her Floppy with her, which was of course her beloved stuffed raven beside her. Her favorite sky blue blanket covered the majority of her body.

Elanaea was unreservedly the most beautiful baby Sedna had ever seen, though she knew that as the mother she was more than a little bit biased. Nevertheless, she believed quite strongly it was true. Could the little darling be a handful sometimes? Most certainly, as all babies were, but caring for her was always a sweet responsibility, which was more than Sedna could say for some of her less personal duties.

But for now, the little baby slept, blissfully unaware of the outside world and all its problems. Her world was one full of adoring family, stuffed toys and fun games to play. Everything a child could ever want... Or so it seemed.

The little form in the crib stirred, and for a moment Sedna thought that her child might wake. But upon turning over just a little, Elanaea stilled and continued to sleep. The mother smiled warmly. No, Elanaea was still too tired from her long day. A moment or two passed, and Sedna heard the soft sound of heavy footsteps upon the carpet coming up from behind her. She knew the gait and did not need to turn her head to know who it was. The exiled princess turned huntress felt a pair of strong arms drape around her waist from behind her.

"Aren't you going to come to bed, love?" Venser asked quietly, not wishing to wake their child. "I put you in one of the guest rooms just like you asked. And I apologize that it's not completely furnished yet... New house and all, ya know."

"In a bit. And it's all good Venser, really." Sedna replied gently, continuing to watch their daughter. She followed it with a soft sigh, hating the idea of sharing a bed with many other women along with Venser. Though, perhaps tonight he could share it with her in the guest room, and only her.

Her bearded lover nuzzled her neck for a moment, kissing her jawline and touching his cheek to hers to join her in watching baby Elanaea. "She looks so peaceful when she's sleeping," he remarked softly. "She's so beautiful... Just like you."

Sedna couldn't help but smile and turned her head to face Venser, then leaned in a little, with him nodding and following suit. The two shared a brief kiss. Exhaling, Sedna rested her head against his chest.

"I am pretty tired..." The azure eyed huntress admitted. She sighed, easing against him just a little more before turning her eyes to the face of her child once more. "Do you ever worry about her?"

"I worry about all my children. Though, I try not to... But I do."

"Mmm," Sedna responded, "I do. She's going to have to watch over my kingdom of Kynareth someday. If my parents ever allow me to come back..."

"The keyword being someday, Sedna. And if." Venser said with a sigh. "That's still a long way's off. And we're going to see to it that once that day comes, she'll be ready. Besides, she's only OUR first. Who's to say Elanaea won't have a new sister or a brother eventually? I mean she's already got her numerous half siblings now."

Sedna felt her stomach churn a bit. She wanted to have more children with him... But she didn't want Ven having children with anyone else, but she knew his man-whorish antics and doubted there was anything she could do about it. And still a mother's concerns are rarely so easily dispelled. "I'm certain of it. This can't be forever..."

"It'll be fine, Sedna." He whispered. "I'm surprised you're even worried about this. You're smart and strong, and so will Elanaea when she grows up."

They then heard a tiny moan emanate from within the crib. They watched as their little one rolled over, then much to their relief, she continued to sleep soundly.

The parents glanced to one another, and Venser gestured to the door with a quick movement of his head, licking his lips a bit. He took the first few steps in the direction he'd indicated and, after she'd cast one last adoring look in Elanaea's direction, and Rowena and Asher fast asleep in their cribs as well inside the nursery. Sedna followed after him. Once out in the hall, Venser quietly closed the door just as quietly as he could manage, he and his lover releasing a nigh-silent sigh of relief at having made it out without awakening their beloved daughter and her siblings.

Venser flashed Sedna a little grin. "I guess those stealth maneuvers were good for something after all. You tried to show me your best when we went on that hunting trip..."

Sedna only grinned back.

"Come on," Venser said, taking her arm in his. "Let's go to bed."

Sedna leaned against her lover's shoulder as they walked leisurely down the hall, the sounds of the rhythmic tapping of their feet against the reflective marble, feeling the cool night air and his warmth as they walked the villa halls of the second floor and to the guest room Ven had set up for her. It was quite a peaceful night in Pryldahn.

"I have to ask again, Sedna. Why are you exiled?"

Her stomach churned yet again, not liking to actually have to discuss it outloud.

"I've told you like five times I think... Must we go over this again?"

Before Venser could answer Sedna huffed and looked away from him.

"I saved my father, Tiberion, from an assassination attempt, got wounded and even though the highest officers knew who I was, they couldn't stop the King and Queen walking in on their savior while he was still being stitched up, so they saw a pair of breasts and black hair and knew who it was. So, I was banished across the Slender Sea, because it was easier to say that I was attempting to kill my father than tarnish the royal reputation of Kynareth and say that the princess was a rebel."

Venser blinked a few times at his annoyed lover.

"That sounds kind of complicated..."

"It really isn't, Ven. And princesses don't partake in hunts, or join the army or take up arms and save their families. Maybe some do for self defense most do not. Look... Can we just... Go to bed?"

And of course, the handsome bearded man would lean on her now, which she was always grateful for. She could never stand those men who refused to accept help of any kind, especially a woman's help, steadfastly denying that anything was even wrong to begin with. Sedna smiled, grateful that the adoration they shared for each other and their daughter. Venser turned his head, glancing down at her. She realized he'd caught her staring, but she didn't bother averting her gaze. One of the perks of having a mate was that after a while she didn't feel the need to anymore.

"I... Adore you, Ven." She told him sweetly, hesitating with her words for a moment.

Venser smiled back at her through sleepy eyes, stopping just short of the door to their bedroom. He planted a brief, but affectionate kiss on her lips.

"And I love you too, Sedna Rosarian.

CHAPTER THIRTY: NIVARAH'S CAVE

Great Blue Lake, Vorland, 1438 ATC

Venser marched inside the cave, letting out a sigh and muttering to himself, mostly about somehow forgetting to visit his dragoness over the summer and now it had turned to fall. To his amazement, the inside is absolutely enormous, and the walls are lined with all sorts of gems. Sapphires, rubies, emeralds, even some diamonds that were the size of his fingernail. No doubt, Nivarah was a dragon that liked to collect herself some shiny objects.

And that's when his eyes fell upon her, seated at the opposite side of the cave in a stone throne of sorts, the stone itself was melted into a crude shape and had a short back. She didn't seem to notice him yet, so he decided to call out to her.

"Nivarah?"

She let out a yawn and made eye contact with him. Her eyes were a slitted bright yellow, and her scaly lips curled into a smile.

"Master."

Her scales were a deep red color, her underbelly being just a bit lighter. She had two horns growing out of her head, and hair that looked like a short black mohawk in between them oddly enough. Her tail hung over the side of her throne lazily.

By the time he was right in front of her she stood up at seven feet tall.

"Master..."

Upon closer inspection her body, her scales had a pleasant smoothness to them and she had just the right amount of muscle to that it gave her an athletic physique, and her sides were feminine, curvaceous in shape that was most pleasing to the eye. And Nivarah had an ample, heart shaped voluptuous rear, most of which was often obscured by her swaying tail. Her strong tail flopped around a bit, smacking against the ground as she regarded him.

"I've been trying to move my collection out... So I could be closer to you and your new home."

"Oh yeah I'd be happy to help you teleport all this..."

"As you know, dragons are very notorious for their want— No. Need of exotic items." Nivarah got up from her throne and flapped over to him, landing right in front of him, and gesturing back to the melted rock throne. Her yellow eyes were about two feet higher up than his own, and he met them as she continued speaking. "And what's more exotic than a human who is not of world? Such an enticing human... Master."

"That's that's alright... You know it."

She advanced towards him a bit, but he didn't back away this time. He felt her strong, draconian tail running up and down his leg, and all he could do was smile and approach her.

Nivarah giggled, as her tail slowly moved up Venser's leg and towards the front of his baggy burgundy pants. "You've missed me..."

"Yes Master..." He shuddered as she rubbed her the tip of her long tail against the front of his crotch.

"Would you like to take a seat on my throne?" She asked, smiling down at him. Venser shrugged. Why not? He moved past her, his hands reaching out to brush her smooth scales for a moment before hopping up onto the throne, putting a leg up on the arm rest and reclining lazily. Nivarah took a seat next to him and continued with her tail's ministrations. He closed his eyes and let out a small moan.

She smirked, giving him a toothy grin. "Nice and slow..."

"Just like I showed you... Real... Massage like." He shuddered. Ven could feel a bit of tugging down there, and he opened his emerald, serpent like eyes back up to see her tail pulling at the legs of his pants. The powerful dragoness able to pull them off entirely with minimal effort, leaving Ven in his leather thong. She leaned toward him, and he licked his lips and felt her hot breath against his own, Nivarah's maw opening.

He locked lips with her, and her long tongue probes around his own. Kissing a dragon is a strange sensation, but not an unpleasant one. As he deepened the kiss, he could feel her tail wrap around his waist, slithering around his body and feeling him up.

A little clumsily she explores his mouth, letting her forked tongue slide against his teeth until tenderly reuniting. Nivarah slid the tip of her tongue across the back of Ven's muscle and he pushed up against her to intensify the contact. Their tongues become intertwined, the narrow, long nature of the red dragoness's tongue allowing her to tightly coil it around his own.

Suddenly Nivarah pulled her big tongue back, dragging him along to more neutral grounds. Eventually though Nivarah's tongue comes back into contact with his and once again she tightly coils around Venser's tongue before retreating back into her own mouth. She repeated this process a couple of times, each time moving the point where their wet tongues meet a little further towards her side.

The handsome bearded man moaned into her mouth as she pulled his pants down, retracting her talons and bringing a large hand down, he helped by slipping off his thong and letting his thick length spring free, allowing her to grip his cock and begin tugging on it.

"There we go Nivarah..."

The smooth scales of her hand were softer than human skin, and the texture of it made it bump along his cock. He pulled back from the kiss, gasping for breath, and can't help but peek down at his crotch as she played with his equipment, this was a first from his dragon mate.

Then Venser simply leaned back as she changed up her motions, opting to slither her tail back and forth on him. She sent him a toothy smirk, and lowered herself down towards his cock. She gave the head a tentative lick with her tongue, and his member twitched in response, before going completely down on him, Venser moaning out and his toes curled reflexively.

Her tongue ran circles around the tip, and she began bobbing her head up and down. Every so often, her snout bumped up against her own tail, which was still wrapped around him and the tip of it running up and down the front of his torso. Nivarah looked up at her master with yellow eyes as she sucked him off, and he couldn't help but rest his hand on her head and caress her.

Nivarah gave the handsome bearded man a little nod as he gripped her horn, then resumed her bobbing.

She let out a low growl of pleasure and winked at him, and immediately began taking more of Ven into her mouth. Before long, she was deepthroating him, and his hips began to thrust towards her mouth of their own volition.

"Good girl..."

A thin line of saliva trailed from her maw to the tip of Venser's thick length, and she licked her lips.

"Female dragons give off an aphrodisiac as they enter their heat cycle... From these." Nivarah informed Venser, sitting up and showing off her perky breasts, erect nipples occasionally coming into contact with him as she leaned in close. Deciding to give them the proper care they longed for, he brought his endeavors down south, his mouth leaving a trail of pecks and kisses in its wake as it neared its target.

Wrapping an arm around her waist, his mouth latched on to her breast, evoking a throaty moan from Nivarah as his free hand kneaded and groped her unattended one in precise, circular motions. As her stifled voice echoed around the chamber, he began to suckle at her nipple, his teeth nibbling it playfully while his tongue poked and prodded at its tip from the inside of his mouth. The night dragoness reduced to shuddering putty by his actions, directed her half sounds towards the cave's ceiling, her unrestrained hand snaking its way unsteadily to the back of Venser's head, her fingers parted through his hair as she helped bob him along on her chest.

Whilst still on the throne the mighty dragoness clambered onto his lap, causing Ven to moan out and adjust himself from Nivarah's weight. Her tail hung by his side as she straddled him, and he leaned up to lock lips with her again. Nivarah returned his kiss with gusto, and after a few moments, they pulled apart from each other.

Nivarah placed her hands on his shoulders and lifted herself up a bit, aligning herself with Ven's cock. He reached down and grabbed his thick shaft, rubbing the head against her folds a bit, droplets of seed dribbling from it. She closed her yellow eyes and turned to the side as he pulled his hand back, then the dragoness dropped herself down.

Pure pleasure shot through the dragoness and the human.

"Ah Master!"

"Oh void there we go... Mhm!"

Nivarah seemed to be lost in her own world of bliss, her large leather wings shuddering on her back as she slowly lifted herself back up. Just like before, she plopped herself back down in his lap. Now deciding that taking it slow wasn't her style, Nivarah began to pick up a rhythm, rising up and down on Venser's thick member. Her dragogina grasped him as tightly as it could without hurting him, and he fell back into the large throne as she began riding the handsome bearded man with fervor.

At this point, the only sound in the cavern was her large, wide hips colliding with his own. Nivarah looked gorgeous, leaning herself back slightly as she began sending him towards that edge he'd been trying to careen over for far too long. Venser moaned out, wrapping his arms around her back and buried his face in her chest.

After several long minutes Ven was dangerously close to the edge, his heavy balls slapping against the underside of her tail as his thrusts began to lose their rhythm. The handsome bearded man's hips slammed against the seven foot dragoness's for a few more minutes before he finally slammed home one last time. White hot pleasure instantly consumes his entire being, as gob after glob of his hot sticky seed rushed into Nivarah's dragogina.

Released in short volleys, rope after rope of Venser's seed fired deep into Nivarah's burning depths, mixing in with her own cum before seeping out from around where the two were joined. Raising his head a bit, he could see the human-dragon concoction slowly leak from her entrance before spreading over his pelvic area. After Venser's member gave one last twitch, it ended just as soon as it arrived.

"That was intense, Master." Nivarah breathed out, her long, forked tongue licking his face a bit, before giving Ven a big kiss.

"We will gather what we can and then I'll teleport us home... Where we can do it again, Nivarah..." Venser said, his head resting in her heaving chest. Wrapping his arms right above her tail, the two let out a satisfied sigh and held each other close.

CHAPTER THIRTY ONE: PRYLDAHNIAN SLAVE MARKET

Capital De Seraphim, Pryldahn, 1438 ATC

Elves were slaves to humans and Pryldahnians. They made themselves useful with the farms, mines and tunnels and wherever else they could. In the previous years after the cataclysm over a thousand years ago a vast army of elven raiders from the Alphonse Islands sailed to Pryldahn and took advantage of the ensuing chaos.

They had slaughtered entire families of Pryldahnians and humans alike while they sacked the capitals. Men, women, and young ones alike. When the rest of Posiil heard of this deed they were horrified and disgusted with this awful act of the elven islanders and for once united the entire continent.

Thus, elves were enslaved. Many of the islandic elves had become slaves to the Pryldahnians after their defeat, much to the disgust of the rest of the world, and though the Oceanic Slave Trade had been abolished many of the Alphonse Islandic Elves descentands still remained in slavery. Some of the native wood elves to the southern lands were even subject. Some masters treated them well and they even earned their freedom although most chose to remain with their masters not knowing what else to do. Others treated their slaves horribly but it was against Pryldahnian law to abuse property, whether it be anyone else's or their own.

"Hmmmmm..."

Venser Karkaldwin stood in the slave market, wearing his usual turquoise and crimson tunic with baggy red pants, bright red boots, and a black cape. Atop his head sat a brand new hat to replace the one that had been taken long ago from the spider centaur women. This one was black, wide brimmed, and had a large yellow feather sticking out of the side.

"Hmmmmm..." He scanned the slave stalls as he browsed, trying to decide which ones to buy.

If Ro were here she'd be attacking everyone. Nuikia too.

He had been wandering through the crowded, fly-shrouded stalls guarded by rough looking mercenaries and a few foreign traders from Leonatina wearing flat brim helmets with a crest from front to back associated with said country, who looked very shady, even for this slave market.

All the elves in the stalls were scrawny and barely kempt, and were all female. They looked unhealthy and malnourished much to Venser's disgust, and they hadn't even been owned yet.

How could anyone do this to them?

It should have been illegal to keep them in this horrible state.

He heaved a sigh and rolled his eyes as the random slave trader, a squat, stout man that wore black hat with a bright white feather similar to Venser's, a necklace, and a brown leather coat with golden embroidery and had a greying goatee and a moustache reached out his grubby hands gesturing wildly and trying to gain his attention, ranting about how good and strong his slaves was, pointing out several of them.

Blatant lies from a little man who was clearly mistreating them.

It was this particular stall that made Venser stop, his face in a frown looking to this man's collection of slaves. All tanned skinned she-elves from the Alphonse Islands. They looked to be in horrible condition... He eyed them all while the squat man continued to ramble.

"These girls, they'll work! They'll show yeh a good time...! I, Joello Delossantos alwayyys tell-a the-a truth! Ask any merchant here." The squat man with the dark goatee and moustache trailed off meaningfully, directing his hands over all of them, about ten in total.

Venser sighed and looked around him. Left to right. Right to left.

The surrounding crowd varied, a lot of foreigners.There are a mix of men and women in finer clothing than him, some alone, some in groups, chatting and surveying the various offerings of the exotic section of the marketplace. More than a few are examining some of the other slaves' stalls as well, though mainly passing on the one Ven was at. The elven slaves standing on their pedestals, knowing that a lot of the owners and potential buyers walking around the market would see them and hopefully someone kind enough would buy them and be better than the man that they were currently owned by.

"You look like someone I know! A crossbow merchant who does allllll of his selling outside of Pryldahn! It's the-a hat!"

Venser shook his head at the slaver named Joello and gestured a hand to the row of elven slaves.

"I'll take them all."

For a brief second, that turned the heads of the many elven slaves and the slaver guards, and Joello went wide eyed.

"All, you-a say?"

"All of them. For my plantation. Perhaps you haven't heard of me? I have a stall I run only once or twice a week while I try to hire and expand. Here, try my greatest variant... I call it the two thousand four Royal Athemyst with the strongest, and best taste." Venser said, reaching into his belt and removing a silver tin, along with a light green cigar with a purple cloth wrap near one of it's ends.

"Here, give it a try." He said, and Joello took it back up a bit, having one of his guards use a tinderbox to light it. He inhaled slowly, taking a few puffs.

"Three spectacular bindings that exclaim the Pryldahnian flavor, which will delight at all times and will make an unforgettable experience." Venser said with a smile, pointing one finger up giving a recited sales speech he had written himself.

"Bahaha! That is-a good my friend! Come, come! I accept this gift and I will offer you fairrrr price for my slaves!"

And Venser followed the squat man as he led him into a nearby tent, his own fine black cape trailing in the early fall breeze.

"Even though my own business is just starting up, I will be having to spend extra to get them back into proper health." He said as the squat man gestured for him to sit across his desk, as Joello continued to puff away at the Royal Athmyst cigar.

"Ah no need to! They are arrows, expendable! How many arrows were broken today, yes? My father said that to me often, and he was a soldier! They work, work, then die."

All Venser could do for now while thinking was nod, his lips curling in further disgust at the man's philosophy. After all, he supposed this was how Joello's business ran. Cheap, ill fed Elven slaves trapped in horrible positions aboard the ships from the Alphonse Islands and...

Did he really have to overthink this?

"I can easily buy all of them. With coin, but mostly jewels and precious metals."

Joello's eyes glittered with greed at those words.

"And not a letter of credit from the-a Silver Bank-a of Avakova?

Venser nodded in negation. "I don't need any of that, I have it and can get it to you all soon enough. All we have to do is haggle the price for all ten of the slaves you have now... And, they are underfed, so..."

He let out a soft grunt, preferring not to tell this man that he personally knew God Queen Y'vonne. The man preferred Joello's sort had nothing else to do with him or anyone else in his life.

And thus negations began.

After several minutes of haggling, and making a few teleporting trips from Capital De Seraphim to Nivarah's cave, Venser walked away with the necessary documents, collars and chains, and ten naked elven slave women.

"I think you'll all be good workers once I get you all settled in and well fed and taken care of. We'll treat you well, but you will remain loyal to me and my family, The Karkaldwins." He explained.

"Can I get a yes, Master?"

"Yes Master... Yes master." A few of them replied.

"Don't worry, any of you. It's all... Uh, good..." Venser peered out past the buildings at the three giant buildings of the Pryldahnian Trinity themselves.

Vayheros. The head of the Trinity. Vayheros was a multi-headed hydra based dragon who is said to have created Laguna as everyone knew it today.

Kore. The god of warfare, destruction, forbidden wisdom, anger, wealth, prosperity, and civilization, who represented himself as a fierce, four armed dragon man with giant wings, a unique war axe in one hand and flaming blades in all his other hands.

Seyr. The goddess of fertility, love, and birth, who was a large breasted naked woman with powerful draconian features and who resembled God Queen Y'vonne. It was Seyr that laid the first egg, which gave birth to the first and from the first dragon the High Dragons such as the ruling De Seraphim family, and then the Pryldanians, a race of tiefling like beings with draconic features rather than demonic features. It was Seyr that breathed life into the sea, that it might flourish with life, teaming for the nourishment of all.

Venser Karkaldwin took a few long moments to watch the ships go by in the harbor, sailing around the giant statues in the bay, each having their own small island. He took time to admire the gods and goddesses.

"All smooth sailing from here..."

CHAPTER THIRTY TWO: SEAFOOD, CHEESECAKE, AND A GIRAFFE

The Dragon's Head Tavern and Inn, Vorland, 1438 ATC

A slight stirring noise was heard as the elven patron that had been graciously given board for the night arose, and she stumbled into the main bar area where Venser and a female she had never met before were. Not being much of a morning person, despite the fact that it was considerably later than she would normally arise, at first glance she would appear to be in a rather bad mood. Her blue eyes squinted tightly, trying to shut out light, a slight scowl upon her face. Nonetheless, as she approached the two of them she did her best to smile in greeting before taking a seat at the bar. "Well... Good morning, maybe? I have no idea what time of day it is. I was dead to the world in there.

It was actually early evening.

Behind the bar was a cardboard cutout of Venser in his original red rubber suit with rubber nipples and an oversized codpiece with a turquoise cape lined with gold fabric draped over his right shoulder. He looked about five years younger and had messy green hair and was clean shaven, revealing an eerie glasglow smile carved into his face. The cardboard cutout said nothing and just stood there being cardboard.

As the sleep slowly washed away from Nuikia's mind, and her eyes began to adjust to being open, she noticed that the "Venser" in front of her was indeed made of a strange thick paper material. She shook her head once again at the man's bizarre ways before turning and giving the female beside her a bigger and brighter smile than the previous one, then bowing her head slightly. "I do apologize, I'm sure I look a mess. My name is Nuikiaa. I'm sorry that you seem to have been left alone here with a weird copy of the bartender."

Sedna was drawing in her blue booklet as Venser did whatever Venser did when no one was around. Traveling and whoring about she assumed. The regal hunteress had just perfected the curve of a herbal leaf that was detrimental to blood clotting when a childish wail was heard from her room. Venser had gone out, and he had left a cardboard cutout in his place. Sedna was a bit disappointed that she had to answer to a cardboard cutout, and when she decided to the mimicking voices of the shadow tendrils.

But Venser clearly didn't want her trying to run the tavern, and Kira had gone to the market and Brea was organizing the basement and had been spending a lot of time writing a cookbook. Before she had come home and given birth to their child, Sedna had been the bartender's protégé at the Port of Morrow in Kaitzur, yet Venser refused to acknowledge her knowledge and training. It seemed that, in his eyes, she was just another huntress who happened to live at the tavern and who shared his daughter. She listened as her daughter's wails grew quieter, and turned to the lady who spoke to her. She was definitely elven, no doubt about that. Quite pretty, in fact. "My name is Sedna, and I was quite aware that the Venser in front of me is made of... Cardboard. Please, sit down, and I'll coax the shadow tendrils into letting me get you a drink."

The blonde elf shook her head, her ears wiggling as what seemed to be either an infant or a very young child was heard in the distance. Curious, was this the child of the woman next to her? She didn't know, but wasn't going to probe her with questions when she had only just met the woman.

"No thank you, miss. I am hardly awake at the moment. Perhaps after my mind clears a bit, I can go back to trying to cloud it."

"I wasn't trying to force the drink on you so early, ma'am. I have a herbal tea that allows me to wake up quicker and concentrate on the day ahead. Would you like me to fetch you some?"

She heard her daughter quieten, but she heard something else in her room. "Excuse me, I need to go and check on my daughter."

The regal huntress jumped up and ran to her room, unsheathing an intricate dagger as she ran. She threw the door open, and saw a shadow tendril reaching over the crib where her daughter slept, gently stroking her hair. Sedna put the dagger away and bowed to the shadow tendril, gathering her daughter up in her arms. Her little girl had grown so much, she could hardly believe it. She walked down the hallway and sat next to the elven girl she had been speaking to earlier.

Nuikia's blue eyes soften as the lady retakes her seat, as her suspicions about the child she had heard earlier were true "You are too kind, ma'am. But it is not necessary. Thank you for your kindness, though." She propped her elbow up on the bar, placing her head upon her raised hand as she quietly observed the two of them, as a small smile graced her face.

"It's weird you know what cardboard is. Oh wait. I told you... I, oh well." Venser said suddenly standing from behind the bar as if he had been there the whole time. There was a lock on the bar in front of him and a tooth and he was holding a bagel, fingering it while he listened to them. "Probing..."

He cleared his throat and tossed the bagel over his shoulder, clasping his hands together. "Nuikia, looking lovely today. Cooking more blackened alligator downstairs." He then moved around the bar and sat down beside Sedna.

"Hello Elanaea. Hows my little girl?" He said with a smile, scratching her stomach.

Sedna smiled as Elanaea shifted in her sleep at the sound of her father's voice. "It's not hard to figure out what cardboard is, some kind of thickened almost wooden like paper. However, it does have a strange name. Why are you fingering a bagel this time? By the way, did you know that the shadow tendrils have gotten a little attached to Elanaea? I saw one standing in my room, stroking her hair while she slept. Is that not strange?"

"Yeah and it's fucking creepy." Venser stated bluntly, clearly weirded out by it.

"I thought it was taking care of her, because she had started to cry, but it soothed her back to sleep. What do you think we should do, Venser? I don't want to offend them by telling them to stay away from our daughter.."

"It's just strange. They don't do anything unless they're summoned. They don't have minds of their own... But, I think you're making a big deal out of nothing." He sighed and stood up. "I gotta go check on the food." He said before disappearing in a puff of thick red smoke.

The regal huntress watched Venser leave and frowned, mulling over his words. "They obviously do have minds of their own, and something tells me that the only reason why they do as they are asked is because they are subservient creatures. Venser, why can't you see that they can evolve? They've stopped hiding, and are interacting with the patrons. With our daughter. Even ask Kira, she'll be able to give you more insight.."

Nuikia remained silent, just listening to everyone else talk, but she turned and watched as a random patron walked past them all, arching a brow at her. Obviously she was no newcomer as she made her way to another room. Nuikia turned back to the bar, and placed her hands together on top of the counter.

"You're being awfully quiet." Venser said, setting a silver platter down on the bar in front of Nuiika. He removed the lid and revealed three plates of well cooked, well spiced blackened alligator, collared greens, and mashed potatoes with butter and a molten lava center. "Ta da. Dig in." He said, pushing on the plates to her, and another to Sedna.

Nuikia's eyes lighting up at the food in front of her as it had been quite a while since she had eaten. she mutters under her breath. "Thank you... You're too kind."

"Well hey," Venser said with a pause leaning up against the bar looking to her, "I told you I'd make my famous blackened alligator a while back. So..." He made a gesture to the food before Nuiika and awaited for her to test the meal he spent a lot of time and effort on.

Nuikia smiled at him, and dug into the delicious food placed in front of her. she starts with the alligator itself, and makes a rather audible "mmm," relishing in the amazing taste of it. The blonde elf moved from there to the potatoes, which have always been one of her favorite foods. Doesn't matter how they're cooked, they always taste delicious. Especially with butter, which these have. She made a noise similar to a moan as she ate, her cheeks flushing a bit at the embarrassing sound. She swallows her food and looks back up to Venser. "Thank you so much. It's simply... Amazing!"

"Eh? Eh!" Venser pounded the bar a few times and grabbed a silver cocktail mixer. "And how about we follow up this delicious meal with a Pink Footed Booby?" He asked, grabbing the ingredients to mix it.

"How'd ya sleep by the way? You must be nocturnal or something!"

"Oh Maker, please. I would love more of that drink." The blonde elven woman chuckled. "I slept like a corpse in there. I must have been more exhausted than I thought... And I'm not that used to beds, to be honest." Nuikia raised her right hand to rub at the back of her neck, massaging lightly at her sore muscles. Her body had been hurting her more lately than usual for some reason. The blonde elf wasn't sure why, though she did have a hunch.

"I don't remember what we were talking about before you went to rest." Venser said adding a drop of the secret ingredient into the cocktail mixer, sliding the vial back into his belt and shaking it up and down for about a minute, pouring it into a glass and passing it to her. "We were getting to know each other... Mhmm." He scratched his chin and tried to recall the previous day.

Sedna shifted Elanaea to her shoulder, looking in appreciation at the food in front of her. "Thank you, Venser. I was just about to get up and grab some venison jerky to eat, but this looks a lot better." She took a fork and dug into her potatoes, which, true to Nuiika's word, was amazing. The handsome bearded barkeep really knew how to cook when he actually did.

Venser nodded and then gave Nuikia a soft kiss on the lips. Before disappearing in a puff of thick red smoke. From outside the tavern, he stood out setting the brick BBQ pit he built on fire before he disappeared again. A few minutes later he set some on the grill and began to cook, his singing was heard faintly inside the tavern.

"Way-oh can't blow the man down! Hey oh! Can't hold the man down, can't hold the man down! Doo! Doo doo doo doo doo doo!" He was enjoying a bottle of huckleberry cider at the same time.

Nuikia looked out the window and simply shook her head again at his antics, though she awaited that swordfish with much excitement. She then turned to her right to look at the male who had just arrived that had said a greeting to everyone. She smiled in his direction giving a small wave, and then looked around the room to see if she could find the pretty huntress Sedna and her daughter.

A few minutes later, Venser appeared behind the bar with a plate of fresh smelling, heavily spiced grilled swordfish and a bottle of Kupid Red and set it down in front of Nuikka, pouring the woman before him a glass of his favorite fine wine. "Well go on," He said, setting down some utensils for her. "Try a piece. Hic!"

Her eyes widened again as the food was placed in front of her. All sense of acting like a 'lady' went out the window as she grabbed her utensils and started scarfing down the fish. About half of it was gone in a few moments, and sounds similar to moans escaped her lips the entire time and she seemed oblivious to the fact. She paused, looking up at Venser with a large smile on her face, her cheeks slightly flushed as she brought up a hand to wipe away any crumbs on her face. "Th...thank you. It's too delicious to describe."

"Good... Good... A way to a woman's heart is through her mouth hole.'" Venser said, walking around the bar, sitting down right beside her. He draped an arm around Nuikia and picked up a fork, popping some into his mouth. "Try the wine too..."

Nuikia pouted, looking down at the fish in front of her. She didn't want anything but more of that in her mouth, but it was only fair to oblige him since he had provided her with such amazing food. She slowly picked up the glass of wine and brought it to her lips, her nose scrunching as it always did at the stench of alcohol as she took a decent sip of the red liquid, quickly setting the glass back down as she gave another pleased sigh. "It's good... But not as good as the swordfish, but still delicious."

"Combined with it, yes." The handsome bearded bartender said, biting into the piece of swordfish on his fork.

The blonde elf gave him a quick smile before digging into the fish again, but much slower this time. However, each time she took another bite, she gave another moan as her tastebuds exploded with flavor, her cheeks flushing with as much pleasure someone could get outside of anything sexual.

"Maybe I- Hic! Maybe I- Hic! Shoulda cooked more than just grilled swordfish..." Venser said, already refilling his glass of wine. "Some sides... Dunno." He turned his head to Nuiika. "But good nuff, right?" He smiled and watched as her cheeks flushed. "Ador- Hic!"

She looked back up to him, her mouth full of a large bite of fish as a rather loud moan emitted from her. She brought a hand to her mouth to cover it while she finished chewing and swallowed what was left in her mouth before speaking. "Better than good enough, Ven. Thank you so much." Nuikia put down her fork and threw her arms around him in gratitude.

Venser wrapped his arms back around Nuikia and held her closer, running a hand up and down her back as they embraced. "Just enjoy the food now..."

The blonde elf pulled her head back just enough to look at his face, shaking her head in agreement. "Okay...." She pulled away from him and went back to devouring the fish.

Of course we're okay... Hic!" Venser hicced a few more times and rested his head on Nuikiaa's while she ate. He kissed her hair and said, "Whyda more wine? Get drunk and... It's fun- Hic! It's fun being dunk and egg..."

Nuikia looked at the glass in front of her that was still about half full and shrugged, saying a 'why not' with a mouthful of food, noticing a fee patrons raised eyes at them before going back to their own drinks and conversations.

Ro walked through the tavern doors without any of her usual caution, her posture slumped, her face near void of expression, and with a familiar cutlass sheathed to her side. She took her time going up the stairs and headed towards the end of the bar in the same manner. Without a word to the others at the bar, she took a seat at the very end and placed a few silver coins on the counter, staring off into space.

"So how bout we go back to my room later for some real vintage drinks? Hic!" The drunken Venser asked, ignoring the woman that he was largely unfamiliar with that was at the bar. "Hey Ro! Roooo..." He waved a hand in front of her face. Nothing. Weird.

Swallowing the last bite of her food, she looks at the plate with a sad look, her eyes actually watering a bit in disappointment at the fact her food was now gone. She turned to look back at the man beside her, trying to muster up a smile as she shrugs. "I suppose we could. But you didn't make enough fish...."

Celeste, a local fairy would bumble in the front doors with her feet padding along the wooden planks of the tavern's floor. Her body from her hair down to her satin and velvet gowning to her bare toes damp with the rain of a spring sprinkle but it didn't bother her. Arms full of fresh flowers and herbs humming softly as her wings beat fiercely behind her flicking the water off them drying themselves. She made her way swiftly up the stairs just to pull out a bar stool at the counter top and then she perched herself into the seat and emptied the flowers and herbs into the countertop and she began to giggle as she shook the rest of the little bits of water from herself.

"I thought I did... Nuff for you mostly..." Venser just now noticed that all the fish was gone. He sighed and got out of his seat. "I'll go make more... For the whole tavern! Uh, you. Take the herbs downstairs we will need them later and I'll compensate you in a bit." He flailed his arms and fell over, hitting the ground with a thud before disappearing in a puff of thick red smoke.

Marvella climbed out of her bed lazily while looking at a time with a yawn escaping her mouth. She changed into her usual black outfit on consisting of a lea-ther jacket, strapless dress with shiny belt, plain leggings and leather boots. She brushed through her hair with her fingers, not caring if it looked bad or not. She walked out of her door as she went down the hall to the bar area while looking around at the patrons, wanting to get herself some food before she went back to Montpelier. Marvella Fullbuster had a slender body and noticeably thick hips, fair skin, strange purple eyes, dark hair tied back, pink lips, a portal ring on each finger, and a pair of earrings consisting of white round with and orange border with sil-ver chains.

Celeste was sorting. By type and then by color the flowers first and the herbs second. Of course the herbs were different, those had to be done by magical uses and which were able to be stored near one another. She hummed happily as she worked and soon she claimed her fingers this way and that and vases began to move up from behind the counter and place themselves before her. After that she carefully filled each of six vases with flowers and then she placed her hands on the vases one at a time and watched as they filled with water.

Nuikia clapped her hands excitedly, bouncing up and down in her seat like a child. "Hurray, more fish!" After Ven vanished, she looked around the tavern to see that it had cleared out a good bit, but new patrons were still coming in. She also noticed a short fairy woman sitting at the other end of the bar, and she raised her brow. She looked familiar, probably had seen her in here before. Nuikia simply waved as she thought or was polite.

Ro the islandic elf finally snapped out of her absent minded trance, watching Ven have dinner with a truly beautiful woman. They had shared girls before... But this one. This Nuikia. She felt a strong sense of attachment to her already.

"Oh Ro, come, come! Actually, I've got something to show you!"

His call from outside was followed by barely audible stomps of something large outside. A long yellow neck with brown spots came into view of the windows on the second floor. "I got that giraffe!" Venser stood atop the back of the giraffe peer-ing in through the window. "I bought the house for it a while back but not... Yeah! You there? I also got cheese-" The giraffe didn't like the man standing on it's back and promptly moved away, letting Venser fall from sight. "Ah!"

Nuikia, propping her elbow on the counter and placing her head on her raised hand as she observed the actions of the beautiful islandic elf beside her. Her pointed ears begin to twitch again, however, as a commotion was heard outdoors. What was Ven doing? Maker only knew what the man was up to now. A what?

"I swear to Marilla..." Ro muttered under her breath before turning towards the window to respond to him. "Again, why a giraffe?! What prompted you to buy a giraffe, of all animals?" She called out as she lept out of her seat and exited the tavern in a hurry, mainly to receive her rum and cheesecake she bought from Brea as soon as possible.

"Nuikia, you come too!" Venser said somehow back on the giraffe, watching it eat fruit from a nearby apple tree. "Rauri." He held a small wooden box in one hand and pulled out a bottle of rum with the other. "I got your rum up here if you want it!" He called.

Brea Rowland the barmaid had emerged from the kitchen and looked out of the window with curiosity, her hazel eyes observing the scene. So that was a giraffe... She quickly made a quick sketch in the cookbook she was writing, on the same page as her scone recipe. Marvella was beside her. "When you're done can I please have a grapefruit beer?"

"And how in Laguna am I supposed to get up there?!" Ruari shouted, glaring up at him. "I'm tired and I just want my food! I'm not climbing one of the tallest animals in the world to get cake and don't you dare throw it at me!"

Hearing the man call for her she quickly exited the tavern to see him indeed sitting upon a giraffe. Nuikia couldn't help but laugh. Why had he bought this giant animal to live in a giant dog house behind the tavern? Where did it come from? They may never know, at least as long as Venser's involved it seemed. "What are you doing now?" The blonde elf turned to the tan skinned elf and agreed that she had no idea how one could possibly climb a giraffe. "He has cake up there? If he throws it, that would be such a tragedy."

"I don't know. Climb up it's legs?" Venser suggested putting the bottle of rum back in the box, shoveling a few huckleberries into his mouth. "Mhmm... Hic! These are good." He said popping a few more into his mouth. "Fresh of void..." He looked down to Rauri with a single berry in between two fingers.

"Want one? C'mon, indulge!" The giraffe still stood there eating. Unconcerned by what was going on around them.

Ro sighed, defeated, and turned towards the woman to respond. "It's cheesecake, too. You know, the best kind of cake? I don't know how he expects me to climb this thing..."

"Cheesecake? Why didn't you say so sooner?!" Nuikia walked closer to the creature in hopes of finding a way up. The blonde elf only saw one, but the animal probably wouldn't like it. She grabbed a fistful of fur on one of its front legs to hoist herself up and try to start climbing the thing. Nuikia was good at scaling cliffs and the like, but an animal was something totally different. "Wish me luck, m'lady. I'm going to try and rescue that cheesecake!"

As the sun began to set the tall animal began to cast shadows that stretched far up the building, the animal didn't like what Nuiika was doing and began to move to the side, trying to shake her off. "Gonna have to try harder than that! Ha ha!" Venser laughed, tossing a huckleberry at her face, before stuffing more into his mouth.

"Never was a fan of cheesecake honestly..."

Nuikia groaned as the berry smacked her cheek, but all it did was make her all the more determined. She tightened her grasp on the giraffe's leg and proceeded to climb upward. the leg didn't have much fur so it was a bit difficult, but she had plenty of experience climbing. She didn't dare to turn and look at attractive islandic eleven woman watching her attempt. She was going to get that cheesecake, whether Venser liked it or not. "Don't count me out yet, Venser! I'm going to get up there. And when I do, you better hope I don't grab a fistful of berries and shove them somewhere."

The giraffe simply laid down in the grass and let out a yawn, smacking its lips after eating the fruit from the tree. Allowing Nuikia to get to Venser easily. He just laid on its back eating the delicious berries while watching the girl like he was being entertained.

Nuikia let out a frustrated sigh, now able to climb the creature with ease. now that she didn't have to worry about the leg, her handling was much more controlled. as she neared Venser, she was breathing a bit heavy, but she was just as determined. "Hand...over that... Cheesecake! Or I can bother Brea to make more..."

"No no no no! I'll tell her not to do that, as her boss!" Come and get it." He said holding the small wooden box close to him.

Nuikia practically screamed in frustration as she tried to hoist herself up onto the beast's back behind him, taking care not to lose her grip in case he decided to try and knock her off or something. With her free hand, she tried to reach for the box Ruari's delicious prize was in.

Venser did nothing to stop her, aside from flick blackberries at her face and let out a playful laugh. When she reached for the box he merely leaned forward and handed it to her. "Woohoo! Ya won the prizeeeeeeeeeeeeeeee!" He let go of the box and began to applaud, stopping for a second to check a pocket watch hanging from his belt.

"Thank Laguna, mother of all. Why are you so difficult?" Nuiika took the chance to carefully slide down the giraffe without dropping the cheesecake while his attention was elsewhere. She quickly hurries back into the tavern, panting as she goes back through the doors. "Ruari, I have the cheesecake!"

"We had fun!" Venser called from behind Nuiika as she walked away. He sighed and looked to the giraffe. "Right Joffery? What an evening..."

"Thank youuuuu...!" The red headed, curly haired islandic elf sang as she glomps Nuiika, peppering her face with small kisses. "You are my hero!" She gives her one final, tight hug before letting her go and taking the box from her. "You can have half, since you put forth so much effort to get it!" Ruari said, taking her by the hand to the bar.

Nuikia's blue eyes widened with glee and she makes a sort of 'squee' sound as she followed the pretty islandic elven woman. Ven was handsome and kind, but Nuikia was simply not attracted to him, or any man for that matter. She only had THOSE kinds of feelings for women exclusively...

CHAPTER THIRTY THREE: THE THREE ARTIFICERS

The Dragon's Head Tavern and Inn, Vorland, 1438 ATC

It was a calm fall day. All around Vorland the swaying trees were just beginning to change their colors, not quite weak enough for the winds to bring the leaves down. For now the country was in a sleepy state of autumn peace.

The black haired demoness barmaid disappeared for just a moment and re-appeared with a tray which held a tea kettle, a black porcelain cup, and hand created tea bag. Setting the tray on top of the bar, her short height about an inch above it, Kira carefully began to put the tea together, "It's always good when people order my tea. This is my... Specialty." Kira giggled and looked up towards one of the patrons in interest, "I would love to try sometime." Once the black tea was crafted with ease, Kira lifted the cup into her hands and placed it in front of the woman from the nearby town of Aline. "Please Enjoy." She tilted her head to the side with a priceless smile as always. Then she moved back to pick up the tray and set it carefully out of the way, all before another nameless patron raised a hand for her, and she clasped her hands and wandered over to help and all the other patrons at their tables.

"Yeah. Later on tonight I just came back to my room for some... Good conversation. That's it, Kira. As usual! Uhhh... Anyone else want some ice cream?" Ven asked, setting a rather large bowl of vanilla ice cream slathered in honey and topped with apricot slices on the bar, casually just eating while he worked. He looked to the tendril and raised a brow, looking at the woman.

"You wouldn't happen to be... What the fuck are they called... Shadow demonesses are as easy as I can say. I don't see a tail and you're too dark to be a Pryldahnian. I mean the horns... Hm."

Selly narrowed her eyes at the man. "Never tie my kind in with demons..." She spat, turning away. "I'm a Soutabulat..."

"Good conversation you say?" Kira then rose a finger and poked at his side as she came back to fill a tankard with grapefruit beer. "Do you want me to meet you there or knock?" The black haired, pale short demon girl rose both of her eyebrows in a sly manner, then gave a light sigh, already feeling the whiskey sour drink Ven had her try earlier flow through her system like a seductive spell. Wandering back over to the male patron and collecting his payment, before whispering to the woman from the town of Aline. "Emer, Venser is nuts. But... In a good way most a lot of the time."

For a moment Nadine almost seemed angered watching the shadow tendril. But settled down. Not what she thought it was. She bit her lip and stared forward at the rain. "No thank you." She said and tapped the bartop. "I don't blame her." Meaning the shadow. Nadine inched away a little.

"A what?" Venser asked, blinking his emerald snake like eyes, grabbing a spoon and digging into the ice cream while watching the ladies at his bar.

"Soutabulat. You'd do well to remember that." Selly snapped her gaze back in his direction for a moment before turning back to Nadine. "Telzar? I don't believe I've heard of a place of that name."

"Consider yourself lucky." Was all the girl with the orange bobcut had to say then decided to say screw it, and ate Some of the ice cream.

"I don't know what a soutaskabulbunt is. But let's get a good look at ya..." The handsome bearded barkeep leaned over the bar to examine the women before him. Venser himself was an ordinary human man in his mid thirties with slicked back raven black hair, a neatly trimmed beard, fair skin, and handsome features.

"Hmm..." The only thing not human about him were his eyes, that appeared to be plucked from the skull of a snake. His orbs traveled all over her body, briefly glancing at her chest.

The girl with the orange bob cut elbowed Selly. "Watch out he's a bit of a perv. Mistook me for a prostitute or some shit a while back."

"That's fine..." Selly smirked. "Even if he were able to seduce me, he wouldn't survive the first five minutes." She leaned against the counter.

Venser rolled his eyes and opened his mouth to speak. "I don't remember that. I think- No maybe I did. Or a mage or a scholar." He chuckled and missed the last part, then said, "Survive the first five minutes. Pffft. Clearly we've never met before. Misss...?"

Nadine groaned loudly. After the day she had, she was not willing to put up with it. Ignoring the two for now, the artifictor grabbed her bag and flipped it open, a bit of weird greasy bright blue substance was flicked at Selly. She didn't notice as she was more interested in finding a book.

"Let me put this in terms you'll understand." Three blade-like tendrils emerged from her shadow with a metallic ring, these however were more white than black, all three stopping a bit before they impaled his head, she placed a finger under his chin. "... See that woman back there?" Selly pointed to the orange haired, golden eyed woman. "She has a better chance with me than you do." She narrowed her dark eyes. "I'm not into men... Especially ones who disrespect my peoples name in such a careless way."

"If you're not into men than that settles it." He said with a shrug, his eyes going over to Nadine before returning to the unnamed woman. Venser remained calm throughout the entire ordeal even with the shadow blades near his head. "We have those here too." He said gesturing to them.

Selly snapped her finger and the blades retracted, feeling the bright blue substance on her hand. "Hmm? What is this?" she stared at it, tilting her head.

"I dont know." Nadine was more distracted by the contents of her bag, she finally pulled out a rather thick book that looked like it shouldn't have been in there and opened it. It was, though.

"Whatcha reading there?" He asked digging back into the bowl of ice cream, acting as if Selly and his exchange didn't happen. Venser was now looking to Nadine's chest, despite the fact she was wearing a rather thick leather blacksmithing apron on.

"You sure do like reading, don't you?" Selly tried to get a look at what the book was called, if the cover even had a title on it.

"Please enjoy it, sir." Kira now took a moment to relax for a moment as she reached for her tea cup and took the final gulp of her own saki and green tea mixture. Those dark eyes gazed upon the patrons while she stood there in silence, until another shadow tendril would appear with a fresh clean full cup of what she was indulging herself with.

"Arigato." She spoke quietly towards the Shadow Tendril whom eventually disappeared into nothing. Kira would then take a few steps to the side of the bar and continue her work, fading into the background.

The book was leather, with a title in a foreign language, symbols not of this world. But once opened it was... A sketchbook. Full of designs for strange arcane machines and scrawled text. Almost as if blueprinting. "It's necessary." She stated and smiled, showing the contents of the page.

"Schematics for an artifact we are working on."

The bearded bartender disappeared in a puff of thick red smoke that quickly disappeared and reappeared behind Nadine, peering over her shoulder silently and looking into the sketchbook, gently trailing his fingertips up her side.

"You certainly have no manners, do you?" Nadine raised an orange eyebrow at the bearded barkeep. The text was not legible, but the drawings were pretty in depth and detailed. The orange haired artifice seemed more interested in the text though. "I don't mind people looking as long as they don't touch."

"I do when it's useful. Or when I feel like it." Venser replied shrugging his shoulders, looking at a silver bracelet the girl wore that has a polished green stone within it. "Lately... It's complicated. Been busy with tedious work here and my farm... I've been so... Hmmm... What's the word?"

"Horny." Selly said with a sly grin, obviously making fun at his expense.

Nadine put the book on the counter and leaned on her elbows. "I can't think of any." Shrug.

"Venser, does the tavern have any rabbit stew tonight?"

"Rabbit? Yeah. We pretty much have everything here. Maybe I can interest you in some fried catfish instead and a Pink Footed Booby?" Venser suggested.

Nadine looked up with wide hazel eyes and her lips pressed into a straight line.

"CAT FISH? YOU EAT CATS?"

Suddenly, there was a sneeze, and out of nowhere a white haired, elven gentleman appeared a little bit away from the bar. "God dammit... That big haired woman got me sick aga- Oh! There you are Nadine!" He stood up and brushed himself off.

"Didn't tell me you went to take a lunch break." He snorted, Selly looked over at her. "Friend of yours?"

Nadine's surprise at the mention of what she thought was fried cat meat faded a bit as her companion Myrin appeared. "Yes, we work together you could say." She then smiled at the elven man with long white hair and patted her open sketch-book. "Needed a quiet place to work... Away..."

Groooaaann...

It was clear she had a long night before and possibly hadn't rested much. Especially since she worked out in the store room in the stables.

"What? No! Catfish not actual cats!" Venser yelled back.

"I do eat a different kind of puss-"

The handsome bearded barkeep was interrupted by the elven gentlemen and stepped away. "Why don't I go make both and you can judge for yourself? I spare no expense when I cook!" He then disappeared in a puff of thick red smoke.

"Pretty rough fight, huh? We almost didn't make it out." Myrin plopped down beside her, Selly doing her best not to laugh at the barkeep.

"There's aquatic cats in this land?" Nadine blinked, relieved and nodded. "Okay then I'll try them." She produced a few coins in order to pay for it. "Almost..." She grumbled and stretched her arms. "And we lost three more of the guards."

"Damn...Those beasts are gaining an edge on us..." He crossed his arms. "At this rate they'll find a way to cross over the other side of Posiil..."

"Apparently this land has cats that are also fish." Selly said. "This makes me want to go to the lake I heard about nearby and seek them out..."

"...That makes no sense." Myrin blinked.

"I know right? Do cats really swim like fish here?"

"No no no no no. There are fish called catfish because they have tentacles that resemble cat whiskers. It's a very ugly fish and looks nothing like a cat." Venser explained, letting out an amused chuckle at the thought of an actual aquatic cat. "I'll have it out in a few minutes... Keep chattering amongst yourselves."

POUT!

Nadine felt deceived. The idea of cute fluffy water cats was better than this. But at least she no longer felt guilty about eating it.

"We should catch some and bring them back to Telzar."

A couple minutes later...

"Chef Venser right here!'" He called moving quickly down one of the hallways, wearing a pair of shoes with wheels on the bottom of them. Along with a giant white chef's hat on his head. Venser stopped behind the bar and set a silver platter down on the bar removing the lid. On the platter were a few pieces of fried catfish, with some salt, paprika, and pepper added to it for taste. Along with a few hash browns and a bowl of hot rabbit stew.

"Ta da! Be my guest, be my guest, be my guest...!"

Nadine sniffed it and took a piece, careful to check if it was hot or not and waved her other hand at Myrin. "Be a good idea. Something for people to look forward to." She then thanked Venser and nibbled on the end of the fish. Obviously she was unsure of it.

Myrin took a piece of the catfish and tried it. "Hmm... Not bad..."

"What are your names by the way?" Venser asked dipping a piece of the fried catfish in some hot sauce, taking a bite out of it

"Myrin of Lapwait! I am a very skilled wizard!" He smiled, plopping a bit of catfish into his mouth.

"You already know my name. You've tried to hit on me before." Nadine said. "Where do you find catfish?"

"The lake behind the tavern if I wanna spend my time fishing. Or the town down the road, Aline." Venser replied.

"Maybe we could spend the night here before going home. We need to stock up on supplies tomorrow anyhow." Myrin looked over at Nadine.

Myrin got a nod. "Yeah. Up early to leave though. I don't think staying away for too long will be a good idea though. Especially not now. I come here a lot but I don't stay too long."

"Three rooms then? Or are you going to be camping out nearby? I know some patrons do that if we don't have any rooms." The handsome bearded bartender said, enjoying a glass of huckleberry cider while listening to them all.

"Yeah, I'll stay up and gather what we need, you can go get some sleep, you look like you need it." The white haired elven man smiled.

"And how do you plan on not dying? Or being kidnapped?" Tsk tsk. At least on Telzar it was dangerous to wander alone. Especially if you had nobility. "Three rooms it seems. Because Myrin can't skip out on sleep. he fought too." She finished off her last piece of fish.

"Awh. Come on, Nadine. I'll be fine."

"So how many rooms, exactly? Two, three?"

"If any more decide to try and come up on us I'm going to need you alert and awake." Nadine gave his childish reaction one of her own and squinted at Venser. "Three" She repeated.

"Fine..." Myrin sighed and placed some coin on the counter, paying for his room.

"Alright... Will need to prepare the rooms. Excuse me, and enjoy the catfish and rabbit stew." Venser took the coin and then disappeared in a puff of thick red smoke.

"What will you do if a land close to here is next? Maybe Vorland itself. And you are too tired to fight." Nadine puffed her cheeks this time. Her small size, standing at five foot three, making her seem an actual child.

"...You make a valid point... Alright then. I'll get some rest and we can head out in the morning." He shrugged and reached into his robes, pulling out a wand and waving it about, summoning a few butterflies.

The girl with the orange bobcut waved away the insects. "Impressive magic." Nadine said and smiled. "I can do something like that."

"Because why not? They make for good distraction." Myrin said standing up. "I'll be right back."

Venser reappeared back behind the bar and adjusted his cravat, handing each of them a small silver key with a tag and a number on it. "All of them are down the left hall. Directly beside each other."

Nadine held out a hand, green energy forming for a moment before she created her own illusions to join the butterflies. Small neon green, shimmering fish that flitted around. "You have to excuse Myrin." The woman with the carrot colored bob cut watched him for a moment, giving him a supporting smile. Venser got a nod and she took her key. "Thank you, rest of the money's on the counter."

Myrin took his key and made his way down the hall without looking back, the green eye shaped rune on his forehead glowing a soft red as he walked passed them.

Nadine sat down with a sigh. Better not to follow him. She knew better than to do that sometimes. Her fish slowly began to fade away as the spell ran out.

In the hallway something appeared. Only momentarily. It was a good six feet tall with glowing blue eyes. Gone as fast as it came. Nadine laughed along and then held out a hand. To add more butterfish, all sorts of shapes and sizes. One a literal butter stick with wings.

Myrim felt the beast emerge, his eyes narrowed and he braced himself. He stood tall and lifted up his wand. "...You..." He bared his teeth, a small circle of flames circling his feet. Grains of salt appeared from mid-air and circling his body, without warning a wave of the salt was launched at the creature with enough force to shred flesh and wear down stone with enough effort.

All his attack would hit was the wall, causing some slight damage to it. Was it even real? Nadine laughed and held out her arms. Illusionary wings sprouting from her back, she too leapt in the air and joined the fish. It felt good to have fun sometimes, that was for sure.

Myrin's eyes rapidly darted around and he cried out.

"YOU WON'T MAKE A FOOL OF ME!" He yelled, going into another of his tantrums.

It never returned. The hallway remained normal aside from Myrin destroying the wall. Nadine heard the screams. "I'll be right back." She nodded a hello at the newcoming deer, and started toward the hallway. "Myrin?" She held up her hands in an attempt to counter his magic use and make him stop before he completely destroyed the wall.

Venser was staring off into space behind the bar and the bowl of vanilla honey ice cream before him had melted. He sighed, and called up the shadow tendrils. Two of them manifested themselves into shadow clones of himself. "Gonna need to repair the wall once he's done..."

"I think you should go to your friend, Nadine."

Myrin was on his knees at this point, head in his hands as the salt began to fade and fall to the floor. "You...Won't." He was mumbling that over and over.

Sighing Nadine knelt beside him and put a hand on his shoulder. "Come on." She planned on taking him to his room and getting him to rest.

"So, seeing things again?" The orange haired artifactor asked quietly and dug in her bag, producing a small vial of liquid. A potion made from some ingredients gotten from the last market she had visited. She waited, not wanting to get up and leave for some water before he answered.

"Interesting... Must be a lot in the forest out there..." He said, pulling his hand back.

"I have to find it Nadine... It teleported all the way over here, somehow..."

"Myrin..."

"I KNOW WHAT I SAW, NADINE! THAT THING APPEARED IN THE SQUARE AND DISAPPEARED INTO THIN AIR!" He sat up, Myrin was never one to lie, especially about The Luektorem.

She just stared at him with bright golden eyes just stared. And handed him the potion. Nah she wasn't going to dilute it. He needed to rest before his crazy obsession got worse.

Myrin took the potion and downed it. "Nadine, I promise you I wasn't seeing things, I landed a hit on it before it disappeared!"

"Okay. I believe you." She agreed. She didn't want to argue with him. Just waited for it to start taking effect.

Myrin opened his mouth as if to say something but quickly shut it, laying back in his bed. "... Maybe I am just seeing things...I mean...I've been so obsessed with them

I could just be paranoid."

She waved at him a bit. "It will all be fine. Don't worry just get some rest, I'll go get what we need from the market." And that included the catfish.

"... I just don't get it... I could sense it, I could SEE it's mana. It doesn't make any sense." He was getting frustrated.

"You've had a lot on your mind and the uncharted lands are full of strange creatures. It could have been anything, if anything. Just get some sleep, I think exhaustion is just getting to you." Nadine started for the door. She needed to go get her stuff from the bar.

"...Right..." He sighed and closed his eyes. "...Thanks, Nadine."

"How's your friend?" Venser asked by removing a small silver tin from his waistcoat, popping it open and pushing a light green cigar in his mouth. He lit it and inhaled, then exhaled greenish white smoke. He let out a cough and called for the shadow tendrils to get him some water too.

Nadine nodded and left. heading to the bar, looking more exhausted than before. She gathered her things along with the now cold rabbit stew and turned to head to the doorway that lead to the room. She wanted to listen in on him, make sure nothing was up. "Myrin... Not good." She mumbled and crammed some stew in her mouth.

Meanwhile outside Myrin's room something scratched against his window.

"What's wrong with the man?" He asked exhaling greenish white smoke that smelled earthly with a hint of citrus. "Heh... Does he like cannabis?"

Myrin's eyes popped open and he hopped up, swinging his hand and causing a salt dagger to fly through the glass. "LEAVE ME ALONE DAMN YOU."

"He's... Got a lot of stuff wrong with his head. Bad things happened. Typical stuff you hear about in taverns. He will be fine, I gave him something to--" Nadine heard the screams. "Oh dear." The dagger hit a tree outside. But there was nothing... But perhaps a slight blue glowing pinprick of light in the shadows of the woods visible from the window.

Myrin jumped through the window and landed on the ground below, raising his hands and causing multiple large spears to form above his head, which he would fire into the woods one after another.

"GET OUT OF MY FUCKING HEAD!"

Venser's head whipped around to look down the hall while his cigar was in his mouth. "Ugh... Yeah. We should go after him."

Nadine was sounding panicked. "Yes, lets." And she darted down the hallway. She wasn't a healer; she didn't know what to do, really. Meanwhile the blue light began to fade.

Venser ran down the hall with the girl with the golden eyes and orange bobcut then disappeared in a puff of thick red smoke and reappeared beside her a few seconds later wearing a nurse's hat and carrying an herb bag with him.

"OOOGIE OOGIE OOGIE OOGIE OOGIE OOGIE OOGIE! I'm a healer! But not the one you were expecting."

Nadine was staring out the broken window, looking back to Ven with a confused look. What was he doing? Did he smoke too many cannabis cigars? "Damnit." She pointed. "He's outside." And she was gone, jumping out the window and gently floating down and over to him.

"STOP ASSAULTING TREES"

The elven man stomped his feet and swung his hand toward Venser, launching a wave of skin shredding salt in his direction.

"STAY OUT OF IT! THIS IS BETWEEN ME AND THE LUEKTOREM."

The shadow tendrils manifested themselves into a shadow replica of Venser himself to serve and run the bar. Meanwhile, he teleported down from the second floor and teleported again to the elven man with the long white hair. "Hey- Ah!" He yelped and flung himself behind a nearby tree avoiding the salt. Barely as some of it caught the side of his pants and coat.

Myrin pointed his blade at the woman who emerged from the woods. "WHERE IS IT! I KNOW IT'S AROUND HERE SOMEWHERE!" He growled in her direction, tears pouring from his eyes.

"WHERE. IS. THE. LUEKTOREM?"

"What the fuck is a Luektorem? Luek? Leukocyte?" Venser called out to Nadine from behind a tree. "Um... I got an idea! Distract him while I go back to the tavern and grab something! Make an octopus!" He disappeared yet again.

Too much was happening. Nadine was frozen in place. She had held out her arms in an attempt to stop his attacks. But paused.

Myrin gritted his teeth. "You're lying...WHERE IS IT!" His eyes flashed red and his body became engulfed in fire, breaking himself free, he would vanish and reappear a little bit away from them. "They won't hurt anyone else...AND IF YOU STAND IN MY WAY I'LL TREAT YOU THE SAME AS THEM!" He swung both arms out, around twenty spears of salt forming around his body.

"TELL ME WHERE IT WENT!"

She had it! Nadine started digging in her bag and slowly approached her elven companion.

Myrin backed away a bit as his orange haired friend approached, the spears parting. "Nadine... Please... Stay out of this...I know it's here." The spears began to shake and collapse, spinning around like a whirlwind.

Venser reappeared in his room and tore the place apart, looking for the item that could help in this situation. Where was it? No, just a bunch of gold and papers littered his desk. He fell to his knees and looked beneath his bed.

"Here it is!" He pulled out a jar of dirt and rolled it across the floor, before grabbing a hand crossbow and a bunch of sleep darts. He loaded the crossbow and teleported back to the forest, at the tops of a tree. He aimed for the elven man's neck, and then fired the sleep dart, sending it flying through the air.

The darts would be shredded by the cyclone of salt now circling him and Nadine. "I...It's here...I can't let it turn everything into a lifeless white dune... We've seen it before."

Nadine ignored his insane babble and just pulled out some sprigs of cannabis, inspired by their friendly bartender. She then slapped him with them, and began smearing them all over his face. It wouldn't do anything but hopefully distract him enough to Ven sedate him.

The salt cyclone slowed for a moment before it dispersed and he collapsed on the ground. He had exhausted himself completely, laying in the grass while the canna-bis took effect, relaxing him before another dart hit him in the neck and knocked Myrin out.

Nadine gave a thumbs up to Venser, brushing back her orange hair and blinking her golden eyes. "A lot of effort..." And then she... Simply fell forward, laying across Myrin like an X. She hadn't slept in nearly three days. It finally took effect.

The handsome bearded barkeep appeared out of a puff of thick red smoke in front of them, letting out a sigh and clipping his advanced hand crossbow to his belt, letting it dangle freely as he approached them.

"Oh great... Good thing I'm used to drunks falling asleep in random places inside the tavern already..."

CHAPTER THIRTY FOUR: A TAVERN FULL OF WOMEN

The Dragon's Head Tavern and Inn, Vorland, 1438 ATC

The blonde elf in hunter's leathers returned to the tavern once again, but this time she had simply gone into the nearby town of Aline to try and see what there was to offer. Turned out, there really wasn't anything there she was interested in. Oh well, it gave her a chance to go on a trek and get some fresh air, so not a total waste. Nuikia strode through the doors and up the stairs to take a seat at the bar, smiling widely at her friend Ruari, a tanned skin elf with larger ears and a mop of curly dark red hair and sticking her tongue out at Venser the barkeep as she approached. "How are we all doing today?"

Ruari was currently checking over her chipped whalebone short staff for any damage. Not taking her attention away from her staff, she answered. "A few dumbasses thought that trying to catch arrows was a great idea and I spent three hours healing them. So exhausted. Also my friend Gale used my staff as a shield of sorts and now I have to fix it."

Nuikia looked at Ruari and the staff sympathetically. "I'm sorry to hear that. Hopefully they weren't the arrows I was shooting off yesterday evening. Laguna the mother of all only knows where they landed." She knew they weren't, but hoped maybe the joke might boost the other female's mood a bit."

Ro chuckled at Nuikia's comment. "No, no, I know exactly who fired off the arrows. Mainly because a shoved him into the nearest pond." After she deemed the staff to be in usable condition, she leaned it against the counter. "Anyways, how was your day? Interesting?"

The window was smashed in and a big yellow bird fell in through the window, sliding across the wooden floor getting glass everywhere. It tumbled and yells of pain were heard before it went still. "Whoo! Douchebag!" Venser yelled jumping up, his part of his costume cut up and falling apart.

"Rather dull, actually. After I woke up and dressed, I figured a nice walk to the nearest town might bear some good results, but there was nothing interesting there for me. I enjoyed the walk, but that was about it." Nuikia went to stretch her arms behind her back, hearing a pleasant pop as she did so. but two seconds later some big red blur came crashing through the window and she jumped in surprise. but once she heard Venser's voice her surprise went away, as she should have suspected he was the cause of the mess. "Never a dull... Venser, what in Laguna are you do- Wearing?!"

Ruari, startled from the sudden noise, nearly jumped out of her seat, knocking over her staff. Ignoring the fallen weapon, she stared at the man as if he had grown a second head. "Okay... What's with... all of that?" She gestured to the damaged costume.

"I'll show you dull." Venser said, walking over to Nuikia, still dressed up as a big yellow bird. He placed his feathery hands on the side of her face and then locked his lips with hers, plating a combo of soft and rough kisses on her face before breaking the kiss with a pop, then he turned to the side and grabbed Rauri's cheeks, doing the same with her.

Nuikia tilted her head to the side in curiosity as he approached her, but her face was grabbed by what she was assuming were his hands inside of two large fake wings and his mouth latched to hers. Her blue eyes widened at the sudden contact and she just kind of sat there and took it, not sure what to really do when a weird man dressed up as a bird starts peppering you with kisses. as he moved from her to Ruari, she just watched him with a very puzzled look on her face. "O....kay. So, my day isn't dull anymore, but now I am so confused. And yes, what was that about a douchebag earlier?"

"And Lhikan kissed it's waves in the sunlight, oh the sweet waves of the sunlight... He tugged at it's reins in the sunlight, and galloped away into legend..." The wind flowed through the strands of her hair, the soft warmth of the setting shining upon her, the gentle caress of thermals and the feverish rush of air currents that pulsed along the sky. The winds of winter were on the tip of this breeze. The courier harpy stretched out her grey wings and made a descent down to the Dragon's Head Tavern and Inn after such a long day of travel, and she had not stopped at his particular tavern and inn before. This would be the perfect place to rest for now. Passing a small party of guards that appeared to have just gotten off duty, she would slip through the thick doors, her pale eyes sweeping around the room, drinking in every detail she could retain. Tavern life was so interesting, she would think as she made her way across the room in a way that made it look as if every person moved out of her path, each step confident and with ease, almost dance like. It would not take long for her to find a seat at the bar, almost as if it magically appeared for her the moment she arrived there. With a frown she would take a seat, her wings sore.

"Did you see that- No not really..." He said with a sigh rubbing his temples. "I spared no expense in buying a giant slingshot, and I had as many shadow tendrils as I could summon pull me back and launch me!" He flapped his wings and ran around in circles making sqawking noises.

"Ohhhhhh no! Men cannot fly! Only birds can fly! Well," He paused and hopped atop the bar, showing off his yellow bird costume, where it was cut on one shoulder and he was bleeding a bit "I proved them wrong!" When the young woman entered he couldn't help but ogle. "And... I have just been proven wrong! Yippity doo! Welcome to the Dragon's Head Tavern and Inn! I'm Venny Karkaldwin and welcome to Douchebags!" He did a backflip atop the bar and accidently hit the shelf, causing him to fall flat on his face behind the bar and several bottles of liquor to fall on him. "Ow! Fuck!"

The courier harpy saw as the male had fallen and heard the loud crash. Her ears perked up in expression of worry. "Oh my are you all right sir...?" Scout would bend down, extending her hand out to the male, she had a body of a woman and some features of a woman, but more characteristics of a bird, a pair of giant, folded grey wings jutted from her back. Her talons would replace fingernails and her hands feathered. She smiled softly at the male, her yellow eyes staring intently at him. "Hey... You kind of look like me."

Ruari hid her burst of laughter behind a tattooed hand. "Pfft... Venser, are you alright?" She asked, her barely controlled laughter making it hard to speak. "Do you need me to heal you?"

Nuikia too found the action to be quite hilarious, especially after the assault he had just given both her and Ruari. The blonde elf chose to not hide her laughter, but she did stand and peer over the counter to make sure he wasn't deathly injured. "Maker Venser, how on Laguna this tavern is still standing with the stunts you pull I will never know."

"I'm fline!" Vensr said jolting up, his costume even more cut now and he was bleeding even worse and had a big bruise on his forehead. He spread his arms out and exclaimed, "Ta da!" He shook his head at Rauri. "Just need to get myself cleaned up and then I'll serve. Entertaining, huh?" He smiled back at the courier harpy and then nudged her a bit, winking and walking away.

Scout Leary chuckled softly for the man sure was strange, but quite exciting. She would gracefully take a seat at the bar, keeping to herself as she adjusted her giant satchel. Her posture would be straight, wings shuddering a bit. She licked her lips for she was itching for something to drink. But what? "Was that the bartender? Uh, I'll have water for now." And then, a snakey shadowy hand rose up from behind the bar and set down said glass of water, causing her to recoil a bit in fear.

"All right then..." Ro's laughter had died down, leaving her with a wide, gap-toothed smile. She turned to see where her staff had fallen and, by using a little force magic, propped it back up against the bar.

"A dooby doo wap! A dooby doo wap! A dooby doo wap!" The head bartender himself sang as he danced his way down the hall wearing his usual crimson and turquoise entertainer outfit, and holding an ivory white cane. The top was shaped like a whale and made out of whalebone too. He set the cane down on the bar and looked at them, a bandage wrapped around his head. "Alright. So who wants what?" He looked at the harpy woman. "Can I interest you in a Pink Footed Booby?"

Scout blinked twice as she looked at the man with a confused expression. "Pardon me....?"

Nuikia turned to the bird-like female beside her and chuckled softly, looking back to the bearded barkeep. "If you enjoy alcohol, don't question it. Just try it." She then turned to Venser and smiled warmly. "I'll have on with her, if you don't mind. It's been too long since I've had one."

"You should take him up on the offer, it's the best thing you'll ever try. And Ven, you should have kept that silly costume on." Ruari told the new patron. "I'll have my usual." She told the barkeep.

"Your usual. Rum. Right. And I'll mix up Pink Footed Booby." He fell from out of sight behind the bar and seemingly disappeared before the patrons. But he crawled around the bar while on the floor, downstairs to the kitchen.

The man stood up about a minute later and set a bottle of rum down in front of Rauri, followed by a random fish. He then pulled a silver cocktail mixer out of nowhere and began to shake it up and down humming to himself. He made an odd clicking sound and two snaky, shadowy hands set down two glasses down on the bar, and Venser then poured a glowing, neon pink drink into both glasses. '

'Four silver." He said to the harpy woman and his friend Nuikia. When they would taste it, they would find it tasted exactly like a strawberry starburst. Only liquid.

The harpy courier would express her thanks as she delicately reached for the glass and sniffed at the drink. She sighed softly because it smelled delicious as she took a sip. She licked her lips in satisfaction and then finished the drinking. Her cheeks became blushed as she hiccupped. "Oh my... That was very good!" Scout Leary giggled a little.

The blonde elf reached into a pouch within her leather folds and procured the desired amount of silver, plus a tip and placed them on the counter beside her drink. She grabbed the glass and brought it to her lips, her nose crinkling as it always did to the scent of alcohol before she downed the entire glass, sighing happily as her taste buds exploded with pleasing strawberries. "That drink never gets old."

Scout would search around in her giant satchel on her side and handed a fistful of assorted coins, one of which happened to be a platinum piece. "Will this be enough sir?"

"I never did ask what you do." Venser said leaning against the bar, looking to Nuikia. "Clearly I'm a bartender, but an entertainer as well and... A stripper if you can believe it." He rarely flat out said that, but he did anyway. "Yes it will." He said with a warm smile taking the coins, he stopped for a moment looking into her eyes with his green snake like ones. A good looking mail harpy, and he didn't often see her kind. "What brings a lady like yourself here?" He asked, tossing the coins over his shoulder into the payment jar, the shadow tendrils catching a few of them out of the air.

Ro picked up the bottle of rum and opened it up happily, taking a swig from it. She glanced down at the plate and cringed.

"Oh, raw catfish... Looking up at me. Great." She stood from her seat, took her staff and rum, and walked over to the stairs. She leaned against the railing, facing the bar and taking a few more sips from the bottle. "Anytime you want to take that abomination away from the bar is great, Ven."

"Well..." The courier harpy paused for a moment before speaking. "I am a simple worker for the Wingtip Express that has traveled many lands away from this one. I go to each town or village and deliver various letters and packages. Once I've done that, I will go to pick up more items to deliver. I came upon this tavern just to rest and relax." She twirled the glass as she glanced down at the last droplet of alcohol in the drink, trying to avoid letting anything slip out.

The blonde elf raised an eyebrow at Ruari, having never seen such actions around a fish before. she looked at the 'abomination' and licked her lips. Fish were the only thing she could stand to eat raw. She ignored Vener's question since he had abruptly turned his attention to the other female and spoke to Ruari. "If I eat it to get it away, will that help? Or is it the smell? Because eating it probably won't get rid of that."

"Ah! So will you be needed a room too, miss...?" He asked the winged woman, cringing a bit and looking to Nuikia. "Eating a fish raw? Like, plucked right out of the water? By the void, ya know you can get diseases like that. Disgusting."

"Eat it, burn it, throw it out the window, I don't care. Just get it out. I just don't like how it looks... That's it. Chopped up and cooked proper like Ven does sure, but not like this." Ro yelled over to the woman. "Preferably, send it back to Coldwrought where it came from!"

"I'll eat it." The harpy courier volunteered raising a feathered hand.

Nuikia turned to the beautiful harpy beside her and smiled warmly. "Shall we split it?"

Scout quickly retaliated for she realized what she said."That is if no one wants it of course. Aha... I love fish." She looked over to the woman and smiled. "That would be lovely. And want a room for tonight, sir."

Taking the fish away from Ruari's general area, she tried to think of the best way to split a raw fish. Nuikia could just tear it in half, but that seemed messy. After hearing Venser's reaction to her wanting to eat a raw fish, she figured she'd just let the lady have the whole fish. She might need it more anyway. "It's okay, you can have the whole thing. I bought something to eat while I was in town. Some sort of weird meat and assorted vegetables on a stick."

"Oh are you sure? I don't want to take your meal away. That would be very rude of me."

"It's free." Venser simply said. "Besides, me or the shadow tendrils can always go cook something up or get more fish."

"I insist on paying, as not a lot of harpies have any sense of value. So... Can I please have about... Ten more fish?" She beamed at the male, for she was excited

Giving her a warm smile, the blonde elf shook her head. "No, it's fine. I could always have Venser make me something else, but I really am not that hungry. I just love fish." The blonde elf woman poked herself in the stomach, her finger squishing at her small amount of fat.

"Need to watch how much I'm eating anyway. I'm trying to gain more muscle, not more chub."

"I think you look great! Fish is very good for you." Looking towards the woman who hated the catfish in particular. "I definitely understand why people don't like it. I hate vegetables... Bleh... Can't stand them. But meat is so delicious..." Scout's mouth started to water as she ordered the ten fish. "How much would that cost sir?"

"Ten fish?" Venser disappeared in a puff of thick red smoke and reappeared a few minutes later with a big tray of catfish from the local lake a few miles behind the tavern. "Twenty silver." He said picking up one of the fish, slapping Rauri in the face with it. "Moo."

"Thank you, sir." The harpy courier greedily took the plate and began eating. When she opened her mouth, her canines would be sharp as she began gnawing the fish. Tearing the meat away, but chewing with her mouth closed. She was raised with the most proper etiquette. She finished the plate in five minutes. She pulled out a small handkerchief from her satchel and dabbed at her mouth. Licking her lips, she sighed for she was pleased and pleasantly full.

"AHH!" Ro screeched, throwing herself out of the chair and onto the floor. "Venser, you dick!" She sent a pulse of magic out from an extended hand to give him a punch in the face, much like the magic she used during their spar.

"Oof!" Venser stood his ground from the magical punch in the face. He wanted to talk to the other two women and get to know them better but a feeling of douchebagitude came over him. "You wanting another spar or something, Rauri?" He asked getting a good idea. "Come on whip it out! You know what I mean, your cutlass!"

"You wanna fuckin' go?!" The red haired islandic elf pushed herself off the floor to lean up on the bar, glaring at the barkeep. "I'll kick your ass even harder this time! And without magic!"

"You know slapping a woman with a fish was probably not the nicest thing to do."

"Go? Go where? To the fair? I only go to the fair to pet the animals." The handsome bearded barkeep said with a smirk crossing his arms. "Hold on, if ya don't like fish then I'm sure you'll like this instead." Venser disappeared in a puff of thick red smoke and appeared five minutes later, holding a leather briefcase to himself.

"A briefcase full of bees!" He said opening it in front of her, before tossing it away to run around in circles with his arms above his head. "Let's start a riot! Whooooooo! Douchebag!" He yelled at the top of his lungs after releasing a shit ton of bees inside the tavern. "And now for my next performance, Castle De Seraphim!"

Scout reacted quickly, unfurling her large grey wings and summoning a cyclone of wind would appear blowing the bees away, opening the window, and outside the tavern. The cyclone would cease and nothing would be damaged. "I feel awful I had to do that, but being stung by one surely is unpleasant."

Seeing the bees fly out of the suitcase, Nuikia jumped out of her stool, running the rail and jumped over. running down the steps would take too long to get away. She hated insects of all kinds, but the ones that fly are the worst. Thankfully, The blonde huntress rolled as she hit the lower floor, not taking any damage but it knocked the breath out of her. "What the Coldwrought are you think releasing fucking bees into the damn tavern?!"

Holding her short staff she cast a weak ward barrier around them before he even reappeared with the briefcase, Ruari awaited the 'surprise' with an annoyed look plastered on her face. When the bees were released, she merely sighed and sat in the midst of the bee hoard.

Venser didn't get the reaction out of Rauri he wanted or for everyone to freak out, but he fell over laughing at Nuikia. He chased after her out the tavern door.

"The bees are gone now!" He laughed as he ran. "Where are you going?!"

"I don't believe you! I was getting the Couldwrought away from those demon spawn called bees that you brought into the tavern in a damned thing, just to release them every-fucking-where! You crazy bastard!" Nuikia stopped running about five feet away from the door to the tavern, trying to catch her breath. She was taking no chances with any of those little shits.

"It was for a stunt! I'm a douche- Whoop!' As he ran after her he tripped over a rock in the ground, hitting his face right on the ground, "Oof!" Venser hit the ground with a thud and then looked up to her, choking out the words, "I'm sorry!"

"Don't do it again! I will yank off your testicles and feed them to you if you even think about it! I don't even know what a douchbag is!" The blonde elf walked over to him a scowl on her face, but nevertheless she held out her hand to help him up.

"No bees or giraffes in the tavern. Got it." He said, taking Nuikia's hand and rising to his feet. "But it was fun right?"

Once Ven was to his feet, she proceeded to smack him once in the chest. "Fun?! That wasn't fun! That was bloody terrifying!"

"It was exciting! I got a real adrenaline rush!" He hooted like a monkey and stumbled back when she smacked him in the chest, then ran back into the tavern. "Ya love me! Everyone does! Ask my wives, ask my kids... Whoop dee dieee...! Stick a wiener in your eye!" Venser called over his shoulder jumping up the stairs three at a time. He plopped himself in the seat beside the regal furry woman and asked, "We had fun right harpy mail lady?"

"Oh um, yes. Actually I have to admit that was the most interesting sight I've seen in a while!" Scout ejaculated.

Nuikia only shook her head as she slowly followed him back into the tavern, looking around her to make sure no bees were left behind. she sat down on the other side of Ruari, trying to keep her distance from the man in case he pulled something else ::

"But seriously what can I call ya, miss?" He asked, wrapping an arm around the winged woman.

A dark eyebrow raised as he was touching her. "My name is Scout Leary. And yes, I know... I could be working as a scout named Scout."

"Scout. Lovely name, And remind me again what brings you-" She wanted a room now that he remembered. He disappeared in a puff of thick red smoke and reappeared behind the bar, looking through the room cards. A snakey shadowy hand refilled her Pink Footed Booby. "What can ya tell us about yourself, Scout?"

Ruari looked down into her bottle of rum to make sure no bees had gotten into it and took a swig from the bottle. "Yeah, why don't ya' tell us about yourself?"

"There is really not much to tell... I have an important job, and harpies that don't try to kill you and take your stuff are rare. I was lucky enough to be found by a kindly human couple south of here." Scout felt a tad uncomfortable with the direct confrontation, she rarely actually socialized. "My job is going to get much harder in about a month when it starts to snow."

"Well I'm Venser Karkaldin, born and raised in Pantia, I'm thirty four, I'm handsome and charming and witty and adventurous and thoughtful and considerate and super muscular and handsome and passionate and hilarious and handsome." Venser said as he leaned up against the bar, an arrogant smirk stuck on his face.

"Oh are you now...?" She blinked her yellow eyes and her wings fluttered a bit, and did have to admit he had a strong ragged look to him.

"So full of yourself aren't you, Venser?" Nuikia crossed her arms on the counter and rested her head on them, looking down at the various patrons again.

Ro rolled her eyes at Venser's arrogance. "I'm Ruari Patel, Marilla's 'chosen' and also an embarrassment to my friends, family and the rest of the Alphonse Islands. Nice to meet you." She smiled throughout her rather insulting introduction.

Venser was nearing his mid thirties, and had fair skin, a black beard that had been trimmed recently, messy black hair that also looked trimmed but was somewhat long, and emerald eyes that looked like they were plucked from the skull of a snake. Despite that, along with the bandage wrapped around his head, he was handsome. "Indeed." He said in both responses to the cute harpy girl and Nuikia. "So tell us this...." He said bending down a bit to meet her level. "Where do you come from exactly, Scout?"

Ro took a swig from her bottle of rum and glanced up at the woman, curious about her in general. She leaned back in her seat and listened to the conversation.

"A tavern full of women. Livin' the dream, eh Ven?'"

"... And then I said, 'Thanks for the dick ya greasy monkey! Ahahahahahahaahahahaha!" The head bartender howled with laughter, slamming his fist up and down on the bar laughing hysterically. "Oh wait- Wait! Ha ha! I already told you that story! Ahahahahaha! Best part is... He was actually a monkey!" Tears formed in his eyes as he clutched the bar in front of Rauri. "Oh- Oh-" He tried to calm down as the woman approached him. "Yeah, room cards right here!" Hearing her situation he tried to calm down and ask a serious question, but he only kept laughing.

The islandic elf shook her head and chuckled. "Doesn't mean it becomes any less hilarious, Ven." She told him, going back to watching and listening in on the conversation.

Scout smiled wickedly at him, enjoying his attempts at humor and his jovial, fun spirit. "I got a bit of coin, how much for the room?"

"Oh I see what ya did there..." Venser said, catching her wicked smile immediately. He looked over the room cards and then leaned over the bar, holding out a small silver key. 'Ten silver a night. 'Right hall, third door on the left." He said stuffing the key down the front of Scout's shirt, causing her to blush and her wings to flitter even more.

A scowl grew on Nuikia's face as a sharp pain shot up her back. She didn't let the fact that something was wrong show, and she quickly made her scowl turn into a smile as the woman to her right looked over in her direction. but the pain in her back was slowly getting worse, and it was starting to spread. Her body temperature was rising as well, her cheeks flushing slightly. she knew what it meant... All the aching her muscles had been going through recently were a warning, and she had been ignoring them. She quickly turned to Venser, trying to act as calm and normal as possible, but she needed to move fast. "Ven, I haven't stayed here the past couple of nights but I didn't take all of my belongings with me. Are they still in the room I was using?"

Scout decided to play with Ven a bit, and sat some assorted coins on the bar and sat down at the end of it, then pulled the key from the top of her uniform top. "Can I get another drink and possibly some more food to eat, unless ya want me eating some sexy ladies..."

"Yeah. Of course, Nuikia. I know you've been coming and going." The bearded barkeep leaned back a bit. "Heh heh... I got something you can eat..." He picked up his silver cocktail mixer from off the bartop and poured Scout more of his famous Pink Footed Booby.

Scout looked at the drink and smiled then sipped it, letting out a hiccup. She laughed when she had done so and watched the handsome bearded barkeep work. "I'm afraid to ask what else you got that I can eat. But thank you for the drink it's delicious, now can I get maybe a steak rare, a bloody steak or some liver or something, I seriously need to eat unless ya want me going all hungry beastie on you."

"Gimme a moment." He said with a smile disappearing in a puff of thick red smoke.

"Take your time sir, I'll just be here admiring the ladies. Ha... Ven is cute. Never seen or met someone as..." Scout waved her arms and flapped her wings rapidly.

Ruari stared at the woman, a smile spreading across her face. "If this is going the way I think it's going, then can I join?" She asked, only half joking.

The harpy smiled wickedly at the tan elf woman with curly dark red hair and placed her elbows on the bar and her head in her hands as she looked down the bar at the woman. "That depends, where do you think this is going..?"

Nuikia stood from her seat, fumbling with her pouch hidden within her dress's folds. she finally found the key and hurried over to the room she had stayed in for a couple nights. Letting herself in, she damn near slammed the door as she quickly stripped herself of her boots, leather hunting outfit, and her short fur cloak. She had just shed the last of everything when her bones began to snap and a rather loud gasp escaped her lips. The blonde elf fell to the floor with a 'thud,' her body was becoming feverish as it became to shift. Her legs stretched and became even more slender, her feet growing in size. Arms did the same, though her hands staying petite, at least for the form she was about the take anyway. as her torso changed, however, much more transitioning had to occur. It stretched as well, and her breasts became non-existent. Nuikia's lower regions... They went through a drastic change as well, but going into detail would be way too graphic. Lastly, as her face caught up with the rest of her body, her hands clasped each side of her face. It felt as though her skull was splitting in two. Her once long blonde hair started shedding quickly, falling as clumps on the floor. But in its place, black hair as dark as a moonless night sky sprouted. Her face began to contort and she tried to muffle a scream by biting down on one of her hands. But her voice, it was no longer the feminine one people were used to. It had dropped to a lower tone. Her body, finally done with transitioning from who she once was to her 'other self' laid on the floor, bare naked for a few moments. for it was no longer Nuikia that laid there, but Daenes.

"Come on, now. I'm not blind.... Yet. Look, what I'm saying is that I'm pretty sure you guys are flirting with each other. Then again, this is Venser Karkaldwin I'm talking about..." Ruari brought her attention back down to her bottle. "I guess what I'm saying is that I'm convinced you guys are gonna 'share a bed', if that makes any sense, and maybe I possibly want in." She took a sip from the bottle, directing her gaze away from her.

"Well then, not a half bad idea, flirting is one thing, sharing a bed is another."

"Well then after a few drinks let's all go have some fun." Venser said, setting down a barely cooked, bloody steak down in front of the woman. "It's on me, Scout."

"And I've... Well a few times, but I've never been with a barkeep." She noted his athletic frame beneath the crimson and turquoise tunic, and his barreled chest.

"A coupla drinks will make ya think otherwise." Venser said, refilling her glass of Pink Footed Booby. Muttering under his breath, "I fucked a queen once..."

"...You what?" Ro turned to the bearded barkeep, now confused more than anything. "How did you manage that?! Which one? The Queen of Vorland? How is the King not putting out a bounty?"

Scout's eyes grew wide and she began to choke on the steak as she looked at him surprised by his statement.

"Well, you see. I started a potato movement which consisted of me persistently uttering the word potato for some reason despite hating doing it, which then led to people calling me that." Venser said dodging the question before letting out a loud, long case of laughter. "Oh Void!" He then ran around the bar and pushed the woman out of her seat. Then put his arms around her waist from behind and rammed his fists into her stomach to get the steak unstuck from her throat. "Mhm! Mhm!"

Scout spit the steak out and turned around to face him after getting a deep breath. She crossed her arms over her chest and frowned at him, her sharp teeth showing once again. "You did what? Are you implying something? What do you know? I also deliver bounties everywhere..."

The body on the floor stirred after a few minutes passed, the initial pains from switching forms subsiding. The elven man sat up and looked around the room for a moment trying to locate the bag with all of his clothes in it. Spotting it, he slowly stood from the floor and half limped over to it, grabbing out the only clothing that 'Nuikia' had bothered to bring, which was a dark brown shirt, and black pants that had matching black leather boots. He put them on as quickly as he could, eager to move around since he had been locked out of his body for long enough. After he dressed, he grabbed the key from the ground and placed it in his pocket before walking out of the door to the room. He just stood there for a few seconds, scanning the tavern with his own eyes. Seeing everything from the back of someone's mind wasn't the best way to look at things. It didn't take him long to find everyone at the bar, with whom he knew to be 'Venser' doing something to some poor woman he didn't know. She had just arrived when the change started happening. The other female at the bar he could recognize as 'Ruari.' Nuiika liked her. She was very kind and had shared her cheesecake with her when the sandy haired barmaid Brea Rowland baked it. He figured it was time to walk over and take a seat himself, so his long legs strode over to the bar and sat a few seats away from the elven female. He wasn't really sure what to say, so he just cleared his throat. Maker, it had been a long time since he was able to actually physically talk.

"What do I know? I just saved your life!" Venser said in response to her frown and her crossing his arms. "I think ya owe me..." He heard someone clear his throat and he looked over to the man. "Welcome to the Dragon's Head Tavern and Inn. What can I get ya?"

Scout raised a brow. "And I think you for that... But I would really like to know the story of how you fucked that queen. Is he joking?"

There was an awkward silence, the tanned islandic elf rolled her eyes.

"I can treat you like a queen...." Venser said with a smile, dragging one of his fingers down the side of Scout's cheek gently.

"I am sure you can sir. Maybe I'd like you to prove it..."

Daenes looked at the man, staring into his emerald snake-like eyes. He could see why Nuikia liked looking at them, since he found them rather pleasing himself. Green was his favorite color, after all. He smiled at him, knowing there was no way he would know that his other self wasn't here anymore unless he spoke up and told him, but maybe he didn't have to be so blunt. The tall elven man could say something that maybe he'd remember Nuikia had said shortly after they had met, but either way, she was still there in the back of his head. "Hmm, I think maybe I would like to try some of your famous Pink Footed Booby, sir. But can I ask you something?"

"if I am gonna sleep with someone I want treated... Differently, not like royalty to say the least. But I wanna see if all this boasting is true. If you're really going to claim that and act like you just won a war." The harpy courier said.

Venser leaned on her back when she leaned over the bar and put his arms around her waist again, trying not to let her giant grey wings hit him or rub against his bearded face. "Tell me how you want to be treated..." He whispered in her ear planting a few kisses on her neck. The man snapped his fingers and gestured to the silver cocktail mixer atop the bar. "Pour it yourself man." He said going back to the woman's neck. "And have as much as you'd like. My good fortune right here is your good fortune..."

Scout smiled and turned her head slightly then spoke softly. "I want to be treated like any other woman, not like I'm anything special, and thus far this works for me."

Dan shrugged, seeing that without a female body Venser was going to pay a lot less attention to them. Nuiika probably wouldn't like that, but she wasn't here right now so it didn't matter. he reached over and grabbed the glass that Nuikia had been drinking from and the mixer, pouring himself some of the drink. he promptly dug four silver pieces out from the pouch in his pocket and placed them on the counter, remembering that's how much he had charged Nuikia for the drink.

Scout looked back to him and placed a small pile of assorted coins on the bar, smiled at the man and slid out of Vensers grasp to sit next to the elven male. "Hi. Let me pay for it, I got plenty to spend and I don't mind paying for a handsome guy like yourself. You can drink for a while with that and I got more if needed"

Venser just sat down beside the woman wrapped an arm around her, and latched onto her neck, sucking and kissing it.

Dan smiled at the woman, taking his gold pieces back and placing them back in the pouch. he grabbed the pink drink but didn't bring it to his lips yet "Hi, I'm gay. But thank you, m'lady. You are far too kind. But I can't let you spend that much money on me. One drink will suffice." He brought the glass up to his lips and his nose crinkled the same way Nuikia's would. his sense of smell was on par with hers, if not better. He downed the whole drink and sighed happily, placing the now empty glass back onto the counter top. He muttered quietly under his breath. "Damn...that really is one of the best drinks you'll ever taste."

Daenes then chuckled softly, shaking his head as Venser was shot down by the woman he was flirting with and promptly slid off his lap to finish her steak at the end of the bar.

"Venser will do what Venser will do, and there simply is no stopping him. At least not from what I've seen."

"Never seen ya before dude." Venser said scooting over to the woman again, wrapping one arm around her and letting out a sigh.

"No, you have not met me. But you have met a part of me. Very pretty. Blonde hair, she has piercings in her nose. She wears lots of feathers as accessories. Don't tell me you've forgotten little Nuiika already, have you?" The elven man smiled at Venser, hoping maybe now he will understand. He really didn't want to have to come out and say 'oh, your friend grew a penis and changed sexes.' He knew that Nuiika had confided in him what might eventually happen, though it was possible Ven simply forgot or did not listen.

Scout looked over at the elven man and smiled. Then back at Venser. "I think this is her, shifted somehow, I did hear noises earlier when she left it was strange noises, similar to the lycans I've met a few times before."

Somehow Venser was eating from a plate of pineapple slices on the bartop, listening to them. He stopped chewing with his mouth full and looked to the man, silent for several long seconds. "Mhmmmhmmm... What?" He got out of his seat and walked away from the two.

Dan looked at the departed male and had a worried look on his face. Hopefully he didn't resent him for something he couldn't control. But he would let the man deal with it the way he needed to. Besides, there was no telling how long Nuikia was going to be gone anyway. He then turned to the female and spoke softly. "You are a smart one. I honestly thought she was able to stay quiet enough for no one to notice. But perhaps your hearing is well above the average mortal, no?"

"I hear very well, I guess most lycans and I heard demons do. I am a hybrid, I guess. I am smart to an extent but its due more to my hearing"

"A harpy, you don't see many employed or just non-hostile in general. Well, as a man who is not always a man, I guess you could say I'm a sort of hybrid, too." He chuckled and held out his hand to officially introduce himself. she could leave him hanging, shake his hand, or place hers in his so that he may place a kiss on it. how it went from here was entirely up to her "I am Daenes, though many people just can me 'Dan.' Easier to pronounce, I guess. I am very pleased to meet you, m'lady."

Venser's bearded face popped up behind the bar looking to the harpy courier. "Uh Scout, after I digest, yeah.... All this, why don't you meet me in my room and I can show you how I wood that queen... And I must tell you, despite my clownish behavior, I can be very convincing..."

"Oh uh, and by the way! It wasn't Queen Y'vonne! She and I are very strictly friends. Yeah."

CHAPTER THIRTY FIVE: SCOUT

Venser's Bedroom, The Dragon's Head Tavern and Inn, Vorland, 1438 ATC

"You actually can be convincing..."

With an arch of her back and straddling the handsome bearded bartender, Scout Leary unfurled her impressive grey wings and the handsome bearded barkeep could see the well groomed state of the powerful feathers. The man reached a hand out to the closest wing, noting the size of the large wing compared to him, several feet in length and could almost touch the walls if she stretched them out all the way. While the harpy girl was about five foot four, and had white skin, yellow eyes, metal gauges in her ears, and black hair tied in a high ponytail.

Venser leaned in close to the wing, eyeing a loose feather to his face. Scout's breath was shallow in her chest.

"Oh yeah... That is molting and needs to go... Could you please pull it for me, Venser?"

"Your wish is my command..." The bearded man nodded and targeted one of the feathers and lightly closed his teeth around the tip of it, waggling his thick eyebrows at her. With a sharp yank, he pulled suddenly on the feather and it came out with a slight resistance.

The harpy courier's response was just a stifled moan that escaped through her clenched teeth. Weeks of careful neglect with her delivery schedule were finally ending. The little tingle of the missing feather from her wing continued down her spine and down to her crotch, her taloned fingers digging into Venser's bare chest as he moved the feather into one hand and set it down on the nightstand. She tried to squeeze her hips together to alleviate some of the heat.

"You've got some really nice wings..." He said, the tips of his fingers trailing over them gently, then switching to the soft skin of her arm, rubbing it up and down.

Her body trembled softly as heat unrelentingly grew in her slit, gently pulsating between her powerful legs as the man kept running his hands across her wings, and over the curves of her body.

"I really never let people touch my wings..." Her voice shook. "There's actually one more that's ready to go on my other wing... I think taking this off will help..." Scout said undoing the straps of her backless top and tossing it aside. Revealing her small, but ample breasts, her tiny nipples perky and a nice shade of dull pink. A small blush formed on her face watching Ven beneath her and admiring his slightly scarred muscular torso.

"Let's get that feather out then..." A grin spread across his face as Scout cried out more and writhed on his lap, feeling his hardened cock beneath his baggy red pants.

"Scout, are you okay?"

"H-huh? Yeah I'm fine..." Rolling her back to try to alleviate the stress building, grinding against his lap..

"You don't have to say anything else... I know." Venser said with a low, comforting voice, placing a hand on her rear.

Instead she let out an extended tortured moan at the slight touch on her flank, and then he started to drag his hands up the sides of her body, and over her chest.

"Enough talk, Venser!" Scout cast a nearly predatory down at the man, cheeks flushed red with lust. Her blush deepened and she did what she wanted her to do. Her breast was plump and her skin was as soft as silk, her gums were in perfect shape and her teeth were white and in good health, the only thing different about her teeth was that her canines were much sharper than a human's. She stood up and quickly kicked off her pants and undergarments, sitting back down on Venser's lap and grinding on his cock again, shuddering with pleasure.

The handsome bearded man fondled her small breasts gently, placing her perky nipples in between two fingers and tugging on them "Lovely..." The handsome bearded barkeep sat up a bit and locked his lips with hers, suckling on her lower lip and kissing her deeply as he continued to fondle her small chest.

The harpy courier shivered softly, eyes widened as she moaned into the kiss, her semi-hairy cunny started to get a little wet from all this attention she was receiving. Her hips wiggled slightly.

He grinned to himself as he nibbled on her lower lip, now moving his free hand to her spine. He dragged a hand down her spine with a gentle and methodical pace, making sure to tease her to the best of his abilities. He would move to her neck and begin to suckle on the flesh, now moving a hand that was once on her neck to her ear, teasing her earlobe with a finger and her spine with the other hand, which trailed towards her lower back slowly.

Venser's rough hand trailing down her body, his right hand slithering down her front and brushing against her wet cunny, using two fingers to open her lips and rub against it, his thumb rubbing in circles around her clit. "Mhmm..." He moaned into her mouth Scout let out all sorts of cute and lewd sounds as they explored her body. Once the man's fingers found her opening she moaned even more and started to wiggle more, her hips moving back and forth on his cock beneath his baggy red pants, she felt like she was going crazy from all this attention. The constant teasing temptations at her hips was becoming too much for Scout Leary. The sensuous teasing of the feather stripping was nearly enough on its own, but the added sensations of Venser's hands on her tender slit plus the tantalizing kiss almost caused her to grip his chest with her talons and rip chunks of flesh from the man.

"Sit up a bit." His fingers twisted inside of her like a little screwdriver, rubbing her more as he took himself out. His thumbs hooked into his baggy red pants and slowly pulled them down, just enough to let her see his V shape as his thick, hard member sprung free, the flaring head of his cock oozing milky white droplets as he kicked his pants away, followed by his bright red boots. "Mhm..." He kissed her again, before laying down on the floor and rubbing his cock up and down. "Sit down..."

The shy harpy courier obeyed and about lost her mind when the man started to twist his finger around inside, such care, she has never had experienced foreplay, feeling his manhood alive and at attention and just waiting for it to enter her. Sitting right above his man hood, a taloned hand reached between her legs and grabbed the man's rod as she guided it to her opening, trying not to scratch him on accident, she bit her lip as she groaned and slowly started to ease herself on. All the way down, as she was taught, til she felt the head hit her cervix. He began to lower himself further as his hand reached her rear. He would cup one of the soft globes of flesh and offer a quick but light spank to her bottom.

As the small harpy woman sat on him, straddling him, the flaring head of his cock brushed against her wet cunny, he grabbed his shaft and used the tip to circle around her lips, her inner thighs, teasing her before pushing himself in slowly. "Mhmmm...!" He reached up and placed his hands on her small breasts, bucking his hips as she rode him. Her cunny was tight, hugging his cock.

"Ahhhahhh...!" Scout moaned as she bounced up and down on the man's thick rod, good thing she was a harpy and she never lost her tightness.

Venser placed his hands on her sides now as the harpy bounced up and down on his cock. Tight, small, the flaring head of his cock kissing her cervix and eventually going past it into her most forbidden portion. The sounds of her ass slapping against his thighs filled the air. "Mhm!"

The harpy girl would moan and make cute lewd noises as she rode the man's rod, feeling him in her womb as not a new thing since she was so small many were able to get past that door, didn't mean it didn't feel good. She was drunk from sex already, her yellow eyes where glazed over and all she cared for was pleasure. He pulled back slowly, gritting his teeth as the pleasurable sensations ran down his cock. Slamming his hips against hers, Venser pushed his cock deep into her tightness, audibly groaning out as the feeling of the heat blossomed through his cock again. Scout cried out in pleasure again, pushing her hips back against him.

"Praise me. Venser, the god of revels and tits and wine and ale and whiskey and mad and wine and spirits and vodka- Mhm! Right there... Yeah," He gave the harpy's rear a hard, firm smack as she continued to bounce up and down on his cock. "And tits and cider. And... Cider." his cock twitched inside of the harpy.

More moans left her lips as her small frame bounced up and down on the man's member it caused more moans and cute lewd sounds to escape from her mouth, placing her talons on his chest and scratching him a bit as she slammed her hips down, intense heat flooded down Venser's shaft, inviting him deeper into her depths.

His features were set, his mind concentrating. Then she could feel it, his cock pulsing as he sped up.

"Mhm! Mhm!" Ven reached under her yet again and grasps his hands around her hips and her plump little ass, digging his fingers into it, and using all his strength he thrusts into her all at once, deep and hard. " He let out a loud yell, feeling himself getting close.

"Oh… Yeahh…"

Relishing the feel of Venser pistoning in and out of her. The moans ever so lightly escaping her lips, flowed with the mewls. Hips still rocking. Grinding herself against his form. She felt a hint of annoyance hearing him speak, saying nothing but the way her body was reacting to his touch said enough of the euphoric bliss that she was feeling for the moment. The feeling of a large cock inside her pussy was incredibly pleasurable to the shy harpy courier, bursts of pleasure rolling up her arching back towards her brain, filling her mind again with nothing but thoughts of agonizingly high pleasure. Scout continued to pant heavily and shout here and there, wings stretched out. Scout's wings flapped erratically as the pleasure mounted in her mind, starting to take over all her usual thoughts, leaving nothing but erotic burning desire. She began to feel her pussy grow hot in her thighs, adding to the solid stream of heat reaching her head already.

Scout let out a load, but muffled moan as the man below her started to pick up his pace, ramming harder into her, her ass was soft and molded to his hands as he groped it. The harpy courier whimpered out, her yellow hues glazed over in pleasure, she all of a sudden threw her head back and let out a moan,and released a wave of her juices all over the man below her as she climaxed. Shuddering her entire frame visibly.

"Aaaaah…!" Scout's wings flared up, flapping as she rode out her exhilarating orgasm, causing Ven to reach his own.

"Oooh ah! Gonna cum!" He growled out, For the moment the first potent load of seed gushed into her belly, Venser's hips began hammering away like there was tomorrow as the harpy exploded on top of him. The sudden shock of climax, the pleasured tingles that run through the body. His cock squirmed inside of her inner walls and nothing but a loud grunt left his lips as his cock erupted with power, painting the insides of her pussy with his sticky seed.

His cum ran down her thighs, and mingling with her juices that soaked the wet sheets beneath them, writhing more when she kept clawing at his bearded chest and collapsed on top oh him, big grey wings going limp. The handsome bearded man gripped the back of her head, lifting it up and he kissed her deeply.

"That was… Mhmmm… That's a good harpy…" The scent of her their sex filled his nostrils, urging a second and third spurt of hot cum directly into her again.

Once his heart rate returned to normal, Venser lifted the small harpy up a bit who was limp with a post love making bliss, managing to free his cock from within her tightness with a satisfying 'pop'. As soon as his cock was free, Scout leaked out his hot semen, gently dripping below them.

"Wow Ven... You really are the most convincing bartender I've ever met..." The harpy girl breathed, licking his lips back before passing out atop him from exhaustion.

The handsome bearded bartender let out a relaxed sigh, adjusting himself beneath her and resting his head against hers.

All before she let out a tired yawn and her yellow eyes barely flittered open.

"H-hey Venser...?"

"Yeah, Scout?"

"Can you finally tell me the story of how you seduced that Queen?"

CHAPTER THIRTY SIX: THE GOLDEN MINX

No Name Port, the island of Pocatellage, 1438 ATC

There were signs that in some other time No Name Port had once been a place of magnificence. Docks that needed repairs, a city full of wooden and stone buildings, blocks of vast grey stone supporting partially ruined warehouses and in the distance a rather large fort that resembled a giant stone mansion. The island itself became a haven for pirates, rogues, scoundrels, outlaws, slavers, and surprisingly traders from every country on Laguna. And was rumored to have been run by the Silver Bank of Avakova. Or rumors had it Carey Webber, the Spider Queen of The Golden Minx. Or there were very few rumors it was run by the elusive cult, the Gods of the Slender Sea. No one was actually quite sure.

Venser and Ruari, accompanied by his succubus friend Cierra passed through a market teeming with peddlers selling everything from shoes to herbs to fish to grilled sharks swarmed a respectful distance away from the softly gleaming white building that stood like a queen among beggars. Beggars there were too, among leather and metal clad mercenaries, sailors and adventurers. More than one drunk passed out or staggering was seen, now and then a well armed looking mariner type, a Pryldahnian woman with unique red facial markings, and their cronies would eye the three warily but for the most part people gave them a wide berth as they made their way through the streets.

"I feel overdressed. But, The Golden Minx is quite the upper class place... So..." Venser said. He wore a crimson velvet longcoat, a white dress shirt with a high collar, red pants with black pinstripes that matched the coat, a floppy bright red cravat with a bronze pin, and a black vest with ten silver buttons on the front.

"I agree, Ven. I've never worn a dress this fancy before. Especially in a place like this..." Ruari wore a long, sparkling cyan gown with golden lines running up and down the sides and the sleeves along with a silver clip. ''... I swear I just saw a man urinating out of his window."

"You two can wait ten minutes and we'll all get out of these constraining outfits soon enough..." Cierra wore the same dress Ven bought for her in Aline. A bright red dress laced with lustrous, pearl beaded fabric with the short skirt and an opening that would expose the navel. "Plenty of merchants and maybe a noble or two to rob... I can't wait."

"Exactly what I want you to do, Cierra. But only steal from the richest, please. Later on we'll be donating some of it to these beggars here..."

"Is that part of how you bought your farm, Ven?" Ruari asked raising a burgundy brow at him, and was answered by both a nod and a shrug.

"It's how I've made MY living all these years, being a succubus and all." Cierra retorted.

"Right right let's not talk about that right now... We're almost there. Either way. This is going to be fun..."

The three made their way up the steps towards the entrance of The Golden Minx, whose double doors were carved with entwined naked bodies clearly meant to be writhing in ecstasy, designs of golden minxes riding upon their shoulders. Looking at the door, and the building, both Cierra and Ruari had to do a double take at the contracting area. Ro herself did a triple take.

The guards were male and female, dressed in effective plate mail of silvered plate and gilded chain, which looked excellently designed and had a six pack and nipples modeled into them, and breasts for the female guards. Each had a short strapped to their sides, and their faceplates were golden with weasel like features.

"We are here for the orgy, and these two have never been here before." Said Venser.

"This is The Golden Minx?" Ro asked looking at the building and the guards and how they contrasted with the rest of No Name Port.

"Yes." A muffled voice came from the male guard. "There is a fee. Twelve gold pieces each."

"Gold pieces? You don't see those often since standard currency is silver." Ro commented again as Venser simply opened one of the pouches on his belt and began to go through it, while Ceirra opened her own purse and counted out the gleaming gold coins.

"Can I pay with gems?" The tanned islandic elf asked.

"No gems. Twelve coins. Gold. Each."

"Don't worry Ro, I've got you covered." Cierra said with a small smile, flashing her sharp canines for a short moment.

Once collected a female guard carefully counted out money. In exchange the doors were swung open and an extraordinary vision greeted them.

The huge chamber was lit with numerous candles which burned brightly. The walls were covered with blue and white curtains and here and there erotic paintings. These were subtle and inviting one that caught Ro's eye showed a woman descending naked into a bath, the painting showing mostly the curve of back and neck and the elegance of her arms rising up to unpin her hair. Cierra noted that Venser had a very similar painting in his study at the villa. The soft pattering sound of water came from fountains that lay at the edges of the room, with gardens of flowers and small trees around them. As they watched they could see a number of naked or near naked folk enjoying themselves on the padded benches that lay about the room.

Here were clearly successful mercenaries and perhaps soldiers off duty, their clothing somewhat worn but their weapons and armor of excellent quality. A shaven haired man with a short beard in Merchant Guild robes was drinking from a goblet and smiling as a serving woman in a linen gown that exposed one breast, her dark hair pinned up and her supple arms bare, made her way past him, smiling flirtatiously.

"There's that woman with the face tattoos..." Ven mumbled to himself watching the armored woman slip down a hallway, long draconian tail flopping behind her.

A young woman with blonde hair pinned up in an elaborate braid approached. Her gown was of a silky material that suggested the shape of her body but revealed little in actual fact. She smiled warmly and said, "Welcome to The Golden Minx. Would you care to come in and relax for a bit? We have a banquet down the hall for all of our event guests."

Venser looked to the tall temptress beside him, and then the tanned islandic elf with curly dark red hair, and they all nodded their head at him.

"Lead the way..." Venser said, wrapping both arms around Ruari and Cierra.

"So what's the occasion? Why are these orgies only every few months?" Ro asked the girl who led them on.

"Winter is almost here. A time of despair, cold and death... But before the snow comes we couldn't be more alive." The girl said happily, smiling behind them, causing Venser to chuckle and nod.

"I couldn't have said it better myself!"

The food was good and fresh, delicious pears and plums, strawberries in cream, hot fresh biscuits baked with cheese and garlic, roasted chicken with lemon and pepper, fish broiled in wine, strips of lamb crusted with spices, warm bread gleaming with saffron oil. They had such a variety of fine wines. Good water they had always but the water that could be brought by soft eyed serving maids here tasted as though it came from a mountain spring.

As they looked round they would see a statue of a girl with wide hips in the garden by one of the fountains. Shown nude, reaching for a bath towel while covering her crotch which, in turn left her hefty breasts exposed. The subtlety of the eroticism of the room startled and enticed them.

They watched the worker girls move around them, hands enticing, hips swaying. Their expressions ranged from calm to ecstatic. This was more like a palace than a whorehouse in a wretched island such as Pocatellage.

Cierra ran her hands through her straight black hair and sighed, looking at the fountains. "It's a good thing we bathed before we came... It was as if we were getting ready for the ball." The movement lifted her bosom and Ruari felt desire make her flush warmly. She loved the tall temptress's contrasting aloofness and softness, the former hid just how cunning a succubus she could be. "We can have one here after the orgy. Now where do we go exactly..."

"Don't know where to go?" A passing serving maid asked pleasantly. "We do have a bathing chamber here if you'd care to. And may I ask how This One can serve you?" she looked between the two as if calculating something.

"Well... We would like to register for the orgy but we'd also love to try your bath afterwards. I'll handle this, both of you... Just go explore." Venser said with enthusiasm, leaning on his new cane. A mahogany finished walking cane, the handle metal and at the top of it an ornament that looked like a golden snake, a sword concealed within the cane itself. He gave both Ruari and Ceirra a kiss on the lips before he was led away by the serving girl. He passed by a smoking room and smelled the earthy scent with a hint of citrus of his cannabis cigar, and smiled to himself knowing that his product had made it to such an establishment as this.

"It's been a while since I've been here. About... A year or so?'"

"I'm sure it has been, sir." The serving girl said as Venser let out a sigh, rolling his shoulders back as he made his way through the debauchery and to the back of the brothel to what looked like the twin doors of a ballroom, converted into a large open area with many cushions and mattresses A few guards stood at the door along with a few workers at a table with ledgers. After signing, "Venser Karkaldwin, Ruari Patel, and Cierra Dusk" on the ledger he went back to find his girls. And when he walked back he couldn't help but notice a very particular woman who bad been watching him since he entered. She had light pink skin with red lips and crimson markings about her eyes. Towards the edge of her jaw and over her ears and forehead were some red scales. She had a black undercut. Combined with the slit pupil, acid-green eyes, the rather obvious horns protruding from her head and the dragon-like features marked her as a Pryldahnian. One who had watched Ven for sometime.

Venser waved to her, and walked away again.

Ruari and Cierra met with the most exotic person they had ever seen to register for the orgy. She wore a hoodlike veil that was beautifully embroidered with gold and scarlet thread woven over the blue material with a web like design, framing older, yet lovely light features and full lips, and pale blue eyes and dirty blonde hair. They sat on a cushioned bench, holding hands as the beautiful older lady asked them discreet but probing questions about their sexual preferences. Ruari blushed and admitted she liked to watch and that she's taken part in group sex before, and Cierra was smiling wide and proud the entire time until Venser came back.

"Shall we go, loves? I'll show us where we need to go. And they told me that there is a new rule. Even though we bathed and everything we've got to do it again before we go into the orgy."

"Can never be too clean, right? And it's much better than a drop in the ocean or in the lake." Ruari spoke up, and Venser silently gestured for both of them to take one of his hands each, as he nodded to the woman with the hood.

"Mistress Webber..."

"Venser."

"Yes. We don't want to be late for the orgy and we want to have as many partners as we can so... Yes. We should catch up later. Yes yes, let's go now" The handsome bearded barkeep said tugging the tall tempress and the islandic elf along, much to Mistress Webber's amusement.

"What was that about?" Ro asked.

"That was the owner, I'm certain of it." Cierra pipped.

"Yes it was. Carey Webber, the Spider Queen... Knower of many secrets and uhh... Head. Lady of the night."

"Ven, did you sleep with her?" Ruari asked before letting out a sigh. "Why should I even ask?"

"You know, actually last week I got asked by this cute harpy mailwoman..." Venser began before Ro cut him off.

"I remember, I was there the story of how you fucked that queen."

"Yeah. I had a fling with the Spider Queen of No Name Port a couple years back when I was still... Well, more nutty than I am now."

"Nutty is an understatement." Cierra said with a giggle, a lot of patrons looking to the six foot tall temptress as her long legs took long strides. "I'm still convinced he's an incubus. A sex demon from the depths of Coldwrought who can't get enough of the warmth of another being close to them..."

Opening the doors to the massive ballroom, they were met by a giant crowd of all kinds of men and women from all different races and walks of life mute evaluating the warm, naked bodies around them.

"I am going to fuck every woman in here..." Venser said through his teeth, licking his lips.

There was a great flurry of activity. There was an athletic man on the floor, on his back, casually straddled by a female elven slave girl, one of the rare dark elves from the Obsidian Islands. Behind her was another man taking up her backdoor, while a third was in front, filling her mouth. Lastly, two other men shuddered hard as her hands squeezed and stroked their trembling, leaking shafts, causing Ro to gasp and watch in awe, stopping in place before grabbing Venser's hand.

"I want THAT."

The handsome bearded man's snake-like, emerald eyes watched that particular scene and he bent down and kissed Ro on the cheek.

"We will get you that..."

A random wiry merchant with a neatly trimmed goatee and moustache and his wife tumbled to a large round bed, limbs entangled and roaming. Two mouths met in a slow, deep kiss, and for a fraction of a second they were at rest.

The wiry merchant, though much lighter than his companion, wrestled his way on top. Their hips met, their urgent, twitching lengths pressed together like molten bars. The heat shocked them both for a moment, then the grinding resumed, back and forth, hot breath across their mouths. One's hand found a soft, bony chest, the other a muscular neck. They both smiled and redoubled their counter-movements as their climax approached like a rising tide.

An elven worker girl rolled onto her back and spread her legs. Another rough looking adventurer woman with a shaved head found her groin, tongue lashing and spreading her supplicant partner's delicious cunny.

"What do you think? Cierra? Ro?" Venser nudged the islandic elf. "Let's get started!"

Ruari bit her lip, standing in the doorway with Venser and his succubus friend as they watched the orgy before them, her hand moved slowly against her own womanhood, teasing herself and getting nice and wet. Around, in, in, up and circle. A long, steady press against her clit. Her blood pressure rose, second by second, and then she moved her hand up and around again. And Venser simply nudged her forward as he wandered off into the lewd crowd, his thick cock, protruded proudly between his legs, and the orange eyed succubus followed.

Venser found a girl, with long curly black hair, tawny eyes and a septum ring, her legs spread and a cock in her mouth, displaying every inch of herself to everyone in the room. And Venser approached, a hand running up and down his cock, slowing down ever so slightly. Spreading her pussy open, then he lined up his shaft and slid inside. She was more than ready for it, and encouraged him on with a long, low moan, all while grasping the cock in her mouth from another man and rubbing it up and down as she sucked.

A bearded barbarian approached on a woman's other end and offered her the tip of his cock. She arched her back and stretched her neck, and the barbarian grunted as she wrapped her lips around both his balls, her tongue flicking out to savor the underside of his shaft.

He took a step back and lowered his hips, and the woman opened her mouth wide, eyes narrowed with desire. He set his head between her lips and slowly pushed forward too slow for the woman's liking, perhaps, as she stretched her head up to meet him, eager for every inch of barbarian meat. He took the hint and began to thrust, slowly, back and forth, in and out of her throat.

The adventurer woman with a shaved head reached back with a hand and stroked her own unattended vulva, fingers parting the lips a little and teasing her clit. She moaned inside her partner and pressed in until her nose was against the hood of the elven worker's pussy. She snaked her tongue deep inside, searching for a spot she knew well.

The elven woman gasped, fire coursing from her belly to her crotch. The heat and the energy of dozens of excited men and women blurred around her. Her cunny clenched tight around the woman's mouth that was thrust inside it, but the woman with the shaved head, her nimble tongue never stopped lashing and poking and caressing her passage. She tried to scream, but the thick cock in her throat turned it into a muted, guttural moan of pleasure.

Everyone all writhing and licking and thrusting and groaning before them. Those whose tastes aligned clumped together, feeding into and off of each other's energy. Most had already gotten started, while others were taking a bit longer to warm up, as it were.

Venser laid on one of the beds, with Ruari straddling his hips and her hand reaching down to grab his cock, rubbing the slick shaft up and down before sliding it inside of her cunny, letting out a please moan as she began to ride his cock while a four foot tall gnome woman with cropped, curled, blond hair shaved on the right side, brown eyes, and a lean build with thick hips sat on his face, Venser's strong hands on her hips lapping at her cunny. From behind two muscular men, recognized as athletes in the Grand Games had wrapped themselves around Ro, one steadily thrust in and out asshole while the other gripped the islandic elf's curly dark red hair, sucking on his engorged organ. Seed trickled out from around their cocks, clearly this wasn't their first round. Ro choked out and withdrew from one of the athlete's cock, quivering with delight and letting out a howl as a few more men approached Ruari and the gnome woman sitting on Venser's face, rubbing their own members up and down as they came closer to them.

Nearby a large Pryldahnian man fucked an stubbled human man in earnest, deep and fast, almost pulling free after each thrust. The slap of hips meeting rump filled the room amidst an ocean of moans of pleasure, punctuated by the grunts and gasps and moans of two horny homosexual man.

An older woman and her chubby partner tumbled to one of the beds, beside several other partners, legs already intertwined, thighs pressed to vulvas and noses to necks.

Every woman in the room was all too willing to offer their bodies as they spread their legs wide, offering their cunts, asses, mouths throats, and hands, and the men all too happily complied. Even the floor was covered in real puddles of the viscous and sticky liquid of everyone's mixed love juices.

All the while back in the patron's storeroom, Cierra had played with quite a few women and teased a few men, sucked a cock here and there and spent a good amount of time breaking into the lockboxes and stealing a few small valuables her group could easily carry out, stashing them in their own box for now before returning to the orgy room.

Meanwhile, a cock had been pushed into each of her tanned brown hands. Ro shivered and twisted her head, circling, licking another cockhead with her tongue and aiming it for her throat. Behind her, another random man had four fingers in her ass, two from each hand, pulling her open, stretching her out, all while below Ruari Venser kept pounding away at her pussy. This man was taller than most men in here, and had broad shoulders, a dark brown undercut, and wore an eyepatch. He grabbed her fat cheeks and pulled them apart, and pressed his monster dick against her open asshole.

SHLAPP!

"AUGH! FUCK MARILLA THE SEA GODDESS'S TITS!"

CHAPTER THIRTY SEVEN: THE MINX'S INFILTRATION

The Golden Minx Brothel, No Name Port, the island of Pocatellage, 1438 ATC

The men and women who walked about moved in slow, deliberate movements, with semen-slick shafts and overflowing holes, sore muscles and burning lungs. Some of the less vital men and women were already beginning to doze off. Dozens of naked bodies were sprawled across the floor and the beds. Each of them, bar none, was coated in some combination of feminine nectar, spunk, saliva, or a cocktail of the three.

After the orgy they went to the larger bathing area to relax and soak. A couple of other female patrons were at the farther end, nodding to them but clearly not much interested in conversation. A fountain stood in the middle of the pool making a soft pattering sound. There seemed to be a current in the water, looking around Ruari could see metal grates on the sides of the pool underwater as she began to descend into the bath.

"How clever... This has better... What's the word? We don't have a lot of drainage back in the Alphonse Islands, or any islands that I've visited."

"Such as an elegant brothel in a cesspit of a city like this? It makes little sense, I know." Cierra said using a sponge to wipe the soap suds off her breasts, giggling a bit.

"Ruari Patel, you strumpet!"

The short island elf stood paused, cum dripping in thick strands from her body as she glared over at the tall temptress, sweating heavily as well as mixed love juices ran down her nearly covered body, huge strings of semen spread across her small chest.

"Shut up... And give me that sponge. And... Help clean me off?'"

In another room, a young muscled woman who was fair skinned with red lips and crimson markings about her eyes, cheeks, and mouth. Towards the edge of her jaw, forehead and over her ears were some bronze scales. Combined with the slit-pupil, acid-green eyes, the rather obvious horns protruding from her head and draconian tail wrapped around Ven marked her as a Pryldahian. She was being pounded away by Venser himself, who hoisted the girl up on a counter and spread her long shapely legs apart while he pleasured her.

"Mhmmm... What's your name, gorgeous?" He grunted out.

"Nodessa... And I know who you are, Venser... Mhm!"

"Oh so you've heard of me..." He chuckled. He pushed forward inch by inch, thick cock sliding gradually into the thin, glossy O of her stretched pussy lips. His arms wrapped around her waist, holding her steady, enjoying the way her lean muscles flexed around him.

"How do you like getting fucked by the god of tits and cider and... Mhm! Melons!"

Nodessa shuddered and arched her back, long draconian tail wrapping around him, as well as letting out a chuckle.

"Mhmm! I heard you were this good... And arrogant... But I need your help with something..." She brought her mouth to his ear and began whispering in a hushed tone, her eyes darting all around them for a few long moments.

"Mhmm... Why me? Why now? Errr come on let's get straight to the point..."

"Straight to the point... Mhm! Good... I know you know your way around here, and you had a fling with the Spider Queen herself... In her archives... Mhm... Just finish up and we'll go find somewhere private to discuss it?"

"Mhm!" He hilted inside of Nodessa. "The baths!"

"So, one of the other main monopolies around here is brothels. Mistress Webber runs the queen whorehouse of them all... Here. As you know. She's something of a mystery, that one."

"Uh huh. Yeah. Telling me what I know." Venser said handing the Pryldahnian warrior woman a cup of special herbal tea that negated pregnancy, and was prized as a good source of birth control for anyone that could get it. And he had gotten a spare one for Ruari as well. The topless server girl behind the table nodded to them and smiled as they both began to walk back to the bath area, silent all the way as they entered, and he couldn't help but smile and nod to all the other women in the baths, who all returned it back or just looked to each other and giggled.

Cierra's long hair damply clung to her bare arms and shoulders, her lovely body nice and wet as she leaned over and licked off all of the mixed love juices that covered Ro's upper body and neck. Unable to resist taking her in her arms, Ro sighed with delight, relaxing as Cierra held a sponge in one hand and washed her just as Venser returned.

"Hey, it looks like you still got a bit of egg on your face, Ro." Venser said descending into the warm bathwater, gesturing for Nodessa to join them.

The tall succubus and the islandic elf both looked at them as Venser handed Ro one of the herbal teas, raising it to her nose and sniffing it.

"This is some really fishy tea..."

"Drink that, we don't want you getting pregnant." Venser said as Nodessa began to settle in, relaxing her tail under the water.

Ro just nodded in affirmation and Cierra opened her mouth to speak, before Venser waved her off.

"Uhhh, me and her are gonna squeeze into that little corner right there and discuss things in private. Just get to cleaning her off, Cierra."

Ro was barely able to comprehend but shuddered and moaned a bit as the succubus's tongue glided over her jawline and cheek, taking a sip of her herbal tea and paying Ven and the muscled Pryldahnian girl no nevermind.

"So, I was hoping you could help me, since I already helped you." Nodessa said.

"Helped you by getting laid? Why ask me and not any of the other higher tier mercenaries here?" Venser asked with a smug smile, relaxing his arms out lazily on the sides of the bath. "You know, I did notice you watching us when we walked over here."

"No... I've heard stories about you, that you're exceptional. I easily recognize you from the posters. And that you know the teleportation spell despite someone of your age, and that you happen to know a lot of the right people as well."

Venser bit his lip and nodded his head up and down. "Yup! That's me! Venser Karkaldwin, Master of the Melon, the God of Tits and Cider and Cannabis, adventurer and Pryldahnian Legend... But like, nowadays I've been trying to town on it since I'm almost forty and I have a business now and a family."

"You don't understand Venser! This is important... I can offer you coin... And it's also about family." All Venser did was raise a brow and waited for Nodessa to continue.

"Have you heard of the Gods of The Slender Sea?"

"Oh yeah, I know Marilla well... My people worship her." Ro commented while Cierra continued to lick all the cum off of her, almost cleaning her completely.

"No no... The Gods of the Slender Sea are a cult that controls all of the seas. Literally. From the pirates that roam them, the shipbuilders, some mercenaries, people of influence and power who want to control everything else as they see fit. And they have my sister. The only thing I know is that the pirate lord The Squall is involved... And they were here a few days ago. And that the Spider Queen has the information since every scrap of information that comes through this city goes through her."

"I've heard of The Squall. He's been terrorizing the Alphonse Island for years, and I've heard some of the weaker islands have to pay tribute." Ro said sitting straight up, her eyes going wide.

"So, you want me to help steal information from Mistress Webber then? Because that's what it sounds like." Nodessa nodded at him, her tail making small movements in the water.

"Yes, you and me. Working together."

A nod of affirmation.

"So you want me to help you sleep with her-"

Nodessa shook her head in negation. "No, I want your help to sneak into archives upstairs. So we can unmask The Squall and figure out who they are, what they look like, and any other information. That might help. As well as any other members of The Gods of The Slender Sea.

The handsome bearded man went silent for a few seconds and gave her a stoic stare, before saying, "Now, as well as I like a good adventure I'm not all for getting involved in unmasking a worldwide conspiracy."

"Wait wait wait..." Cierra pipped with a hushed tone. "First we are stealing from the rich... And now the Gods of the Slender Sea? Who exactly is this... Cult?"

"I'm not too sure exactly... Basically, they are a group of people that hide in the shadows and seek to unite the entire world under one banner by any means necessary... Including brainwashing using ancient Kundalandian artifacts. From common brigands to empires. They gather influence and wealth, spinning their webs of lies and deceit in the shadowy heights of society."

There was an eerie silence between Venser and his girls, Ro was looking quite clean now. Venser broke the silence by saying, "Sounds about right. I'll help you find information on The Squall. And that's it. I'm not interested in getting caught up in getting me and my lovers here caught up in some global hunt."

"Oh I would love a shot at The Squall..." Ro muttered.

"That's the thing..." Nodessa began. "I enlisted your help so you could teleport us up there and bypass all the security easy."

Venser leaned forward as they conversed in the bath. "The Golden Minx has a suppression field that specifically prevents teleportation. So, either it's the work of mages or a weirdstone... But either way, the only say to actually get to the second floor is to sneak... So, that's what we're going to have to do. Though, I have one ability that actually does work here..."

Still in the nude, discreetly as possible, Venser and Nodessa slipped past the armored guards who patrolled the inner hallways, avoiding brushing against servants, and knocking out a pair of guards and taking their armor. The place was big, well appointed, elegant and very clean. It was floored mostly in the inner halls with soft beautiful carpets. It was lit almost everywhere with everburning candles.

"This armor is too small..." Nodessa commented.

"Not to mention it was a pain to get on." Venser said behind his golden weasel faceplate.

"I'm used to armor. Being a Koran mercenary." Nodessa said. Venser nodded as they walked side by side acting like guards down the hall.

"Kora? Right. North of Pryldahn, and I heard everyone there is a fanatic of Kore the war god and all of you are basically born to crave battle. And I mean... All of you are ripped too."

"All Korans are born to be warriors, grow up as warriors, and find no greater honor than to die as warriors. Though, I loved playing in the sea more than anything with my sister. One day she left to join the Koran Navy and never came back... I did the same, not sure about my place in this world."

"Have you been back since?" Venser asked listening to Nodessa explain her origins. "And those markings..."

"Not for many years, no. I was a member of the Hydra Monks for a few years, and I left them as well. Despite all the training and time I spent there... I just wasn't fulfilled."

He had listened and peered in when possible in the assignation rooms. Oddly the madams who supervised the place treated the prostitutes, male and female, as though they were ignorant savages or animals, speaking to them sharply, with snapped fingers and warning glances, much to Venser's distaste. They all wore shiny black leather collars with a gold ring on the front of them, both a sign of slavery and bondage. The very sense of order and calm in such a place as this was strange to them, as a majority of the guards were downstairs watching the large influx of patrons.

"You remember where you're taking us, right Venser?"

"Yes. I've been up here before once or twice. Or... Thrice."

They entered a library of pornography which seemed to also have records of the activities of patrons and began to peer through the most recent volumes.

"So... What exactly do we have to go off of? Since the entire purpose here is identifying The Squall."

"The Squall is Koran, just like me... So, dragon-like features, fierce eyes... And three scars on the right side of their head. I have no idea if The Squall is a man or woman, the tales are never clear."

Some of the highly detailed pornography he read made Venser get an erection within his armor, closing one volume and noticing a display marked, "Private Collection."

"You'd think this would be in the Mistress's Chambers..." Nodessa commented, looking to the chain and the lock. "Is anyone coming? I'm going to rip this right off."

The handsome bearded man turned around and held up his left hand, his mark began to glow greenish white and emit steam until it quickly dispelled, Venser's strange slitted pupils became so thin they almost disappeared. Everything around him now became blue silhouettes, and the bodies of every living thing through the walls were yellow outlines of their bodies. He noted a pair of guards passing the doors to the library, and a majority of others were either absent or guarding the other women in the other rooms.

"And... We should be good for now."

"Venser, push back against the display. Otherwise it will all come tumbling down." Nodessa ordered, and Venser complied.

"So are you just-" And the strong Koran warrior woman simply yanked the lock and chain off, much to Venser's surprise. He simply shrugged as they both began to pour over the pages, noting the detailed drawings of Mistress Webber and her many sex partners.

"A note... From last night. I am happy you are so impressed with what I have shown you. The Foul Fury has been rebuilt. Stronger. Faster. And we now openly sail under the squid banner. We will disembark from Pocatellage tomorrow early morning. What I long for is battle, a chance to crack open the hulls of my enemies. And I shall return to you soon Mistress Webbers with many spoils in the form of jewelry, you will see. And I will give my regards to The Squall for you my Mistress. I heard he set sail west, maybe near The Alphonse Islands. That's where I'm headed. - Captain Tylar Pereira." A sketch of the man was provided. Shaved head, a short beard, and an edgy bland face.

"We have a clue. All we've got to do is find this Captain Pereira as well as the Foul Fury." Nodessa said as Venser looked to the sketch for a few seconds.

"I don't recognize this man... And most likely he's already gone back to the ship since I know many of the sailors do that once they are done with business here."

"We can go grab our gear and race back to the Freeman's Paragon, follow him out of the harbor, and then seize him and all of the cult's plunder." Nodessa said with a nod taking the note and hiding it in her chestpiece.

"Not let's get out of here..."

CHAPTER THIRTY EIGHT: THE FREEMAN'S PARAGON

No Name Port, the Island of Pocatellage, 1438 ATC

"... The ship ye be boardin' is called the Freeman's Paragon, as there be treasure beyond closed doors that awaits the infamous ERB-all-ist recently acquired. And I be Captain Willem Wake." The captain had bright blue eyes, was in his sixties, and wore a large grey sunhat and had a bushy salt and pepper beard.

As Brayden Buckyton climbed the Jacob's Ladder and landed upon the polished wood with a resounding 'thud', Pip, Lager and the ship's dog, Cranberry, all promptly sat up from their nap- hurriedly rubbing the sleep from their eyes to erase the evidence of their naps. The dog attempting to follow suit, however failing due to his lack of coordination and thumbs. "Alright ye maggots,-" Brayden began, tossing a look over his broad shoulder to see the rest of the crew stiring to life and begin to prepare to set sail. "Let's ready the anchor, ready the oars and let loose the ropes. I've a feelin' our Koran mercenary will aboard within minutes, with a new addition and hopefully a feckin' destination." He declared, though his chest felt short o' breath as he realized Nodessa would only be bringing one new mate aboard and not two. "Aye, aye!" Were the resounding echoes the crew's response, all sixteen o' them plus the dog running around like eejits in preparation for their next journey.

"Joining us as well, Ruari? Cierra?" Nodessa asked, one brow arched to perfection. "We sail within an hour."

"Yup!" Venser pipped up speaking for all of them. "For now we are all in this together."

"Brayden be the boss, right behind Captain Wake. He'd tan my hide if I barked an order your way without a second though, I reckon." She smiled back. "As you all are passengers for now until we take down the Foul Fury."

"The life of a pirate pays pretty well." Ro commented. "Er, not that I... I've dealt with pirates many times before. I am from the Alphonse Islands."

Blue hues trained upon the crew hard at work readying the ship at berth. Were they...? With a roll of those eyes, Nodessa smacked his palm against her forehead and gave a groan. "Fuckin eejits, the entire lot o' you!" He wailed, shaking his grey haired head.

"FIRST the anchor, THEN the rudder, THEN THE BLOODY SAILS! We get the oars out once we're out of the harbor!" With a stomp and huff. He shook his head when Brayden glanced up to curse back at her for yellin' at him, only to watch his jaw drop when his dark gaze settled upon the lass she'd brought with her. For him. "Aye, aye!" A resounding chorus echoed from the ship, and Captain Wake was back to rolling those blue hues upward. "NO, NAE!" He yelled back, more-so growled. Were they truly all daft? Had they even heard her right?

Brayden looked up from uncoiling the rope thicker than his skin, aiming to strip them up and down with his words for yelling at him like he was a bloody moron. Until his gaze landed upon the new man and the two girls. He felt his lips part at the surprise, his mind whirring with all the possibilities as to why they'd be heading this direction. As if there'd been a fire lit under his ass, Brayden hopped the deck-railing and landed on the dock below.

The young sailor noted his heart didn't skip a beat at the sight of Nodessa again, though he had the foresight to determine that would eventually change the more he became convinced she was here to stay. There would be mornings when she would step out of their bedchamber, the sunrise upon the horizon framing her beautiful figure as if she were a divine beauty. His heart would skip a beat then. Or when they were readying' the ship to sail from another port. He would look over and she'd be there beside him, leaning across the banister with a smile too-big for her face as she reveled in the salty air and the beautiful view. She would be his view... He thought, smiling to himself as he freed the coiled rope and set to work upon another.

Nodessa moved to the helm and set her slender fingers upon the wheel- fingertips sliding over the polished, cherry oak finish smoothly. She'd dreamed of commandeering a ship ever since she was young, and the appreciation that she'd finally won it was not lost on her. Her strong draconian tail swishing back and forth happily.

Cierra smiled and settled against his side after they were aboard the ship. The breeze blew her hair around her face as she stood beside Venser. She was not in love with him but drawn to him in a way she could not explain. This man stirred something inside her. She was void of a need to feed from him or entice him. She bared herself around him. She looked up at him and chuckled. She stepped back a little on her unsteady legs and looked down at the deck, not used to being on ships as they watched everyone scurry about. The tall temptress stood there with her head hung down, her burnt orange eyes lowered with a glimmered, her red dress billowing round her legs and her raven hair billowing about her like some wild halo as she let out a sigh.

"Came here for naught?" Captain Wake asked the new people aboard his ship. "I hope you all 'ave a thirst for adventure. It would be a droll voyage without it." Looking back down at the ropes. "Bloody damnation!" He swore, realizing he'd supposed to have been coiling instead of uncoiling. How else were they to take off?

"Brayden!"

With a deep exhale, Brayden set re-coiling the ropes he'd just uncoiled.

"We've got a target! Not far from here is a ship with a squid on it's sails, the Foul Fury! And today we board them, kill every God of the Slender Sea cultist aboard, and take their cargo!"

"Oh this is going to be fun!" Venser ejaculated looking to Ro and Cierra.

Cierra simply smiled while Ro brushed back her hair and sighed.

"Exactly what I am used to."

"An adventure on the high seas!"

"Oars ready! Sails ready! Prepare to cast off ye dogs!"

CHAPTER THIRTY NINE: THE FOWL FURY

The southwestern Slender Sea, 1438 ATC

Far into the southwest, there sailed a single ship in the deep blue sea. She was on a mission, soaking in the feel of the waves on this peaceful trip so far. However this was no ordinary ship, this was one of the finest vessels to ever sail the Slender Sea. Led by a renown captain, any who gazed upon the red sails of the ship and dared face them in combat would be in for quite a challenge.

There was always new land out there, waiting to be explored, and plenty of plunders and bounties. With that settled, Captain Wake put away his spyglass.

"Let's move everyone!" The Captain shouted. "Every scrap of deck on the wind!"

The Freeman's Paragon began to move at its fastest speed toward the ship with the squid sigil in the distance.

Taking in the brisk salty air. As they got closer to the enemy ship, The Fowl Fury, Captain Wake turned the ship abroad, he steered the ship towards around them from the side to flank them and give them enough room for arrows.

"I could sneak onto the ship and set it aflame."

Venser said standing on the deck with Nodessa, Cierra, and Ruari. He had teleported himself and Ruari away to go change and get their equipment since they now knew where they were before they set sail. Venser wore his usual crimson and turquoise entertainers tunic , his utility belt, his wrist bow, and not much else. While Ro wore a dark blue shirt and matching pants with a matching sash and a few pieces of metal armor she had borrowed from Ven, tightened around her arms and torso, and a helmet borrowed from the Nodessa's crew. Meanwhile Cierra had slipped into a simple all black dress and opted to stay away from the fighting.

"That would defeat the purpose of salvaging the ship and everything they have, Venser." Ruari pointed out, the wind blowing through her curly burgundy locks.

"She's right. But if we could get close enough you could teleport aboard, cause some chaos while we fire on them and board them with little resistance." Nodessa said with a nod readying her shield and short sword, giving Ven a strange look before pulling down the faceplate of her helmet. She wore a bronze metal corset with a short collar, and light armor with steel plates on the hips, and shoulder protectors complemented with a torn, bright red short cape over one shoulder.

"You know you could lose an eye or lose your head going into combat without a helmet, Venser. Or anything else to protect you."

The handsome bearded man himself did a double take at Nodessa's outfit when she pointed that out.

"Ah naw, it'll slow me down when I fight and what if I get knocked overboard? It'll all weigh me down so I'll be good either way."

Ro shook her head and scoffed, trying to for her unruly curly locks underneath the simple leather and metal helmet handed to her by one of the crew.

Nodessa stared at him with her acid green slitted eyes and let out a sigh. "Let's hope you're as extraordinary as the rumors say..."

"We're in range Captain Wake!" First mate Brayden yelled to the salt and pepper bearded Captain Wake. "They see us as well!" The massive ship with the squid on their sails began to advance and turn to get in range with their own archers.

"Battle stations everyone! Arrows! Pick up the rowing!"

Ro tensed up as they came closer and closer in range, her cutlass sheathed and holding her whalebone staff close to her.

"Arrows!"

Both ships were closing fast as the pirate crew of the Freeman's Paragon readied their bows, while the soldiers of the Fowl Fury were all armes with Pryldahnian repeating crossbows, which would lose their power with a longer distance.

The sounds of arrows and bolts whistling through the air and shouting of orders from both ships were nothing compared to the heavy waves of the slender sea, and it took about thirty seconds for any of the projectiles to actually make contact.

"Duck!"

"Slow the oars!"

"Venser, get over there!"

Venser jogged across the deck and disappeared in a puff of thick red smoke, reappearing on the back of the deck of the Fowl Fury much to the surprise of everyone on board. Venser unhooked the strange sword hilt on his belt and twirled it in a three sixty motion, allowing the blades to telescope into a short sword.

"What the- Get him!"

"Archers! Loose!" Cried the first mate of the Fowl Fury as he stood beside the helmsman at the wheel.

Bzzzzzt!

When a cultist sailor rushed at him with a sword, Venser pushed out his left hand and a stream of magical green lightning burst from his fingertips and struck the man, sending him flying back against the walls of the ship. He teleported back away and when he reappeared he ran his blade over his left palm, coating it with his blood. Venser then struck his sword with magical green lightning and reinforced it with the same power.

Another soldier drew his sword and started to run towards the man. Rushed rushed and when he raised his sword, Venser thrust forward and impaled the soldier in the lower chest ending his life quickly.

After the body dropped, two more soldiers swung at the handsome bearded man, but Venser quickly sidestepped one swing, while parrying the other with surprising swiftness, all while the helmsman tried to stay calm at the wheel and pilot the Fowl Fury, and the archers kept firing on hia companions. Venser pushed the opposing blade away, waving about his unstable green lightning blade. After he pushed, Venser stepped forwards, making a backhand motion and blasting the off-balanced cultist soldier with a powerful gust of wind. He turned his attention back to his other attacker and did the same. Before rushing at the helmsman and screaming, causing the cultist crossbowmen to lose their focus and all aim their fire to the man with the lightning sword causing chaos on deck.

"We've got them softened up! Let's board them!" Captain Wake let out a hearty laugh and got the Freeman's Paragon closer.

"Let's board the bastards!"

More of the cultists in dark purple and copper armor lay dead compared to the ragtag pirates as a harpoon from the Freemans Paragon punched through the hull of the Fowl Fury and bound them together.

Jumping aboard and ducking, a blade passed over Nodessa's head. She slashed at the soldier's ankle, making him fall backwards. Standing up straight, the Koran pirate plunged her short sword downward into the fallen soldier's chest, killing him and raising her shield to block a couple of incoming bolts, and the cultist crew began to drop their crossbows as they began to run out of bolts, drawing their swords and clashing.

A soldier turned and swung with a sword, with Ruari just barely dodging, blocking another swing with both her whalebone staff and cutlass, kicking her foot out into his groin and slashing at his neck, killing the man.

"Oof!"

Venser was struck in the head by a the butt of a Pryldahnian autocrossbow, falling back against the railing and leaving him disoriented as he began to pass out.

A large masked cultist swung at Nodessa with a battle axe, missing and smashing a nearby banister, causing broken splinters to fly everywhere. The Koran pirate shook himself off and started circling the man, trying to find an opening to attack, all before jumping forward and shield bashing him, and Ro held out the tip of her staff and pushed the massive man over the edge of the ship with a powerful gust of wind.

"You're welcome!"

A balding man with a shaved head, blue eyes and extremely round features burst out of the captain's cabin, a sword in each hand. This was Captain Tylar Peraira, one of the members of the Gods of The Slender Sea.

"Come now, which dares challenge the Scourge of The Slender Sea?!"

He couldn't be heard over the chaos, and was promptly shot in the throat by a stray bolt, falling dead as the crew of the Freeman's Paragon overtook the Fowl Fury.

"Search the ship! We will drag all the cargo aboard and then have the Fowl Fury sold and scuttled!" Nodessa yelled once the enemy cultists were dead, and many of her own crew were looking for them. As the Koran mercenary was searching Captain Peraira's body as well.

"C'mon Ven stay awake..." Ro mumbled kneeling in front of the handsome bearded man, shaking him and trying to keep him conscious while wiping away the blood on the side of his head.

"Oh wow fuck my cock that's a concussion... Oh wow that all happened so fast... Urgh." Venser mumbled sitting up and coughing a bit.

"Like what the fuck happened during all that?"

Ro sighed and shook her head.

"Everyone told you to wear a helmet..."

"Bottles of wine, rum, sugar and spices... A chest or two of silver coins but no gems. And... Holy... These will sell well." First mate Brayden muttered to himself checking below deck while Nodessa herself went to rummage through the captain's cabin.

A random crew member opened one of the many crates and found several crossbows and hand bombs, enough for a small army. Captain Peirara had been an arms dealer all along.

While the numerous, miscellaneous treasures were nice, her acid green hues widened at a simple treasure.

A journal filled with precious information on the Gods of the Slender Sea, and her target, the infamous Squall.

Who was The Squall really?

"Nodessa, we need to grab all we can and find the nearest port to sell the Foul Fury. There's a storm coming in!"

CHAPTER FORTY: STARGAZING ON THE SLENDER SEA

The southwestern Slender Sea, 1438 ATC

The chill of the early winter nights lingered despite the blooming flowers on the islands who were due to wither and die any moment now. Clouds dissipated from the day storm leaving a clear dark sky with a bright moon and thousands of stars. There was better time to enjoy the stars than after a storm. Everything was quite calm as they drifted back towards the nearest port, and Venser, Cierra, and Ruari all sat near the railings, watching the calm waves of the ocean and the sky.

A seagull landed on the railing nearby, a fish clutched in his talons. It squawked before it began to peck and eat it, causing Cranberry the ship's dog to bark and chase it off, claiming the fish for himself, much to the laughter of a few crewmembers of the Freeman's Paragon. They heard the heavy thuds of boots on the wooden deck and they knew it belonged to the six foot tall Koran warrior woman.

"Enjoying the stargazing? How are you all holding up?" Nodessa Narada asked, the black undercut between her small horns was looking quite unruly.

"It's going good." Ro said, sighing, letting out a yawn and closing her eyes, breathing in the salty air.

The sea is peaceful at night with gentle waves rocking the ship, sometimes breaking audibly on a nearby rock.

Venser only gave a simple nod and kept looking at the many colorful galaxies and stars that dotted the sky. He would never get tired of this view. He blinked a few times and looked down, distracted by a piercing green glow around that side of the ship, and a few other sailors bent over the railing to admire it.

''What's that?'' One sailor asked another.

''Luminescent plankton! Now you've seen your fair share lad!''

''What's plankton?''

''Oh it's amazing...'' The handsome bearded man said, still distracted.

"Venser?" Nodessa wrapped his back with her long draconian tail, causing him to jump a bit.

"Uhhh well... Head injury, it's... I'll have to get back to you on that... Fellow mercenary friend."

Nodessa nodded and said, "You did good. It was brave. It was madness that you were so willing to do that but... It paid off being both brave and mad."

"I know these stars... We're near the Alphonse Islands... Near... Home." Ruari mumbled falling onto her back, and Venser and Cierra did the same. Nodessa just chuckled and sat cross legged near them.

"Venser knows a lot about madness..." Cierra commented, her burnt orange eyes looking to him.

Venser Karkaldwin reached out for the islandic elf beside him, his fingers wander over her soft, sun-kissed arms, and she slapped his hand away.

"I got a small cut on my arm and it's your fault... Hmph."

"Hey now... You and Cierra chose to come along on this voyage too."

Ro pushed on his shoulder, and Cierra smiled and silently did the same on Venser's opposite side.

"So, did you find any more clues to try to find out more about this cult and your sister?" Cierra asked and Nodessa noticeably winces at her very high pitched voice.

"I did. And plans for a weapon that I've never thought about before... But these could work."

"The wooden penis cannon?" Venser asked.

"Uh what no you... You really got your head rung like a bell. The plans are for a cannon... But small ones that you can hold in your hand."

Ro spoke up, "They even rarely get used because powder in a long metal tube is too unstable. Like, bombs are enough but a cannon you can fit in your hand? You might as well be asking to see Marilla's tits..."

Venser snorted and sat up.

"Not a problem for me... All I have to do is drop my pants and speak sweetly to the ocean to make her some of my famous Pink Footed Booby and the sea goddess herself will rise up and..." The handsome bearded man gestured to his crotch. "Ya know."

"Hand cannons will never catch on. Or cannoks in ships unless you want to blow up your own ship or have them do nothing because of wet powder." Ro said backing up a bit and pushing Venser either her bare foot.

Venser laughs, low and deep, only for a moment staring into the waters again. No. They couldn't get those to work and mass produce firearms. But what could he do? Destroy the plans to keep the planet of Laguna from advancing like this? He enjoyed the simple ways of everything around him, and felt urged to snatch the blueprints from Nodessa and toss them overboard, but he ultimately decided not to.

"Venser, were you listening?" The Koran mercenary woman asked, blinking her acid green hues.

"Errrrr uh. No. Concussion, sorry. And a lot on my mind right now... Little ones at home cigar business tavern work..."

"Right. So, we should dock in the Port of Zeff in a couple of hours. There we will be selling our loot to make end's meet. Along with paying for a dock for the Foul Fury until we figure out what to do with her."

"Didn't you say you've always wanted your own ship, Nodessa?" Venser asked, looking back to her.

"Yeah! You could keep it and captain it yourself with your own crew!"

Nodessa looked at them all, before standing up and leaning over the railing, letting out a sigh and trying not to whao anyone with her tail.

"As good as the prospect sounds... Maybe one day when this is all over. For now I just enjoy piloting the ship when I can and being a simple passenger. As I can go off on my own whenever I like at the end of the day."

There was a silence for a few moments as they all nodded, and Ro sat up and reached out for an open a bottle of rum, taking a swig and finishing the precious drink she had helped herself to earlier.

"Can never go wrong with spare money. It looks like we all need it. I need another bottle..."

The tall temptress stretched out her legs and sat up, adjusting her dress and yawning. She said, "I can go get some. Two bottles?"

Cierra Dusk nodded in affirmation as she walked off to explore the Freeman's Paragon and bring back some rum, shaking off her sea legs in the process.

"And why not? Let's drink and celebrate! I mean, get really drunk before we dock. Like..." Venser's voice trailed off before he shook his head.

"What this big pervert was going to say... How often is it that we capture a ship like the Fowl Fury? Alphonse Island elves don't get drunk. We absolutely gods be damned smashed!" Ruari jumped to her feet with a wild giggle and began to shake off her sea legs as well, pacing in circles, swaying back and forth in her steps.

Nodessa smiled and crossed her arms with a nod, simply taking the two in and staying quiet for now, enjoying the peace. She noted the infamous dimension hopping man whore mercenary with exceptional magical abilities was enjoying the peace all to well, admiring the beauty of the ocean while lost in thought.

"Are you excited to go home, Ro?"

The tanned islandic elf stopped and looked to the Koran mercenary woman, and then to Venser, and then to the sea before them, and then back to Nodessa, watching Cierra return behind them, handing a bottle to Ro and holding up another.

"This is special. This is some strong smelling mead... Definitely not made with regular honey."

"Actually... I might stay and visit for a few days. And Venser can come teleport back to me then."

Nodessa looked back to Venser, and felt a light wind pass them by. She said with a new raised, "Little ones at home?"

"Hence why... Yeah. A lot of odd jobs and business to make a lot of coin to feed them and my lovers and... I know. Family is everything. And... Well. I am with them when I can and..."

His slitted emerald eyes watched a star shoot across the indigo sky filled with multicolored nebulas and far off galaxies.

"I admit it. Sometimes I can't just help the urge to go out and adventure. To go out and... Do all this. Rather than stay home most of the time with the loves of my life."

"But what... What matters most is in the end I will always go back home to them."

"Always."

CHAPTER FORTY ONE: AMA

Villa de Karkaldwin, The Farmlands, Pryldahn, 1438 ATC

"Ama? Aaama... Mama!"

"That's right my love... Mama is here."

The little daughter of Venser and Sanna, Rowena, looked up at her mother and paused herself in playing with some blocks. Their living room chamber was vast in the new home they'd purchased, having been living here for nearly a year now. The golden-skinned mother of the girl stopped cutting onions for their dinner and turned to look at her, offering a smile that could only be described as a mask. Yet it was one that a child so young wouldn't be able to see through. The golden gypsy walked over and knelt in front of her infant child, who eagerly took the chance to slide into her mother's opening arms and embrace her.

Sliding a hand through the little girl's small tufts of black, glossy hair, Sanna was silent for a moment before speaking with a tone that was gentle and yet... It held pain the child couldn't possibly understand.

"I know, darling. I miss your father too. Let's get you something to eat, hm?"

Despite saying something so warm and comforting, the darkness that threatened to overtake her mind started to creep in as Sanna realized she hadn't seen her lover in more than a week. It seemed like even when he was gone more than a day she missed him dearly.

"How can I raise a child all alone? A girl needs her father, right? I know it won't be long... It never is..."

Standing with the little one in her arms babbling away, the golden gypsy sat with her in a chair which was made to rock and put her to the breast. Looking out to the window upon the vastness that was their beautiful new home and the snow that began to fall, Sanna's mind wandered. In her intense, bright green eyes laid a pain that she couldn't explain, a loneliness that she didn't want. They were in the section of the villa that held their personal quarters, as Sanna had taken particular fondness in Venser's room while he traveled, the master bedroom they shared with other lovers. It smelled of him, everything reminded her of him... Which was a fantastic comfort on nights such as this. The gentle rhythmic suckling of her infant daughter's feeding calmed her a little, though she couldn't stop herself from reflecting further on her feelings.

"I don't mind the lovers... Alex, Kari. Everyone else... They're all so wonderful, and this place is a beautiful home for us all. So why do I feel so alone, despite them being here? Am I truly good enough to be the lover of a man so grand? He comes home and tells such fantastical tales of his adventures, and a lot of coin, spending so much time with us, yet he is also gone so much..."

Before she knew it, Sanna's eyes were filling with tears and blurring her vision. She was thankful that the other lovers and younger children had gone to bed, for she loathed being seen crying. Drying her eyes slowly so as to not disturb Rowena, she took a breath and looked down to watch her for a moment. The snow fell so fast, lulling the girl into a slumber as the wind wheezed outside like a sort of sad lullaby. The tiny wafts of black hair were soft against Sanna's arm, her darling baby's tiny chest rising and falling with deep breaths as she slept so calmly. Using a finger, Sanna tenderly unlatched her daughter's mouth from her breast and adjusted herself carefully before standing from the chair, heading to the nursery humming a soft, soothing Krimeakhetan lullaby all the while. She stopped for a moment and sighed.

"I miss the days when we would spend so much time together. Just us. I was gone a lot too... Perhaps this is my karma for my own absence. I know he must have been lonely, and not having the chance to get to know his daughter in my sickness did not help. Perhaps it is what I deserve... But an innocent child does not need such abandonment. I know the other lovers are here with me, but... A girl needs her father as much as she... Venser can be here for."

Arriving in the large nursery for Rowena and approaching one of the many cribs that lined the walls, Sanna placed the sleeping one-year-old in it and laid a blanket up to her chest carefully after giving her forehead a kiss.

"Goodnight, my darling. Sleep well," She whispered to her before leaving the room quietly and headed for the atrium. The moonlight bathing the land, a thin white sheet covering the open area which allowed the sky to bear down. The little pond was starting to freeze over with a thin film from the coming cold of winter, a clear mini-glacier fixated to the fountain's former stream as an icy centerpiece to a somber scene of white. Her amber gown of furs mixed with the flakes and grew damp as she sat upon one of the benches which surrounded, her gaze moving to the sky. She did not bother to brush away the petals of white that fell upon her raven locks, a youthful face showing a few signs of stress from self-reflection and daily life.

"Venser, my love... I know I've never wanted for anything, yet there is one thing I cannot hope but yearn for. I miss you, beloved. I wish you were here to see your daughter grow. Some small part of me even wishes that I was your only lover, but... I am content with not being so. I am not selfish and hope to never become so, for you have given me a better life and a chance at love than I ever knew possible. If not for you, I would have never had the adventures I've had or have birthed our beautiful daughter. I hope someday that I might even bear you another... I understand you must do what you have to, though I wish there was another way. Perhaps... Perhaps I shall dance again. Would that help to give you peace, so that you might spend more time with all of us?"

Lowering her head, her shoulders shook with cold and with grief. Venser's absence weighed heavily on her, but she was resolved to stay strong. This new land of different cultures, slave legality and decorum... She was still getting used to it. Sanna and the others, Venser especially cared for the slaves, and in turn, the elven slaves that worked the fields and around the house cared for them in return.

"Perhaps, then, I simply need to give things more of a chance... The Pryldahnian culture. This is how things are done in this region."

Letting out a calmed sigh, she realized that having spoken her desires out loud had helped to ease the ache in her heart. It was as if she'd spoken to him herself, as if he'd been right in front of her and she could feel his presence. Clutching her furs to her chest as she stood, Sanna took a shivering breath and headed inside quickly.

"It is getting plenty cold tonight... I do hope the winter eases. It cannot be good for the gardens; I'll check on them tomorrow. I cannot leave it to the slaves alone, it would be unruly of me and cruel." She mulled aloud as she traversed the hallways of the estate, working her way to Venser's massive bedroom.

The large bed they shared, with a multitude of other lovers, looked so inviting that she swore she could almost see Venser within the sheets and beckoning to her. Stripping herself of the wet furs and leaving them by the fire to hang and dry, her naked form slid between silken sheets and grew warm again. Her hand laid upon the pillow upon which his head normally rested, pulling it close to her chest as her eyes drifted shut.

"Sleep well... My love."

This lasted only a few minutes before the golden gypsy sighed and sat up, sliding out of bed and walking out to a balcony that faced towards the harbor of Capital De Seraphim, out towards the Slender Sea. The golden gypsy beckoned her attention towards the dark purple sky speckled with stars, feeling the soft wind against her face. She thought of the wind from her home of Krimeakhet, and a saying from her gypsy family. As a woman of the desert, the desert winds would blow the dunes away, and then blow the shifting sands back. The wind was free, and she knew Venser loved to wander just as free as the wind that shaped the world.

Nothing but the faint light of a full moon behind a few clouds cast upon Sanna's beautiful features. Her eyes were so bright as she looked out past the capital city and out to the endless sea. And then the moon, and wondered if her love was watching the moon at the same time she was.

Somehow, though, she knew as she blew a kiss on the wind and hoped it found Venser's lips, wherever he was.

And it did.

ABOUT THE AUTHOR

V.M. Mouchas resides in Idaho's capital and coolest city with his forty wives and forty slices of cake. He is an adventurer at heart and once conquered the wilderness with nothing but the clothes on his back, a tomahawk, a stool, the high ground, and a ballpoint pen. He loves Arby's and will use the earnings from this book to buy more Arby's sandwiches. He also thinks 80's synth is cool.